CAUGHT BY PASSION

"Aye," Philippa said. "'Tis vitally important that I marry Drogo, Lord Oldcastle. That is why you must tell him that I am a virgin. Because I am!"

Adrian answered with a throaty chuckle. But the laughter quickly faded as his gaze bored into her. Rain pattered on the thick, leaded window panes, and Philippa shuddered as a chill insinuated itself into the room. Unable to tear her gaze from Adrain's intense scrutiny, she pulled the counterpane over her knees and clutched it to her shoulders.

He stood, towering over her, his expression inscrutable. Then he reached for a marten pelt draped over the end of her foot-board and arranged it at her feet. Bending over, his face was scant inches from Philippa's. She saw the bristles on his jaw and the creases bracketing his mouth.

Plastering her spine against the headboard, Philippa held her breath, fearful of her body's reaction. Adrian's nearness affected her drastically and he leaned so close that his chest brushed her knees and hands. Fire blazed through Philippa's fingertips and spread throughout her body.

A crack of thunder ruptured the silence.

At the same time, the door to her solar exploded inward and a scowling Drogo, wet hair plastered to his head, burst into the room.

THE MAIDEN BRIDE

CINDY HARRIS

LEISURE BOOKS NEW YORK CITY

This book is for SRS, my friend.

A LEISURE BOOK®

December 1999

Published by

Dorchester Publishing Co., Inc.
276 Fifth Avenue
New York, NY 10001

ISBN 0-8439-4650-4

Chapter One

England, 1362

Sir Adrian Vale drifted back to consciousness. His swollen
eyelids blinked against the harsh glare of a rushlight held high
above his head. For a moment, he couldn't remember where
he was, or why his body hung in mid-air, arms pulled in one
direction, legs pulled in another. He knew only that his physical pain had become something palpable, inescapable, as
closely connected to him as a malignant tumor. It mirrored
the deep, silent pain that had been gnawing at his heart the
past four years, ever since his wife Jeanne had died attempting to give birth to their son.

The light and its bearer moved away, and the low stone
ceiling Adrian stared at receded into blackness. The levers
behind his head creaked. His muscles stretched yet again,
impossibly, and a streak of fresh pain brought startling clari-
ty to his memory. He remembered where he was—in an
underground chamber in the Tower of London, delivered a

sennight ago to answer for his crimes. The stench of standing river water and his body's foul reaction to encroaching death tainted the air he gasped.

Muted voices filtered through the clot of pain in his head like curdled cream through cheesecloth.

"Hast thou no mercy?" asked a trembling voice. "The man's body cannot withstand this brutal punishment. Kill him if you must, but put the wretch out of his misery, I beg of you."

"Spare me yer pious sermons, priest," came the reply. "Good King Edward has ordered you to gauge the man's endurance, not to plead his case. Now, dost thou believe the fool can be punished further, or no?"

The answer was vague. "The wretch's body hangs a hand's width above the rack's bed. Stretch him more and I fear you'll crack his bones!"

"A turd in yer teeth, you pious coward. I ain't even broken a thumb!"

Adrian pictured his tormentor's face, pocked and gnarled to match the malicious voice. He imagined the creature's expression, pouty and sullen, one hand resting on the tantalizing lever. Another ounce of pressure tightened the ropes that bound his body, and Adrian felt his nerves unravel.

"King Edward wants him alive," warned the clergyman.

"And alive he'll be, fer all that I should care. This one's as strong as Satan, I tell ye. 'S'blood, the man ain't made so much as a peep, and I been racking him on and off fer nigh a week." The subjugator gave his lever a hard crank, tightening the ropes another notch.

A low moan echoed through the dark, vaulted chamber before Adrian realized the eerie sound came from him. Everywhere there was a muscle or a bone in his naked body, searing pain existed.

The shuffle of leather on stone brought light again. Adrian squinted against the glare. His struggles only served to worsen his pain. Invisible weights compressed his chest, crushing his rib cage, squeezing his heart. Suffocating, he sucked in fetid air and stared up at a doughy face, grim beneath its tonsure.

"Sir, why don't you confess your sins? At least, I might then be able to pray for your soul, even if your body be condemned."

"I have not sinned," Adrian managed between clenched teeth.

Behind him, his torturer chuckled. "He defiles women's bodies and cavorts with demons. And yet he says he has not sinned."

The priest's frown deepened. "Why, sir, do you defy the laws of man and nature by practicing midwifery? You thumb your nose at the law by engaging in this woman's job. Foreswear your deviltry and make your obeisance to the king. Perhaps Edward will be lenient!"

Adrian stared, considering his response. Why should he argue his beliefs to this, or any, man? He knew what he was about, and he wasn't compelled to apologize. Besides, there was a part of him that truly wished for death, craved the nothingness it would bring. Only death could erase the suffering Adrian had lived with these past four years. Jeanne's death, and that of their infant son, were like a hair shirt prickling at his soul. Adrian's bereavement was far worse torture than this damned rack.

He worked his jaws and spat in the priest's face.

The priest drew back, his dignity assaulted. He wiped a coarse sleeve across his face, then made the sign of the cross. His eyes narrowed to slits like those cut in a knight's helmet. Clutching the rushlight, he turned his head from Adrian, and said in a shivery voice, "Truly, we are in the presence of Satan. Go ahead, then, man. Stretch the bastard till his limbs snap like faggots in a bonfire!"

The next few minutes were a blur of suffering and confusion, but at last, Adrian's body went limp and darkness overtook him.

He awakened in another place, this one warm and dry. Adrian's fingers stretched and coiled, his fist closing around a handful of straw and fragrant herbs. Licking his cracked lips, he tasted sweat and blood. His tongue was ulcerated and tasted metallic—he must have bitten it when he was thrashing against the ropes. Opening his eyes, he saw an expanse of rush-strewn floor beneath a traffic of boots and buskins and pointy-toed shoes. So, he'd been saved from the rack after all. But he didn't know where he was, or why he'd been delivered from that wicked contraption in the Tower's basement.

He was on his stomach, nose pressed to the floor. Adrian drew his knees to his chest and inhaled, wincing at the girdle of pain lacing his chest. He was alive and his limbs hadn't been separated from his body—that was something to be grateful for. He lifted his throbbing head and scanned the hall. Every sinew in his body screamed in protest as he struggled to all fours. Crusted with grime and stink, he drew looks of disdain from all around him. A lady wearing an elegant sur- coat and jeweled headpiece sniffed, then averted her eyes. Except for a filthy rag tied around his groin, Adrian was stark naked.

"He's come to his senses," someone whispered, and the crowd parted, clearing a path. Adrian lurched to his feet, wobbly as a newborn colt. He saw the dais at the far end of the hall where, in a high-backed wooden chair studded with jewels, lounged King Edward III, whose orders had sent Adrian to the Tower's pit and almost killed him.

The soldier-king was a statuesque man enjoying the prime of his life. Highly esteemed for his warrior prowess, regarded by his knights as a *man's man*, Edward was fair-haired with an aquiline nose and keen blue eyes. He commanded silence with a mere arch of his brows. "Bring the prisoner to me," he intoned, cutting his eyes at two brawny knights sporting the king's heraldry on their tunics.

Adrian half-stumbled, half-leaned on the men who flanked

him as he made his way toward King Edward's chair. When they released him, his knees buckled and he crumpled to the floor, which was just as well since he would have refused to kneel before the monarch on whose whim he'd been tortured nearly to death.

"Are you too weak to stand?" asked the king.

Summoning a strength he hadn't known he possessed, Adrian stood. He squared his shoulders and thrust out his chin. "Nay. I stand before you, Your Grace. The rack has not conquered me. Nor have you."

A gasp went up among the courtiers. Adrian's lack of remorse shocked them; his fearless baiting of the king horrified them.

"Everyone out!" Without taking his eyes off Adrian, the king dismissed his entourage with a wave of his hand. "Lords Raeburn, de Champignac and Bishop Gramonti shall remain!"

The room emptied quickly, leaving three distinguished-looking men surrounding the king's throne. They stared down their noses at Adrian, and he in turn pinned his distaste on each of them. Matching titles to men was not difficult. The bishop was clearly the Italian in long, flowing, silken robes. Lord Raeburn had to be the Englishman, in a rust-colored tunic and low-slung dagger belt. And no one but a Frenchman, de Champignac, obviously, would have worn so flamboyant a feather in his flat beaver cap.

"Are you not afraid, sir?" Edward asked, his tone mocking. "Didn't your encounter with the rack impart some sense to you?"

Adrian uncoiled his fists, rubbed his aching neck and sighed heavily. The fire in his belly belied the cool repose his slight smile indicated, but he was loath to show his apprehension to the king. Crossing his arms on his chest, he said, "I regret my encounter with the rack, Your Grace, but not for the reasons you would wish. Indeed, it is the time spent away from my vocation that troubles me. When you see fit to

11

release me from my captivity, I shall go immediately to my modest dwelling outside the walls of St. Katherine's and continue my work."

Edward's eyes darkened. "God's blood! What brand of insolence is this that you dare defy me even now. To think that I knighted you on the battlefield at Crécy and entrusted you with the duty of protecting the prince at Poitiers! You were as beloved to me as a son, Adrian. Your disobedience pains me greatly."

"I served you well, Your Grace." Adrian glanced at the three men surrounding the king's chair, their faces as implacable as alabaster effigies. Then he leveled his gaze at Edward, adding, "I didn't ask for much in return, sire. Just a small manor house near my family's home in Tenterden, a few sheep and enough arable pasture to support the needs of my serfs."

" 'Twas ample recompense for the homage of a brute like you. You should have been happy to live out your days as a gentleman farmer."

Something roiled up inside of Adrian. In a blink, he was standing in the doorway of his plaster-and-frame house, surveying his *demesne*, its cornfields, its green pastures, the rolling meadows where marigolds rioted. The smell of sheep, the clatter of cow bells and the noisy chaos of the kitchen came rushing back to him. His wife—Jeanne, sweet Jeanne—kneeled in her herb garden, filling her basket with rosemary and peppermint; she looked up from her work, met his gaze and smiled.

Opening his eyes, Adrian was taut with rage. His fingernails cut into his palms and his heart thundered against his aching ribs. He read Edward's expression, disapproving, disappointed, shrewd. The king's displeasure was nothing compared to the deep bitterness Adrian felt at having lost Jeanne.

"I *was* happy in Tenterden, sire, until my wife Jeanne

died." Adrian heard the hoarseness in his voice, and hated exposing his emotion to Edward.

Sucking his teeth, the monarch gave Adrian a lazy appraisal. "I seem to recall hearing something about the Lady Jeanne's death. Damn me, what was it?" He snapped his fingers to summon the errant recollection, as if news of Jeanne's death were some trivial scrap of gossip tossed about like offal in the barracks dining hall.

"She died in childbirth," Sir Adrian said. The memory of it twisted in his gut, tightening his muscles with a violence the rack could never imitate.

"Ah, yes, so she did." Steepling his fingers beneath his chin, the king eyed his once-most-trusted knight. "Many women do, Adrian. Giving birth is a risky business. God hath wrought it so for a purpose. 'Tis the Lord's punishment on all women for the sin committed by Eve."

Adrian spat onto the ground.

"I'll give this upstart a thrashing, sire," Lord Raeburn said, making to descend the dais. "Just say the word!"

Edward raised his hand, checking the marcher baron's protective impulse. "Down, Raeburn, down." To Adrian, he purred, "You disagree with what I have said?"

"Aye, sire. I disagree."

The men surrounding Edward all looked at one another, then back at Adrian as if he had suddenly sprouted horns.

King Edward said nothing, but pursed his lips and stared down at Adrian with gleaming eyes. Only the chirping of starlings nesting in the rafters pierced the silence that threatened to engulf the great hall.

Sir Adrian struggled to contain his outrage. It was not Edward's fault that Jeanne had died, but it was the king's Parliament that had enacted the law that prohibited men from practicing midwifery—the law he'd been accused of breaking.

Inhaling, Adrian forced himself to speak with a civil tongue despite the anger coloring his thoughts. He locked his knees against the muscle cramps that shook his body.

"Your Grace, the lady folk of England suffer overmuch in childbirth. The finest physicians in the country are denied the right to intervene in the tomfoolery that passes for legitimate medical treatment of pregnant women. You have only to allow trained doctors, men as well as women, to practice midwifery and the cloud of superstition cloaking childbirth will be lifted!"

"You cannot save your precious Jeanne, Adrian. You cannot bring her back."

"No, but I can prevent other needless deaths. Since Jeanne's death, I have traveled to Montpelier and Paris, where I have studied with the greatest physicians in Europe. In addition, I have apprenticed with the most skilled midwives in England, sire. I know that scores of infants die each year who don't have to. Hundreds of women sacrifice their bodies each year attempting to bring life into the world! Your Grace, I can not ensure the viability of every child conceived, but if you allow me to continue my studies, I can save some women . . . mayhap one day, I can save your sister, or your daughter!"

"I'll have no man touching my sister or my daughter save their rightful husbands! 'Tis diabolical, your proposal. 'Tis unnatural that a man should touch a woman thusly!" Edward's booming voice faded as he fidgeted, drumming his fingers on the wide wooden arm of his jeweled chair.

At last, the king shrugged one shoulder and said, "But I cannot forget your faithful service, my boy. I've brought you here to offer you terms. You should consider yourself doubly blessed, for I am giving you another opportunity to redeem yourself, to prove yourself worthy of the blue garter you once wore round your thigh."

Adrian flinched at the king's forgiving tone. He knew Edward hadn't ordered him tortured seven days straight only to release him just as his bones were about to snap and send him on his merry way. Whatever Edward's terms were, they were bound to be onerous and second in discomfort only to the scaffold.

"What is it you would have me do?" Adrian asked.

"Spy for me." Accompanying these words was a rustle of velvet and brocade among Raeburn, de Champignac and Gramonti. An epidemic of throat-clearing broke out among them.

"You want me to be a spy?" asked Adrian, incredulous. "But England is no longer at war. The peace with France was signed at Brétigni two years past. On whom would you have me spy?"

"There are some Englishmen who are not as committed to the French peace as their sovereign is," the king replied.

A snort of derision escaped the bishop's lips, but he paled when King Edward shot him a scorching look. The slightest of smirks twisted at the French lord's mouth.

"And this individual on whom you wish me to spy, he is one who undermines your efforts to keep the peace with France?" asked Adrian.

"That is what you are to find out." Edward rubbed his under-lip and his eyes glittered mischievously. "This man's name is Drogo, Lord Oldcastle, and he holds his lands in Sussex at my sufferance. You are to go there, infiltrate his household, and learn whether the rumors circulating about him are true."

"What rumors are those?" Adrian asked.

Edward flipped his wrist in Raeburn's direction.

The man spoke with a heavy Welsh accent. " 'Tis said the lord does keep a company of trained knights in his employ, and that from his castle on the Sussex coast near Rye, he does launch raids across the channel, sending them through Normandy and Brittany to terrorize the populace of France."

De Champignac spoke up. "He pillages French towns and

razes resisting villages to the ground. This Lord Oldcastle has raped and plundered a swath through the northern country-side, destroying more fields and confiscating more loot than all the English armies put together."

While Raeburn and de Champignac talked, the Italian bish-op nodded, arms folded and hands tucked into the sleeves of his crimson robe. Adrian listened, thinking of his Gascon war bride, Jeanne, whose love had blotted out the horrors of the battlefield, but whose death had ripped his soul asunder.

"But why me, sire? Why send a knight whom you've dis-graced and nearly tortured to death when there are hundreds of able warriors more worthy of this task, more eager to win your favor than I?"

Edward smiled wryly at his candor. "I have chosen you, Adrian, because you are the perfect knight for this mission."

"I am not, sire, for I do not relish the thought of spying on my fellow Englishmen."

"You want to continue your midwifery, don't you, Adrian?"

"Of course, sire."

"I am giving you that opportunity, sir. I am offering to bestow upon you the title of"—Edward rolled his eyes heav-enward and clucked his tongue—"King's Physic!" he said, snapping his fingers. "Specially licensed to attend to the ladies of the realm."

Lord Raeburn's cheeks flared red while the Frenchman chuckled and the bishop swallowed convulsively. The barely suppressed tone of merriment in Edward's voice raised the hair on Adrian's neck. He distrusted the king's sudden gen-erosity in sparing his life. Something told him that his ascen-sion from the Tower basement to Edward's luxurious hall had only brought him closer to hell.

"But you dragged me from my quarters a sennight ago, and ordered me confined for daring to assist women in delivering their babes. 'Twas on your command that I was tortured on the rack for seven days straight. Seven days, sire! And now, you spare my life and even condone my practice of midwifery—all in exchange for my spying on a Sussex lord? 'Tis unbelievable, sire! There must be some clause in this contract which you are hiding from me. What is it?"

The bishop gasped, crossed himself and muttered something in Italian.

"Yes, yes," the king murmured. "It is amazing that he is still alive, and I am not referring to his ordeal on the rack. I should have your tongue cut out, Adrian, for daring to speak to me in such an insolent tone. Mayhap, you truly *are* the spawn of the devil. I am willing to overlook your defects only because I require your services—and because of the loyalty you once showed me. You see, Drogo seeks a physic skilled in women's complaints. And I require a spy who can insinuate himself into Drogo's castle without creating undue suspicion."

Lord Raeburn cleared his throat. "Do you not think Drogo will be suspicious of a man practicing midwifery, Your Grace?"

Edward shrugged. "It just so happens that a Sussex knight named Sir Killian Murdoch arrived this morning in London with news of Drogo's need for a lady's physic. The knight had instructions to scour the city, and then the countryside, and return with the most skilled midwife in the land."

"Drogo is not expecting his knight to return with a male midwife," the bishop gently suggested.

"Am I not known to be a generous and innovative man?" Edward returned. "Raeburn, you will explain to this Sir Killian that I am allowing Sir Adrian to practice midwifery because he is the most knowledgeable lady's physic in the land. And I wish to spare his life. Who is Drogo to question my judgment?"

Adrian ignored Raeburn's satisfied smile and the conspiratorial look he shared with the bishop and the Frenchman. "Drogo seeks a midwife?" he asked. "For his lady?"

"Aye," the king replied. "Drogo needs a midwife and you need a royal pardon. 'Tis a very tidy venture, is it not?

Everyone gets what he wants from this enterprise. You get to go on practicing your profession, Adrian. You receive my blessing in spite of my disgust! And I get the perfect spy."

"Is Drogo's lady anticipating a difficult birth, sire?" Adrian asked. "Is that why you have chosen me for this spy mission?"

Lord Raeburn interrupted, his expression oddly triumphant. " 'Tis a stroke of genius, sire."

"But, my leniency is not without limits, Adrian," King Edward warned. "Should Drogo send you back to London 'ere you gather the intelligence I require, I will revoke the pardon I am granting you! If you fail in your duties as spy, I'll not only strip you of your title and license, I'll order you disemboweled, drawn and quartered. Your head on a pike-staff is all the same to me. Do you understand, Sir Adrian?"

Adrian clenched his fists at his side and stared into Edward's thunderous features. His heart galloped at the thought of being allowed to practice midwifery without fear of being hauled off to jail in the middle of a difficult birth. Here was an opportunity not only to continue his practice, but to do so with the king's condonation.

And the only condition was that he keep an eye on this troublesome Lord Drogo and discern whether there was evidence the man was terrorizing the French countryside. How difficult could that be? What did the danger matter if Adrian was allowed to pursue his calling? Assisting women through the hazards of childbirth was the only thing that mitigated the enormous sense of loss he'd suffered since Jeanne's death. If he couldn't practice midwifery, Adrian would as soon die. If he could live, he would do anything to continue his calling. It was as simple as that.

He made a leg, lowering himself to the floor in obeisance. "Your Grace, I accept your offer."

"Hah! As if you had any choice, Adrian."

The knight straightened. "A man always has a choice, sire. I only pray that I have made the right one."

Chapter Two

Lady Philippa Gilchrist lay on her bed, half-asleep and dreaming of her father's return to Oldwall Castle. With one arm thrown over her eyes, she blocked the late afternoon sun that filtered through the thick glass windows and indulged her favorite fantasy. She pictured her father striding up from the village, pounding across the drawbridge and marching through the outer bailey as if he were still Drogo's most trusted knight and vassal.

It was sheer nonsense to think Sir Casper might one day show up, and Philippa well knew it, but when the clamor of servants downstairs drifted to her ears, she thought for an instant her father had returned from France.

She sat up, listening. Gib, the baron's valet, and Hilda, who served as both scullery wench and Philippa's personal maid, were issuing orders willy-nilly to serfs. Philippa crossed the solar's floor and flew downstairs in a trice. She was half-certain that her father had made liars of those who claimed he would never reappear in England.

She came to a halt at the bottom of the staircase, drawn up short by the sight that greeted her.

A man, taller and darker than most of the Norman stock populating this coastal area, stood at the opposite end of the hall. Surrounded by a cluster of servants, mostly women, he wore an expression of weary amusement that accentuated the sensual curve of his lips. As she approached, Philippa watched Hilda flutter around the man, bowing and ducking her head as if he were royalty.

"The lord's ale is of the finest quality, sir, I assure you," the wench said. "Or would you prefer wine from Burgundy, sir, to quench your thirst?"

The stranger smiled at Hilda, his eyes lighting on her swollen belly. "Ale will be fine, woman. And some bread or meat pies, if you have them. By the way, how far are you from your lying-in time?"

Even from halfway across the hall, Philippa could sense Hilda's confusion. Judging from the cut of his clothes and the dignity of his bearing, the stranger was hardly low-born. What would compel a man of quality to ask a serving wench such an impertinent question?

Hilda's murmured answer was inaudible to Philippa, but the stranger nodded in response.

"Hast thou had many babes before this one?" he asked the servant.

Something in his voice halted Philippa in her tracks. Kindness, compassion, intelligence. These were unusual traits among the men who inhabited Oldwall Castle.

Clearly embarrassed by the attention she'd drawn, Hilda answered in muted tones.

The stranger laid a hand on her shoulder and in a low voice, said, "Do not overtax your body these next few weeks, woman. Ask the others in the kitchen to lift the heavy pots and crank the rotisserie for you."

The servant bobbed a quick curtsey, then pivoted and fled toward the screen that concealed the hall's passages to the buttery and pantry. As she passed, Philippa noticed her pink cheeks and heaving bosom. The stranger's probing questions had agitated the maid. Men of his quality rarely showed interest in women below the salt. When they did, their motivations were generally driven by base impulses.

Philippa drew nearer the stranger, unnoticed amid the chaos surrounding him. Ordinarily, her distrust of men would have caused her to turn away from him, but his tenderness toward Hilda, a woman Philippa considered her dearest friend, intrigued her.

She smiled as Old Gib fussed like a mother hen, brushing the visitor's dusty tunic, directing him toward the trestle table, inviting him to rest his feet while Hilda fetched ale and dry bread. Three other women, all cleaning wenches who had left their duties to ogle the newcomer, buzzed like bees round him, offering him a wash basin and towels. When he finally did lower his body onto the hard wooden bench, he had to wave off the tittering womenfolk just to make room to stretch his long legs.

Emptied of serfs, the hall grew still. The stranger, unaware of Philippa's presence, bent forward and rubbed his legs. A dim ruckus could be heard coming from the buttery where Hilda and Gib rallied their troops of underlings in preparation for supper. Rays of late summer sunlight slanted through the high, arched windows, illuminating motes of dust that floated in the air like sighs.

Or had she actually heard a sigh? Philippa tensed as the stranger's head jerked up, and his gaze met hers. He froze, big dark hands motionless and wrapped around his outstretched thigh. Ten paces away from him, Philippa saw his lips tighten, his jaw clench. If he had sighed, it was from pain, for despite his dark complexion, there was a certain gauntness to

21

his features that spoke of illness or suffering. In the shadows creeping across the stone floor, he was a statue, his muscles carved from stone, his eyes as hard as rock.

She felt him studying her, his stare momentarily riveted to her flat stomach, her hips, and breasts. The heat his frank appraisal produced in her was unprecedented, inexplicable. A stab of guilty pleasure nearly sent her fleeing from the hall. She burned with embarrassment, and yet something compelled her to stay and learn who this strange man was. His scrutiny was familiar, intimate, disturbing. Even when he began kneading his thigh muscles again, he didn't take his eyes off her.

"Are you the Lady of Oldcastle?" He rubbed his hands hard down the front of one leg.

His muscles were sore from riding, Philippa surmised.

Wincing as his fingers kneaded his own flesh, he exhaled a breath so ragged it scraped Philippa's flesh and stippled her skin with apprehension.

"I shall be soon. I am Lady Philippa, Sir Casper Gilchrist's daughter," she replied. "And who might you be?"

For a long time, the man withheld his answer, so absorbed was he in massaging his own muscles. Coarse woven hose outlined the curves of his lower legs and the bulging muscles of his thighs. There was something vaguely unsettling about the way his hands moved over his legs, grasping flesh and muscle, kneading hose and skin with strong, skillful fingers.

He rearranged his limbs, bending one knee and straightening the other. Then he pressed the heel of his hand into the top of his thigh and grimaced. Another half-sigh, half-moan escaped him, and Philippa's pulse quickened. Accustomed to averting her eyes from Drogo's lumpy, misshapen *chausses*, she swallowed hard against the urge to stare at this man who moved like a sleek cat, stretching and flexing, rubbing the ache from his travel-weary bones.

When she finally repeated her question—"Who are

you?"—she was chagrined to hear the husky sound of her voice.

"I am Sir Adrian Vale, come from London with Lord Oldcastle's knight, Sir Killian."

"Killian brought you here?" Philippa stepped closer, curiosity overwhelming her well-conditioned distrust of men. "From London? Why, whatever for? Do not tell me Killian has dragged home another knight seeking honors! Drogo will be furious! *Dieu*, no wonder the man has run off to hide himself. He won't be safe across the channel when Drogo hears of this."

"Do not fret, lady. Killian is surely safe from Drogo's displeasure, for he serves his lord faithfully. He has brought me here at Drogo's request."

A crash sounded in the northern wall as the hall's great oaken door was flung open. Philippa turned to see Drogo darkening the threshold, blending with the shadows as if he were some malevolent ghost. Then the short, stocky baron fully materialized, thundering across the floor in his tilting armor, a brace of knights and squires in his wake.

Scrambling behind was a scrawny lad wearing a parti-colored tunic and carrying Drogo's helmet as if it were a treasure box. When the entourage reached the trestle table, the lesser vassals filled the benches while Sir Killian stood protectively a step behind his liege-lord.

Drogo propped his fists on his hips and scowled at Adrian. Philippa had always considered the baron an oddly proportioned man, with a head too large for his body and eyes too small for his face. His eyebrows were black and bushy, his hair an incongruent red, and to Philippa he looked as if he'd stood too near a roaring brazier and roasted his own skin.

Staring from one man to the other, she couldn't help but notice the disparity between the tall, handsome newcomer and the barrel-chested Lord Oldcastle. She sensed Drogo's awareness of it, too. The older man's mouth turned downward as he scanned the knight's muscular legs, broad shoulders, and thick black hair.

"So! Sir Adrian Vale, is it? Killian informs me you hold a license from the king. 'Tis true?"

Sir Adrian half-stood, but Drogo pushed him back down on the bench. "Rest, sir." His tone was not polite.

Adrian nodded. "To answer your question, it is true that King Edward has licensed me to practice."

"Practice what?" Philippa asked. "If you are a physic, you should know that I am a skilled practitioner myself. I have taken great care to stock the infirmary with a vast assortment of herbs and powdered-plant concoctions."

Adrian shot her a startled look, but said nothing. Nor did Drogo, but that hardly surprised Philippa—the baron held all women's opinions in contempt. He wouldn't bother to answer his future wife's silly questions.

Staring at Adrian, Drogo beckoned Killian with a curl of his fingers. "Did you make proper inquiries in London as to this man's qualifications?"

"Aye, my lord." Killian sounded quite sure of himself.

"He understands what services are required of him?"

"For the most part, my lord."

"He has had experience in such matters?"

"In what matters?" Philippa asked.

Adrian's mouth was set in grim lines. "You did not send word ahead, Sir Killian? The lady has had no forewarning that a *man* was retained?"

Drogo huffed his impatience. " 'Tis not the lady whom Killian must answer to, sir. 'Tis I. And if the king's men have recommended you, then I have no quarrel with such an unusual arrangement."

What the hell were these men talking about? Why should Philippa have been warned that a *man* was being retained—for what? She turned her gaze on Adrian. Her sense of dread tripled when she saw the pained expression on his face.

Before, she had thought his taut features a result of physical exhaustion. Now, he appeared to be suffering from some inner hurt, an anguish that centered around whatever he'd been brought to Oldcastle's manor for. Whatever it was, it must be an unpleasant chore if even he were loath to put it into words.

"Mother of God," Adrian said, his voice whisper-soft.

A tense silence yawned while the three men appraised each other warily. Were Drogo a man commonly in good spirits, his belligerent mood might have been remarked upon by his men-at-arms, whose duty it was to protect him. Given his general ugliness, however, not a one of them noticed that he'd suddenly gone rigid, or that his mouth had turned upside down in a hideous frown.

Servants poured ale and passed trenchers of viands and gravy while knights and squires banged tankards and cutlery, sang bawdy songs and swapped off-color jokes. Still, the din of the supper table paled in comparison to the silent thunder of Drogo's hostility.

Looking from him to Sir Adrian, Philippa was alarmed to find the handsome knight staring at her.

Fear of Drogo's reprisals—fear, in general—tempered her reaction to Adrian's stare. Still, Philippa found, to her surprise, that she liked the knight's penetrating gaze on her. Which was odd—exceedingly so—because her experience with men had been so unpleasant as to convince her that all of them were violent, lecherous creatures. But there was something in Adrian's gaze that was different from the others', something anguished and puzzling with which she identified.

She looked at Drogo. He was staring at Adrian as if the knight had maligned the English king and sworn allegiance to the French King John. Killian was loudly reiterating the excellence of Adrian's qualifications, whatever they were, and Adrian—*Adrian was simply staring at her.*

And, God, did his eyes mesmerize her. Conveying an

unfathomable depth of emotion, they filled her with a shivery warmth and turned her knees to butter. They held the hint of an apology mingled with regret.

Or was Philippa simply seeing in the knight's lambent gaze a dim reflection of her own pain—a pain so immense that it dogged her heels like a fawning page? Did this man have any notion what it meant to consider oneself unworthy of love?

"What is it that you are licensed by the king to do, sir?" she finally managed, appalled once more by the husky quality of her voice.

Drogo drowned out her question. "I do not like his looks, Killian. He is too handsome by far. God's fish, he is as pretty as a woman!"

"He is the highest qualified practitioner in all of England, my lord. I was fortunate to have found him." But Killian didn't sound so sure of himself anymore.

A tiny spark of courage—a little candleburst—ignited in Philippa's heart. She took a big step and planted herself between Drogo and Adrian. The lord had no choice now but to look at her. Indeed, surprise widened his eyes. The Philippa he knew shrank from his glare, never invited it. But instead of meeting her stare, his gaze slid to the neckline of her tunic and lingered there.

Disgust and fear fanned a flame in Philippa's stomach. As a rule, she avoided attracting the baron's attention; having suddenly demanded it, she found his interest in her sickening. Good lord, what had she been thinking about? Stepping aside, she hugged her body. That old, familiar anger kindled in the pit of her stomach. It was a rage that smoldered inside her and never died away. At that instant, she hated Drogo, Killian, and even Adrian—because he was a man, too.

Drogo's chuckle was low and sinister. "Now, Lady Philippa do not get yourself in a huff over this. You will soon learn why Sir Adrian has arrived at Oldwall Castle."

Killian snickered.

Adrian's stare shot to Drogo's second-in-command like a flaming arrow. "I see no humor in this situation, Sir Killian. If I am to safely deliver the lady of her babe, she must trust me. She should have been given a choice in this matter. If she does not prefer a male midwife, she has every right to be attended by a woman."

Philippa rounded on Drogo, her chest tightening, her breath coming in short puffs. *What the devil was going on here?* She wasn't even married to Drogo and already the baron had sent for a physic? And what kind of physic was this? Everyone knew that only women could practice midwifery.

"A male midwife?" she asked, incredulous. "Deliver me of my babe? I prithee, tell me what he is talking about."

"Haven't you figured it out yet, Philippa? Sir Adrian is come to be the midwife at Oldwall Castle. He shall deliver your babe—my heir—when the time comes."

A fusillade of poison arrows could not have ripped a bigger hole in Philippa's heart. Reeling from the impact of Drogo's words, she turned on Adrian.

A cord of muscles rippled beneath the smooth dark skin of the knight's jaw. Yet the gaze he turned on her was immeasurably deep, disturbingly intense. "My lady, you have nothing to fear. I am well qualified and by the time your babe arrives, you will be accustomed to the idea of a male midwife."

"No, I will not!" The pleasure Philippa had taken in Sir Adrian's stare dwindled to ashes. Now, his frank gaze filled her with trepidation, repulsed her. Did he really intend to deliver her babe, to see her naked body, to touch her *there?*

Drogo waggled a thick finger, as if admonishing a naughty child. "Now, Philippa. Methinketh you should hold your tongue. For 'tis my command that rules this roost, not your petty wishes. And, the more I think on it, the more I am satisfied that Sir Adrian is the perfect midwife for Oldwall Castle."

Philippa averted her eyes. She couldn't stand to feel Adrian looking at her any more. How could she have entertained the silly notion he might be different? Hadn't she learned by now that all men were the same? Even the ones with the liquid brown eyes, gleaming hair and broad shoulders. God, she felt betrayed! Stupid and insignificant, just as she'd been told those many years ago. And she despised the newcomer for having reminded her of it.

"Killian, why did you not inform Sir Adrian of his first duty?" Drogo asked, his tone infuriatingly coy.

Philippa's blood roared so loudly in her ears she could barely discern Killian's smug reply. "Sir Adrian had no inclination to talk during our journey, and so I thought it wiser to allow you to brief him on his expected duties here, my lord."

Drogo clapped his hands and guffawed. "Left the fun part for me, did you, Killian? I should have known! You old jester, you!"

Killian's short bark of laughter tightened the knot in Philippa's belly. Through clenched teeth, she said, "What nasty little surprise have you in store for me now, my lord? Do you truly think I will allow a male physic to attend the birth of my child? If and when one is conceived, that is?"

"Oh, I'll get a child on you, my sweet. My heir will be born nine months to the night after our wedding, if I have anything to do with it."

The thought made Philippa shudder. She knew she was going to have to allow Drogo his husbandly rights, but she was hoping he'd take one of the wenches as a lover and leave her alone. The thought of having the hideous man's baby—well, she'd vaguely allowed herself to admit that would have to happen, too, but it wasn't something she liked to dwell on. It was simply too distasteful to imagine.

She felt Sir Adrian rise to his full height. Daring to look at him, she was thunderstruck by the way he towered over Drogo, dwarfing the bantam cock who was to be her husband.

Gulping a quick breath, her eyes took in the width of Adrian's shoulders, the hardness of his long legs.

He was indeed a handsome man, his skin unblemished, his hair thick and gleaming. She thought if he ever smiled, he might be the most handsome man in Christendom. But she doubted seriously that she would ever see Sir Adrian Vale smile.

In fact, she hoped he never did smile again. She reminded herself that he was her enemy. He was Drogo's agent in this malevolent scheme to embarrass and humiliate her. She hated him.

Adrian bowed before Philippa. When he straightened, he looked her straight in the eye, and said, "I was brought here to serve as Oldwall's physic and midwife. 'Tis a most unusual situation, I know, but King Edward has recently granted me the title of King's Physic, specially licensed to tend to the ladies of the realm. You have no reason to fear me, my lady."

"I thought there were laws forbidding men to practice midwifery," Philippa stammered.

Drogo snorted. "So did I!"

Killian cleared his throat. "This is a special case, my lord. According to the king's man, Sir Adrian has studied all over the world—"

"I am the best midwife in England, my lord. You can find no better than I. 'Twas my impression you wanted only the best for your wife."

"But I am not his wife!" Philippa clamped her hand over her lips, horrified that she'd revealed her disgust for Lord Oldcastle. Fighting a wave of nausea, she muttered, "Not yet, anyway."

"You soon will be, talkative chit." Drogo puffed out his chest and winked at Adrian.

"I am confused, my lord," Adrian said. "Then why do you need the services of a midwife, now? Killian led me to believe that I was needed at Oldwall Castle immediately."

29

Glancing over his shoulder, Drogo said, "You really didn't tell him, Killian?"

"No, my lord."

"Tell him what?" Philippa cried.

"Tell me what?" Adrian demanded.

Drogo looked from his future bride to the handsome knight, and chuckled again. "That you, Sir Adrian, are charged with the delicate duty of validating my future wife's virginity."

Philippa felt such a streak of horror pass through her body that her knees wobbled. "He is to do what?"

She vaguely heard Sir Adrian's terse question. "And how do you propose that I do such a thing, my lord?"

"Why, examine her, of course," Drogo replied, obviously amused by the notion of Philippa, his virgin bride, subjected to a physical examination by this tall, handsome, virile knight. "And since you are such a strapping specimen, rather than the wizened old hag I'd expected, I fear I shall have to be present when you perform this examination. Wouldn't want anything untoward to occur, now would we?"

Philippa's throat closed. She couldn't suck a single breath of air into her lungs. She heard the sound of her own sobs choking her, then she buried her face in her hands. Shame, that old companion of hers, wrapped its frigid arms about her.

Chapter Three

Watching Philippa's beautiful green eyes widen in horror, Adrian couldn't help but think of the French women he'd seen brutalized by English soldiers who considered them the spoils of war. Though Adrian had never taken a woman without her consent, most of his fellow knights routinely had. 'Twas the right of conquering soldiers to ravish the female population, raze the peasants' villages and destroy crops in the field. Only Adrian's personal code of honor criminalized such behavior.

"No!" Philippa gasped, her pale complexion turning even more ghostly. She clutched the front of her dark blue velvet surcoat, fingers curling around a jeweled cross that lay upon her smallish breasts. "For the love of God, my lord, please do not do this to me."

"Pipe down, woman. You should have known such would be expected of you." Drogo reached beneath the short skirt of his jupon and scratched vigorously. His wide smile revealed a lifetime of poor dental hygiene. Whether his pleasure was taken from the probings of his fingers, or from Philippa's humiliation, Adrian couldn't tell, but one thing was certain—Drogo was enjoying himself.

Repulsed, Adrian weighed his conflicting duties. His personal vow to safeguard the health of women warred with his duty to carry out Edward's orders. Like as not, both endeavors held hidden danger.

"I didn't know, my lord. You never told me!"

"I'm telling you now, lady. Sir Adrian will find your maidenhead, or there'll be no wedding. And to ensure this strapping brute of a fellow doesn't try nothing funny, I'll be present during the examination *to keep a close eye on everything he does.*"

Adrian's muscles stiffened at the playfulness in Drogo's voice. Had any man ever dared look at Jeanne the way Drogo ogled Philippa, Adrian would have killed him. But, a challenge to the lord of Oldwall Castle would only win him a one-way trip to London, accommodations at the Tower, and all the torture he could stand. Not exactly a holiday. So Sir Adrian stood still and silent, though ever fiber in his body ached to plow a fist in Drogo's leering face.

Chanting, "No, no, no," Philippa shook a strand of hair loose from the dainty chaplet that encircled her head. Adrian's fingers itched to smooth it back into place among the thick flaxen braids coiled at her ears. Hands clenched at his sides, he saw Lady Philippa in a way he hadn't noticed before.

She was a beautiful young woman if a trifle frail-looking. A dark blue tunic hugged her slender body, a gold girdle accented her shapely hips. Perhaps her neck was a bit long, and her moon-shaped eyes set too close together, but Adrian thought her the loveliest woman he'd ever seen, aside from his Jeanne. That she should suffer because of him filled him with remorse. That she should unwittingly arouse him shocked Adrian. Shifting his weight, he discreetly rearranged himself.

A sob shook Philippa's body, nearly bending her double. Head bowed, she pled with Drogo. "Oh, no! Please, my lord. Do not do this to me! Do not allow this . . . this *man* to touch me!"

Her outburst silenced the knights and squires who were dining. Eager to hear such a titillating debate, they turned and stared. Hilda, the pregnant scullery wench, edged away from the trestle table, a jug of ale perched on her hip. Maintaining a watchful eye on Philippa, she sidled closer to Drogo than the other servants dared. The air in the hall thickened with tension and the smoke pouring from the poorly ventilated kitchen.

Drogo gestured toward his gaping men, his voice booming like an actor's. "Straighten up, my lady. There is naught to be upset about. 'Tis a routine formality that many brides undergo."

Philippa lifted her face and glared at Drogo through glistening eyes. Adrian thought he'd never seen such rage and fear on a woman's face. Mesmerized, he watched her square her shoulders and meet Drogo's gaze head-on.

"Why, my lord?" Though she beseeched him, her words resonated with dignity. "Why are you doing this to me?"

Adrian's pulse quickened in response to the nakedness of her emotions, the strength with which she reined them in.

Drogo tilted his head, his black eyes darting from Philippa to the spectators at the trestle table. "Why am I doing this to you?" he mocked her. "Why, girl, isn't that as obvious as the nose on my face? I am lord of Oldwall Castle, and my wife will bear my legitimate heirs. Don't I have a vested interest in determining whether the wench what shares my bed is a virgin, or not? Lord Drogo isn't interested in messy leftovers, my lady. Drogo don't want no bastard blood in the veins of his first man-child."

A great burst of laughter went up among the lord's men. Behind Drogo, Sir Killian smiled broadly.

Adrian could contain himself no longer. "Surely, my lord, you do not hold to the belief that a woman can bear a child fathered by two men?"

Drogo faced his new midwife, black bushy brows drawn down into an inverted V. "I've seen it happen in pig litters, sir. A sow what ruts with two male pigs can get pregnant by both."

"Women are not sows," Adrian argued.

"Some are, some ain't," Drogo conceded. "But the fact remains, I've got a right to know whether I'm wedding a virgin."

"For God's sake, my lord. *I am a virgin.*" Philippa's jutting cheeks darkened; her lips whitened.

"Then you have nothing to fear, my lady," Drogo said.

"Can't you take the lady's word for it, my lord?" Adrian asked. There was no doubt in his own mind that the girl was a virgin; the thought of being touched by a man clearly scared her to death.

Drogo puffed out his chest and stared at Adrian. "A right cheeky bastard you are, Sir Adrian. Been here less than an hour and already you're tweaking my nose. As for Philippa's credibility, let's just say she's her father's daughter, that one. And Sir Casper couldn't be trusted to utter a truthful word if his life depended on it."

Philippa's voice was whisper quiet. "Leave my father out of this discussion, my lord."

Drogo's gaze shot to her, the back of his arm raised to land her a blow. Hilda scuttled through the rushes and stood beside Philippa. Protectively, the servant wrapped her arms around a waist half the diameter of her own. Adrian admired the courage and solidarity of these two women. Quietly, he said, "You wouldn't slaughter a prized pig 'ere it was fat enough to eat, would you, my lord?"

Drogo froze, and Oldwall Castle held its breath. Slowly, the man lowered his arm and turned to Adrian. "Point well taken, sir. I should like to joust with you some day. Or are the hands of a midwife too delicate to don a pair of gauntlets?"

"I have not lost my fighting skills," Adrian said. "But I am a physic first, a knight second. I prefer saving lives over wasting them."

Adrian's gaze flickered to Philippa's then, and he caught the hatred in her eyes. Looking her full in the face, he was stunned by the power of her emotion. She blamed him as much as she blamed Drogo for what was going to happen! Adrian couldn't explain to her why Drogo's wishes ruled him. He could only meet her gaze, and Hilda's, trying wordlessly to convince them of his honor.

Drogo ambled to the trestle table, grabbed a leg of roasted pheasant from a squire's trencher, and ate while he talked. "So you enjoy delivering babies, do you, Sir Adrian? That is passing odd business for a knight. And against the law. But Edward has given you a special license, I am told by Killian, so you should be happy to practice at Oldwall Castle."

"I am, my lord."

"Do you accept my offer of a position in this castle? And with it, all the terms of a retainership?"

"Aye, my lord," Adrian answered. The words felt like treason beneath Philippa's furious gaze.

"Then, as lord of this castle, I order you to examine Lady Philippa and determine whether she is a virgin. Do you understand?"

"Aye, my lord."

Philippa shuddered in Hilda's embrace. "Drogo, why are you doing this? Is it further punishment, my lord? How long must I suffer for my father's disappearance?"

"Punishment? Why, child, do you not wish to marry Drogo?"

The lady's nostrils flared. The lord's question deserved no

response. Adrian reckoned that Philippa's parents had long ago promised her to Drogo, or that she'd been captured from a rival baron's castle. Whatever the cause of her betrothal, Philippa obviously was not the willing participant of a love-match. But then, few people were as lucky in marriage as Adrian and Jeanne had been.

Memories of Jeanne unexpectedly deepened Adrian's resistance to Drogo's orders. "My lord, why do you not let one of the local women examine Philippa? Surely there is a qualified midwife in the village who can perform the examination?"

"You will examine the girl and I will watch!" Drogo thundered, much to the enjoyment of his vassals.

Philippa turned into Hilda's embrace, shuddering against the raucous laughter which erupted.

"And what if I refuse to perform the examination?" Adrian's hand hovered perilously near his sword belt. Momentarily, he forgot about King Edward and the rack. For a farthing, he'd have plunged a knife through Drogo's heart then and there, releasing Philippa from this miserable lot in life.

The baron lifted his chin. "I shall send you back to London, sir. I have no need for an insubordinate servant."

For a fleeting second, Adrian thought of killing Drogo, then fleeing the castle. He could live in the forests as a hermit.

But Sir Killian uttered a warning that chilled Adrian's blood. "Sir Adrian, do not think to betray my lord's trust or to shirk the duties he assigns you. The king's man who brought you to me in London made it clear that your licensing was an experiment. I have been charged with the additional duty of reporting your activities to the king."

Adrian clenched his teeth. Lifting her head from Hilda's shoulder, Philippa flashed him a look that could have pierced a coat of plate armor.

Drogo tossed his cleanly picked bone on the floor, and two sinewy hounds lunged from beneath the table to descend upon it. Drogo watched them with interest, shouting encouragement as if he were witnessing a cockfight or a bear-baiting. When he was bored with the dogs' noisy contest, he walked over and gave them both a healthy kick to the ribs. Both animals yelped, retreating beneath the trestle table with tails tucked between their legs. Satisfied, Drogo lazily strode back to where Adrian stood. "You'll do what I say, Sir Adrian. Or I will kill you."

"Those are the castle rules," Philippa added coldly before Hilda's squeeze silenced her.

"The examination will be performed in the morn," Drogo pronounced. "In Philippa's solar."

"Why must it be tomorrow?" Philippa asked.

"Give the girl more time, my lord," Hilda begged. "She's an innocent thing, and she needs more time to get used to the idea of being touched by a man."

"Silence, whore!" Drogo roared. "She'll get used to being touched by a man soon enough. And not by some soft-peckered knight who prefers slapping baby's bottoms to jousting and hunting and hawking!"

"Then let Hilda be present, also," suggested Sir Adrian.

The servant nodded, while Philippa hugged the woman's waist tightly.

"No!" Drogo strode to the head of the long trestle table, apparently more comfortable with his rowdy men than on the raised dais behind them. He quaffed a tankard of ale next to the place that was his, and belched before he turned and made a dismissive gesture in Philippa's direction. "Enough of this silly chatter. Go upstairs, women, both of ye. The lady can eat in her solar this night. I care not to see her hateful stares and listen to her sniveling! I shall see her in the morn when she is in her rightful place—on her back!"

Amid the laughter that followed Drogo's jibe, Philippa, wrapped in Hilda's arms, glided toward the staircase. Killian took his place at Drogo's right hand, while Adrian watched the women ascend the stairs. Philippa held her head erect, but her composure was belied by the rigidity of her spine and the mantle of scarlet skin about her neck. Her movements were graceful, contained. Even in the thick of battle, Adrian had never witnessed such dignity under brutally trying conditions. He wondered what kind of woman Lady Philippa was. He wondered whether he could touch her body intimately without showing the effect she had on him. He had to.

If Drogo could have known what he was thinking, Adrian would already be a dead man.

Dawn. Philippa heard a rattle outside the thick oaken door of her solar. Clutching a counterpane to her chin, she pulled her knees to her breasts and snuggled close against the great carved headboard. Her chest tightened painfully, and her head ached with the pressure her galloping pulse produced. The moment had come. She would have shrieked if she thought hysterics might alter Drogo's plans, but she knew him well enough to know a show of fear would only excite him. A night without one wink of sleep had galvanized Philippa's determination to deny him the pleasure of her fear and shame.

Hilda slipped into the room; the door pulled shut behind her and a bolt rasped into place.

Sighing with relief, Philippa said, "Thank God, 'tis you."

Hilda waddled across the room, a small tray balanced on her gravid belly.

Philippa had no appetite for figs or stale bread, but she sipped the steaming, fragrant posset her servant offered her. "I am surprised that oaf outside allowed you to visit me," she said, her heartbeat returning to normal.

"The lord sent orders that you was to be brung some food, my lady. He didn't say who should bring it." A sad smile curved the woman's lips as she took Philippa's empty cup and replaced it on the tray. After a moment, she lowered herself awkwardly to the edge of Philippa's bed.

"Is this babe giving you trouble, Hilda?"

"Forgive me, my lady," the servant replied, starting to rise. "I should not presume to rest my feet in your presence."

Philippa laid a restraining hand on Hilda's forearm. "Stay! I need you, Hilda."

The older woman struggled to sit comfortably, then turned her ruddy face toward Philippa. "My lady, I am so sorry I can not be with you during your . . . examination."

"We are made stronger by our ordeals." Sighing, Philippa flipped a long golden braid off her shoulder.

"Are you terribly afraid, my child?"

"Afraid? Of Drogo? Ha! He is a worm, nay, worse than a worm! Lord Oldcastle is a worm in a mule's behind!"

"He is to be your husband, my lady," Hilda whispered.

"Aye, my father contracted my marriage when I was a child. Methinketh when Father returns, he may find a way out of the bargain when he sees what an ogre Drogo has become."

Her confidence was a sham. She was fantasizing again, and Hilda's downcast eyes affirmed her foolishness. But Philippa needed something to hang on to at that moment, some thread of hope, no matter how slender.

"Your father may not make it home before you must wed Drogo," Hilda said. "And even if he does come home. . . . "

Philippa's heart lurched. She knew what Hilda meant to say even though the poor wench couldn't bring herself to say it. Plucking at the counterpane bunched in her hand, Philippa blinked back the hot tears that threatened to spill down her face. When she trusted her voice, she said, "I know, Hilda. The contract is binding. I shall not disgrace Father. I cannot. By the terms of my marriage agreement, if I refuse to marry Drogo, Father will forfeit his interest in Drogo's shipping company. I can not allow Father to return home a pauper, can I? Can I, Hilda?"

"No . . . no, I suppose not." Hilda didn't sound so sure.

"Besides, being Lady of Oldwall Castle won't be so bad. Will it, Hilda?"

"No, my lady. You shall have everything a lady should want. And as long as I am here, you will be regarded as a princess by the servants."

"Thank you, Hilda." Philippa reached out and clasped her friend's hands. "I am not afraid, I promise. This examination will not take very long. Will it, Hilda?"

Despite having given birth to several children, all stillborn, Hilda's cheeks reddened at the thought of a man performing such an intimate examination. She lowered her eyes and bit her lip. "I don't know for certain, my lady. A virgin test wasn't required when I was wed. To be certain, my Denys had no illusions about the condition of my maidenhead. 'Twere more chinks in it than in a rusty coat of mail."

Philippa forced a smile at Hilda's earthy humor. Breathing deeply, she clutched the woman's hands, taking comfort from her chafed skin, her strong fingers. She edged forward on the bed and whispered. "What will he do, Hilda? What will this Sir Adrian do to me?"

Hilda swallowed convulsively. "I suppose you will lay on your back, child, with your skirts pulled up to your waist."

Philippa felt a blaze of heat streak through her body. Her skirts pulled up to her waist? "*Dieu*," she whispered, silently praying for strength.

Stammering, Hilda continued. "And then, the physic will most likely ask you to spread your legs . . . very wide."

"Oh, God." Philippa gulped in air as her throat constricted.

"And then," Hilda said in a tiny voice, "then, he will touch you . . . down there."

The thought of Sir Adrian touching her anywhere, much less *down there*, filled Philippa with anticipation. Even though she hated him, she couldn't ignore that he was a handsome man. *Before* she'd even had reason to hate him, she'd been attracted to him, surprised at her own reaction to the stony set of his jaw, the liquid warmth of his eyes. Now, he was going to touch her intimately, and she didn't know how she was going to live through the humiliation of it.

"He will put his finger inside you, my lady."

Hilda's frankness startled Philippa. She stared at the servant's tight lips, hoping that the woman was joking. A moment of silence passed. Hilda was not joking.

"His finger . . . inside . . . me?" The words alone sent a shocking tremor through Philippa's body. She couldn't imagine anything more vile and intrusive. Sir Adrian Vale's fingers inside her body! She wanted to die. "I hate him."

Hilda started to say something else, but a loud rapping startled both women.

Drogo's voice could be heard bellowing from the corridor. "Are you ready, Philippa? We are coming in."

Hilda grasped Philippa's shoulder and planted a kiss on her forehead. "Be brave, my lady. 'Twill be over soon enough, and you will forget all about it."

Philippa nodded dumbly, preparing to slip out of her body while this horrible ordeal played itself out. She'd learned long ago how to disassociate herself from unpleasant things. Hilda's pitying face registered somewhere deep in her brain, and Philippa heard her own voice squeak. "I will be all right, Hilda. Do not fret over me."

But in her heart of hearts, she knew she would never forget what was about to happen to her.

The door burst open. Hilda scurried out as Drogo marched in. Sir Adrian slowly entered the room, a look of stony disapproval on his face.

Masterful at concealing her feelings, Philippa aimed at giving off an air of haughty resignation. She regretted her wildly emotional response to Drogo's announcement last night in the hall. By the time she had pulled herself together and masked her fear, Drogo had taken his satisfaction from her. But he would get no more from her today, she vowed.

Calmly, she said, "Close the door behind you, please, Sir Adrian."

A moment passed while the knight studied her with those dark, liquid eyes of his. Then he pushed the door closed against Sir Killian's gaping face.

Drogo stood at the foot of the bed, grinning. "Well, sir. Go to it. What shall you have her do? Disrobe completely? Lie naked and spread-eagle on the bed?"

Philippa noticed the protuberance beneath Drogo's jupon, and shuddered. The man's eyes gleamed avariciously and his tongue darted over his lips in a way that made Philippa recoil in disgust. Instinctively, she wrapped her arms about her shoulders and huddled against the head board. She thought of making one last appeal to Drogo's sense of honor.

"Well, come on, man!" Drogo cried. "What are you dawdling for? Get on with it."

It was futile to beg.

Philippa wouldn't relinquish her dignity no matter what Drogo and his minion, Sir Adrian, did to her.

She felt the tall knight's presence by her bedside. Leaning over her, he said quietly, " 'Twill not take long, my lady. Lie back now and try to relax."

Every muscle in her body contracted. Drogo stood at the foot of her bed, staring, licking his lips. And this dark stranger, whose compassionate gaze had just the day before sent tremors of pleasure up her spine, was going to defile her. Her vision blurred and the room swung like a corpse at the end of a rope.

"Breathe, my lady," Sir Adrian urged her.

She realized she'd filled her lungs a moment ago, but had failed to exhale.

"Breathe, or you will pass out."

She looked him straight in the eye. "Would that be so terrible, sir? Must I be conscious in order for you and my husband-to-be to enjoy this spectacle?"

She saw him cringe, but she had no sympathy for his offended sensibilities. So, he thought Drogo crass and perverted, too—well, that meant he possessed an ounce of decency, at least. But not enough to compel him to refuse Drogo's orders. She recalled the way he'd told Drogo that, yes, he wanted to stay on at Oldwall Castle as midwife, and she whispered, "Toady," just loudly enough so that he could hear it.

His eyes snapped to hers and a cord of muscle twitched along his jaw. His lips parted, as if he thought to rebut her accusation, but they were both aware of Drogo's presence, his escalating arousal. Philippa tossed one of her braids over her shoulder and slid beneath the counterpane. There, she lay on her back, sheet pulled to her chin, glaring up at Sir Adrian. She had no intention of making his job easier for him.

Never taking his eyes from hers, he peeled the counterpane from her body and folded it loosely at the foot of the bed. Philippa's thin night rail afford little protection against the warmth of Adrian's hands; so large a newborn babe could have fit in his palms, they brushed her waist and hips. Coiled at his sides, they reminded her of the man's power, his masculinity.

She shuddered at the mingled feelings of guilt and fear that accompanied her thoughts. Despite her humiliation, she felt a nervous tingle race from the tip of her bare toes to the middle part in her blond hair.

Sir Adrian straightened, towering over Philippa. His eyes quickly scanned the length of her figure, then met hers again. A flash of awareness passed between them, but in an instant, Adrian hardened his eyes and glanced away. The silence in Philippa's solar was chokingly thick. She masked her fear while deep within her a whirlwind of emotion raged. She wanted to hate Sir Adrian, but she was desperate for a sign of her subjugator's compassion. And she couldn't bear to look at Drogo, who interrupted his harsh breathing only to urge this unholy ritual forward.

She searched Adrian's face for a sign of warmth, but his features were all hard planes and angles. His jaw was carved from stone; his eyes hooded. Sir Adrian's only visible reaction to Philippa's probing stare was a darkening of his complexion.

She folded her arms across her chest and lay as still as a corpse. Drogo's breathing grew more ragged, and, from the corner of her eyes, Philippa saw him rub his hands in anticipation.

Sir Adrian shot the baron a look of reproval, then said to Philippa, "You must lift your tunic, my lady."

Her heart leapt in her throat. When she spoke, her voice was barely a whisper. "Nay. I will not."

Adrian's features tightened, his Adam's apple bobbing convulsively. Good. He was as repulsed by Drogo's perversions as Philippa. But he was not protesting the baron's orders, so Philippa cared not a whit whether his liege-lord's noisy panting disturbed him.

"If you do not remove your night rail, my lady, I shall be forced to remove it for you."

Philippa's entire body prickled beneath the knight's hard gaze. She inhaled deeply, considering her options. She could participate in his tawdry ceremony and do as she was told, or she could lie there like a limp rag which, she supposed, would deny Drogo the pleasure of her fear and would have the added benefit of inconveniencing Sir Adrian.

Through clenched teeth, she said, "Do what you will, sir. But do not expect any cooperation from me."

Adrian answered her with a curt, guttural sound. He leaned down, lifted the hem of her tunic, and rucked it around her pale, shapely thighs. Her knees clamped together like mortared bricks. Philippa's refusal to lift her hips made it impossible for Adrian to pull her shift past her waist.

"Come on, man!" Drogo exclaimed. "I ain't got all day!"

Philippa made her body as stiff as a pike-staff. Her green eyes, blazing with hatred, cut to Adrian.

With a heavy sigh, he grasped the neckline of her tunic with both hands. With one violent movement, he ripped the flimsy cotton panel off her body, leaving her naked and exposed.

Chapter Four

Cold air hit her body like a splash of icy water, tightening her skin like an astringent. She knew what he was about to do but found herself shocked that he was going to do it.

"How dare you?" Philippa gasped, hugging her shoulders, drawing up her knees. Rolling away from Adrian, she instinctively tried to cover her nakedness.

Adrian's hot fingers clasped her arm, preventing her from turning, banding her limbs with coiled heat. "Do not fight me, my lady. 'Twill go much easier and faster if you allow me to do what I must."

With the heels of his hands, he flattened her shoulders to the mattress. The weight of his body rendered her helpless; he hovered over her, his rocky jaw prominent, his nearness eclipsing everything else. Swathed in his scent, a combination of leather and man, Philippa's senses swelled to near bursting.

Warm breath, redolent of ale and spearmint, fanned the sensitive skin of her neck. Goose bumps sprayed across her collarbone and down her arms. Arousal, deeply resented but powerful nonetheless, exploded like star-bursts everywhere Adrian's skin touched hers, and even where it didn't. But Drogo's heavy breathing intruded, reminding Philippa why she hated Adrian. She did hate him, even more so because of her body's response to his touches. She grabbed his wrists, shocked by the strength of his pulse and the fine, silken texture of the hair that covered his forearms.

Warmth flowed grudgingly into her. Philippa's fingers melted into Adrian's skin. She clung to him, her uneven breath mingling with his. Beneath his linsey-woolsey tunic, Adrian's chest bulged hard as plate armor. His animal strength—barely under control—boiled in veins that mapped his arms and throbbed at his temples. Glistening biceps strained the sleeves of his tunic. The sweaty aroma that wafted from Adrian's dampened clothing was intoxicating. Philippa's back arched as she hungrily sucked the air they shared between them.

In response, Adrian's fingers dug deeper into her flesh and his gleaming eyes fastened on her parted lips.

Her arousal sparked guilt, which in turn drew an instant of lucidity. Philippa writhed like a madwoman in the tangled sheets, wrenching herself free of Adrian's hold. "Don't touch me," she hissed.

He released her as if she were a cauldron of boiling oil. Snatching his hands to his sides, he said, "I am afraid it cannot be helped, my lady. If I am to examine you, I must touch you."

Anger bubbled up inside Philippa—anger that her emotions could be manipulated with such careless disregard; anger that she couldn't quell her body's responses to Sir Adrian's touch. With lightning quickness, she kicked her leg outward and thrust her heel into Sir Adrian's stomach.

"Ooomph!" Doubled over, his hands flew to his groin.

Drogo's huge guffaw hurled Philippa past the edge of reason. She scrambled toward the side of the bed opposite

Adrian, desperate to escape the torture of his hands on her body. She heard her own frantic panting, the sounds of terror as she squeaked and grunted. One foot landed on the cold floor, one hand grasped the wooden footboard of her bed. Five paces to the door . . . she would fly down the stairs . . . seek sanctuary in the chapel. . . .

A cold blade of steel pressed against her throat.

Philippa froze, and through the loose strands of hair flowing over her brow, she recognized Drogo's grinning face. Her eyes traveled downward to the puddle of hose at his ankles. Reeking like a gong-farmer, the man ran a thumb along the ridge of Philippa's lips. Philippa's physical senses were so confused, she wasn't sure whether revulsion or arousal caused her tongue to find Drogo's calloused skin. But when she tasted the pungent filth of his nails, she choked back a surge of bitter bile, then bared her teeth and sank them into a meaty pad of flesh.

He could have slit her throat.

Instead, Drogo dropped his dagger to the floor and slapped her so hard that she went sprawling back onto the bed, her limbs akimbo. Colors, along with a jolt of pain, exploded in Philippa's head. When her sight returned, the side of her head throbbed and the room spun precariously. She struggled to her elbows, but strong hands pushed her down again. Strong, kind hands—not Drogo's. At the baron's snarl, the door to her solar flung open and Killian rushed in, his eyes agog. "My lord, shall I restrain her?"

"No!" Drogo bellowed.

In her dazed state, Philippa watched the ensuing tableau with horror. Sucking his injured thumb, Drogo sifted through the rushes for his knife. Releasing her, Adrian crossed the width of the solar in panther-like strides, his own dagger drawn. Killian stumbled backward, a blade at his throat. The door slammed shut.

Drogo leaned heavily against the footboard, cursing and

clutching his loins. "A spirited wench, ain't she? I'll have a time of it taming this little snapping puss! God's blood, this is monstrous good entertainment!"

Adrian reappeared at the side of Philippa's bed. Through the fog in her head, she heard his voice, deep and soothing. "Are you all right, Lady Philippa? Can you see me?"

"Aye, both of you." Philippa tried to focus on just one of the Sir Adrians that floated before her.

He bent forward. His palms, warm and calloused, and smelling of soap, framed her face. Philippa would have closed her eyes to blot out the multiple troll barons that paced beyond the footboard, but Sir Adrian held her in his somber gaze. Her head slowly cleared and she blinked away the double images that crossed her eyes.

There was no point in attempting to hide her nakedness. Philippa lay motionless on the mattress, hot tears filling her eyes. Adrian sat on the edge of the bed and held her hand. Strangely, she calmed beneath his touch—though she hated him now more than ever. His hoarse whisper sent shivers through her skin. "My lady, how many fingers am I holding up?"

"Two." And at least one of them, Hilda had said, was going inside of her. *God, why was this happening?*

He felt her head again, fingers palpating her scalp.

"Hurry up, then, man!" Drogo shouted. "I ain't got all day. My men are waiting on the jousting field, there's hunting to do before the noon meal, and I have important business to attend."

Adrian shot a venomous glance over his shoulder. "Would you care to postpone this examination, my lord? 'Twould be most agreeable to me, and I am certain the lady would not object."

"Christ's knuckles! Nay, Sir Adrian. I want this matter done, and I want it done proper. Now, leave her skull be. I barely touched the chit!"

"Get on with it." Noting Adrian's startled look, Philippa added tightly, "I, too, have more important matters to tend to."

Adrian nodded. He scooted toward the foot of the bed and patted the top of one of Philippa's thighs. Drogo leaned over the carved oaken panel, leering. Philippa's skin crawled beneath the baron's wolfish stare, but she couldn't will herself to float to the ceiling, as she'd learned to do years ago. She knew she couldn't disassociate herself from Adrian's probing fingers. He was too overwhelming to be relegated to some distant place in her mind. Nevertheless, she gulped back a sob and managed to block Drogo's heavy breathing from her mind.

Adrian's fingers scored her flesh. "You must lift your knees, my lady."

She knew if she didn't, he would do it for her. Clutching the shreds of her bedclothes beneath her, Philippa slid her heels to her buttocks and bent her knees.

"You must part your legs, my lady." Adrian's voice was rough-edged but not unkind.

Philippa closed her eyes, humiliation pouring through her like lava. She felt the pressure of Adrian's hands, one on either knee, as her limbs splayed and opened like a butterfly. Cool air whispered against her most sensitive parts, heightening the sensation of her nakedness. Totally exposed, a tremor of apprehension rippled through her body. And strangely, a throbbing tingle pooled beneath the thatch of golden hair that concealed her womanhood.

Adrian's voice penetrated the cloud of emotion swirling in her mind. "My lady, I am going to touch you now. I am applying some ointment to my fingers. . . . "

Philippa opened her eyes. The knight rubbed his hands together, perhaps to warm his hands, then dipped his forefinger in a jar of thick, oily salve taken from the pouch attached to his belt. Philippa drew in a ragged breath as he coated his finger with the glistening jelly. Then his hand was between her legs, his fingers brushing her bristly hair.

"If you feel any pain, you must tell me," he said.

She closed her eyes once more, determined to shut out Drogo's presence. A million nerve endings screamed as Adrian's fingertips, warm from the friction of his own hands, touched her skin. She felt the tentative parting of her outer flesh, swollen and tingling. Adrian's finger probed, seeking her opening.

The heavy aching in her loins increased. Philippa instinctively squeezed her muscles, tightening her body, creating an impassable barrier through which Adrian's finger could not easily pass, even with its sheen of lubrication. "Relax, Lady Philippa," he told her. "You must relax."

But she didn't know how. Her fingers grappled with the counterpane, her legs spasmed and cramped with tension.

Adrian clasped her knees again. He gently spread her legs further apart, widening the cleavage of her womanhood. The cool air that kissed her skin was met this time with a trickle of liquid heat. Philippa's lashes flickered, but Adrian's voice was firm. "Keep your eyes closed, my lady." And so she followed his advice.

His finger probed again, this time sliding between the folds of her flesh and into her body. A tingly warmth impaled her, confusing Philippa's senses. A tiny mewling sound, which could have been mistaken for pain, escaped her lips. She flung her arm over her eyes to hide the hunger building inside her. Her inner muscles clutched at Adrian's finger; the liquid heat that was at first a trickle now gushed from her.

Sir Adrian slid his probing finger deeper, the heel of his hand cupping Philippa's throbbing mound. Fire streaked through her, and everywhere Adrian's finger explored, flames of wet heat exploded. He reached so deeply within her, she ached, and for the first time in her life experienced a mindless hunger, an obsessive longing for something she'd never known existed. Aware of her jagged breathing and her heaving breasts, she whispered, "I hate you," as scalding tears welled behind her eyes.

He said nothing. Philippa peeped from beneath her fore-arm, watching Adrian's face. A frown tugged at his lips. His eyes met hers and the awareness that crackled between them drowned Drogo's urgent gasps. Philippa swallowed the lump that had risen in her throat and willed her body to ignore the crescendo of arousal building in her loins. It was impossible; she shut her eyes and gritted her teeth against the torturous pleasure-pain that wracked her body.

Jostled by Adrian's movement, she peeked again, and saw that he'd repositioned himself. One shoulder was lowered so that his head was between her knees, so close to her woman-hood that her scent would fill his nostrils. He had angled him-self as if to burrow deep within her body. Burning with desire and hatred and humiliation, Philippa bit her lip as his finger explored parts of her body she never knew existed.

She felt his free hand flat on her belly, pressing down hard.

"What are you doing?" Philippa shivered as his warm cal-loused skin molded itself to her stomach.

"Examining you, my lady. Your birth canal is tipped back-ward, I fear. Giving birth will not be an easy chore for you."

His fingers palpated the smooth expanse of skin between her jutting hipbones, and the pressure of his hand on her belly intensified the sensations created by his finger, still deep within her. The throbbing in Philippa's loins sharpened to an agonizing ache. Contractions started, wave after wave of them, and the urge to buck her hips and arch her back seemed irresistible, but somehow Philippa managed to control her movements. She tried to think of something that would dispel her erotic thoughts.

Drogo's heavy breathing . . . his fingers itching with lust-ful eagerness.

The image Philippa conjured tempered her body's reaction,

but still she could not help how she was clutching at Sir Adrian's finger! Horrified by her body's betrayal, she glanced from beneath her forearm and watched him scrutinize her exposed body. Lord, he was staring at her tender pink flesh and white thighs with the cool detachment of a monk dispensing alms. But Philippa could not detach herself from the sensations roiling through her body. When Sir Adrian at last unsheathed his finger—slowly, gently—she almost grabbed his wrist to keep his hand captive between her thighs.

But, it was over! Saints preserve her, at last the ordeal was finished! Attempting to disguise the liquid warmth seeping from between her legs, Philippa rolled onto her side. A shudder quaked her body as Adrian slid the counterpane to her shoulders and gently tucked the covers around her. Burying her face in her pillow, knees pulled to her chest, she gave in to the tremors threatening to erupt within her. With a stifled cry, she finally allowed herself the release her body craved.

"I am sorry, my lady," Sir Adrian's voice was as warm as fleece.

Philippa hid her tears, hoping that the knight would think she sobbed because of her humiliation, or because he'd caused her pain. His firm, warm touch lingered on her shoulders until Drogo's voice peeled it away.

"Aargh, leave her be, sir. She's a coddled, spoiled brat, that one. Sir Casper couldn't break a horse, nor tame a woman properly. But she'll make a fine wife, anyhow, that one! Upon my word, her loins were damn near drooling for me. Ha! Methinketh this wench will fancy the marriage bed when she's grown accustomed to a man's ways."

There was satisfaction and satiation in Drogo's voice, and Philippa knew he'd savored every moment of her nakedness, gloated at every second of her suffering.

She tried to breathe normally, but her body still trembled from the shock of her unwanted arousal and the shame of having experienced pleasure beneath the goatish gaze of Drogo.

Reminded that it would be the baron's fingers next probing her womanhood, she curled up in a tight ball, shivering with dread. "Please, my lord, send Hilda in to attend to me," she mumbled into her pillow. "I beg of you."

As usual, Drogo ignored her request. "I am late for the practice fields," he said, stamping across the room. At the door, he paused, and said, "Do see me this evening, Sir Adrian, so that we may discuss the results of your examination. I'll want to hear more about the chit's backward birth canal."

"Aye, my lord."

Philippa heard her solar's door open and close. Drogo's footsteps faded down the stairs, along with Killian's and those of the guard who had been stationed at her door throughout the night.

Philippa lay still, her senses adjusting to the aftermath of her shock, her heart decelerating. Sir Adrian's silence, punctuated by a heavy sigh, filled the room. She knew he watched her; his distress was palpable, the crunch of straw beneath his pacing boots strangely comforting. The musky smell of her body intertwined with the soap on his skin, the pungent salve on his hands. Philippa prayed that the knight was as miserable as she.

A muted cacophony filtered through the cracks in the solar's window. In the lower courtyard, smithies pounded sheets of metal into plate armor, while pie-makers hawked their wares. Drogo's hunting party departed the castle grounds in a dim rumble of horses' hooves and celebratory whoops. Life went on, the world oblivious to Philippa's anguish.

Sobered and restless, she turned and watched Sir Adrian clamp the lid on his ointment jar and slip it into the leather pouch at his belt. His skin glistened from salve and her body's juices. The sight of his big hands and supple fingers, wet from her desire, filled her with embarrassed apprehension.

Even an unskilled midwife's apprentice would have recognized her body's reaction for what it was. There was no doubt in Philippa's mind that the King's Physic, specially licensed to tend to the ladies of the realm, had recognized the hot fluid of her arousal, the clutch of her inner muscles. He was probably laughing silently at her inability to control her body's physical responses.

Oh, how she despised her body for betraying her! And how she hated Sir Adrian for manipulating her emotions so heartlessly, so skillfully.

He turned abruptly, staring. "Are you all right?"

Philippa snorted derisively, struggling to her elbows amid the rumpled linens. "You are no different from every other man. I hate you, Sir Adrian."

The knight inhaled deeply. "I don't blame you for hating me, my lady, but I am Drogo's servant as much as Hilda, and I cannot refuse his commands. I tried to make the examination as painless as possible."

"I hardly felt a thing."

"Good. Then I shall leave you be, my lady." Sir Adrian nodded curtly, pivoted, then strode from her bedside. But he paused with his hand on the door latch, then slowly returned. "There is just one thing I wish to say."

He sat on the opposite side of Philippa's bed, his long legs stretched before him, one hand on the mattress supporting his weight. Time crawled, and Philippa held her breath, not trusting herself to speak above the clot of fear in her throat.

"What would you have me tell the baron, Lady Philippa?"

Coughing, she toyed with a flaxen braid. Heat scored her cheeks. "What do you mean, sir?"

His voice was icy, his jaw a glacier. "I believe you know precisely what I mean. What shall I tell Lord Drogo when he asks me whether you are a virgin?"

"Tell him that I am a virgin," she replied tightly.

"You would have me lie, then?"

" 'Tis no lie, Sir Adrian." But Philippa's heart raced like a huntsman on the trail of blooded prey. She fixed her eyes on a point in the center of Adrian's forehead, refusing to be shaken by his hard, penetrating gaze. "I *am* a virgin, and you are an impudent scoundrel if you suggest otherwise."

"I have examined hundreds of women, my lady, and while the lack of a maidenhead does not prove you have been with a man, what I felt inside you certainly does. You are no virgin."

Philippa crushed a fistful of linen, anger deadening the arousal she'd felt just moments before. Her mask of cool displeasure concealed the desperation of her inner thoughts. Frantically, she recalled snippets of a discussion she'd once had with Hilda. "If I lost my maidenhead, sir, 'twas from rigorous exercise, mayhaps even from horseback riding."

"You do not ride side-saddle, my lady?" His gaze was as tight as a shrunken wimple.

"In my youth, I did not," she replied. "You cannot be certain that I did not lose my maidenhead that way."

A tense, prickly silence overlaid the chiming of the chapel bells and the call to morning Mass. Philippa prayed that Adrian would not challenge her further; her sanity could not survive another examination, and she couldn't imagine what would become of her if Drogo got it in his head she was damaged goods.

Adrian twisted his lips and averted his gaze. For a moment, he rubbed his lower lip, apparently in deep contemplation. Surely, he didn't suspect she'd been taken by another man! Why, Hilda had once said in passing that it was impossible, even for a midwife, to know for certain. . . .

The knight's gaze focused on her again, besieging the fortress so carefully constructed around Philippa's heart. She sat up and pulled the counterpane to her chin. Despite the unnerving effect Adrian's scrutiny had on her, she forced herself to meet his gaze.

"Why do you stare at me like that?" Her teeth chattered noisily, while her shoulders trembled with fright.

"Are you cold?" Without waiting for an answer, Adrian pushed off from the bed and strode to the fireplace on the opposite wall of Philippa's solar. Deftly, he created a spark with steel flint, touched tinder to wick, then tossed a flame on the dry faggots. He grabbed a fire-iron, squatted, and poked the crackling logs until a tendril of warmth lifted from the hearth and curled around Philippa's shoulders.

She inhaled deeply, feasting her gaze on Adrian's broad back, the muscles bunched beneath his tunic, the contours of his strong, muscular haunches swathed in snug woven hose. When he'd finished with the fire and cracked a window, he returned and sat on the edge of the bed nearest her, his skin bronzed by the warmth of the flames, his brow furrowed. If Philippa hadn't hated him so virulently, she would have laid a palm on his burnished cheek to soak the heat from his skin.

As it was, she hugged her knees tighter to her chest and donned a mean expression.

"Thank you for tending the fire, sir. 'Twas unnecessary. Hilda would have done it."

"Ah, Hilda. I am glad you mentioned her, my lady. I fear that she is due for a difficult delivery. If it would not inconvenience you too terribly, I would suggest that Hilda be relieved of her kitchen duties and allowed to tend you solely as a personal maid, or dressing woman."

"You are asking me to lighten Hilda's duties?"

"Aye, my lady. I know she has had several stillbirths before this pregnancy, and she appears to be suffering much discomfort already."

Philippa's concerns for her own welfare vanished. Hilda was more than a servant to her; the woman was a treasured friend despite the disparity in their social ranks. Nodding, she said, "Sir Adrian, I want Hilda to have the best of care while she is lying in. Will you attend the birth of her child?"

"Aye, that is my duty as the physic and midwife of Oldwall Castle. I shall do everything for Hilda that I possibly can."

"I thank you."

Unthinkingly, Philippa laid her hand on Sir Adrian's arm. The heat that shot through her was like the pinch of a red-hot blacksmith's tong, and she recoiled with a gasp. An almost indiscernible curve appeared at one corner of Adrian's mouth, but he did not remark on Philippa's unease. Instead, he leaned back against the footboard of her bed and crossed his arms over his chest. A sly, half-teasing look glimmered in his eyes.

"For the second time this morning, sir, why are you looking at me like that?"

Should he tell her? Sir Adrian stretched his aching legs and met Philippa's round, inquisitive gaze. He would like to tell her why his gaze was riveted to hers. He would like to see her expression when he said she'd unwittingly stirred the loins of a man who'd been celibate for four years.

The throb beneath his chausses for once surpassed the ache in the muscles of his arms and legs. Philippa's parted lips, and the blush that darkened her swan-like neck, increased his physical discomfort tenfold. Four years without sex had not squelched his desire for women. Now, he felt like a schoolboy awkwardly attempting to conceal an irrepressible erection.

"I am looking at you," he began, silently cringing at the hoarseness of his voice, "because I am trying to understand why you have not been honest with me."

"I don't know what you are talking about," Philippa said.

"But I think you do." Adrian was impressed by how quickly the woman regained her balance.

"Let us not play games, sir. What is it that you think I have failed to be honest about?'

"You said you were a virgin, my lady."

Her eyes snapped, her bottom teeth flashed. "I *am* a virgin! I swear it!"

Emotions warred within Adrian's breast. On the one hand, he wanted to believe the girl was telling the truth. On the other, he hated to see her married off to Drogo. But Philippa's future was not for him to decide. He'd foresworn the pleasures of loving women when Jeanne died. His commitment to remaining unattached was as strong as a monk's. And even if it weren't, falling in love with Drogo's future wife was hardly a prudent move in light of his directive from King Edward.

"My lady, I care not whether you are a virgin. If I were marrying you, it would make no difference to me." Jeanne certainly had not been a maiden, and he'd loved that woman with a passion that continued despite her death.

Philippa chewed her lower lip, intensifying Adrian's urge to take her in his arms. He wanted to slide across the bed, and lean her back against the rumpled covers. He wanted to hold her face in his hands and ravish her lips, her tongue.

But he could not. Philippa was a woman posing as a virgin, and Sir Adrian was a physic dedicated to saving women's lives. And both of them were under Drogo's thumb. They could not be lovers, and if Philippa continued to deceive him about her virginity, there was little chance they'd even be friends.

Adrian ran his hands over the tops of his thighs, smoothing the kinks in his muscles. When it was obvious that Philippa was staunchly adhering to her story, he unfolded his stiff legs and stood.

Staring down at her, his fingers ached to trace the rivulet of white scalp on the top of her head. "I shall try to postpone telling Drogo what I have discovered, my lady. Perhaps you will change your mind and confide in me what has happened to you."

Hands fisted at his sides, Adrian moved toward the door, all too aware that Philippa's gaze tracked him like a hunter's loosed arrow.

"Nothing has happened to me," she said. "I am a virgin."

Adrian nodded, his back to her. As he stepped across the threshold, he hesitated. The needs of his body warred with the dictates of his conscience. His teeth clenched so tightly, his jaw ached. But he pulled the door behind him, whispering a sanguine oath. He didn't want to care what happened to Lady Philippa Gilchrist. Her welfare meant no more to him than Hilda's.

Liar! He raced recklessly down the uneven steps, then crossed the great hall in long, angry strides. The truth of it was, he cared intensely about Hilda *and* Philippa, though in very different ways. The truth was, he saw much in Philippa that he could love, if his memories would release him.

But, wasn't he the one clinging to the past? Wasn't he the one so steeped in guilt and pain that he couldn't bear to think of loving another woman?

Frustration seized him, filling his head with images of Jeanne, fantasies of Philippa, and the horrible specter of a life spent alone, without the love of either woman.

He'd been blessed to have been loved by Jeanne. Perhaps Providence would bless him again. Perhaps it wasn't treasonous to want to love again.

Quickening his pace, he thought of Jeanne, so brave in the last few moments of her life. Yes, he still loved her. He still respected her courage and integrity. But, he realized, with a heart-thudding shock, that Philippa was courageous, too, perhaps more so. Philippa was facing a future worse than death, a marriage to the most cruel brute Adrian had ever known. And her dignity amazed him.

Indeed, Adrian's fascination with Philippa was growing increasingly consuming. Exhaling a harsh breath, he wondered how long he could conceal that fascination from the world. If Drogo ever understood the complexity of what was going on between him and Philippa, their lives wouldn't be worth a farthing.

And King Edward III wouldn't lift a finger to save them.

Chapter Five

Adrian thundered down the curving stone stairwell, bursting into the courtyard with clenched teeth and a pounding heart. Stunned by the glaring daylight, he halted. The quiet in the middle bailey was eerie, like the silence of crickets before a storm. The dense black hair on his arms bristled and his warrior instincts instantly revived.

His rattled emotional state had heightened his senses. His gaze swept the courtyard. Only the clatter of cooking pots echoing from the kitchen broke the stillness. In the baron's absence, Oldwall's occupants seemed to be exhaling a collective sigh of relief. All except Sir Adrian, whose every breath pained his chest *and* his conscience.

He stretched his aching muscles and filled his lungs with crisp, smoke-scented air. The northern wind sweeping off the channel stung his cheeks, but the sun was bright. Avoiding the long cold shadows cast by the castle's towers and turrets, Adrian headed toward the arched gateway that opened into the lower bailey. A guard wearing a thick, padded gambeson and clutching a halberd stared intensely at Adrian, then nodded him through the gate.

A black foreboding snaked up Adrian's spine. Concern for Philippa was imprudent, dangerous. That he couldn't cease worrying about her infuriated him. Drogo's degradation of her had sickened him, but he had more to worry about than the future of a pretty little lying minx.

He stood in the middle of the lower bailey, surrounded by craftsmen peddling their wares. Without warning, his anger erupted. Adrian slammed a fist into his open palm. God's blood! What was he going to tell Drogo?

He could lie and say Philippa was a virgin. Then, later, when Drogo detected the truth—not an unlikely event—both Adrian and Philippa could wind up hanging from a gibbet.

And if he told Drogo the truth? Philippa would be exempt from the ogre's tyranny, but was that what *she* wanted? She seemed determined to marry the man. Adrian hesitated to expose her lie before he understood why she was so determined to marry the man. Which left him with one option: Before he disclosed his findings to Drogo, he would consult further with Philippa.

Wending his way through the congested courtyard, Adrian felt a loosening of the invisible pincers squeezing his temples. But nothing could pry free his mental image of Philippa naked, spread-eagle on her bed, her arms thrown over her face to conceal her humiliation. Allowing Drogo to leave Philippa's solar *alive* had required herculean restraint, a trait ordinarily eschewed by Adrian. Not killing the man had stretched his patience to the limit.

The heaviness in his loins simply blackened Adrian's mood.

A glint of metal drew his gaze upward. Guards clad in light mail hauberks, armed with swords and crossbows, paraded along the elevated walks lining the battlement topped curtain walls. Scanning the surrounding moat and the throngs of people milling below them, they reminded Adrian of Drogo's power over him. Meandering through knots of fletchers, furriers, weavers and chandlers, Adrian felt the guards' eagle-eyes mark him. Their hostile stares were like grease thrown on the flames of his lust.

The watch tower, with its fluttering banner of yellow and blue, loomed above him. Adrian stood in the center of a crowd, alone. The physical reactions he'd experienced in Philippa's solar filled him with self-loathing. Images of her flashed brighter than the polished helmets of Drogo's guards.

He closed his eyes, imagining her smooth, flat belly. The memory of her small breasts tightened his chest. A vision of her hard little nipples choked him. Her creamy thighs . . . her pink flesh, swollen and moist and warm . . . the pictures Adrian conjured pumped boiling blood to the focal point of his manhood.

He heard a groan and realized it was his.

Rubbing his face, Adrian opened his eyes to the horizon. Beneath his chausses, his arousal was thick and throbbing. What the devil had he been thinking when he'd agreed to act as King Edward's spy? He should have refused this impossible mission. At the moment, being racked until his bones snapped seemed preferable to walking around with a red-hot lance pinioned between his legs.

A shadow on the ground caught his attention. Short and curvy, it merged with his own. Aware of the presence behind him, Adrian tensed, his muscles coiled.

He pivoted slowly, looked down, and gazed into a pair of heavy-lidded, feminine eyes.

"Care to keep me company for a bit, sir? Forget your burdens for a while?" Smiling seductively, the young woman ran a finger down the front of Adrian's tunic.

For a whore, she was not unattractive. Her teeth were in reasonably good condition and her breath didn't stink. Adrian's throbbing manhood strained beneath his braies.

Ever since he'd laid eyes on Philippa's naked body, so young and unblemished, Adrian had been heavy with desire. A quick tumble with this willing bawd would, temporarily at least, slake his thirst.

Temptation flicked its wicked tongue along his nerve-endings. He grasped the woman's wrist more roughly than he intended. Her eyes widened, but so did her smile.

"What is your name, woman?"

"I am Belinda, Sir Adrian."

"How is it that you know my name?" Releasing her, Adrian stepped back to scrutinize Belinda's ample breasts and wide hips. The urge to use her cushioned body for his own selfish needs was strong.

"A little bird told me, sir. And I know all the little birds in this castle, them what matters, anyway." Belinda swished her hips from side to side.

"Ah, now that intrigues me. You sell information as well as love?"

Belinda flicked her tongue over incriminatingly swollen lips. "I keep my eyes and ears open. My legs, too, if that's what you're in the market for."

Adrian chuckled. Stepping closer, he clutched the back of the girl's neck in one hand, tangling his fingers in her thick black hair. *Making love*, at least in the way he wanted to make love to Philippa, was the furthest thing from his conscious mind. But his body ached for a woman's touch. "I am not as familiar with the layout of the castle grounds as I should be. Could you also furnish me with a tour of Lord Oldcastle's manor?"

Belinda sucked in a deep breath. "Is it a tour of the castle you want, sir? Or a little love-jousting?"

"Luckily, I have enough gold coin for both." Adrian released Belinda's neck and smiled. He liked her pluck and her sense of humor. "The tour can wait, however. I confess I am sorely in need of your more *womanly* skills at the present."

She nodded toward a wooden outbuilding. "That's where the guards store their weapons and plate armor. 'Tis empty at present, and for a cut of my earnings, we can take advantage of its privacy."

"Lead the way, then." The hoarseness in Adrian's voice startled even him.

"Been a long while, has it, sir?"

"Aye, a long while." But even as Adrian ached to release the tension building within him, a warning bell pealed in his head. Touching Belinda's arm, he asked, "Are you healthy, woman?"

"Ain't got no diseases, if that's what you mean." Walking toward the ramshackle storage shed, she looked at him sideways.

"Do you have your menses on a regular basis?"

She gasped, but didn't slow her pace. "What kind of question is that, sir?

"I am a doctor—"

"A midwife is what I heard."

Adrian appraised her, wondering what else she'd heard. "You weren't joking when you said you keep your eyes and ears open. Then, you know I am well-acquainted with the workings of a woman's reproductive system. I want to be certain that I do not get you with child, Belinda."

She scoffed. "There ain't no certainty you won't, sir! But if you do, I know a wise-woman in the village who traffics in concoctions brewed from tansy, parsley, willow seeds and the bark of white poplar. 'Tis said the potion brings on a woman's menses."

"Have you ever been pregnant, Belinda?"

"Once, sir," the woman said softly, her cheeks eyes darkening. "But the babe didn't live out the first night. 'Twas better that way, I suppose. . . . "

Belinda led Adrian into the ramshackle lean-to, pungent with piles of well-worn gambesons and tunics, casks of oil and banks of plate armor. She closed the door, then pressed her back to it. A narrow window set high in the opposite wall focused a ray of dusty light on her upturned face. Belinda beckoned to Adrian with a curl of her fingertip. "What pleases you, sir?"

The damn containing his composure burst. In a blink, Adrian was on her, his body pressing her back against the door. His forearms framed her face, while his arousal prodded the coarse linen of her tunic. With a cry of surprise, she clung to him, her fingers grappling his neck and face.

The sounds of their frantic struggle filled the tiny storeroom. Hands groped and grasped, skirts were lifted, braies unlaced. Adrian closed his eyes, suddenly desperate to rid himself of the image of fair Philippa, young and innocent, naked and exposed.

But he could not forget Philippa. The memory of her body, wet and warm and tight, drove him to a frenzied state of arousal. He'd felt the clench of her muscles around his finger. *Mon Dieu*, he'd inhaled her musky, feminine odor. With his shoulders wedged between her legs, it had been near impossible to resist burying his nose in her golden budge. Philippa's intimate perfume still filled his nostrils, inciting him to dangerous heights of carnal passion.

Belinda's fingers closed around his naked manhood, jolting him with erotic pleasure. He reached down between them and covered her hand with his own. A lump the size of a boulder formed in his throat; he struggled to control his rapacious urges. He wanted to lift up Belinda's skirts and thrust into her, but he was a physic, for God's sake, dedicated to alleviating the pain women suffered in childbirth. To negligently impregnate a woman, even an enterprising leman, was contrary to everything he stood for.

"We must not . . . " he heard himself croak.

In one practiced movement, Belinda yanked her skirts to

her waist, gave a hop, and wrapped her legs around Adrian's middle. He had only to plunge into her to take his satisfaction.

She tightened her grip on his manhood, urging him to delve into her. "Heaven 'elp me, you're the biggest man I've ever seen," Belinda said, stroking Adrian to blinding heights of pleasure.

His forehead thudded against the rough wooden door. Every natural, animalistic impulse in his body roared in protest as his hips stilled. "Belinda, wait." The words were ripped from his throat.

A small, choking sound escaped her lips. "Bloody hell, man, what are ye waitin' fer? The king to give his blessin'?"

Prying her fingers from his arousal, he captured her hand between them. "Do you know when your menses are due, woman?"

"My what? Are ye daft, man? What the hell has that got to do with anything?" Banging the back of her head against the door, Belinda leveled an incredulous look at Adrian. "You ain't some kind of pervert? You ain't like the baron, is you?"

Adrian vaguely wondered what kinds of perversions Drogo indulged in, but now was not the time to ask. "Nay, woman. But I do not want to get you with child. If you do not know when you had your last period, I cannot spill my seed inside you."

"Not come inside me? After getting me all primed?"

"Primed? Bloody hell, is this your idea of—" Snorting his frustration, Adrian banged his fist on the door. "Well, I'm not going to put you out of your misery just because I pity you."

When he pulled away, Belinda's feet clapped the floor. "Now, what's this? We ain't finished yet! We struck a bargain!"

"Don't worry, I've never reneged on a bargain," Adrian said, clamping her hand on his erection.

Her fingers barely closed around him. She said, "Oh," very softly, then stroked him, slowly at first. When his breathing deepened, and he swelled to near bursting in her hand, she pumped like a milkmaid.

Adrian gnashed his teeth and groaned. Arrows of tingly heat streaked through his body. Eyes closed, he imagined himself thrusting into Philippa's golden-thatched womanhood. Then he shoved Belinda against the door and stained her cheap smock with his seed.

When his vision cleared and his body ceased its convulsive shuddering, he pressed his lips against Belinda's ear. "Are you still aroused, woman?"

Her voice was husky with desire. "Aye, you have succeeded in arousing me, sir. And 'tis not an easy feat."

Nor one frequently attempted, thought Adrian with pity.

She stroked the hard planes of his back and sighed.

"Pull up your skirts," he instructed her.

Belinda hiked her damp tunic, then wound her arms around Adrian's neck. Supporting her bottom with one arm, he slid his free hand to where her thighs parted, inserting two fingers between the drenched curls. She threw back her head and moaned as he expertly brought her to fulfillment.

Satiated, Belinda looked up at him, smiling. Adrian was amazed to see a blush on her cheeks. Her skirts fell and she adjusted her leather girdle. "You do not have to pay me, sir," she said.

Adrian fished in his pocket for a couple of coins and pressed them into her hand. "I am a man of my word, Belinda. Besides, there is something else I would ask of you."

Her eyes lit. "Name it, sir. I am at your disposal."

"You said that nothing goes on in this castle without your knowing it. Is that true?"

"Aye, sir. The baron's soldiers are my best customers, and their lips are loose. Not a single one of 'em has a lance so big as yours, though."

Adrian suppressed a smile as he tied the drawstring waist of his braies. At his instruction, she fetched a pail of water from the well outside. When he'd washed his hands and face, he asked, "Could you give me a tour of the castle grounds, Belinda?"

She nodded happily, and a few moments later, the two emerged from the storeroom into the bright sunlight. Adrian glanced upward, certain that the guards above were noting his every move. Which made Belinda the perfect tour-guide: Anyone watching them would think they were searching for another place to lie together.

Drogo had not returned from his hunting expedition by the time the noon meal was served. Adrian sat at the trestle table among a half-dozen squires, pages and men-at-arms omitted from the party. He ate silently, aware of the curious glances and side-long stares slanted in his direction. It seemed the other knights didn't know how to react to a male midwife. They eyed his bulging muscles and lifted their brows, then whispered to each other and erupted in snickers.

It was just as well. Adrian was immersed in his own thoughts, turning over in his mind what he'd learned from Belinda, committing to his memory a visual map of the castle grounds. She'd been an excellent guide. She'd shown him the servants' quarters and knights' barracks, the ale-house, and the stables, where she'd tried to talk him into giving her pleasure again. She'd even pointed out the gatehouse prison tower at the corner of the lower bailey opposite the watch house, and explained that it was strictly off limits to all but Drogo's select first guard.

But, despite his urgings, Belinda had refused to venture near the prison tower. Adrian had studied the tall, turreted building from afar. Surrounding its perimeter was a circular wooden fence with an iron-banded gate manned by two guards. Ten feet tall, the fence was topped with iron spikes, upon which, according to Belinda, were occasionally picketed the heads of Drogo's enemies.

Dipping a stale hunk of bread into his stew, Adrian considered the prison tower. What could Drogo be storing there that was so secret only his most trusted personnel were allowed entrance? The thought puzzled him, almost pushing from his mind the troubling memory of Philippa's plight.

The sight of a servant scurrying up the steps reminded him of her. Recognizing Hilda's pregnant figure, Adrian called out. The woman halted halfway up the stairwell, turning a startled, harried look on Adrian. The men around him fell silent when he left the table, but their talk of hunting and fighting soon resumed when they couldn't overhear his conversation.

"Are you taking that tray to Lady Philippa?" Adrian asked, starting up the stairs.

"Aye, Sir Adrian." Hilda continued sideways up the steps, clutching the tray possessively. Adrian followed. When they reached the landing, Hilda stopped outside Philippa's door. "Was there something else you wished to ask me, sir?"

"Is Lady Philippa all right?" Adrian took the tray from the woman, though her fingers reluctantly released it.

"As well as an innocent girl could be, after what she has been through, I suppose." There was an accusatory note in Hilda's voice. Adrian could hardly blame the woman for being protective of her mistress. He wondered if it would surprise the maid to know that he was as worried about Philippa's welfare as she was.

But Philippa was no innocent girl, and her lie had yet to be dealt with. "A warm posset and bread. That is good, she needs nourishment. May I take it in to her?"

Hilda gasped, aware his request was purely ceremonious. "Why, whatever for? Ain't you done enough harm for one day, sir? My lady is hardly recovered from the shock she suffered this morning! And you would remind her of the ordeal she's just been through? I think not!"

Smiling over the tray, Adrian shoved open the unlatched

door with his foot. "Go and rest, Hilda. It will do you and your babe a world of good."

He entered Philippa's room, then kicked the door shut in Hilda's gaping face.

Philippa had thrown on a simple linsey-woolsey smock and returned to bed. She lay on her side, her back to the door, wondering if Sir Adrian's hiring as physic signaled her eviction from the infirmary. Hilda's quavering voice and the succeeding door-slam jarred her senses. Her eyes flew open. A tall, broad-shouldered shadow loomed on the wall opposite her. Him!

She sprang to her feet, hands held up defensively. "What are you doing here, Sir Adrian? Where is Hilda?"

"I have prescribed rest for the poor woman." Adrian strolled into the room as if this morning's travesty had not occurred. Holding up the tray, he cocked his brow, inviting Philippa to eat.

She shook her head, arms wrapped around her roiling belly. "Nay, I am not hungry. Put it over there." She nodded toward a small chest beneath her window on the opposite side of the room.

Adrian glanced at the chest, then strode toward Philippa. She wedged herself in the corner while he placed the tray on the table beside her bed. The very nearness of him jangled her nerves. The morning's ordeal was excruciatingly fresh in her mind. How could she have allowed her body to betray her so? How was she going to convince Sir Adrian she was a virgin after reacting to his touch like a wanton bawd?

She averted her eyes, but not before she caught a glimpse of sinewy leg and muscled forearms. *Dieu*, but he was handsome! Philippa breathed a sigh of relief when he backed away from her.

He found a sturdy stool and dragged it to the foot of her

bed. He sat with his powerful leap spread, arms folded on his broad chest. "Get back in bed, my lady. I only want to talk to you."

She tip-toed back to the huge four-poster, easing onto her soft mattress without taking her eyes off the strange knight. Knees to chest, spine against the headboard, she said, "What do you want to talk about, sir?"

His stare probed deeper than his hands had done. "You are not a virgin, my lady. I wish to know what you have to say on the matter."

Instantly, her cheeks burned. Philippa's stomach flip-flopped, but she maintained a cool facade. Tossing a braid over one shoulder, she said, "You are not as skillful a midwife as King Edward thinks, sir—not if you believe I have enjoyed relations with a man."

"I know not whether you enjoyed those relations," Sir Adrian replied. "Judging from my examination, I suspect not. I know only that you are not a virgin."

Philippa stared in disbelief. How could this man know so much about her merely from touching her *there*. She felt he was peering right down into her very soul and yet she was determined to hold to her story. There was nothing to be gained by being truthful with this man, everything to be lost.

"I *am* a virgin," she said.

Adrian shifted on the stool, pushing one long leg out before him. Wincing a bit, he massaged the top of his thigh. He must have ridden an untrained horse, or a near crippled one, to be so stiff after a ride from London to Sussex.

"You are lying to me," he said, rubbing his leg.

Silence stretched uncomfortably between them. For a moment, Philippa thought her throbbing pulse was audible. A boom of thunder penetrated her jumbled thoughts and gave her a shiver. Outside the weather was changing. Inside, there was a friction in the air that crackled and popped, raising the hair on her forearms.

"I am not a liar, sir."

She saw from his expression that he didn't believe her. "If I tell Drogo that you are a virgin and he later discovers you are not, we may both forfeit our lives."

"He won't find out—" Philippa bit her tongue. "That will not happen because I *am* a virgin. Therefore, Drogo will not be disappointed on our wedding night."

"You are certain you are not with child?" Adrian's gaze raked her figure.

Even with her knees pressed firmly to her breasts, Philippa was aware of a warmth spreading through her. "I am certain."

He nodded. "You could probably trick him into believing that you are a virgin, then. If you are a good actress, and skillful at sleight-of-hand tricks, you can still collect your morning gift in exchange for sacrificing your virginity."

Your morning gift. Philippa's mind flashed on a bone-paneled wedding casket, the treasure box that contained her soul's salvation and the key to winning back her father's honor. She feared saying anything incriminating, so she merely lifted her brows.

"You could smear some chicken blood on the streets on your wedding night," Adrian continued. "I am certain you could contrive a way to do that without the baron being any the wiser."

Chicken blood. She'd have to remember to tell Hilda to obtain some, and hide it beneath the mattress in a small bladder pouch.

Sir Adrian leaned forward, his expression earnest. "But if you intend to deceive the man, then I must become your accomplice."

The implications of his suggestion reverberated through the small room, more deafening than the roll of thunder that outside creased the night sky. A wind picked up, rattling the precious glass panes of Philippa's window. Releasing a pent-up breath, she chose her words carefully.

"You would do that for me? You would certify to Drogo that I am a virgin?" Nothing in her request implied she wasn't a virgin, she told herself, just that she acknowledged Adrian's power.

"I might."

"What would convince you?" She was afraid she knew; a knot formed in the pit of her stomach at the thought of some dastardly proposition. "Are you suggesting that I allow you to have your way with me in return for your endorsement?"

His jaw tightened. He stared at her longer still, as if he were attempting to solve a puzzle. At length, he said, " 'Tis odd that you would jump to that conclusion. On the contrary, I was offering to forsake my physician's oath and lie for you. *If* lying to Drogo is truly in your best interests. That is what I am unsure about, my lady."

Philippa's hopes surged. She leaned forward. "I must marry the baron of Oldwall Castle. I am contractually bound to do so!"

"What happens if you break that contract?"

"I must not!"

Adrian's eyes hardened to granite. "Is it so important to you to be mistress of Oldcastle? Would you marry a man you do not love in order to secure a comfortable future for yourself?"

Philippa opened her mouth to protest, but quickly clamped it shut. It was none of Adrian's business what drove her to marry Drogo. She wouldn't disgrace her father by divulging the terms of her marriage agreement. Nor would she reveal why she was so determined to preserve her father's honor.

She had the urge to lunge forward and rake her fingernails down Adrian's smooth, olive complexion. But she overcame her rage in order to calm her voice. "Aye, 'tis vitally important that I marry Drogo, Lord Oldcastle. That is why you must tell him that I am a virgin. Because I am!"

Adrian answered with a throaty chuckle. But the laughter quickly faded as his gaze bored into hers. Rain pattered on the thick, leaded window panes, and Philippa shuddered as a chill insinuated itself into the room. Unable to tear her gaze from Adrian's intense scrutiny, she pulled the counterpane over her knees and clutched it to her shoulders.

He stood, towering over her, his expression inscrutable. Then he reached for a marten pelt draped over the end of her foot-board and arranged it at her feet. Bending over, his face was scant inches from Philippa's. She saw the bristles on his jaw and the creases bracketing his mouth. She inhaled the scent of him, curiously musky, and wondered if he'd spent his morning wenching. A vague jealously rumbled in her loins.

Plastering her spine against the headboard, Philippa held her breath, fearful of her body's reaction. Adrian's nearness affected her drastically. He fussed with the covers more than necessary. When he finally lowered himself onto the mattress, her heart thumped like a nervous rabbit's foot. His weight upset her balance and she pushed backwards, resisting his lure.

Adrian leaned so close that his chest brushed her knees and hands. Fire blazed through Philippa's fingertips and spread throughout her body.

She masked her burning desire with a wall of ice. "Pray, do not touch me," she said, her voice a cold hiss. "Or I shall scream rape."

Adrian froze. His gaze searched hers, lingered on her lips. Philippa saw his nostrils flare, his forehead furrow as he considered her warning. Then, slowly, he retreated the length of the bed.

Eventually, he stood and stared down at her.

One part of her wanted to cry out, "Touch me, don't leave!"

Another part of her begged him to go.

Emptiness flooded the vacuum in Philippa's heart. But her long-conditioned instinct to shield her emotions prevented her from speaking. Outside, thunder rumbled and lightning hit so close that the crumbling old castle seemed to tremble and groan. Gray sheets of rain curtained the window. Despite Philippa's fur blanket, cold numbed her toes.

A crack of thunder ruptured the silence.

At the same time, the door to her solar exploded inward and a scowling Drogo, wet hair plastered to his head, burst into the room.

Chapter Six

"Like mother, like daughter!" The baron stood at the foot of the bed, staring first at Sir Adrian, then at Philippa. "Well, what have we here?"

Sir Killian, wearing a bemused expression, hovered in the threshold, arms crossed on his chest.

Drogo's darkening scowl terrified Philippa. Surely, he didn't think there was anything untoward going on between her and Sir Adrian. Hadn't it been his idea to have the male midwife examine her in the first place?

Unable to trust her voice, she said nothing.

Sir Adrian gave Drogo a deferential nod. "Lady Philippa required my services, my lord. I was just leaving."

"Required your services?" the baron echoed, throwing a lewd grin over his shoulder at Killian. "She looked healthy enough to me this morning!"

Killian, Philippa noted, returned his liege-lord's smile with a crudeness that chilled her. Keenly aware of Drogo's incisive stare, she squirmed beneath the counterpane and pelt.

Sir Adrian's voice was smooth, his face devoid of alarm. "This is a personal matter, my lord. Between the lady and her physician."

The baron guffawed. "Can you believe this, Killian? Now, the Lady Philippa has secrets from old Drogo!"

Sir Killian snorted. "Nay, my lord. I cannot believe it."

Drogo sidled up to Adrian and slapped his back. "What sort of secrets is my future bride keeping from me?"

"My lord," Adrian said, jerking his chin in Killian's direction. "This matter is one of some . . . ah, delicacy."

Drogo huffed. "Whatever you can say to me, you can say in front of Killian."

With a sigh, Sir Adrian leaned closer to Drogo. Philippa could barely make out the whispered words, but she heard the physic refer to her "menses" several times.

Drogo's giggle was strangely child-like, annoying.

Sir Adrian straightened, shot Philippa a quelling gaze, and in a louder voice, concluded, "That is why the examination was inconclusive, my lord."

"Inconclusive?" Drogo appeared as surprised as Philippa was to hear that pronouncement. But he chafed his hands together, and licked his lips. "Does that mean we shall be forced to perform another examination when her monthlies have passed?"

Sir Adrian rubbed his lower lip. "Possibly."

Philippa felt as if someone had knocked the wind out of her with his fist. Another examination? Why didn't Sir Adrian just go ahead and tell Drogo that she was a virgin? Why was he so concerned about whether it was in her best interest to marry the odious man? What business was it of his?

"How long will her menses last?" Drogo asked.

" 'Twill be five days before the examination can be performed again," Sir Adrian said.

Five days. Philippa felt as if her death sentence had been delivered. Her head fell forward onto her folded arms. She

80

heard Drogo's grunting departure, his heavy footsteps crossing the threshold of her solar. The door closed. Adrian's presence in the room was palpable, but she dared not look at him. Her feelings for the man were so conflicted, she couldn't bear to see his face. She despised him for arousing her, but his concern for her welfare seemed genuine. Was it possible that he truly cared whether Drogo mistreated her?

On the other hand, it was outrageously presumptuous of him to insert himself between her and her marriage to Drogo. She was almost twenty years old, certainly old enough to know whether she wanted to marry the man. Besides, whether she wanted to marry the baron was immaterial; she *had* to marry him. Her father's fortune, his honor, and her honor, too, depended on it.

And, she reminded herself, she was not worthy of a decent man's love. The secret she held tucked to her heart had robbed her of the most precious gift a bride could give her husband.

So, how dare this Sir Adrian Vale upset her marriage plans—and with the scurrilous report that she wasn't a virgin? Drogo would disavow Philippa in a second if he thought his heirs might be tainted by another man's blood.

She felt Sir Adrian's presence beside her, his big, capable hand atop her head. His touch was gentle and soothing. When he drew away from her, the emptiness in her chest seemed greater.

His footsteps crossed the room, paused at the door. The rain died down, leaving a silent coldness in the air. When Adrian left, the door shut behind him with a gentle click.

Alone, Philippa gave way to her emotions and sobbed convulsively. She wished to God Sir Adrian Vale had never come to Oldwall Castle. The emotions he'd awakened in her could only cause her grief. His kind, loving touch had reminded her of the cruelty to which she'd become so accustomed.

She had set her expectations low to avoid disappointment.

Sir Adrian had upset everything by causing her to hope, to want, to feel. God, how she wanted him to hold her in his arms, to take her away from this gray and crumbling castle. But she knew he wouldn't do that, so her only choice was to hate him.

Adrian crouched in the shadows, watching the door of the rickety storehouse just inside the main gate. Through the daub and wattle walls, a duet of grunts and groans wafted to his ears. Occasionally, a guard on the walkway above glanced down and chuckled, readjusted his cod-piece, and continued pacing.

The door opened, Belinda emerging with her client in tow. In the moonlight, money exchanged hands. The man bent to kiss Belinda's lips, but she turned her head and he stalked off. Shrugging, she dropped the coins in a small purse attached to her girdle and patted her hair.

Glancing upward, she gave the guard who'd been watching her a two-fingered hand-signal. He nodded, then returned his gaze to the surrounding moat. Belinda made her way across the bailey, passing a wooden outbuilding almost identical to the one she'd just vacated, inches away from the shadowy nook where Adrian hid.

"Belinda!" he whispered, stepping out of the shadows.

She whirled. Grasping her elbow, he pulled her into the darkness. A quick glance at the guard above confirmed they hadn't been spotted.

Her hands instinctively flew to Adrian's face. When she recognized him, her body relaxed into his arms. "You frightened me, Sir Adrian. Why do you jump at me from the darkness? Don't you know I would come to you anywhere?"

Adrian's body reacted to the feel of Belinda's curvy warmth in his embrace. But he hadn't the time or the inclination to indulge his physical appetite. He gently pried her from his body, and said, "I need your help."

"I am at your disposal," she purred, leaning into him again. She pressed a palm to Adrian's jaw and gazed at him with eyes so doting, it brought a flood of warmth to his cheeks. He pitied the poor woman her infatuation, and knew her ardor for him was a reflection of the callousness of other men.

Capturing her fingers, he covered them with his hands. "I need to know how to gain entry into the gatehouse tower, where prisoners are kept."

Belinda's eyes widened. "I cannot do that, sir. 'Tis dangerous to defy Drogo's orders. No one is entrusted to enter the prison tower without express permission from Drogo. Or from Sir Killian, I suppose."

Adrian lowered his head and peered into Belinda's luminous eyes. "Please, there is no one else whom I trust."

"And why trust a whore like me?" Her tone was flirtatious, yet self-deprecating.

"I do not regard you as a whore, Belinda, merely as a desperate woman. I am desperate also—to gain admittance to the prison tower."

She lifted her eyebrows and smiled suggestively. "Did you know, sir, that you were the first man who ever—"

Just then, a guard marched by, his heavy-mail hauberk and plate armor creaking. Adrian wrapped his arm about Belinda's waist, yanking her farther into the shadows beneath an overhanging thatch roof. Her breath was hot and pungent on his face. When the guard had passed, he peeled her arms from his neck, and whispered, "Belinda, I shall pay you for your time, but I have no time for this tomfoolery."

"You don't have to pay me, sir. I'll tup you for free."

Adrian grasped her shoulders, gently shoving her an arm's length away from him. "No! I want to see the inside of the guardhouse."

Sulking, Belinda swished her hips from side to side. "Impossible. There are two sentries that stand guard outside the fence which encircles the small yard outside the tower.

The men are well known to me, and they never leave their gate-post until relief comes in the morning."

"Bloody hell!" Adrian's mind spun, then locked. "Belinda, how well do you know these men?"

"Why, they are two of my best custom—" Her eyes lit with comprehension. Smiling, she put her fists on her hips. "If I lure both men away from their post, sir, what will you give me?"

"More gold than you can earn in a month, girl."

Belinda stood close to Adrian. " 'Tis not gold I want from you, sir. You should know that by now."

"Belinda I do not want to—"

"Nay! I am not asking you to tup me." She placed her fingertip on Adrian's lower lip, and despite himself, he grew slightly aroused at the hungry expression on her face. "I want you to do something no other man has ever done for me, Sir Adrian."

"What is that, Belinda?" Against his will, his voice deepened.

"I want you to kiss me."

Adrian brushed away the tear that slithered down her cheek. "Ah, sad little minx," he whispered, wrapping his arms about her.

The rasp of a dagger unsheathed from its scabbard raised the hair on the back of Adrian's neck. He pivoted, his hand flying automatically to the dagger at his own belt. In the shadow of the gatehouse tower, Sir Killian's teeth glowed white.

"Care to tell me what you are doing here at the prison entrance?" Killian asked. "In the middle of the bloody night?"

Adrian ignored the scrape of the peep-hole sliding open behind him. Drogo's second-in-command suddenly fascinated him. The man's silence during the arduous trip from London to Sussex had been a relief for Adrian's muscles had shrieked in protest each time his horse stumbled over a rut.

Now that his senses were alert, however, he thought it wise to examine Sir Killian Murdoch a bit more closely.

"Is there some reason I should not be here, sir?"

Raven-haired with a spray of silver at his temples, Killian possessed a refinement of speech and manners at odds with Drogo's overbearing brutishness. "You are dumb like a fox, Adrian. Do not think your handsome face fools me."

A gravelly voice spoke through the opening in the door behind Adrian. "Who's there? What do ye want, stranger?"

Stepping past Adrian, Killian showed his face to the guard. " 'Tis I, Wat. The stranger here is Sir Adrian, the baron's new physic. He has made an honest mistake, knocking on the prison door. Never mind him, man, find out what has happened to those two numbskulls who are supposed to be guarding the gate!"

The peep-hole clacked shut. Squaring his shoulders, Adrian stared pointedly at Sir Killian's drawn dagger. "Do you draw your weapon each time someone knocks at this tower door?"

Killian's grip tightened around the hilt of his knife, but after a moment, he slowly resheathed his weapon. His mouth curved in an uneasy smile. "Nay, Sir Adrian. But you are new to Oldwall Castle, and you do not yet understand the rules which apply to Drogo's realm. No one is allowed to enter the prison yard without express permission from Drogo himself."

"I was told of no such rules," Adrian replied, noting the padded gambeson that emphasized Killian's muscularity.

"Drogo asked me to brief you on the castle ordinances," Killian said. " 'Twas negligent of me not to do so before now. I apologize. Come, I will walk with you back to the great hall. That is where you should be. There, or in the infirmary, tending to patients."

Adrian fell in beside Killian and the two men strode through the sleepy compound. Killian's gait was quick, his gaze constantly shifting from right to left, occasionally darting over his shoulder.

"Is there some reason I should be confined to the castle keep and the infirmary, Sir Killian?" Adrian asked, passing beneath the portcullis that led to the inner courtyard.

"Security measures." Killian's tone grew friendlier. "This is a coastal area, as you know, and Drogo has invested heavily in shipping concerns that transport goods—wool primarily—from the staple ports to Flanders."

"Drogo's ships sail from Rye, do they?"

Killian slanted him a curious stare. "Aye, sir, but that is none of your concern. Stick to your baby-doctoring, and you will get along just fine."

"Has Drogo's castle, or his shipping concern, been threatened by French raiders? I should think I have a right to know if the castle security is endangered by pirates."

"The threat from French pirates is always a real one, sir. That is why Drogo insists on strict security measures. You wouldn't want to see poor Wat lose his head just because you wheedled him into allowing you entrance into the guardhouse, would you?"

"If I am to be Oldwall Castle's physic, I should know my way around the castle," Adrian said. " 'Tis more to being a physic than birthing babes, you understand. What if I am called upon in the middle of the night to attend to some poor prisoner's wounds, or to witness an interrogation? Shouldn't I have some knowledge of where I am going?"

"Drogo does not torture his prisoners," Killian replied.

"How many prisoners does he maintain?" Adrian knew that many coastal barons made fortunes capturing wealthy Frenchmen, then ransoming them back to their families. The practice was not taboo, though King Edward had ostensibly outlawed it since the inception of peace.

"The only prisoners in Drogo's prison *donjon* are men-at-arms guilty of one dereliction or another, a few whores, and some serfs wont to settling their disputes with knives instead of words."

Killian's reply was delivered with finality just as the men approached the stairwell leading to the great hall. Adrian paused on the bottom step, reluctant to end the conversation. "Tell me what kind of man Drogo is. You must know him better than any of his retainers, isn't that so?"

"Aye." Killian studied the tip of his leather shoe. Shoes that made not a sound as he crept around the castle grounds. "Drogo is a rough brute of a man, but fair to those who serve him. Do not get on his bad side, Sir Adrian, and you will be fine. He honors his bargains. Just ask Lady Philippa. Her father has been missing in France for years now. In Sir Casper's absence, there is no one to force Drogo to wed Philippa. Yet he will, because he is a man of his word—provided she is a virgin."

"I understand," Adrian replied. "How fortunate for Philippa."

"I shall not tell Drogo that you wandered to the gate-house, Sir Adrian, for it will infuriate the man beyond all reason. And I do want to see you succeed in your new position. Oldwall Castle has suffered the loss of many babes lately, many born dead, some succumbing after just a few days. If you can deliver the Lady Philippa of a healthy son, I am sure Drogo will make you a rich man. You haven't taken a vow of poverty, have you, Sir Adrian?"

"I am not immune to wealth," Adrian answered.

Killian gave a short bark of laughter and clapped Adrian's shoulder. "Stay out of trouble, then, and worry about Lady Philippa's maidenhead," he said, with sudden mirth. Backing into the shadows, he added, "And if you have any further questions, Sir Adrian, please do not hesitate to seek *me* out. You must be careful in whom you place your trust. These old castle walls have ears, you know."

After the man faded into the blackness, Adrian turned and trudged up the stairs. His pallet, hard and lumpy as it was, was welcoming after the day he'd had. His muscles still ached, but at least his body wasn't thrumming with cooped-up sexual arousal. Belinda had temporarily eased his suffering in that regard.

Tomorrow, he would seek her out once more, this time to ask her more questions about the occupants of Oldwall's prison. It was odd that Drogo didn't want his physic to enter the gatehouse tower where prisoners were traditionally housed.

There was much disturbing about Oldwall Castle. A secrecy pervaded its shadows. A malevolent mood simmered just below its surface. And not the least of the mysteries surrounding Oldwall was Philippa's determination to marry Drogo, Lord Oldcastle. Why would such a pretty young woman, cultivated and well-mannered, be so determined to wed such a foul man?

Adrian rolled to his side and stared into the rustling darkness. Drogo would demand a verdict on Philippa's virginity in five days. That didn't leave him much time to decide whether he should lie for her, or tell the truth and ruin her chances for marriage to the prosperous baron.

King Edward's spy mission had taken on a new dimension. Learning more about Drogo would assist Adrian in deciding whether Philippa should marry the man. But, as his lids closed, Adrian cursed the king for sending him to Sussex. Caring about a woman was the last thing in the world he'd ever wanted to do again—and here he was, risking his neck for one who hated him.

His breathing had just deepened and his first dream of Philippa had begun to unfold, when a woman's blood-curdling scream pierced the night.

Bolting to his feet, Adrian grabbed his dagger belt and scanned the darkness for signs of danger. The men surrounding him scrambled upright, clutching their weapons and shoes. Someone hurriedly lit a rush, casting light on the scene. "Is the castle under attack?" one of the young squires piped up.

The sound of feet pattering down the stairwell snapped Adrian's head around. Philippa's face, terrified and pale, glowed in the semi-darkness. When her eyes found Adrian, she pushed through the crowd of men, ignoring their curious stares. She clutched her skirts in one hand, a single pricket candlestick in the other.

"Come quick, sir. 'Tis Hilda!" She whirled around without waiting for his answer.

Adrian snatched up his leather medical pouch and followed Philippa toward the stairs. A burly knight—bleary eyed, his tousled hair full of straw—stepped in his path and stopped him with a hand flat on his chest. The two knights stood eye to eye, so close Adrian could smell the decaying teeth in the other man's mouth.

"What is going on, sir? I ain't heard no warning bells and Lord Oldcastle ain't summoned us to arms. What the devil is all that screeching and screamin' upstairs all about?"

At that instant, another blood-curdling yell shattered the night. The knight, who had probably killed many men, flinched.

"Go back to sleep, sir," Adrian advised him. " 'Tis a serving wench giving birth."

Cursing, the knight stood aside. "Well, try to keep the bitch quiet, will ye? And what the devil is she doing in the keep having a babe anyway? Drogo will severely punish anyone who disturbs his sleep, don't you know?"

Philippa's candlelight bobbed up the winding staircase. Adrian caught up with her, and said, "The knight asked a worthy question. What *is* Hilda doing in your solar?"

"I asked the woman to sleep in my room tonight."

"You weren't feeling well?"

At the upper landing, Philippa turned and looked him full

in the face. "I have bad dreams," she said, then whirled and pushed open the door to her solar.

Adrian found Hilda lying on her back on Philippa's bed. The woman's face was pinched with pain; her skin was drenched in sweat.

"I never had such pain, sir," the wench said, gasping. "Not with any of the others!"

Taking her forearm in his hands, Adrian pressed his thumb against her inner wrist. Hilda's faint, irregular pulse caused his own to quicken. Over his shoulder, he said to Philippa, "Get two or three of the other women. We need hot water and clean towels, lots of them."

Not hesitating, Philippa fled the room.

"I am here, Hilda," Adrian whispered. "There is nothing to be afraid of."

Her voice was already weakening. "Sir, help me! I do not want to lose my baby!"

"I will help you." Adrian pressed her hand, then moved to her feet. He lifted the hem of her smock and wedged a hard pillow beneath her hips.

Even though Hilda was in the most intense pain of her life, she possessed the decency to be shocked by the probing hands of a male midwife. She gasped. "Sir, I beg of you—"

"Hush, Hilda." Adrian gently forced Hilda's knees apart to determine the extent of her dilation. "If I am to help you, I must touch you. If you want to deliver this babe safely, then I am your best chance."

He was surprised to see that although she was in the later stages of her labor, her cervix was not dilated sufficiently for the child's head to pass through her birth canal. Reaching beneath her loose tunic, Adrian ran his hands over her belly. He was grateful her eyes were closed. He could not have concealed the look of alarm on his face.

Cupping Hilda's belly, he hoped his suspicions proved ill-founded. Gently, he inserted one finger into her body.

Her eyes flew open, and she lifted her head to stare at Adrian. "For God's sake, sir. Can you not allow one of the women to examine me?"

Adrian smiled up at her, his hand groping for the top of a head. But what he felt was a tiny foot.

Instantly, he was bathed in a cold sweat. Hilda's child was going to be born upside down. And the birth was progressing too quickly. In footling births, it was important to delay the baby's descent into the birth canal and allow the cervix time to dilate. But the puddle of water and blood staining the bed-clothes told Adrian that Hilda's membranes had already ruptured. And the babe's toes were already within Adrian's reach. So, if the cervix didn't widen soon, there wouldn't be enough room for the child's head to exit.

Hilda sensed his concern. "What is the matter, sir? Is my babe all right?"

"The babe appears to be fine, Hilda. But—"

A wave of pain hit her. Adrian held her hand through the contraction. Hilda was in for a rugged night. He hoped she had the stamina to withstand the agonies that awaited her.

Philippa entered the room with two older women, servants whom Adrian had seen in the great hall. Pausing in the door-way, they crossed themselves. Scowls marred their features and one of them actually balked at coming into the room.

"Get in this room, Gertrude and Blodwyn!" Philippa's voice took on an authoritative edge that stunned Adrian. "Hilda is in need of your assistance, and I will not allow your silly superstitions to stand in the way. Sir Adrian is a quali-fied physic and midwife—the best in England! He knows what he is doing."

She dropped a bundle of towels on the bed while the serv-ing women hauled in buckets of hot water. Then she sent them into the corridor to await further instructions. "How is she, sir?" Philippa asked, standing at Adrian's elbow. "Is she going to be all right? Is the child going to survive?"

Between pants, Hilda said, "Something is wrong, my lady."

Adrian glanced at Philippa, then focused his gaze on Hilda's bulging eyes. "Your cervix isn't widening sufficiently. When a child is born in the normal position, its head acts as a wedging device, forcing the cervix to dilate. When a babe is born feet first, however, there isn't enough room in the birth canal for the head and shoulders. Which means the infant's head can get stuck and dangerous complications may result."

Hilda's features contorted in a rictus of pain.

"What can you do to help her?" Philippa asked.

"I can try to slow the birth process," Adrian replied. "Otherwise, the child might die before it ever gasps its first breath of air." He dipped a washcloth in the basin and dampened Hilda's glistening brow.

Hilda's head came up, chin to chest. "I don't understand," she eked out between gasps.

"Your babe is turned around," Adrian repeated, in as soothing a voice as possible. "The little bugger is going to enter the world upside down."

"Just like his father, Denys," she whispered, her thin smile turning to a grimace.

Adrian traded places with Philippa. While she held Hilda's hand, he emptied the contents of his medical pouch. On the bedside table, he arranged his powders for pain, analgesic salve, a scalpel and a ball of twine. He tried to make Hilda more comfortable with fresh towels beneath her bottom and a cool compress on her head.

Hilda's next scream was weaker in volume and strength. Her fatigue raised the stakes. Adrian knew that if she lost her fighting spirit, both she and the babe could be lost.

"Is my babe going to die?" Hilda asked, between deep, jagged breaths.

"Not if I can help it. But you must stay alert and do what I tell you," Adrian urged, leaning over her as Philippa scooted away. He smiled down into Hilda's frightened eyes.

"I will try, sir," she said.

Adrian pressed his fingertips to the pulse point in her throat. The gray cast to Hilda's face troubled him. If the babe's head got stuck in her birth canal, he might have to cut open her belly and take it. It would be an agonizing ordeal for Hilda, one that only the strongest of women survived. If loss of blood didn't kill her, the subsequent infection probably would.

Adrian looked at Philippa, reading fear in her eyes. "I am doing everything that I can do, but the birth is going to be a difficult one."

"Upside down," Hilda mumbled.

He laid his ear against the woman's chest. Hilda's heartbeat thumped erratically; and her breathing grew more irregular. Her cries of protest were lessening. Her head lolled from side to side and her expression took on an otherworldly look.

"Don't let Hildee die, sir!" For a moment, Philippa's composure threatened to snap. She gripped Adrian's arm, her fingernails gouging his flesh.

He gave her hand a squeeze. Their eyes met in the flickering candlelight and a shared intimacy passed between them. Then, wordlessly, Philippa released Adrian's hand and backed away.

He returned his attention to Hilda. "You must try not to bear down on the child—not until I tell you to," he told her in a loud voice, attempting to pierce her fog of pain.

To Philippa, he said, "Bring the other women in, and instruct them to hold her down, flat on the bed, until I say otherwise. Hilda is most likely not going to cooperate with me when she realizes what I am about to do. But 'tis necessary."

Philippa instructed the servant women to pin Hilda's shoulders and arms to the mattress. Adrian sat on the bed between

Hilda's parted legs. The woman cried out, her eyes widening in shock, pain and outrage.

A muffled sob came from Philippa, but Adrian could not look at her. He merely said, "Everything will be all right," a dozen times over, hoping he wasn't lying, attempting to calm everyone's nerves, including his own.

Virulent curses streamed from Hilda's lips. "You curse as well as some of the London ladies whose births I've attended," Adrian said with a wink.

Hilda's body was slowly dilating, but not quickly enough. Adrian gently probed for signs of the child's progress. "Try to be still, Hilda, while I tickle the soles of your baby's feet."

One of the women holding Hilda's arms said, " 'Tis indecent! We'd be more help to Hilda if we tied knots in all the ropes in the castle!"

The other said, "She oughtta be in a birthing chair! It'd be easier on her!"

"Nonsense," Philippa admonished them. "Keep quiet, or I shall instruct Drogo to punish you with a hundred lashes when he returns."

Adrian was surprised to hear the steel ringing in her voice. He had wondered vaguely where the lord was; his absence certainly explained why Hilda was being allowed to give birth in the comfortable surroundings of Philippa's solar. If the lord of the castle were at home, he wouldn't allow this hurly-burly to interrupt his sleep.

His fingers found an ankle, then touched the lower part of the child's leg. Withdrawing his hand, Adrian observed the widening of Hilda's cervix. "Thank God," he muttered, but he knew this birth was going to be difficult, still.

"Hilda, you must fight," he whispered through clenched teeth. His heart thudded in his chest, while sweat poured down his brow. "For yourself and for your babe."

She screamed in response.

Hilda was trying not to bear down, but the pain was so

intense it stole her breath. Tension hung in the room like a shroud and the air grew dense and prickly. Adrian felt terror. Jeanne's face flashed in his mind and he blinked, confused. Adrian feared the struggling woman wasn't going to survive.

Looking down, he saw a tiny foot emerge from Hilda's body.

Philippa saw it, too. "Hilda, the babe's foot is coming out!"

Clasping Hilda's knees, Adrian told her to push. She grunted with the exertion, then another foot emerged from between her thighs. Adrian cupped his hands beneath her bottom and supported the weight of the tiny legs next appearing. But Hilda's cervix wasn't dilating quickly enough to accommodate the child's head. Soon, he would have no choice but to take it.

Adrian spoke quietly to Philippa. "Take that knife from the bedside table and hold it in the fire till it glows red."

Without question, she did so, despite one of the serving women's disdainful snorts. When she reappeared at Adrian's shoulder, she clutched the small, pointed knife with a towel wrapped around its handle. "Douse the knife blade in a bucket of hot water," he told her, "then prepare to hand it to me when I ask for it."

Hilda's breathing scraped like a razor on a strop. Her moans raised the hair on Adrian's arms. Then, in the grip of a contraction, she fell silent. The baby's bottom slid out, and Philippa cried, "Hilda, the child's bottom is out. Just a while longer, and it will all be over."

Only Adrian knew how far from a safe birth Hilda was. He had slipped two fingers inside Hilda's body in an attempt to maneuver the babe's shoulders a bit. A sanguine oath escaped his lips. The umbilical cord was tangled around the babe's neck.

The room spun around him . . . for an instant, Adrian couldn't focus, couldn't concentrate. Jeanne's body, naked and huge with child, her back bowed by pain, moved beneath his hands. Blood roared through his veins, deafening him to Hilda's miserable cries.

Another scream pierced the room.

But it was Jeanne's tearful voice that echoed in Adrian's mind. "God, help me, Adrian!" his wife had cried. "I don't want to die . . . I don't want to die!"

Suddenly, he was back in Tenterden, and it was Jeanne writhing on the bed, her knees flung wide apart, her face streaked with tears. Adrian ducked his head and closed his eyes. What was happening to him? Was he losing his sanity?

Every nerve in his body stretched to the breaking point. He lifted his head, and Jeanne stared back at him above her swollen belly. From the depths of his soul, a shuddering groan rumbled through the room. Jeanne's death was happening all over again. She was reaching out for him and he was losing her! Jeanne was shrieking his name, begging him to save her! And all he could do was stand by impotently while some hag of a midwife tore his child to bits with her dirty fingers!

What kind of man was he that he couldn't prevent a woman's death, couldn't rescue an innocent child? Had all his training and education been for nought?

Philippa's voice brought him back. "What is the matter, Sir Adrian? Why is the babe not coming out?"

His head snapped up. His gaze locked with Philippa's. Tears glittered behind her green eyes, her lips were thin and white.

As quickly as the nightmare had come, it vanished.

Adrian released his memory of Jeanne, turning his attention to the sensation at his fingertips, the feel of a squirming infant struggling to be born. "I am trying to loosen the cord from around the child's neck," he said, hoarse with emotion.

Hilda's breath rattled; her color grayed. One of the women cried, "Call the priest, Lady Philippa! He is the only man who can help her now!"

"Shut up!" Philippa commanded, pressing a moistened cloth to Hilda's brow.

Adrian heard her whisper softly and he, along with Hilda, took comfort from Philippa's soothing words. No longer a frightened girl, Philippa suddenly showed the strength of a hardened warrior.

He felt the child's life slipping away. Inside Hilda's body, his slippery fingers struggled to uncoil the cord from the babe's neck. Philippa was at his side, and he turned to her. "The babe's head is stuck. If it is not born quickly, it will die."

"Hilda isn't strong, Adrian. Can't you do something? For God's sake, can't you cut the child out?" She held up the knife, and its blade glittered in the candlelight.

"The loss of blood would kill her. And if she survived the procedure, infection would probably take her life."

Philippa's eyes flashed and her jaw clenched. "Can you uncoil the cord from the child's neck?"

"I am trying," he ground out.

A moment passed, while Hilda's gravelly breathing underscored the thick, tense silence.

"Save Hilda," Philippa said at last. "Try to save the babe, too. But, for God's sake, save Hilda first."

Hot tears stung Adrian's eyes. He'd be damned if he'd lose Hilda *or* her babe. Turning away from Philippa, he gritted his teeth. His heart thundered rebelliously—he would not allow this woman to die!

A terrible roar, leonine and ferocious, reverberated through the room. Opening his eyes, Adrian realized the sound had come from him. Philippa's hand clasped his shoulder. He heard her say, "You can do it, Adrian. You must. Hilda has been my friend since childhood, and I shall die without her!"

He focused on the sensations at his fingertips. Holding his

breath, he unwound the cord from the child's neck. Then he grasped the infant's tiny shoulders and turned them in a corkscrew motion. Hilda's cervix widened another fraction and the child's chest emerged.

Sweat poured off Adrian's brow, temporarily blinding him. He shook his head, exhaling a silent prayer. He'd done it. He'd uncoiled the noose around the babe's head and repositioned its shoulders for a safer birth.

Glancing at Philippa, he allowed himself a slight smile.

Wrapping her arms around his neck, she kissed the side of his head.

The servant women sobbed, prayed out loud, and urged Hilda to push.

Seconds after Adrian withdrew his hand from Hilda's body, the child's shoulders emerged.

"How are we doing up there?" Adrian asked Hilda.

"Bloody awful! When—I get me hands on Denys—I'm going to—strangle—him for gettin' me with child!"

Philippa shooed the serving women away from the bed. It was no longer necessary for them to restrain Hilda. She had struggled to her elbows in an effort to expel her baby.

Adrian spoke to her in a loud, sure voice. "Hilda, you must try very hard to push, now. Push!"

Some inexplicable, miraculous burst of energy roused the woman. Her strength was superhuman. But her body refused to cooperate with her efforts to thrust her child into the world. Adrian watched with growing trepidation, his gaze flickering to the knife Philippa held in her hands.

Mentally counting the seconds, he knew the child would suffocate if its head didn't emerge soon. Adrian wondered, not for the first time, what urge compelled human beings to produce children. The brutality he'd witnessed on battlefields paled in comparison to the pain he'd seen in birthing rooms.

He looked into Philippa's eyes and prayed she would never experience the kind of pain Hilda was undergoing.

Then, he looked at Hilda, drenched in sweat and blood.

"Is my babe going to live?" she asked again, hope glimmering in her eyes.

Chapter Seven

The next minute passed like an hour. Adrian's body was drenched in sweat, his hair plastered to his neck. Hilda's body was turned sideways on the bed, her feet braced on two upturned chests. The serving women hovered in the recesses of the room, alternatingly muttering their condemnation and whispering prayers. Philippa stood shoulder to shoulder with Adrian, the sleeves of her tunic pushed to her elbows, strands of damp hair stuck to her cheeks.

"Here it comes," said Adrian, his hands poised between Hilda's legs. The serving women rushed over to the opposite side of the bed. They supported Hilda's neck and shoulders as she struggled to a half-sitting position and made one last heroic effort to push her child from her body.

"Hilda, push!" cried Philippa. The woman's face turned beet red, her cheeks puffed out like two balls. Her strangled gasps alarmed Adrian, but he knew if her babe emerged without further complications, the odds were respectable that she would survive also.

"Oh, Mother-of-God-have-mercy-on-me!" Hilda cried.

The babe's head squeezed from between Hilda's thighs. A writhing bundle of red and purple flesh slipped neatly into Adrian's big, bloody hands.

"It is a big child!" Adrian said,

"Oh, Hilda, it's a beautiful girl!" Philippa cried.

"Is my babe all right? Ten fingers . . . ten toes?" whispered Hilda, falling back on the bed. Her face was pale again, her voice a tiny squeak.

Philippa held her breath, watching Adrian's expression. He held the child in his arms and peered down at it. She squalled, and a wide smile spread across his face.

"Yes! The child is all right, Hilda!" Tears of joy streamed down Philippa's face. She crawled onto the bed, and bent over her friend, clasping her hand, smiling into her creased face. Hilda gave a weak smile, and tears slid from beneath her closed eyes. The serving women clapped their hands and hugged each other.

Philippa's eyes met Adrian's. He held the babe gingerly, rocking it in his arms. A sob bubbled up in her throat, but she swallowed it and clambered off the bed. She dipped a towel in warm water. Then she turned to Adrian, and gently wiped blood from the baby's soft skin, cleansed her pink face and tiny fingers while he held her.

Within minutes, the child's limbs flailed impatiently, and her cries gained strength. Adrian took advantage of Hilda's unconscious state to cut the umbilical cord, and sew up a rip in her flesh. Philippa wrapped the babe in swaddling strips of soft linen.

Her heart was in her throat when Adrian slipped his hands beneath Hilda's arms and slid her body across the bed. He tucked a small pillow beneath her head, then turned to the serving women. "Take some warm rags and wash Hilda's body," he said, then gave them explicit instructions concerning the disposal of the afterbirth. The women acted quickly and efficiently, suddenly in awe of Adrian's skill. Fresh linens were placed beneath Hilda's body and a warm blanket tucked around her.

While Hilda slept, Philippa held the babe. Adrian stood over them, and there was a certain paternal pride that shone in his face. His breath was warm on Philippa's skin as he gently leaned close to caress the babe's cheek. He held the infant's tiny hand between his thumb and forefinger.

"Look, the child's fingers are so tiny . . . and almost translucent," he said, his voice filled with awe. Philippa smiled at him, amused.

Adrian's touch trailed from the child's cheek to Philippa's forearms, lingering a trifle longer than necessary. In the dimly lit room, his eyes locked with hers; something warm and intimate flowed between them.

Hilda revived with a moan. "My babe. . . . " Her arms reached out, grasping for the touch of her infant.

Philippa placed the babe in her mother's arms. " 'Tis a girl, Hildee," she said, her voice quavering with emotion. Her own body ached from the tension and excitement and fear of the birthing process; she couldn't imagine what Hilda's must feel like.

Hilda's heavy lids flickered, and her chin quivered. "A girl? God help the little brat! Me old Denys said he'd drown the next girl-child I delivered. Says he's tired of bein' laughed at because he ain't got nothin' but split-tails."

Pressing her palm to the woman's cheek, Philippa was appalled to feel the heat blazing beneath her wan skin. "Don't worry, Hildee. You can stay in the castle as long as you want to. I won't let Denys take this one away from you, I swear it!"

"Why can't I ever produce a male-child?" keened Hilda, half-delirious. At first, Philippa feared she wouldn't accept the child. But, soon the woman's fingers gently stroked the top of her daughter's head.

Philippa felt Adrian's gaze on her. Without turning, she

answered his unspoken question. "She's given birth to five children, three of them still-born. All have been female, and her husband warned her if this child was not a boy, he'd drown it in the ocean."

"I shall speak with this man. What is his name?"

"Denys Terrebonne."

Indignation grated in Adrian's voice. "The babe will not be drowned, I assure you."

Moving aside, Philippa allowed Adrian greater access to his patient. Now that Hilda appeared to be past the most dangerous part of her ordeal, Philippa's awareness shifted. As her shoulder brushed his, she felt the heat of his body. In the calm following Hilda's crisis, Philippa couldn't tear herself away from Adrian's side.

He tested the temperature of Hilda's cheek, then frowned. "She has a slight fever. This woman must have total bed rest until her body has recovered from this ordeal."

Philippa looked down at Hilda's contented expression, and then at Adrian's blood-speckled tunic. She felt an intimacy with the knight that she'd never felt with any other man. Having seen him tend to Hilda with such skill and professionalism lessened the embarrassment she'd felt after her examination. Without warning, Philippa's perspective had radically shifted. Now she viewed Adrian as a gifted physician, a compassionate man with a rare talent.

But the severity of his expression worried her. "Hilda and her babe will need constant attention." Stepping around Philippa, he reached for his medical supplies laid out on the bedside table.

He told one of the serving women to fetch a flagon of warm red wine. When it arrived, he poured a powder into the liquid, then held the earthenware vessel to Hilda's lips. Hilda choked and sputtered, but not before Adrian managed to get some of the concoction down her throat.

Philippa held the flagon while Adrian stoppered his medicine bottles and tied his leather pouch to his dagger belt.

"Is Hilda going to be all right?" she asked.

His gaze bore into hers. Muscles rippled beneath his stern, unshaven jaw. Quietly, so that Hilda and the serving women couldn't hear him, he replied, "Mayhap. But she is not out of the woods, yet. If her fever comes down, and her body has the strength, she will survive. The babe looks healthy, for all the trouble she caused her mother. That is to be thankful for."

"Even if Hilda does survive, she will risk her own death, and that of the child's, just by taking it home."

"How long can she stay in the keep?"

Philippa hesitated. "She must be gone from my solar before Drogo returns, or he will pitch a fit. His private chamber is just across the corridor, you know. And, I don't think he will tolerate the sound of a baby wailing while he tries to sleep."

"And when is the baron scheduled to return?"

"Your guess is as good as mine. Drogo and Killian rode from the castle shortly before the onset of Hilda's contractions, according to the servants. 'Tis not an unusual occurrence."

"And you don't know where the baron rode to?"

Philippa shrugged. "I assume to handle some business relating to his shipping concerns. Dover or Winchelsea, perhaps. While he is gone, Hilda will be safe from Denys's retribution here. When Drogo returns, however, I shall be forced to think of some other place for Hilda. She is not well enough to defend her daughter from her brutish husband. And she will not agree to leave the child here while she convalesces at home."

Biting her lip, Philippa recalled an empty provisions room on the top level of the castle keep, just above the stairs. "I think I know of a small storage room where Hilda can stay until she is recovered. It is above our heads, and with a little cleaning, will serve quite adequately as a temporary nursery."

Adrian nodded absently.

The room was quiet, save for Hilda's labored breathing. Her babe, snuggled in the crook of her arm, seemed as exhausted as she. The two serving wenches had departed the room, leaving Adrian and Philippa alone. Through the window panes, streaks of pink and orange signaled the beginning of a new day. And for all that Philippa was bone-tired, she felt a quickening of her pulse and a tightening in her chest.

Adrian's hand clasped her shoulder, and she inched nearer him, drawn by some irresistible force. The man she'd hated seared her skin with his touch, inspired a longing she'd never known. Her chin lifted a notch as she stared up at his hooded gaze, the sensuous curl of his lips. Something about his bleak expression was both compellingly attractive and deliciously dangerous. She shivered with dread . . . and excitement.

His voice was low and deep. "How long does Drogo usually stay gone when he makes these unannounced trips?"

"He is usually gone for two or three days. But one never knows. He may return tomorrow." She was disappointed when he released her.

"How often does he make these mysterious forays into the darkness, in the middle of the night?"

"Not often," she replied, her gaze fastened on the sharp angles of his face. "Every other month or so."

"And when he leaves the castle on such trips, does he take Sir Killian with him, always?"

"Always, sir. And no one else."

"You have no idea where they go?"

"Nay." Nor did she care at the moment. All Philippa could think about was the strange sensation snaking up from the tips of her toes to the top of her head.

"How long have you been acquainted with Drogo?" he asked.

"Since I was a young girl. My father was—is—a partner in a shipping business with him and Killian." Philippa noted the narrowing of Adrian's eyes. She wished he would speak of something other than the baron's strange habits and business practices. His sudden dispassion sobered her, and she inched backward, the spell broken.

For a long moment, the two stared at each other, their silence punctuated by Hilda's ratchety snores. Philippa chafed beneath Adrian's incisive gaze. She felt he saw more in her than she wished to expose. She clasped her hands at her middle, and turned her face away.

The sounds of activity in the inner courtyard filtered through the window. The castle was awakening, and servants were flowing through the middle gate. Knights and squires and men-at-arms were shouting to be fed in the great hall below.

Adrian's whisper cut through all the background noise, sending a shiver up Philippa's spine. "I am curious, my lady. Why would your father and mother promise you to a man like Drogo?"

Her cheeks burned. Facing Adrian, her heart hammered in her chest. With barely suppressed rage, she whispered, " 'Tis none of your concern, sir. I prithee, do not ask me such impertinent questions ever again."

"You want me to lie for you, to tell Drogo that you are a virgin, and yet you do not wish to confide in me *why* you must marry the man?"

Philippa opened her lips to speak, then clamped them shut. She'd experienced so much intense emotion in such a short period of time that her nerves were as brittle as fall leaves. She'd wanted to hate Sir Adrian because he'd humiliated her, and because he'd aroused her. Then, he'd saved her dearest friend and servant, proving himself a compassionate, skillful healer. Now he was probing the most secret parts of Philippa's life, prodding her for answers she would never willingly furnish.

She drew back her hand to slap him.

Cindy Harris

Catching her wrist, he yanked her body to his. Her breasts crushed against a rock-hard slab of chest. She twisted and pulled away. But with one hand, Adrian effortlessly held her captive.

"Philippa, why are you lying to me?" His wintry voice sent shivers through her body.

"Leave me alone," she whispered urgently, begging him with her eyes.

"I cannot leave you alone, my lady. Would that I could! But you are under my skin, woman. You are like a haunting, and I cannot acquit myself of your spirit! Don't you know that I burned with desire when I touched you? Don't you know I could have killed Drogo with my bare hands?"

Eyes shut tightly, Philippa shook her head. She tried to push away from Adrian, but he refused to release her. His grip tightened around her throbbing pulse, a spiral of heat scoring her flesh. "You are hurting me," she said in a tiny voice, afraid to breathe, afraid to fill her nostrils with his scent.

"I would never hurt you, Philippa."

She opened her eyes. "Then quit asking me those damn, fool questions! You don't know anything about me, Sir Adrian. You don't know what you are meddling in!"

"Tell me, then. Tell me, and I can help you!"

"No!" Philippa rocked back on her heels, pulling away from Adrian. He straightened his arm, allowing her some distance. "Let me go, you madman! Let me go, and leave me alone."

He snatched her back to his chest, and lowered his head. Roughly, his mouth covered hers. He released her wrist, and framed her face with his hands. Philippa made a muffled protest, but when Adrian's tongue penetrated the barrier of her compressed lips, her knees wobbled. A casket of emotion, buried deep in her heart, split open. Erotic sensations spilled through her body like precious jewels from a plundered treasure chest.

She kissed him back, eagerly. Her hands moved up his chest and over his shoulders, testing all the textures and planes of his hard body. Tilting her head, she drew his tongue deeper into her mouth. Thank God Hilda was senseless from her ordeal, she thought, rising to her tip-toes.

Heavy footsteps pounded up the stairwell, and jolted her to her senses.

Philippa jumped backward, her gaze riveted to the door. She guiltily touched her burning lips and stared at the servant who burst into the room.

"What is it, Gertrude?"

The servant's chest was heaving almost as much as Philippa's.

Philippa skirted Adrian's formidable body, and stood beside the trembling woman.

" 'Tis one of the castle whores, my lady. Found dead, just inside the front gate. And one of the guards has brung her body to the castle keep."

"Why?" Philippa asked. "Her body should have been taken to her family. Or to the infirmary if there is some question about the cause of her death."

"She has no family," replied Gertrude. "And the girl was murdered. The guard what found her says Drogo must be informed."

"Drogo is not here," Philippa said. "And he will not return for several days, most likely. Besides, why would Drogo care if one more unfortunate whore were killed?"

"One *more?*" echoed Adrian.

Gertrude drew her sleeve across her nose and sniffled. Philippa shot Adrian a quelling glance, put her arms about the older woman's shoulders, and patted her back.

"Have there been other women murdered in the castle?" Adrian glanced at Hilda, grateful she was oblivious to this conversation. He looked back at Philippa and Gertrude soon enough to catch the conspiratorial look they exchanged.

"Gertie, stay with Hilda," said Philippa. "Until we can find another room in the keep for her, she can stay here."

"Or until the baron returns and evicts the woman from the castle completely," observed Adrian, his patience slipping. He followed Philippa from the room, and quietly shut the door behind him. On the landing, he gripped her elbow and gave her a little shake. "How many others have been murdered, my lady?"

" 'Tis none of your business, sir. Drogo does not look kindly on gossip mongers, and I shall not run the risk of provoking his anger by passing on unsubstantiated rumors to you."

Adrian released her arm roughly. "You are trying my patience, woman. Why are you so secretive? First you refuse to explain to me the cause of your deception. You insist you must marry Drogo, but you cannot tell me why."

"Isn't it enough that I want to be lady of this castle?"

"I do not believe you. You are not that greedy. And you are not the type of woman who can pretend she loves a man when she despises him. I learned more from examining you than you think I did. I touched more than your body, Philippa. I put my finger on your soul. . . . I felt the essence of you, woman!"

"Stop it!" Philippa clamped her hands over her ears. "I will not listen to this nonsense."

"You will listen! Women are being killed inside the castle walls. And you know something about it, don't you? Tell me what you know, Philippa! You are too compassionate a woman to seal your lips and ignore the suffering of others."

Dropping her hands, Philippa hugged herself. Adrian, impressed by her stubbornness, returned her scowl. The morning sun shone through a narrow arched window high in the vestibule, illuminating Philippa's soiled tunic, the smears of blood on her cheek, her tousled hair.

She made her signature gesture—a braid tossed defiantly over one shoulder. Adrian lifted his hand and ran his thumb along her jaw line. Philippa drew a quick breath, and her lashes flickered. Her skin quivered, and myriad emotions flashed in her eyes. One of them was fear.

Slowly, Adrian drew back his hand. Not the least of the mysteries at Oldwall Castle was why Lady Philippa Gilchrist was so terrified of men.

Whirling, she bolted down the steps. Adrian followed, his gaze pinned to her rigid back, slender hips and graceful shoulders. The great hall was abuzz when they entered, the trestle table flanked by men-at-arms breaking their fast, all of them speculating loudly on who killed the girl and left her body just inside the castle gate.

Adrian rubbed his weary eyes, and Philippa disappeared behind a screen into the kitchen. He couldn't fault her for not wanting to dine with Drogo's men. They were a rough and rowdy lot, and in the absence of their lord, more coarse-mannered than usual.

But he was hungry, so he beckoned a serving woman to bring him a trencher filled with sausages and boiled quail eggs. He tore off a piece of bread, and filled his mouth. The man beside him, a young, strapping fellow with a thick neck, nudged Adrian's elbow.

"Have you heard, sir? Another whore murdered! This one right beneath the watchtower, or at least that's where her body was dumped. 'Tis passing strange, how so many bawds can be killed and not a single person claims to have seen a thing!"

Adrian washed his food down with a swallow of ale. "How many, then?" he asked.

The man belched before he answered. "This makes five or six in the last three months. That's more'n usual, though to tell the truth, whores don't have such a long life expectancy in Oldwall Castle."

Adrian's ears pricked. So someone in the castle had a penchant for murdering prostitutes, and no one—even the legion of guards who seemed to be everywhere within the castle walls—had ever seen the perpetrator of these dastardly deeds? He turned to the man, raising his tankard in a friendly toast. The man grinned back and quaffed an entire vessel of Oldwall's finest brew.

Adrian asked, "Do you happen to know how it is the poor women are killed?"

Grinning, the man drew his finger across his throat.

Adrian tensed. "They all died the same way?"

"Aye, but this one is cut worse than usual. 'Pears she struggled more than most. Put up a good fight, they say, judging by the cuts on her forearms and hands."

"Young, was she?"

The man dug a bit of food out of a back molar. He examined the nugget before poking his finger back in his mouth. "Oh, Belinda wasn't no young thing—"

"Belinda?" Adrian's heart stopped, and the air in the hall suddenly thinned. A roaring waterfall inside his head drowned the other man's remaining words. "Belinda?" he heard himself croak.

"Aye, she was a handsome minx, Belinda. And generous. Willin' to bargain a bit if a man's pockets were to let. Practically a legend round here for her abilities to please a man. 'Tis said Belinda could polish the shine off a warrior's sword—"

Adrian cut the man off with a fist planted in his nose. He acted without thinking, but once he'd lunged at the man who'd disparaged Belinda, he couldn't control the rage that poured out of him. Blood squirted from the man's nose and lips, spraying Adrian's already soiled tunic. The two men went crashing over the table, and onto the floor.

Food slid into the rushes. Wine and ale spilled everywhere as Adrian and the thick-necked man rolled and tumbled in the straw. The other men at the trestle table backed away, clearing a space in the center of the hall for the first fight of the day.

At last, both men scrambled to their feet and faced each other. They circled each other like big wary cats, crouched, their gazes locked. Adrian's anger gorged his muscles; it felt good to use his fists after a night of relying solely on his wits.

He sneered at the brute across from him. "Come on, you yellow dog! Come and get a piece of me, if you dare!"

The man unsheathed a gleaming sword.

Adrian's hand flew to his belt. *No sword.* When Hilda had started screaming the night before, he'd jumped up from his pallet, grabbing only his dagger belt and medicine pouch. His fingers found the hilt of his short knife at his back, and he drew it. A murmur of amusement rippled through the crowd.

It *was* comical to think Adrian could ward off the blows of a killing sword with his puny dagger. He was like a quintain swiveling in the wind, his chest a glaring target for the murderous beast preparing to charge him.

Surprise was Adrian's weapon.

He tossed his dagger into the straw.

A collective gasp went up and someone blurted, "He's as good as dead, that one!"

The thick-necked man's jaw dropped. His eyes flickered to the knife embedded in the straw, then to Adrian's waist. His hesitation cost him dearly.

Adrian reached inside the leather pouch at his belt. His fingers uncapped a jar. In a blink, he emptied an oily lotion into the floor rushes. Then, he faked a quick move toward the man whose sword tip hovered in the air.

He hopped backward as the man's sword slashed the air, a hair's width from Adrian's nose. Adrian's leg lashed out like a whip. The heel of his leather boot struck the man's hand, but he managed only to loosen the man's grip on his sword hilt.

"Aargh!" Lurching backward, Adrian's combatant wielded his sword wildly, loosely. The crowd parted to allow him room to retreat. When he regained his balance, he charged.

Calculating, Adrian paused; the other man's momentum could not be checked. With a graceful side-step, Adrian allowed his foe to gallop past.

The thick-necked man's feet slid in the liquid Adrian had emptied on the floor. For a moment, he glided through the rushes, his face a mask of confusion. Then his boots slipped out from under him and he landed on his arse. *Hard.*

His sword slipped from his fingers, and he lay on his side, clutching one hip and groaning. Adrian quickly snapped up the weapon, and handed it to one of the onlookers. "Give this back to him when he no longer wishes to kill me," he said wryly.

Then he bent over the man. "What is your name, man?"

"Denys Terrebonne."

Good God, Hilda's husband! "Well, congratulations, Terrebonne. You are this day a father."

"What?"

The surrounding crowd erupted in guffaws. Men who had previously eyed him with suspicion now buffeted Adrian with claps on the back. Kneeling, he peppered Denys Terrebonne with questions to determine how seriously injured the man was.

Fearing a broken hip, Adrian instructed a couple of squires to find a cot and transfer the man to the infirmary where he might tend to him as soon as possible.

Then he strode out into the courtyard, where Belinda's body, covered by a blanket, lay on the ground. He ordered her body be carried to the infirmary, also.

Chapter Eight

The infirmary was a tiny low-ceilinged room beneath the hall. Silently bemoaning the lack of ventilation, Adrian paused in the doorway with an herb-scented handkerchief pressed to his nose. Then, he stepped backward as the servants who'd carried Belinda's body from the courtyard made their quick retreat.

When the young men had passed, Adrian ducked his head and entered the alcove. On opposite sides of the room were two raised cots, both occupied, one by Denys Terrebonne, the other by Belinda's lifeless body. Warped plank shelving lined the third, rear wall. To Adrian's surprise, the shelves sagged beneath the weight of brown glass bottles, stoppered vials and crockery pots.

Striding toward Denys, Adrian extended his hand. "Sorry to have done you in so thoroughly."

The man frowned, sat up, and reluctantly accepted Adrian's hand. Perched on the edge of the cot, he glanced nervously at Belinda's lifeless body. "So I got a new babe, then? Is it a boy?"

"Hilda delivered a girl, Denys. You should be happy. There's nothing sweeter than a little girl's love for her father."

Denys's bottom lip puffed out and his expression darkened. "Damn. Wanted a boy. Told Hilda I wanted a boy. A man ought to have a boy!"

" 'Tis no reflection on your manhood, if that's what you're thinking," Adrian said gently. "And in case you're wondering, the baby is faring considerably better than your wife."

Blinking back angry tears, Denys turned his head. After a moment, he cleared his throat and looked at Adrian. "The men said ye were a sissy midwife, but I think you're a mountebank. Couldn't even deliver me a boy! Well, don't worry, I'll prove meself the better man one day!"

"All right. Drop your braies and let me have a look at that hip, now."

" 'Tis not necessary. I can walk fine now. Step back, and let me give it a try."

With one eye pinned on Belinda, Denys shuffled the length of the tiny room, then hobbled back. "See? Good as new! I'll be going now. I've got work to do. I'm an armorer, you know."

Adrian laid a restraining hand on the man's arm. "Hammering plate armor is a strenuous job."

Denys puffed out his chest. "Not fer a man like me! Hammered two suits last week! Made one fer meself the week before that and it's as fine as any Drogo's knights would wear."

With a sigh, Adrian said, "You took a pretty hard fall on that stone floor. You could have dislocated your hip, or broken a bone."

"Nay, I am all right, I assure you. Stronger men than you have come at me, sir, and have wound up in, er, *her* condition."

Backing out of the room, Denys muttered his thanks. Once

over the threshold, he pivoted awkwardly and called over his shoulder, "Mayhap I shall prove myself more of a man than you on the jousting field one day."

"Mayhap." Adrian might have taken the man more seriously had Belinda's presence not been so disturbing. Turning, he stared down at the woolen blanket that covered her. Death had never frightened him. He'd dissected several cadavers, all illegally obtained, without so much as flinching. But his feelings for Belinda interfered with his professionalism.

Not that he'd loved her, far from it.

Still, he'd pitied her, trusted her . . . had perhaps even led her to her death. Guilt singed Adrian's throat like an acid spring. He choked back his emotion with a harsh cough, and yanked the makeshift shroud from Belinda's face.

The sound of a female gasp sent shivers up his spine.

Adrian stared at Belinda's ashen face, half-expecting her to draw a breath.

A hand clasped his elbow.

Whirling, his free hand instinctively caught the intruder's slender neck.

Philippa's eyes bulged, and she made a choking sound.

"God, forgive me!" Adrian's stranglehold eased, but his fingers lingered on her skin. He pressed his thumb to the pulse that throbbed in the hollow of her throat. He said Philippa's name on a sigh, reluctant to release her.

She grabbed his wrist, but did not push him away. For a moment, the two stood so close their breathing mingled in the space between them. Then, Philippa's gaze shot to Belinda's body, and she shuddered. "I am here because this is my infirmary, and I have an interest in whomever is brought here. Do you know who the girl is?"

"Her name is Belinda. I know little about her, except that she earned her living prostituting herself." Adrian's fingers surrendered Philippa's elegant throat.

"Inside Oldwall Castle?"

"Are you shocked?" he asked, confused by the mixture of Philippa's innocence and worldliness. Terrified of men, but not a virgin. Submissive to her parents' wishes, but willing to flaunt Drogo by allowing a servant to give birth in her solar. What kind of woman was she, so full of contradictions?

"Shocked?" Philippa echoed. "On the contrary, I have nothing but gratitude toward the women who earn their living by slaking the carnal thirst of men."

"Do you mean that you are grateful for women who will have sex with your husband if you choose not to?"

As she flipped a braid over her shoulder, Philippa said, "That is exactly what I mean."

"You abhor the idea of making love to your husband, then?"

"Do you blame me, given that my husband is to be Drogo?"

"Hardly," Adrian admitted. "But you don't have to marry him, you know. No one is holding a sword to your pretty throat." His gaze fastened on the mottled handprint his grasp had left on her long neck. He reached towards her, but her chin reflexively jerked upward and her eyes widened. Another tense moment passed with his hand hovering near her collar bone, then he let his arm fall to his side. "What are you afraid of, my lady?"

"Nothing."

Then why do you lie to me? The words were on the tip of his tongue, but he clamped his jaw shut. Now was not the time to challenge her.

He looked down at Belinda. The dead woman stared straight ahead, a rictus of shock frozen on her face. Adrian gently closed her eyes, then slanted an appraising look at Philippa. "You do not appear afraid, my lady. Are you not offended by the sight of death?"

"I am not so delicate or genteel that the facts of life—or death—offend me, sir. Surely you must know that, after last night. Besides, before Drogo retained you as the castle's physic, I spent much of my time here in the infirmary."

"Was it you who filled those jars with herbs?"

"Aye, my mother was a skilled herbalist before she died."

"How old were you when you lost your mother?"

"Ten years. Shortly thereafter, father and I moved from our home in Rye to Sussex and Drogo's castle. Father needed to be close to his business associates, I suppose."

An awkward silence followed Philippa's reminiscing; she abruptly halted her speech, apparently embarrassed that she'd revealed any of the private details of her past.

Adrian resisted the impulse to draw Philippa into his arms. His urge to protect her was mitigated by the stubborn, independent attitude she projected.

"You were an able assistant last night, my lady. Much more useful than those two superstitious hags who felt a man shouldn't be allowed within a mile of a lying-in room."

Philippa gave him a wan smile. "You mustn't be too hard on them. They have never heard of a male midwife, and they think you are some succubus, some deviant, who meddles in women's work for the sheer deviltry of it."

"I have been called the devil's spawn by mightier people than they. And did you set them straight on that score, my lady?"

Philippa's eyes gleamed in the dimly lit infirmary. "I didn't have to, sir. They saw with their own eyes what a dedicated physic you are. Not even the old midwife in the village would have had the skill or the temerity to do what you did."

Adrian shrugged. "I am glad I didn't have to cut the child from her belly."

Philippa nodded toward Belinda. "This one never even had a chance, did she?"

Adrian followed Philippa's gaze. Belinda's throat had been cut. Adrian bent lower, examining her as closely as possible in the inadequate light.

Lowering the blanket, he cringed at the cuts and slashes on the woman's arms. Her limbs were stiff, but he managed to lift an arm to display Belinda's bloody palm. "This woman fought valiantly for her life. Her death did not come quickly."

"She saw her assailant, then," said Philippa.

"Yes, and probably knew him to have allowed him to get so near her," said Adrian. "Look, her girdle is askew, as if she'd pulled up the hem of her dress. She must have thought her murderer a potential customer."

"Can you tell by examining her whether she had sex with the man who killed her?"

"Nay, she had sex with many men. I have it on good authority that she sported with the top-ranking men in Drogo's service. The presence of a man's seed in her body will not tell us whether her killer used her for his own pleasure before he took her life."

"Look in her purse," said Philippa, pointing at the small leather pouch attached to Belinda's leather girdle. "Has she been robbed?"

Adrian untied the pouch, and emptied its contents into his hand. He recognized the shiny gold pieces he'd paid Belinda, and a hard knot formed in his throat. Engulfed by guilt, he closed his fingers around the coins and struggled to modulate his voice. "The motive was not robbery, my lady."

"Then this murder was motivated by pure evil. Like the others."

Adrian nodded slowly. "Mayhap."

"Sir Adrian, are you all right?"

Beads of sweat dotted Adrian's upper lip, and his head throbbed. He pulled the blanket over Belinda's head. The small infirmary floor tilted precariously beneath his feet, and he stretched out his arm to brace himself against the stone wall.

He supposed his body was suffering a delayed reaction to the exertion of his fight in the hall, lack of sleep, the residual effects of his ordeal on the rack, and the overwhelming sadness he felt as a result of Belinda's death. Nausea gripped his stomach, his head ached, and his vision blurred.

Philippa clasped his elbow—her grip was stronger than he'd expected. "You need some rest, sir. You can finish examining Belinda's body later."

Adrian shook his head, attempting to clear his vision.

"And forgive me for saying so, sir, but you stink."

Adrian managed a weak laugh. His tunic was blood-spattered and stiff with dried sweat.

"Come, sir, I shall instruct the servants to prepare a hot bath for you in my room. Hilda can be moved to the empty storeroom on the upper floor of the keep. Gertrude has already set about converting it to nursery."

"A bath?" The idea of soaking his aching muscles in a tub of hot water tantalized Adrian. He knew his body was signaling its fatigue, telling him he'd gone beyond the limits of his endurance. A bath sounded wonderful. Suddenly, he craved it.

Pushing off the wall, he followed Philippa out of the dank infirmary. Even with his stomach roiling and his skull pounding, the gentle sway of her hips beneath her low-slung girdle mesmerized him. Her spine was straight and her carriage as elegant as any queen's. Lady Philippa could have led him over a path of hot coals, so vulnerable was Adrian to her charms at that moment.

But as he watched her move down the darkened corridor ahead of him, a warning sounded in his head. Philippa existed in a no-man's land, at least for the male midwife who'd taken a vow of celibacy and sworn never to impregnate another woman.

Visions of Jeanne, sweating and struggling in the throes of a fatal childbirth, flashed before his eyes. *Dieu*, but he had loved that woman! Yet it was his love that had robbed her of her life. The guilt he suffered for failing to save Jeanne's life, for trusting the village midwife to assist her during her ordeal, was like a hungry wolf hounding his heels. It nipped at his flesh, plunging its teeth into the marrow of his soul each time he gazed upon another woman with desire.

So how could he risk inflicting such a wicked punishment on another woman—especially one so wounded and skittish as Lady Philippa? How could he jeopardize another woman's life in exchange for a few moments of selfish sexual pleasure? Squeezing the bridge of his nose against the pressure raging behind his eyes, Adrian exhaled.

Why was he even entertaining such foolish fantasies about Lady Philippa, a woman spoken for by the baron, Lord Oldcastle? If she wanted wealth and social status, then Drogo was her man. Sir Adrian could give her nothing but heartbreak. And so it was ludicrously cruel for him to thwart her marriage plans, either by seducing her or by disclosing her lack of a maidenhead.

On the other hand, how could he possibly resist touching this alluring female whose beauty tempted him beyond human endurance? Watching the proud set of her shoulders, he marveled at her strength and grace. Committing the curves of her body to his memory, he realized that her physical loveliness was merely a dim reflection of her inner beauty.

As long as he lived, he would never forget the moment she had turned to him during Hilda's ordeal and said, "Try to save the babe . . . but for God's sake, save Hilda first."

In that birthing room, Philippa's determination to save the life of a serving wench had bolstered Adrian's courage. Her fortitude had drawn him back from the past, an awful place of remembrance where he'd relived the torments of Jeanne's death, suffered the agonies of a despair so bottomless it threatened to engulf his sanity. Philippa's strength had imbued him with renewed vigor, filled him with hope and optimism. Her tiny frame was but a shadow of his hulking figure, but her spirit had eclipsed his own. And he had changed forever in that instant when she wrapped her arms around his neck and kissed his head, willing him to reach within himself and find the skill and courage to save Hilda and her babe.

Even on the battlefield, Sir Adrian had never seen such loyalty among soldiers who'd trained, slept and fought together against a common enemy. Philippa had the heart of a lioness and the strength of a thousand warriors. If he never touched her, he would always be proud to have her as a friend. Yet if he never touched her, he knew that his soul would always thirst for her, his flesh would always ache for her.

He knew then that he would risk his own life to guarantee Lady Philippa's future happiness. Sadly, he determined that refusing to make love to her was the surest way to protect her. But that did not prevent him from giving her a sexual pleasure that few men took the time to explore.

Philippa supervised the moving of Hilda and her babe to the upper level of the castle keep. Adrian slumped against the window embrasure while servants filed in and out of her solar like ants, hauling enough buckets of steaming water to fill a small lake. By the time the huge wooden tub was full, fresh linens had been placed on Philippa's bed and Adrian's headache had diminished. When the last servant backed out of the door with an empty trough, he unbuckled his dagger belt and let it fall to the floor.

Philippa started out of the room.

"Where are you going?" Adrian asked.

She looked over her shoulder, and a ripple of apprehension threaded through her. He looked so masculine, so forbidding with his features tightened by pain. Yet, there was something compellingly vulnerable in his voice. Philippa was terrified by her inability to resist his animal appeal.

"I must tend to Hilda," she said, faltering.

"She has Gertrude. If you are needed, the servants will find you."

True enough. Still, Philippa hesitated. "I must leave you,

123

sir. 'Twould be improper for me to remain here while you bathe."

"Gertrude and the others will not betray you if you instruct them to remain discreet. Besides, I want you to stay."

" 'Tis unwise."

"If you want to be the lady of this castle," Adrian warned, "do not leave me." His threat was implicit; her future was in his hands.

"I have my duties in the infirmary, sir. I cannot stay. I pull teeth on Tuesdays, and there are many in the village who will suffer if I do not see them today."

"You pull teeth—" Adrian snorted. "I suppose I shouldn't be surprised by now at anything you tell me," he said, kicking off his boots to step out of his braies.

Philippa's eyes widened at the sight of his strong, lean legs encased in tightly woven hose. When Adrian pulled his filthy tunic over his head and tossed it on the window sill, her pulse fluttered like a dazed moth. Then, he unlaced his garters and peeled his stockings off, exposing perfectly muscled legs, taut and brawny. The effect his near undress had on Philippa was disturbingly similar to the effect his hands once had on her flesh; her knees wobbled beneath her tunic and her heart hammered beneath the jeweled cross on her bosom.

The room shrank to a suffocating size. But it wasn't the hot water in the tub that caused a trickle of liquid warmth to seep between her thighs. It was the ripple of muscle and sinew in Adrian's strong limbs. More frightening still, it was the hungry, alluring look that gleamed in his eyes.

Philippa's chest tightened painfully and she cleared her throat with difficulty. Scooping an armful of dirty linens from the floor, she frantically clutched them at her middle as if to ward off her predator's charm. Then, she forced herself to look at the door, vainly attempting to ignore the sound of Adrian's footsteps padding toward the tub. But a shiver of desire prickled up her spine. She glanced over her shoulder and held her breath at the sight of Adrian's nakedness.

He was perfect, broad-shouldered and trim-waisted. His chest was smooth, but dark silky hair trickled from his navel to his manhood, which even now, though not fully erect, was impressively large.

Philippa had heard from the servants that he'd bested one of Drogo's most ferocious men-at-arms in the hall even though he was unarmed and the other man wielded a deadly sword! She wouldn't have believed such a tale had she not seen Adrian's magnificent naked figure. Sir Adrian was like a spirited warhorse, powerful and untamed, his black gaze as furious as a charging steed.

Standing beside the wooden rim of the tub, he looked at her. "Come and rub my back," he said softly.

Like a sleep-walker, Philippa dropped her bundle of laundry and went to the tub. She knelt beside the great oaken mazer and watched him step over the rim, where he stood knee-deep in the hot water. From her vantage point, she stared straight up the length of his sinewy legs, covered lightly with the same black silken hair that surrounded his manhood. Steam moistened her cheeks, but her throat was as dry as parchment. Her gaze traveled upward, over Adrian's flat belly, hard nipples and bulging chest muscles.

When her gaze locked with his, a shudder of awareness forced Philippa to cling to the edge of the tub.

Water lapping at her fingertips, Philippa groped along the rim of the tub for a washcloth. Her fingers closed on the thick, coarse rag as she noticed a subtle movement beneath Adrian's navel. He stood as still as a statue, staring down at her, while his manhood lengthened and swelled.

Horrified, Philippa gulped convulsively. The lump in her throat solidified, constricting her breathing passages. The air was heavy and rife with tension.

125

"Are you all right?" Adrian asked, lowering himself into the bath.

His haunches bulged as his arousal disappeared beneath the surface of the water. Grasping the edge of the tub, he lowered himself slowly with a movement that accentuated his arm muscles and the veins that mapped his dark skin. The water reached his waist, exposing his hardened nipples and glistening chest. He slid toward Philippa and turned his back to her, inviting her to wash him. Her stomach roiled wildly.

In the ensuing silence, Philippa's stomach calmed. Finally, Adrian sighed heavily and slid further beneath the surface of the water, allowing his arms to float freely beside him. He leaned his head against the hard wooden edge of the tub, then abruptly lifted it. "Could you put a towel beneath my neck, my lady?"

She snapped out of her reverie to pad the tub's rim with a towel. Then she sat still as a cat beside the tub, staring at Adrian's profile. His lashes were as thick as a girl's and, as his breathing deepened, they fluttered against the dark circles beneath his eyes. Beads of sweat dotted his upper lip while his hair curled riotously from the humidity of the bath.

The rhythm of his breathing soothed her. Soon, Philippa's panic subsided. Like a sleeping giant, Adrian was not a present threat to her safety. Still, the aura of power and sensuality surrounding him stirred something in her that she hadn't known existed, a hunger she'd never felt before.

His eyelids flickered and his forehead creased. He was dreaming. Philippa watched while his lips twisted and his expression changed from one of repose to agitation. The muscles in his neck corded and his hands, floating on the water, suddenly fisted. He slapped the water, spraying Philippa and sloshing a wave over the side of the tub.

With eyes open wide, Adrian turned abruptly to face Philippa. The look of rage in his eyes frightened her, repelling her from the side of the tub.

But after an elongated instant, recognition shone in his eyes. Adrian reached over the side of the bath and clasped her arm, drawing her near again.

"I am sorry," he rasped. "I was having a bad dream."

"You have them, too?" Philippa whispered. She hadn't thought anything could frighten a man as strong as Sir Adrian. She scooted closer, half-leaning over the tub, her face a mere whisper's distance from Adrian's. The water slapped the side of the wooden basin, spilling onto Philippa's tunic, drenching her breasts, molding the woolen material to her nipples. A strangled gasp caught in her throat. "Sir, you are hurting me!"

Staring in disbelief at his grip on her arm, Adrian loosened his fingers. Then, he half-stood, and reached over the side of the tub, gathering Philippa in his arms before she could protest.

Suddenly, she was in the tub with him, water up to her shoulders, braids floating on the surface of the bath. Her tunic floated upward, rucking about her hips, exposing her naked limbs beneath the water.

He unbuckled her girdle. Water splashed and frothed as Philippa struggled against Adrian's groping hands. She couldn't believe what was happening to her. Her tunic was a heavy tangle beneath her arms. She twisted her body away from Adrian, reaching for the tub's rim to pull herself out of the water.

"Don't fight me, my lady. I just want to hold you."

Philippa opened her mouth to scream, but Adrian clamped his hand over her lips. The texture of his skin, the warmth of his fingers, seared her with longing and fear. Writhing out of his arms, she managed to fling an arm over the side of the tub.

He pulled her back, capturing her in his arms. "Take off your tunic, sweetling. Or would you rather that I rip it off, as I did your night rail?"

Philippa's heart thundered against her ribs. Adrian would stop if she wanted him to, if she told him to. But she didn't.

Wordlessly, she lifted her arms over her head, while he pulled off her tunic and slung it, sopping wet, to the floor.

Cheeks burning, she turned her head. Philippa's hands instinctively covered her tiny breasts. The water calmed, and Adrian's breath caught on an inhaled oath. His limbs moved beneath the water. He grasped her by the knees, parted her legs, and pulled her body toward him. The sensation of her legs wrapped around his waist shocked her thoroughly, rendering her incapable of intelligent speech, much less a spirited protest.

She felt his manhood thicken and harden against her body. Adrian quickly rearranged himself, laying his shaft against her belly, and Philippa gasped, partly from indignation, partly from the overwhelming power of her emotions.

Her voice was a squeak compared to the thudding in her chest. "What are you doing, sir?"

"I believe you can call me Adrian without fear of breaching some ridiculous rule of protocol. *Philippa*."

The way he said her name, breathlessly, urgently, raised chill-bumps on her neck and shoulders. Philippa pressed her hands against her cheeks, willing herself to remain calm. She should cry out for assistance. A servant would come and rescue her from this rogue, but . . . she didn't want to be saved. Not yet.

Adrian's gaze slanted to her exposed breasts. They tingled beneath his stare, the tips of them aching for his touch. Her hands flew from her cheeks to her bare chest. Adrian's mouth tightened when she covered her nakedness.

But his gaze, when it met hers, filled her with warmth. He took hold of her hands, peeling them away, baring her breasts. Then he caressed her neck and shoulders and back. Philippa felt his strong hands lifting her, supporting her, as her breasts rose from the water. Adrian lowered his head and took one of the hard little buds of flesh in his mouth, first rolling it about on his tongue, then sucking, then scraping his bristly jaw across it.

Philippa shivered, and her loins throbbed with liquid heat. Her back arched involuntarily, and Adrian cradled her in his hands as if she were a rag doll. Weightless, her body drifted closer to his, her legs locked more tightly around his waist. The cleavage of her womanhood pressed against his hard belly. The coarse curly tuft of hair surrounding his manhood tickled her open thighs.

The hard shaft of his desire prodded her bottom. Unthinkingly, Philippa responded with a little bounce of her hips and her movements brought a strangled rasp from Adrian's throat. He lifted his head from her breasts and pulled her closer to his hard, hot, slick, muscled body.

His lips were wet, glistening. Philippa's breasts tingled and ached for more of his kisses, but she was too shy to tell him what she wanted. A tiny mewling sound bubbled up from deep within her as Adrian's nose touched hers. He kissed her bottom lip gently, igniting a flame of erotic hunger in her blood.

After sucking and nibbling at her lips, Adrian drew back to look into Philippa's eyes, to gauge her reaction before taking her deeper into uncharted territory.

Philippa, embarrassed by her inexperience, didn't know how to signal her pleasure. All she could manage was a whispered, "Aye, 'tis good."

Which seemed to be the magic words, for Adrian drew a ragged breath and claimed her lips ferociously. Wrapping her arms around his strong neck, Philippa pressed her fingers into the hard muscles of his back. She clung to him as he held her tightly, his lips fastened to her mouth, his hard manhood nudging her bottom.

He kissed her savagely, then softly. His tongue entered her mouth with deep, probing strokes, then flicked lightly along her jaw and traced the outline of her lips. Adrian urged her to dizzying heights of passion, then cradled her in his arms, soothing her frazzled nerves with sweet words. What he said was immaterial; the honeyed tone of his husky voice thrilled Philippa to unknown heights and comforted her at the same time.

Never in her life had she welcomed a man's touch. Never had Philippa hungered for a man to kiss her. She pressed her face in the crook of Adrian's neck, tasting the salty, manly flavor of his skin. At first, her request was a mere whisper. "Make love to me, Adrian."

A moment later, she repeated her request. Louder. Bolder.

She thought he didn't hear her. "Adrian, please. I prithee. Make love to me."

But when his body stiffened, she prayed he hadn't heard. She wished she could reach out and capture her words, force them back into her mouth. She thought her brazenness had repulsed him.

Tipping her chin, he forced her to look at him. "Philippa, I cannot make love to you," he answered tersely.

"Aye, 'tis understandable." She gulped back a sob. She was damaged goods; she was accustomed to rejection. But still, she hated herself for showing this man how foolish and vulnerable she was.

" 'Tis too great a risk for a few moments of stolen pleasure," he said, at length.

Clearly, he wasn't a skillful liar. "You're the one who insists I am not a virgin. If that is true—and I'm not saying it is!—what risk is there for me in making love to you?"

"The risk of pregnancy." Adrian's voice was rougher than the ashlar blocks of the castle walls.

Certain that her unladylike proposition had angered him, Philippa countered, "Making love once with a man . . . underwater . . . will not get me with child."

A burst of mirthless laughter escaped Adrian's lips. "Is that what you have been taught? *Mon Dieu!* Do you not understand that you could become pregnant any time that you have intercourse with a man?"

"You are becoming tedious with your superior knowledge of women's bodies, sir."

"Adrian," he corrected her.

"Adrian."

A chill swept across Philippa's shoulders, causing her to shiver violently. Adrian drew her closer to him, the warmth of his body enveloping her. She lowered her arms, pulling herself tightly against him so that her nipples pressed against his naked chest.

"I want to make love to you so much, Philippa, you would not believe it."

"A man takes what he wants." Philippa spoke from experience.

He drew back an inch. "I am sorry if you believe that."

Avoiding his penetrating stare, she focused on his lips, the stubble on his chin, the ripple of muscles beneath his hard jaw. When his hand moved between her legs, she flinched with surprise. Adrian easily lifted her from his lap, switched places with her, and positioned her against the edge of the tub, her head against the towel. He leaned against her, his lips on hers, his hand beneath the water.

"I know now why it is illegal for a man to practice midwifery," Philippa whispered. In answer to his questioning look, she added, "You have gained more knowledge about a woman's body than 'tis safe."

Adrian's chuckle was as warm as the bath water. He caressed the flat planes of her belly and stroked her inner thighs. "And 'tis criminal how alluring you are, Philippa. We are both guilty of wanting each other, are we not?"

She nodded. The heel of Adrian's hand cupped the mound of flesh at the top of her legs. Philippa's head lolled back and she groaned. Adrian's breath was hot against her neck; she clung to his strong arms to steady herself, finally closing her eyes in sheer ecstasy.

"That is right, Philippa. Relax, and let me give you pleasure." His fingers tangled in the wet hair at the top of her legs. Then his hand slipped between her thighs, and he stroked the slippery furrow of her womanhood.

She shivered with arousal, her loins throbbing and aching with pent-up emotion. Adrian's breathing grew more ragged in response to her gasps. Burying her face against his neck, Philippa hid the grimace of agonized pleasure that contorted her features.

Hooking his arm beneath her knee, Adrian slipped lower into the water. Pinned against the wall of the wooden tub, Philippa's leg draped Adrian's shoulder, widening the crevice of her womanhood, exposing her burning flesh to his probing fingers.

A burst of pleasure exploded in Philippa's body; her hips rocked forward, grinding against Adrian's hand. He massaged the tiny nub beneath the folds of her skin. Her inner muscles spasmed and quaked. Philippa felt a growing emptiness that longed for fulfillment, completion.

Her fingers groped beneath the water for Adrian's erect muscle, but he shifted his body, leaving her with nothing to focus on but the sensations cascading through her body.

Then his fingers entered her. First one, and it stroked her slowly, in and out. Then two, and they filled her, pushing against the walls of her body, reaching deep inside her. Contractions pulsated and quickened in her, building to a throbbing crescendo. Philippa's hips bucked convulsively while Adrian held on to her, urging her towards an exquisite explosion of pleasure.

Philippa curled around Adrian's hand and arm like a shell around an oyster. Her inner body gripped his fingers. She gulped air like a drowning person, half-aware that Adrian's breathing was as ragged and shallow as her own. He was a rampart of muscle beneath her, his hands and fingers impaling her with pleasure-pain. The need to have his huge erect arousal inside her was suddenly unbearable, overwhelming.

In her need, she cried out, her words muffled and incoherent. She wanted Adrian, all of him. She had never wanted any man like that before, and she knew in her heart that she would never want another after knowing the exquisite pleasure only Adrian could give her.

Her tongue found his skin, the pulse beating in his throat. She tasted the nectar of his sweat, licking and suckling and clinging to him while deepening contractions rocked her body.

Adrian's fingers quickened their movements in response to hers.

Too soon, her release came like a lightning bolt of pleasure. Liquid heat gushed from her thighs, while tiny aftershocks rippled through her loins. She heard herself moan, heard Adrian's guttural reaction. Then, she inhaled deeply, her body as limp as melted wax. Floating in a dream of contentment, her leg slid from Adrian's shoulder and her head snuggled against his breast.

He sheltered her in his protective embrace. His breathing slowed and Philippa's pulse normalized. By the time she lifted her head, a drowsiness had nearly overtaken her, and the water in the tub was tepid.

Adrian's beard was darker, more stubbly, than Philippa remembered. His eyes were soft, deep-set in shadowy hollows. His jaw was set firmly, the muscle beneath it twitching convulsively. He wore a haunted, tormented look. Philippa shivered, suddenly afraid.

His whisper was abrasive. "What am I to tell Drogo, now, my lady? Would you have me lie to him so that you can marry the fool and be miserable the rest of your life?"

Philippa's breath caught in her throat. Adrian's eyes turned cold even as she stared into them. The menace in his voice was unmistakable. He was reminding her that her fate was in his hands, that he controlled her, had the power of life and death over her. It was a threat she understood all too well.

As she pushed away from him, water sloshed over the sides of the tub. She'd acted foolishly, throwing herself at this cruel man, Drogo's minion. She'd offered herself to him, but he hadn't wanted her. If his rejection wasn't humiliating enough, the consequence of her actions was. Her blind, incautious passion had probably convinced him beyond doubt that she wasn't a virgin—when what she needed most from him was an endorsement of her innocence.

What kind of idiot was she?

Angrily, she stood, grabbing a towel to cover her nakedness. Stepping over the side of the tub, she stared into Adrian's granite eyes. Shame rolled through her, adding sting to her harsh words. "I hate you," she hissed.

He lunged over the side of the tub, grabbing for her.

Leaping backward, Philippa avoided his touch. When she spoke, her voice was so quiet that Adrian froze, one leg over the side of the tub, one knee-deep in water.

"Do not come near me," she said. "Or I shall scream. And when the servants come, I shall tell them you raped me. And they shall tell Drogo—"

He held up his hand. "Stay, woman! I comprehend. I shall not harm you."

She watched him climb from the tub, water dripping off his body. He roughly toweled his chest and legs, then tossed on his soiled clothes. Philippa's emotions simmered like witch's broth, searing her insides and making her sick. What a mooncalf she'd been. To think she'd trusted him!

Now, the coldness in his black eyes frightened her. The coiled tension in his muscles paralyzed her with dread. She'd been wrong to trust this man. He was like the other one who'd touched her—cruel and unfeeling—and she hated him for it

Chapter Nine

Adrian flattened his back to the wooden outbuilding opposite the storeroom where Belinda had conducted her business. A full moon illuminated the lower bailey, complicating his attempts to remain hidden from the omnipresent guards. Periwinkle clouds scudded across the purple sky, and the flag atop the gate tower flapped noisily in the icy breeze. Drogo's guards marched along the elevated runways lining the curtain walls, their helmets glinting like stars, their plate armor twinkling in the silvery night.

Two hours of standing motionless, cloaked by shadows beneath the overhang of a thatched eave, stiffened Adrian's muscles and numbed his toes. And not a single woman had passed. Impatience was gnawing at his gut. News of Belinda's murder had obviously thinned the ranks of prostitutes who milled around the courtyard after dark.

His extremities tingled, and his body shuddered with cold. Fearing frostbite, Adrian decided to abandon his post for the night. Blowing on his hands, and chafing them, he looked up at the walkway. Then, he slid down the side of the building, as quiet as a stalking panther. When the guard he was watching turned to scan the moat, Adrian slipped around the corner, poised to dash towards a spire of shadows thrown down by the middle towers.

He collided with a small mountain of lumpy curves.

His body reacted on instinct. In one liquid movement, Adrian spun the cloaked bundle on its heels, and drew his dagger. He pressed the knife blade against a thin woolen gorget covering his captive's neck and shoulders. The weight in Adrian's arms sagged, and he pulled it into the shadows, hissing in its ear, "If you scream, I will slit your throat."

Slamming his captive against the wall of the outbuilding, he leaned against it, knife to gorget. A guard ambled past. Ten feet away from where Adrian stood in the shadows, the man in light armor clapped his hands, warming them with his breath. He surveyed the moonlit courtyard, his gaze passing without remark over Adrian's hiding place.

The guard shrugged his shoulders, raised the dagged hem of his tunic and pissed on the ground. Urine splattered the packed dirt, releasing a piquant smell in the cold air that Adrian thought would revive a dead man. The heavy odor filled his nostrils.

When the guard was finished, and had continued on, Adrian exhaled. He lessened the pressure of his knife blade against his captive's throat. He stood back, and peered into the folds of a black hood. His grip tightened on the handle of his dagger.

"Who are you?" he demanded.

"My name is Cecily." The woman's voice stunned Adrian.

"Are you a working woman?"

"Aye. Are you a killer?"

Adrian quickly resheathed his dagger, and released his hold on Cecily. "Don't you know that I almost killed you?" he asked.

Her laugh was a high-pitched girlish tinkle. She pulled her hood off her head, and her pale nondescript features shone in the dark. "I all but peed down my leg 'ere I realized you wasn't going to slit my throat."

"I almost did cut you," Adrian admitted. "Sneaking up on a veteran of the French wars will buy you a winding shroud quicker than a kiss from a plaguey rat."

Shaped like a barrel of ale, Cecily shifted her weight from one foot to the other as she spoke. "Ah, I ain't afraid of ye, sir. If you was wantin' to cut someone, we wouldn't be standin' here waggin' our tongues, now would we?"

Her equanimity angered Adrian. "There is a murderer loose on the castle grounds, woman! What are you doing skulking around in the shadows alone?"

"I might ask you the same question, sir. The guards are looking for someone to pin these whore murders on, you know. Belinda's death was particularly upsetting to them; many of Drogo's guard were her faithful customers. If I tell the guard-captain that you grabbed me, shoved me against the wall, and held a knife to my throat, what conclusion do you think he'll draw?"

"Are you blackmailing me?" whispered Adrian.

"I am asking what it is worth to you for me to keep quiet."

"Bloody hell, woman, I *should* have slit your throat!"

"You're not a killer. We've established that."

Adrian reached inside his heavy cloak, and fished some coins from his pocket. The woman's pudgy hand opened and closed, then disappeared within the layers of her voluminous clothing. "Thank you, sir. Now, would you like to tup me? I'm not as pretty as Belinda, but I'll give you a better bargain for your money."

Adrian tried to disguise his shudder of disgust. "Bloody cold out here," he mumbled.

"I'll happily warm yer bones, dearie—"

Prying her hands from his hose, Adrian replied, "Thank

you, no. But, I would like to buy some information from you."

She huffed indignantly. "Too fat for you, sir? Well, there's some what like a woman with a little meat on her bones."

Her remark reminded Adrian of something Belinda had said. "Is Drogo one of those men? Has he ever been one of your customers?" he asked.

"Nay, he likes 'em skinny and young and *virginal*."

Goosebumps popped out on Adrian's neck. So, virgins were Drogo's fetish. Well, no wonder the baron was so eager to learn whether Philippa possessed her maidenhead. The wicked man couldn't wait to deflower his virgin bride. It was the fantasy of defiling an innocent that heated Drogo's blood.

"But Belinda was no virgin," Adrian said. "And I was under the impression that Drogo was one of her customers."

"Drogo didn't always plow virgins; after all, there are only so many to go around these days, lessen you favor children."

The thought made Adrian nauseous. "Is the baron so perverted that he defiles children?"

"Nay, not that I know of. Never heard of him taking a chit younger'n thirteen. He likes 'em developed, see. He ain't *that* perverted!"

Adrian leaned against the building and pinched the bridge of his nose. At length, he said, "Cecily, do you know who Belinda's other regular customers might have been?"

"Belinda tupped all the guards, all Drogo's highest-ranking men. Drogo himself, when the lord couldn't find a virgin. But, I done told you that."

"Was Sir Killian Murdoch one of her customers?"

Cecily shrugged. "Probably. Now there's a handsome man, but a might womanly about his looks, wouldn't you say? Vain as a rooster, he is. Damn, he'd never look twice at me. Too fat, I am. Though some men like a woman—"

"With a little meat on her bones. Yes, but Cecily, did

Belinda ever tell you that any of her customers frightened her? Had any one of them ever got rough with her?"

"They all get rough from time to time, sir. This job ain't for the faint of heart. Just a few months ago, a man jumped out of the shadows, much as you done, blindfolded me and dragged me to someplace cold that smelled like underground. He stripped me naked, then dressed me in dog-mail coat and a snout-nosed bascinet. Then, do you know what he did? He shoved the basket hilt of his sword up my—"

"Christ on a raft! Who would do such a thing?"

Cecily shrugged. "Damned if I know, sir. I never saw his face, and he never plowed me, not the entire time I was with him. I thought he was going to kill me when it was over, but he filled my purse with nobles, and dumped me back here, where he'd found me."

With a sigh, Adrian plucked some more coins from his purse and pressed them in Cecily's hand. "I'm the new physic, woman. Should you ever have need of medical assistance, please come to the infirmary."

Cecily pinched his biceps, and twittered with delight. "You sure you don't want to tup me? You've paid your money, sir, and I'm not one to cheat a customer."

"Thank you, Cecily. And if you hear of any other strange goings-on, or if any of the other women encounter a man who seems capable of committing murder, please report it to me. Only me."

"Drogo is the lord of this castle, sir. 'Twould be improper to report such goings-on to the physic and not the baron what has dominion over me."

"Please, Cecily." How could he tell the woman he suspected the lord of the castle was a perverted murderer? Especially when he had no evidence, just the conviction that Drogo was an evil man who enjoyed seeing women humiliated, and perhaps killed.

The fat woman nodded, then spotted a lone guard standing in the middle of the courtyard. She waggled her fingers at Adrian, and said, "If you ain't going to tup me, sir, I shan't stand here all night flapping my jaws. I have business to conduct."

Adrian grasped her elbow just before she stepped out of the shadows. "Why aren't you afraid that this murderer will slit your throat also?"

"His victims have all been young and pretty, sir," she replied wistfully.

"God be with you, woman," Adrian said as Cecily's woolen cloak slipped from his fingertips, and she stepped boldly into the circle of moonglow illuminating the lower bailey.

Adrian watched the prostitute approach the guard. After a few minutes of haggling, she led him toward Belinda's storehouse. He wondered who owned the whore concession in this lower bailey. Was it Drogo, or the guards who watched from above?

Every breath he took filled his lungs with icy air, and he winced as the wind picked up, snapping the banner on the guard tower, whipping his cloak about his legs. King Edward had only asked him to find out whether Drogo was supporting raids on the French countryside, and here he was, investigating the death of a whore. One had nothing to do with the other, yet he couldn't in good conscience abandon Belinda. He owed it to her to find out who'd murdered her. He considered it as much a part of his duties as delivering babies.

The guards above were looking out over the moat, their backs to the courtyard. Cecily was occupying the attentions of the guard who'd pissed at Adrian's feet. Except for the two sentinels stationed at the gate outside the prison tower, Adrian couldn't see any other guards. He crouched in the darkness, and sped across the open courtyard, darting from one bank of shadows to another.

He made it to another shed, a ramshackle stable thrown up

to accommodate the few horses and asses ridden by the guards deployed in the lower bailey. The main stable, where Drogo's destriers were housed, was in the middle bailey adjacent to the castle keep.

Adrian stood with his back to the outer wall of the stable. Hidden in shadows, he heard a single horse whicker in its stall. Peering around the corner, he saw the two guards outside the prison gate. About twenty feet away from where he stood, they passed a leather flask between themselves. Adrian gave a silent chuckle, then slipped inside the horse barn.

Aromas of hay, horseflesh and manure assaulted his nose. Adrian scanned the walls and found a coil of coarse hemp hanging on a peg. With his dagger, he cut several lengths, enough to bind the ankles and wrists of two men. He opened the horse's stall gate, and squeezed into the tight space next to the animal. Snorting nostrils and laid-back ears signaled the beast's distrust.

Adrian stroked its flanks, quickly noting the animal's gender. His whispers calmed the skittish mare. Ruffling the horse's thick mane, he smiled in the darkness. His knack with females came in handy at the strangest moments.

Opening his cloak, Adrian grabbed two handfuls of hay and stuffed them down the neck of his tunic. He borrowed a leather strap from the horse's harness set, then cinched his waist to accentuate the mounds of his chest. As he unsheathed his dagger, he apologized profusely to the mare whose cooperation he depended on. With one deft stroke, he shortened her long black tail considerably. Grinning, he clumsily wound the horse's tail into a poor imitation of Philippa's beautiful braid.

He used the twine in his medical pouch to fashion a crude chaplet that anchored the braid to his head. From a distance, in the dark, provided the guards were drunk enough, he thought he could pass for a woman. After adjusting his sagging hay-stacks, Adrian stepped outside the stable and peeked around the corner.

The guards' laughter underscored the silence of the lower bailey. One of them leaned his head back, flask to his lips, then flung the empty bladder to the ground with a mirthful curse. Adrian inhaled, waiting for a cloud to darken the moon, then he emerged in the silvery light and gave a short whistle.

Whirling, the guards signaled instant awareness. Another shadow scudded across the moon, momentarily cloaking Adrian in darkness. The guards' hands flew to their sword belts, while Adrian's muscles tensed. He turned sideways, and arched his back to show his hay-mound breasts to their finest advantage. One of the men made a wolf-whistle which sent them both into peals of laughter. The shadows shifted, and Adrian pivoted, tossing his braid over his shoulder as he'd seen Philippa do.

He heard them arguing over who was going to be first. Adrian knew if Drogo weren't absent from the castle premises, the two men wouldn't dare risk leaving their post.

"But what can happen in the time it will take us to plow that pretty thing?" one of them reasoned.

His companion offered to stand guard while the other took his pleasure with the whore. Afterwards, they would trade places. "No one will ever be the wiser," promised the first, urging his friend forward.

Adrian cast a come-hither look over his shoulder, then darted toward the stable door. He picked up a loose board lying on the floor, then pressed his back to the wall. When the eager guard rushed in, he slammed the plank against the back of the man's neck.

Ten minutes later, the second guard came looking for his companion. "Are ye gonna swive all night, man?" he groused, stumbling through the door with his hands at his crotch. "My turn!" The blow from behind sent him sprawling face-down into a pile of horse turds.

With the guards securely bound, their mouths gagged with rags, their bodies propped against a hay trough in the empty stall, Adrian released his cinch belt and hung the horse's leather rein on its peg.

Quickly, he strode to the opposite end of the stable. Reaching inside his clothing, he grabbed the clumps of straw that clung to his woolen under-tunic and tossed the prickly stuff behind a bale of hay. He untied his braid, and threw it there, too.

Adrian sauntered through the unmanned prison gate. He strolled through the small yard surrounding the turreted tower, and hesitated at the heavy oaken door.

He banged his fist on the iron-banded door and bellowed for Wat to let him in.

Philippa pulled her cloak tightly about her throat and lowered her hood. As she passed beneath the portcullis of the middle gate, an iron grip clamped her upper arm.

"Where do you think you're going at this time of night?" a menacing voice demanded.

When she showed her face, the guard released her arm. "Since when are the castle inhabitants restricted to the middle bailey?" she demanded with more cheek than she actually possessed.

The guard's tone softened. "I am sorry, Lady Philippa. But with the death of another girl, security measures have been increased. For your own safety, you should stay within the castle keep, or take a servant with you for protection."

"I can take care of myself," said Philippa, pushing past the guard.

He quickly stepped in her path, making his coat of mail an impenetrable barrier. "I'm afraid I must insist, my lady. I cannot risk the ire of Drogo coming down on my head. If some tragedy should befall you, 'twould be my neck on the chopping block!"

"I am going to speak to the captain of the guards," said Philippa. She pulled her hood over her face, willing her voice to remain calm. Inwardly, her stomach twisted in knots. When had she become such a facile liar?

The guard slanted her a quizzical look.

Philippa's knees quaked beneath her tunic, but her voice remained level. "The captain has sent word that he has a sick man in need of my herbal remedy for flux. Now, if you please—" she said, skirting the man's puffed chest.

With a quick side-step, the guard planted himself in Philippa's path once more. "Captain Quince summoned you?"

Philippa was grateful her hood concealed her uncertainty. "Aye, that is the one."

Her gambit paid off, and the guard let her pass. "If you do not return through this gate within an hour, my lady, I shall send someone to look for you."

Philippa smiled over her shoulder. Didn't the man wonder where her basket of remedies was? When she visited sick people in the village, she carried a covered straw basket filled with herbs, phials of powders and various bottles of liquid concoctions. All that was beneath her cloak tonight was a bundle of raw nerves and fear.

Quickening her pace, she entered the lower bailey, her breath coming in quick, frosty puffs. She must be crazy, trailing after Sir Adrian like a bitch hound in heat. Though she'd spent the afternoon in Hilda's temporary lodgings on the upper level of the castle keep, she'd been obsessed with thoughts of Adrian. Pictures of his naked body flashed in her mind even while she'd held Hilda's baby girl in her arms and rocked her to sleep.

Hilda's condition was still guarded, her fever dangerously high. The woman had been allowed to soak in a tub of cool water, scented with violets and herbs, a luxury affordable to her only because of Philippa's generosity. But Hilda's fever still raged.

And so did Philippa's.

She'd sat at her friend's bedside, watching her sleep, praying for her recovery. But her silent thoughts had wandered to images of Adrian, the sensations she'd experienced when he kissed her, scraped his bristly jaw across her tender skin, and touched her deep inside. She never would have believed a man could incite such passions in a woman. She never would have believed she was capable of relishing a man's touch.

Dieu! How she'd thrilled to Adrian's touch! Even as Hilda and the baby dozed, Philippa squirmed in her chair, unable to rid herself of her carnal thoughts, her unprecedented desires. She'd been angry with Adrian when she'd told him to leave her room, angry because he'd been so presumptuous to mention her lie. His question—*What am I going to tell Drogo now?*—reminded her that her fate was in Adrian's hands. The fact that he had the power to decide her future infuriated her.

That any man would presume to exercise his control over her set Philippa's stomach to burning. It was a man who'd taken her innocence from her, and it was a man who'd dishonored her mother. Philippa was not going to let another man control her destiny. She was going to manipulate her own future, restore her family's honor, preserve her father's fortune. She would not allow her sexual attraction to Sir Adrian, compelling as it was, to alter her focus.

Whispering an unladylike curse, Philippa winced as a chill wind buffeted her. She had no business sneaking down the stairs to find Sir Adrian. Only a crazy woman would have snaked her way through rows of snoring men, poking and prodding the ones who were face down, lifting hoods and blankets to peer into dirty, ale-reeking faces.

She had raced upstairs to retrieve her cloak, whispering what a fool she was. She had no right to hunt down Sir Adrian, no reason on earth to seek his company.

Except that she couldn't get him off her mind, couldn't erase the smell of him from her memory, couldn't dispel the hope that he'd kiss her again the way he had in the tub.

So by the time she lunged into the harsh north wind, Philippa had reasoned she must find Adrian. She had business to conduct with him. After all, he was the one who'd so rudely reminded her that his verdict would decide whether she married Drogo. She had to secure his endorsement. She would promise him money—lots of it—in exchange for his complicity. She would be rich when she married Drogo.

Philippa had spied Adrian in the inner courtyard, mingling with a group of kitchen servants who'd stayed late to carve and dress the venison slain by Drogo's hunting party the day before. He'd easily passed with them through the middle gate.

She'd thought it exceedingly strange that he would hide his identity to slip beneath the eagle-eye of the guard manning the middle gate. Obviously, he didn't want anyone to know where he was going. Why the secrecy? she'd wondered, her curiosity piqued.

Then, she'd lost sight of him when the guard delayed her.

Now, she scanned the empty lower courtyard, noting a short, squat woman crossing the open space to meet an idle guard. Inside the curtain walls, several wooden outbuildings offered shelter from the blistering northern wind, and protection from curious eyes. She scurried to the one on her right, nearest the prison tower, and hid herself in the shadows of the stable.

When she saw Adrian crossing the courtyard, headed straight for the wedge of darkness she was hidden in, she slid around the corner and into the stable. The single horse occupying it was still neighing in alarm when Adrian entered just seconds after she did.

Crouched behind a bale of hay at the far end of the stable, and opposite the two stalls, Philippa watched, fascinated. She almost revealed herself by laughing when Adrian stuffed his tunic with straw and cinched his waist with a leather strap. When he lured the two guards into the stable and knocked them both unconscious, her heart thudded painfully.

146

Terrified that one of the guards might get his sword unsheathed, she held her breath till they were both securely tied and gagged. It shocked her that she cared so much for Adrian's safety. Even when Drogo went on dangerous boar-hunting excursions, or trips to the coast to conduct his business, she'd never given the baron's welfare a second thought.

When Adrian disposed of his costume, he showered the top of Philippa's head with hay. His horse-hair braid fell across her head with a dull slap.

Adrian heard the scrape of the peep-hole door sliding open. A bulging eye suddenly stared out at him. "Who are you?" came the same gravelly voice he remembered from before. Sir Killian had called the man Wat.

"Where are the oafs who are supposed to stand guard at this gate?" Adrian demanded.

Wat's eye blinked, then the peep-hole snapped shut. Within seconds, a latch clinked, and the oaken door creaked open. Adrian brushed Wat aside and entered.

He found himself standing in a low-ceilinged corridor, unusually thick with fragrant rushes that covered his ankles. He knew from Belinda that the corridor wound around the circumference of the building. But the detached circular staircase was not accessible from the interior of the *donjon*, he realized with dismay. Finding the landing that opened onto the stairwell was his first objective.

While Adrian stood in the threshold, accessing the situation, Wat rushed outside to confirm the guards' absence. Returning to the tower entrance, he shouted down the corridor for help, summoning two brutish looking men clad in the armor that all Drogo's guards and soldiers wore. The military atmosphere of the castle was unmistakable; if Adrian hadn't known better, he would have thought England was still at war.

Wat frantically explained that the gate sentinels were missing, and sent the two guards out the door to find them. Then, turning to Adrian, he said, "Who are you, sir?"

"Sir Adrian Vale, the castle's new physic. I have come to inspect your prisoners. Rumor has it that an infectious respiratory disease is being passed among them."

"A what?" The old man blinked and gulped in the dim torchlight.

"Have you had a cough lately, sir?"

The old man's rheumy eyes widened, and he gave a little convulsive snort.

"I feared as much," said Adrian. "Spreads like wildfire, this particular disease. Worse than the plague once it hits you, and there's no certain cure. I've seen strapping men half your age drop dead less than three hours after being exposed."

Crossing himself, Wat whispered, "*Mon Dieu!*"

"You'd better show me the prisoners. All of them."

Wat hesitated, but fear for his own welfare overwhelmed the orders he'd been given not to allow anyone in the prison tower.

He jerked his head, indicating Adrian should follow him. They trudged down the damp corridor, their boots rustling through the rushes, and emerged in another yard at the back of the tower. A flickering rushlight in a sconce attached to the outer stone wall illuminated the circular wooden fence surrounding the tower, and the small apron of compacted dirt identical to the front prison yard.

After lighting a smaller rush from the wall sconce, Wat started up the covered stairwell, glancing over his shoulder as he wound up the steep steps. The stairs spiraled upward in a clockwise direction that allowed defending swordsmen to wield their weapons freely but impeded an attacker's ability to employ his right hand while leaning around corners.

At the first landing, Wat paused, and Adrian stood beside him. The older man huffed and puffed from the exertion of climbing the stairs.

"You say a man could die within hours from being exposed?" Wat's face wrinkled with concern.

"Aye, so you'd best leave me alone with the prisoners. Just show me where they are, then return to your post."

Wat led him beneath an arched doorway, and showed him a corridor lined with tiny cells, each seemingly carved into the stone wall. Noses poked through curtains of iron lattice-work, and terrified eyes glimmered in the semi-darkness.

Then, in a twinkling, Wat vanished, leaving Adrian to wander the corridor, peering into the musty, damp cells. They were inhabited by some of the dirtiest, smelliest, most pathetic-looking wretches he'd ever seen.

None of the vacant-eyed men talked to him or reached out as he passed. Most of them sat slumped in the straw, their backs against the stone wall, while others clung by skeletal fingers to the iron bars of their cages. Having circled the entire perimeter, Adrian estimated there were fifty prisoners crammed into the tiny cells. The air was foul with unwashed bodies and human excrement. The rushes on this level were moldy, and rustling with vermin.

He paused before the cell of one man who leaned against the iron bars of his cage. The man's gaze was not as blank as many of the others', and his cheeks were not as gaunt. "Why has Drogo imprisoned you here?"

The man sighed, and shrugged his slumping shoulders. His clothes hung in tatters on his emaciated frame. He shook his head.

Adrian asked the question again, this time abandoning his Norman French for English, the language slowly being adopted by King Edward's court. The man wearily lifted his brows, and said nothing.

"Can you not speak, man?" Adrian demanded, grabbing the bars and pulling himself nose to nose with the man. It made him furious that this waifish prisoner would tell him nothing.

And still, the man stared dumbly in response to his anger.

Adrian's voice was a ferocious growl. "Have you not a tongue in your head, man?"

The prisoner responded to this challenge with a slight twist of his lips. Then, he opened his mouth wide to show Adrian that his tongue had, indeed, been cut out of his head.

Chapter Ten

Adrian pressed his face to the cold iron bars and peered into the prison cell at a dozen or so men, all of whom had opened their mouths to show their tongues were severed. It was a hellish scene, and it angered him to the point of violence. He saw black spots before his eyes, felt his muscles burn with outrage. Pushing off the metal latticework, he stumbled backward against the stone wall. For a moment, he stared at the tongueless men, met their blank hopeless gazes. Then, he turned and ran toward the stairwell.

At the landing, he paused. There was another floor above this one, and one below. Adrian reckoned his time was limited; it wouldn't be long before the guards were found tied up in the stable. Though he'd disposed of his costume, he knew it eventually would be found. Even if it wasn't, there was a possibility Adrian would be suspected of the ambush. He would plead his innocence, of course, claiming to have heard a rumor of sickness in the prison. But whether anyone believed his alibi was entirely up to God.

Racing up the stairs, he encountered another oaken door with a barred squint at eye-level. He grasped the door handle and pulled, straining his muscles to no avail. Then, he reversed his momentum and rammed his shoulder against the door. It didn't budge.

Stepping back, Adrian became aware of a chaotic hub bub in the lower bailey. The heavy, impatient sound of destriers' hooves was unmistakable. Orders barked by angry men increased Adrian's agitation. He thought there was a search party turning the courtyard upside down for the two guards. It surprised him they hadn't been found yet. His time was running out.

As he raced back down the steps, Adrian cursed his predicament. He didn't even know what he looking for—all he knew was that Drogo forbade all but his most trusted guards to enter the prison tower. And that he wasn't going to get any answers from the prisoners. Whatever Drogo was hiding, he was making sure no one tattled his secrets to the wrong man.

Adrian was more convinced than ever that Drogo was a sinister man. He passed the second landing and descended to the ground level, emerging in the tiny back courtyard of the prison tower. The sounds of a rowdy crowd gathering in the bailey were growing louder. As he wound his way around the stone corridor, he thought it strange there were no prisoners housed on the lower level. Stranger still was the fact that the rushes strewn on the floor were so thick, fresh and fragrant.

He looked down at his leather boots sweeping through the scented straw. The stone floor was hard through the thin soles of his shoes. He took long strides, anxious to be out of the prison tower, eager to merge into the crowd in the courtyard. If he could blend with the soldiers, he could make his way back to the castle keep without anyone ever knowing he'd left his pallet.

Unless his disguise had been found, the guards were probably still searching for a stocky whore with a long black braid.

Adrian's feet scraped something unusual, something that definitely wasn't stone. He froze in the semidarkness, then backtracked, feeling the hard uneven stonework beneath his feet. There! Holding his breath, he looked down, kicked the rushes from his ankles. He stooped and swept the thick straw aside.

A leather hide covered the stones. When Adrian lifted one corner of it, he saw a rectangular grate set in the floor. Kneeling, he peered through metal bars, and saw a stone staircase descending into total darkness, seemingly into the bowels of the earth. He lowered his face to the grate, then quickly jerked back, his nose wrinkling. The stench rising from this strange hole in the ground was as foul as any he'd ever encountered, and distinctly human.

The din of the commotion in the bailey grew stronger. Adrian started to stand, then paused. He thought he heard a sound coming from the hole. Bending closer, holding his breath to avoid inhaling the stench, he cocked his head. A low moan wafted upward, chilling his bones to the core.

There was someone down there! Ignoring the footsteps pounding down the stone corridor, Adrian frantically brushed more rushes aside, looking for a handle to pull up the grate. His fingers tightened around a small metal ring. He braced himself on his haunches, and pulled.

Footsteps pounded the stones behind him, but he ignored the sound of approaching danger.

He'd lifted the grate an inch when he felt the razor-sharp point of cold metal prodding his temple.

"Release the ring, Sir Adrian."

The grate fell shut with a heavy clap. Turning his head, Adrian stared straight down the gleaming shaft of a sword. The hilt of the sword was grasped by a leather gauntlet, its knuckles studded with metal points. Adrian's eyes moved upward, past the man's yellow and blue tunic, his capmail gorget and his strong, handsome jaw. The sharp tip of the sword slowly lowered till it pointed at Adrian's throat, then his thudding heart.

"Come, Sir Adrian, you are needed in the keep." Sir Killian smiled chillingly and resheathed his sword. He jerked his head toward the open door where Wat stood goggle-eyed and palsied with fright.

Adrian stood, his gaze locking with Killian's. He stepped over the exposed grate and followed the man into the outer courtyard of the prison tower. As they passed through the gate, manned once more by the guards whom Adrian had tricked into leaving their posts, Killian clapped Adrian soundly on the back.

"If you would but tell me what it is you are seeking, Sir Adrian, perhaps I can help you. I know everything that goes on around here, you know. A man like you could use a friend like me."

"Who is down there in that underground prison?" Adrian barely glanced at the dozens of soldiers streaming through the middle gate. Rushlights were lit everywhere, making the castle grounds as bright as day.

Killian sighed. "I assume you have heard about the latest rash of murders in the castle."

"Aye, someone is slitting the necks of whores. A girl named Belinda was killed just last night. Any idea who is responsible for these evil crimes?"

Puckering his lips, Adrian appeared in deep thought. Then he turned a hard glance on Adrian, and said, "I suppose it would not be wrong to take you into my confidence. Drogo and I believe there are two men responsible for the murders. One of them is imprisoned in the pit you found. He was tossed into that *oubliette* until he confesses the identity of his accomplice. You aren't going to suggest we're being too harsh on the wretch, are you, Sir Adrian?"

"On the contrary. Whoever killed Belinda should be drawn and quartered. I should like to do it myself if I find the man."

Killian stopped dead in his tracks, halting Adrian with a hand on his shoulder. "Wat and his men have perfected the art of extracting the truth from hardened criminals, Sir Adrian. 'Tis not a job for the likes of me and you. We are decent men, schooled in the principles of fairness. Let us not stick our noses where they don't belong."

"I have no aspirations as a subjugator," said Adrian. "But wouldn't it be wise to have a physic look at the prisoner in the pit to determine how much physical punishment he can endure before the torture silences him forever?"

"Forget about the prisoner, Sir Adrian. Your services are needed elsewhere." Killian's tone of urgency matched his quickening pace. Nearing the stairwell of the castle keep, he added, "Drogo suffered an injury during our trip, and you—as Oldwall's physician—must tend to his wound."

Philippa hovered in the landing, just outside Drogo's solar door. Averting her eyes, she murmured greetings to Sir Killian and Sir Adrian.

Killian instructed Adrian to wait outside while he had a private word with Drogo.

When the door to Drogo's solar closed, Adrian faced Philippa. "What is the matter with Drogo?"

Philippa clasped her hands tightly to keep them from shaking. "I saw him briefly when his men carried him up the stairs. It appears that he has a crossbow bolt embedded in his knee."

"Who shot him?"

"Highwaymen, bandits . . . French pirates, for all I know."

"Has there been much loss of blood?"

Philippa nodded, shivering. "Aye, his hose and boots were covered in blood, and his face was as pale as white birch."

Adrian stepped across the small landing and held Philippa's shivering hands. The strength in his touch calmed her, but it reminded her of their previous intimacy. She looked into his dark gaze, smoldering in the dimly lit corridor, and forgot she was frightened. Steeling her nerves, she was determined more than ever that her past sacrifices would not be in vain.

"You must save him, Sir Adrian. Please, do not let him die. I will give you all that I have if you will keep him alive!"

The knight's eyes widened. He drew back his hands, and stared at Philippa. "You want the man to live that badly? After what he has forced you to endure? Do you think when you marry him, he will change? Damn, woman, you should hate him!"

She stammered, certain that Adrian could see right through her. "I do hate him . . . nay, I don't! He is to be my husband, so I must love him!"

Adrian shook his head. "You are a curious woman, Philippa. You seem to despise Drogo. You defy him by sharing your passion with me. And yet, you plead with me to save Drogo's life that you might marry him yet."

"Is it not your duty as a physician to save his life?"

"Of course. And it is also my duty to report to Drogo that you are not a virgin. Not every medical issue is black and white. So you had best be truthful with me. I shall not lie for you until I understand why you wish to marry Drogo."

Tension had been building inside Philippa ever since she'd stood in the lower courtyard and watched a squadron of guards search the stable for a murderous whore who lured two guards away from their sentinel duties. Suddenly, a damn had burst in her chest, and anger flooded her body. She balled her hand into a fist and pounded Adrian's arm as hard as she could. He did not blink an eye.

"I hate you," she whispered. "What you did to me today in the tub was despicable. You were playing a trick on me to see whether I was, in fact, a virgin. Well, even a virgin can experience a *petit mort!* Hilda told me so."

"What you felt had nothing to do with the condition of your maidenhead, child. I fear that you need a lesson in the facts of life."

"Aye, perhaps I do. I was foolish not to scream for help when you assaulted me."

"I did nothing to you that you didn't *want*."

Philippa drew back her hand to slap Adrian's face, but this time he caught her wrist in his iron grip. The heat of his fingers seared her flesh. Her body steeped in a mixture of lust, anger and remorse.

He yanked her to his chest, and lowered his head. His lips were hard and hot. The smell of him was strong in Philippa's nostrils. He ravaged her mouth and bruised her lips. She felt his hot breath on her skin and his hard chest against her breasts.

With her heart racing Philippa arched her back and twisted her face away. But Adrian's arm encircled her waist. He captured her chin with his fingers and forced her to look at him. When she gasped, his palm covered her mouth.

"Hush," he whispered. "Unless you want to get us both killed."

Philippa's lashes blinked back hot tears, and she froze, terrified of being discovered in Adrian's arms. Still, her fear of Drogo was mild in comparison to the intensity of her need for Adrian.

Silence thickened around them. Adrian's hand slid from Philippa's lips, and cupped her cheek. He lowered his head, kissing her more gently, tracing her lips with his tongue, nibbling the corner of her mouth. The tip of his tongue raised gooseflesh on her shoulders, and she shivered. Her head tilted backward while he rained tiny kisses down her long neck.

Her breath caught in her throat, and she clutched at Adrian's cloak for support.

Wild images of Adrian's naked body danced through her mind. Unthinkingly, Philippa reached down and found the hard bulge beneath his dagger belt. He drew in a quick, ragged breath and whispered her name. The sound of it filled her with longing, and she rubbed the heel of her hand along the hard shaft, thrilling to the irregular gasps her movements induced.

He grasped her buttocks, and pressed himself into her. Philippa felt his lengthening arousal prod her soft belly. She wound her arms around his neck, tangling her fingers in his thick hair. His mouth closed on hers again, and the taste of him, the smell of him, the rock-hardness of him, overwhelmed her.

Philippa felt the first twinge of a contraction deep within her loins.

Then the scrape of footsteps on the other side of Drogo's door jolted her senses. Her eyes flew wide and met Adrian's startled look. He shoved her roughly from him, and she stumbled backwards, her face burning with shame and desire.

The door flung open. "Come in," Killian said, glancing from Adrian to Philippa. "Just you," he added to Adrian, as Philippa stepped toward the solar's threshold. She'd assumed she would be needed also; until Adrian arrived, she'd been the one summoned in medical emergencies.

"But I need her," rebutted Adrian, his voice huskier than usual. Belatedly, he added, "as my assistant."

Nodding, Killian reluctantly admitted both of them. Drogo's solar was richly furnished, much like Philippa's. It contained a huge, carved four-poster bed, a fireplace that opened up into a chimney, and an arched window with real glass panes. The only lordly addition to the room's decor that distinguished it from Philippa's was a massive mantel piece wide enough to hold several pricket candlesticks and a small wooden wedding casket paneled with bone. Intricately carved, the bleached-white panels depicted wedding scenes. A fitting receptacle for her morning gift, the sight of it gave Philippa a sudden chill.

Drogo's voice quickly drew her attention from the casket. Amid a tangle of bloody sheets and towels, he lay writhing. "God's teeth, man! Do something before I bleed to death!"

Adrian tossed off his cloak and unsheathed his dagger as he crossed the room. Bending over Drogo, he flayed the man's boot and hose with quick ripping actions. Then he grimaced at the damage the barbed-metal arrow-tip had done to Drogo's knee.

Drogo cursed a blue streak. "Cut the bloody thing out of me, now!"

Straightening, Adrian turned toward Philippa who wavered just inside the door. "Come, look at this."

"What the hell does she need to look at it for? You're the physic. Damn, if you've been trained at the finest universities in Europe, as Killian says you have, you should know how to gouge an arrow out of a man's knee."

Philippa cringed when she saw the injury. The barbed point had pierced the skin beneath the knee-cap. Someone had snapped off the feathered end of the ash arrow, but at least five inches of it protruded from Drogo's leg.

Adrian spoke to Drogo slowly, as if to a child. " 'Tis not such a simple matter to remove the arrow. If I pull the arrow out, I will do more damage to your leg than has already been done."

"Cut it out, I said! Anon! Pain doesn't frighten Drogo! Killian, get me some strong wine and a coin to clinch between my teeth."

"Cutting it out will also widen the area of damage, my lord." Adrian's features were taut, his gaze hooded.

Philippa watched him, slightly in awe of his cool professionalism. He seemed not the least bit cowed or flustered by Drogo's histrionics.

The baron pounded his fists on the luxurious feather-stuffed mattress, saturated with blood. "Then what do you intend to do, sir? Damn, whatever it is, do it quick! I can't lay around in bed forever with an arrow sticking out of my knee!"

Adrian turned to Killian. "I shall need half a dozen clean towels, boiling water, a thick wooden plank, and a heavy stone, large enough for me to hold in my hand."

"A stone?" echoed Drogo. "What the devil for?"

"You will know soon enough," said Adrian, untying his leather medical pouch from the back of his belt. He laid his instruments and palliatives atop the table beside Drogo's bed, then turned to Philippa. "Have you ever concocted a dwale, my lady?"

"Nay, but I am familiar with its reputation as a sedative."

"Sedative?" Drogo's voice was a strong as ever. "You think you're going to put Drogo to sleep?"

Through a clenched jaw, Adrian replied, "Believe me, you will not be asleep for long. But at least this concoction will dull your pain. Somewhat."

"Tell me what you need, sir, and I will make a trip to the infirmary." Philippa mentally noted all the ingredients the physic listed, then darted through the door. She was grateful to escape Drogo's bellowing, and relieved for a respite from the roiling emotions that attacked her every time she was in Adrian's presence.

And she was glad for the chance to calm her nerves after the splash of excitement she'd received when she saw the wedding casket sitting atop Drogo's mantel. She knew what that precious box contained, and her determination to own its contents was what drove her toward her marriage to Drogo.

As she scanned the sagging shelves in the infirmary, her trembling candle cast eerie shadows on the walls. Belinda's

A Special Offer For Leisure Historical Romance Readers Only!

Get Four FREE* Romance Novels

A $21.96 Value!

Thrill to the most sensual, adventure-filled Historical Romances on the market today...

FROM  LEISURE BOOKS

As a home subscriber to the Leisure Historical Romance Book Club, you'll enjoy the best in today's BRAND-NEW Historical Romance fiction. For over twenty-five years, Leisure Books has brought you the award-winning, high-quality authors you know and love to read. Each Leisure Historical Romance will sweep you away to a world of high adventure...and intimate romance. Discover for yourself all the passion and excitement millions of readers thrill to each and every month.

SAVE AT LEAST *$5.00* EACH TIME YOU BUY!

Each month, the Leisure Historical Romance Book Club brings you four brand-new titles from Leisure Books, America's foremost publisher of Historical Romances. EACH PACKAGE WILL SAVE YOU AT LEAST $5.00 FROM THE BOOKSTORE PRICE! And you'll never miss a new title with our convenient home delivery service.

Here's how we do it. Each package will carry a 10-DAY EXAMINATION privilege. At the end of that time, if you decide to keep your books, simply pay the low invoice price of $16.96 ($17.75 US in Canada), no shipping or handling charges added*. HOME DELIVERY IS ALWAYS FREE*. With today's top Historical Romance novels selling for $5.99 and higher, our price SAVES YOU AT LEAST $5.00 with each shipment.

AND YOUR FIRST FOUR-BOOK SHIPMENT IS TOTALLY FREE!*

IT'S A BARGAIN YOU CAN'T BEAT! A Super $21.96 Value!

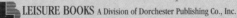

LEISURE BOOKS A Division of Dorchester Publishing Co., Inc.

GET YOUR 4 FREE* BOOKS NOW— A $21.96 VALUE!

Mail the Free* Book Certificate Today!

---

4 FREE* BOOKS 🌹 A $21.96 VALUE

*Free * Books Certificate*

YES! I want to subscribe to the Leisure Historical Romance Book Club. Please send me my **4 FREE* BOOKS**. Then each month I'll receive the four newest Leisure Historical Romance selections to Preview for 10 days. If I decide to keep them, I will pay the Special Member's Only discounted price of just $4.24 each, a total of $16.96 ($17.75 US in Canada). This is a SAVINGS OF AT LEAST $5.00 off the bookstore price. There are no shipping, handling, or other charges*. There is no minimum number of books I must buy and I may cancel the program at any time. In any case, the 4 FREE* BOOKS are mine to keep—A BIG $21.96 Value!

*In Canada, add $5.00 shipping and handling per order for first shipment. For all subsequent shipments to Canada, the cost of membership is $17.75 US, which includes $7.75 shipping and handling per month.[All payments must be made in US dollars]

Name _____

Address _____

City _____

State _____ *Country* _____ *Zip* _____

Telephone _____

Signature _____

If under 18, Parent or Guardian must sign. Terms, prices and conditions subject to change. Subscription subject to acceptance. Leisure Books reserves the right to reject any order or cancel any subscription.

(Tear Here and Mail Your FREE* Book Card Today!)

Get Four Books Totally
F R E E* —
A $21.96 Value!

(Tear Here and Mail Your FREE* Book Card Today!)

PLEASE RUSH
MY FOUR FREE*
BOOKS TO ME
RIGHT AWAY!

Leisure Historical Romance Book Club
P.O. Box 6613
Edison, NJ 08818-6613

AFFIX
STAMP
HERE

body was beginning to stink, and its presence sent a chill up Philippa's spine. Hurriedly, she yanked jars and bottles from the shelves, dipping into her well-stocked inventory. She mentally checked off her list: dried gall from a castrated boar, opium, juice of hemlock, briony. She'd get lettuce and wine from the kitchen.

Moments later, she returned to Drogo's solar with a laden tray. Killian arrived with a rock, while servants trailed in and out with clean towels and hot water. Adrian mixed the dwale under Drogo's keen scrutiny. Then he instructed the man to drink the concoction.

Drogo was a compliant patient, much to Philippa's surprise. Only after he downed the medicine did he questions its ingredients.

"The opium will put you to sleep," Adrian said. "But since opium is deadly in too large a quantity, I have mixed it with a purgative. The henbane and briony will flush the sedative out of your system. Otherwise you would go to sleep and never awaken."

Mumbling a vulgarity, Drogo relaxed into his pillow. Just before his lids flickered shut, he managed to ask Adrian how he was going to extract the arrow.

"You don't want to know, my lord," Adrian said, hefting the rock in one hand and the wooden plank in the other. Drogo's breathing deepened while Philippa's grew more shallow. At Adrian's instruction, Killian rolled the baron to his side and positioned the plank beneath his injured knee.

"Hold the wood steady," said Adrian. "Place your hands on either side of the knee and bear down, that's it."

The room fell quiet, except for the distant drone of men carousing in the hall, and the thunderous staccato of Philippa's heart. She watched Adrian test the weight of the stone in his hand while the whites of Killian's eyes glowed like two full moons. Then, Adrian slowly lifted the rock above his head; and, with a violent downward thrust, he hammered the jagged end of the protruding arrow through Drogo's knee, embedding the arrow tip in the wooden plank.

Drogo's eyes flew open, and he howled in pained surprise. Blood spurted from his wound, splattering Adrian and Philippa. She jumped back, a muffled cry of horror in her throat. The baron's spine arched, and his flailing hands attempted to grasp the board his knee was now pinned to. Adrian dropped the rock and cuffed Drogo's wrists in the air.

"Help me! Keep him flat on his back!" he ordered Killian, whose face was suddenly as bleached as driftwood.

Moving in slow motion, Killian pinned Drogo's shoulders to the bloody mattress. Adrian released his hold on Drogo's wrists and turned his attention to the board now nailed to the baron's knee. He grasped the plank, and would have pulled it away from Drogo's knee, extricating the arrow cleanly from the wound. But Drogo, in his pained madness, was throttling Killian, shaking him as if he were a rag doll. The baron's body bucked and convulsed, and blood spilled everywhere, coating the wooden plank, Adrian's hand, the sheets. It was a hellish scene, and Philippa edged away, her stomach rising in her throat.

She pressed her back to the wall, and though dizzied by nausea, was unable to tear her gaze from carnage before her. Her knees wobbled beneath her skirts, but she was frozen by Drogo's acid curses and animal strength. Killian's face was turning purple, and his eyes were bulging. In a few seconds, he would be dead.

Wrestling Drogo's kicking legs, Adrian managed to glance over his shoulder. "Philippa, come here. I need you."

Swallowing the bile that scoured her tongue, she hesitated. Ordinarily, she wasn't squeamish, wasn't frightened by the sight of blood. But this was too much. Knitting her slippery fingers together at her waist, she locked her knees and held her breath.

Adrian turned and impaled her with a black gaze. "I need

you, Philippa. You must hold Drogo's leg while I wrench the plank from his knee. Hurry—he is strangling Killian!"

So be it! Philippa almost screamed. Blood dotted the wall behind Drogo's nightstand, and puddles of it were smeared on the floor. The front of her gown was soaked, and her cheeks were wet with blood. Adrian's leather boots made bloody prints as he moved along the edge of the bed, struggling to keep Drogo still so that he could complete his task. His hands clamped Drogo's thigh, strong fingers digging into flesh as fatty as a winter duck's. He couldn't get a firm hold on the plank, though, not with Drogo fighting him, not with blood spurting everywhere.

Killian's tongue protruded through thick lavender lips. Another few seconds, and he would be dead . . . God, how Philippa wanted him dead! How sweet it would be to see him buried next to his dear father, Faustus, Drogo's brother!

Drogo's meaty fingers tightened on Killian's neck, reducing Killian's voice to a chafing whisper. "Help me," he managed to eke out.

"Philippa, don't just stand there!" Adrian's command boomed, rattling her senses. "Come here, woman! Help me!"

Something snapped inside her. She was not a murderess, though she harbored a hatred that glowed hotter than the fires of hell. Pushing off from the wall, she stood beside Adrian. He wrapped his hands around Drogo's leg and held the bloody limb while she grasped the plank. Phillipa braced herself against the bed with her foot, and pulled. Every muscle in her body strained, and her back arched. Suddenly, the plank came loose, the arrow exited Drogo's knee and she careened backward on her heels.

Releasing Drogo's knee, Adrian lunged for her. He held Philippa tightly against his chest for an instant, but Killian and Drogo were in no position to notice the brief intimacy.

"Aargh! You bloody bastard!" Drogo yelled, loosening his hold on Killian's throat and turning his vitriol on Adrian.

Killian slumped, then slid to the floor, his eyes rolling in his head.

"You no-good-baby's-bum-slapping-paper-sculled-son-of-a-bitch!" the baron finished.

The bloody plank, with its embedded arrow, slipped from Philippa's hands and fell to the rushes with a thud. She felt faint, sickened not so much by the crude surgery she'd witnessed as her wicked desire to see Killian choked to death. Her last meal threatened to resurface, and her ribs ached from the abuse of her pounding heart.

Bent over Drogo's knee, Adrian staunched the flow of blood with clean compresses. From the floor on the other side of the bed, Killian's gurgling breaths could be heard. A sigh escaped Philippa's lips; this ordeal was over, but she wasn't certain who had suffered more—her, Drogo, or Killian.

She felt Adrian staring at her over his shoulder. She was grateful when he snatched a clean towel from the nightstand and tossed it to her.

While Philippa wiped her face and hands, Adrian doused Drogo's wound with ale, then bandaged it. Killian slunk out of the room, hollow-eyed and greenish. As the opium took effect on Drogo, his curses became more garbled, less venomous. Once, he jabbed the air with his finger, then his hand fell lazily to his side. Soon, the rattle of his snore filled the room.

Philippa willed her limbs to carry her to her room, where she barely managed to prevent her knees from buckling as her servants peeled off her bloody clothes.

Chapter Eleven

What a fool she'd been to let Sir Adrian pleasure her! And what a fool she was to be thinking of him even now!

Philippa's bare shoulders shimmied uncontrollably as she slipped beneath the now tepid surface of her bath water. She couldn't believe her stupidity. Since the age of ten, when her entire world had fallen apart, and her father had been publicly disgraced, Philippa had thought of nothing except avenging her father's honor.

She'd not voiced a whimper when her father entered into that vile contract with Drogo, Lord Oldcastle. And she'd never openly voiced her disgust for the misshapen creature who, if he was to become her husband, would restore her father's good name and her family's fortunes.

So what on earth had compelled her to risk squandering everything she'd worked for in exchange for a few moments of guilty pleasure? Kissing Adrian outside Drogo's bedroom was surely the height of recklessness.

Had Killian swung open the solar's door a second earlier, he'd have caught Philippa in Adrian's arms, and he'd have seen the rapturous expression on her face. Her reputation would be ruined, Drogo would expel her from his castle, and Sir Casper Gilchrist, Philippa's father, would forever be a ruined man.

Bone-tired when she'd left Drogo's bedchamber, she had nonetheless insisted her servants draw her a bath after they'd stripped off her fouled clothing. Philippa's request, issued in the middle of the night, caused a minor ruckus among Gertrude and the maids. The sight of three slump-shouldered women hauling buckets of steaming water up the stairs piqued her conscience; after all, they were as weary as she. And Drogo's bellowing rattled everyone's nerves, leaving the servants edgy and exhausted. But the notion of crawling into bed with Drogo's blood crusted on her skin was unthinkable to Philippa.

A thorough scrubbing left her skin shiny and pink. Ordinarily, there was something about a bath that cleansed more than the skin. Philippa thought of Pilate's futile attempt to wash the blood of Christ from his hands. But, like Christ's persecutor, she couldn't rinse away the guilt and panic she felt at having succumbed to Sir Adrian's charms. She felt like a fool, having allowed her body to respond to his touch. And for that reason, she despised him once more.

Philippa leaned her head against the wooden rim of the tub. A single candle burned on the floor beside her, washing the room in a weak, flickering glow. Her mind was filled with torturous recriminations: Why had she allowed Adrian to kiss her? Why had she allowed him to touch her intimately in the bath? Why on earth had she allowed her body to writhe and buck like a harlot's? Hadn't she learned enough about men to know that all they wanted from women was sex?

Sex and babes, she silently amended.

Eyes closed, Philippa revisited the scene that took place when she was ten, just before her mother died, just before her father linked his fortunes with Drogo's. As she sank lower, the bath water rose to chin level. Hugging her shoulders, she saw a female child, her hair bleached white by the sun, cheeks as red as apples. Philippa yearned for the innocence buried deep within that child's heart. But she knew that naive sense of security was lost to her forever.

Sleep came unexpectedly. In the cloudy confusion of her imagination, a strange but familiar sensation rolled over Philippa, separating her body and soul. Floating upward, she hovered just beneath the oak-beamed ceiling of her bedchamber. But her ten-year-old body remained in the tub. With peculiar detachment, as if she were watching a drawing come to life, Philippa saw the door to her bedchamber slowly creak open.

The child in the tub turned her head to the window, away from the door. As was often the case in her dreams, the room in which Philippa floated merged with another place. Fading into view was her old room in her father's house in Rye. Thick oil-cloth, rather than expensive panes of glass, blotted the sun and blocked the frigid northeastern winds. A straw pallet replaced Philippa's ornately carved four-poster bed. Against the side of the tub sat a rag doll, smiling incongruously.

The man who entered the room smiled at the little girl. He pushed the door shut behind him, then dropped the latch into place. The little girl's eyes shut tightly, and her slender arms crossed protectively over her chest. The man ambled toward the tub, unlacing his britches as he walked. When he reached down and grasped the little girl's shoulder, a tiny sob filled the room, but Philippa, hovering among the shadowy rafters, felt nothing as she watched.

Nothingness swelled in her heart, deadening her to the little girl's emotions. She was invisible, a vaporous cloud of nothingness invisible to the man who'd entered the room. He couldn't see her, and so he couldn't hurt her. And she knew nothing of what the little girl felt. It was all happening to someone else.

Sir Faustus Murdoch, Killian's father, couldn't hurt her any more.

Then a jolt of pain splintered her dream, and Philippa's eyes flew open. Her shoulders shuddered uncontrollably, and her teeth chattered so violently she feared biting her tongue in half. With shaking hands, Philippa splashed cool water on her face. She grabbed a wet towel off the rim of the tub and began scrubbing her body again, working on her chest and stomach so furiously that she left her skin raw and reddened.

She ducked her head beneath the water, and came up gurgling and spitting. Only after soaping and rinsing her hair did Philippa slowly climb from the tub. Then she dried herself off and pulled her night rail over her head. She was still shivering when she jumped beneath her covers and pulled the marten coverlet around her body.

Turning her head to the wall, she whispered her prayers, but no solace came to her. Peace of mind was a fantasy. But the presence of the man she'd dreamed of was just as real to Philippa as the sound of the wind banging at the window, threatening to shatter the glass panes and invade her room.

Adrian's candle cast a muted glow in the corridor outside Philippa's solar. He raised his fist as if to pound the door down, but instead, sucked in a deep breath and allowed his knuckles to rest lightly on the gnarled wood. Beneath a crashing wind, the sleeping castle groaned and squeaked, hinting at the secrets locked within and beneath it. Adrian leaned his forehead against the oaken door, and with his fingertips, traced a furrow in the planks. He drew strength from the grassy aroma, the rough splintery texture of the wood. His need for something real, something *incorruptible*, had driven him to Philippa's chamber. Yet he loathed himself for being there.

He was a fool to come to her now, in the middle of the night, just hours past the bloody spectacle in Drogo's room. Still, he could not stay away. He knew Philippa was exhausted; so was he. But he'd spent two nights with her, tending first to Hilda and then to Drogo, and in that time, she'd become a powerful presence in his life. In forty-eight hours, he felt he had lived a lifetime with her.

His muscles burned and his temples throbbed. The only antidote for his misery was the sight of Philippa, the sound of her voice. He was drawn to her by some ancient life force, and all the destriers in England couldn't have pulled him away from her door. Just knowing she was nearby filled Adrian with a fiery longing.

A faint sigh, then the rustle of covers, sounded through the cracks in the door. Adrian's body tensed in response. How could a woman's sigh raise gooseflesh on his arms? How could the mere mental image of her turning in her bed cause his loins to harden? Digging his nails into the wood, he held his breath and shut his eyes, desire building in his gut like a storm. Even with Jeanne, whose love was given sweetly and without inhibition, Adrian's sexual needs had never been so overwhelming. He ached with the urge to cleave to Philippa, protect her, bury himself within her.

He loved her. *Loved her and thought he couldn't live without her*. And the realization was so shocking, it snatched his breath away.

From the moment he'd met her, he'd been obsessed by her beauty, grace and dignity. But he supposed he'd begun to fall in love with her during Hilda's childbirth, when she had put her hand on his shoulder, and shared her strength with him.

Her strength had flowed into him like a potent dwale, suffusing his blood with passion and need. He now loved Philippa more than he loved himself—so much so that he would even vouch for her virginity if he thought she loved Drogo, and if he thought the baron would cherish her and care for her.

But Drogo was a blustering pervert with a fetish for deflowering virgins. Though tradition required a husband to give his bride a wedding gift in exchange for her surrendered maidenhead, Drogo would bestow upon Philippa nothing but a lifetime of neglect and humiliation. Philippa's captivity at Oldwall Castle would be a far greater affront to justice than the torture of a suspected murderer in an underground *oubliette*.

No, Adrian simply couldn't allow Philippa to marry the man. In no way could he participate in a fraud that would facilitate her marriage to Drogo.

Confusion blurred his reason. He was on a spy mission for the king, but so far he'd spent his time chasing a prostitute's killer and brooding on the mystery presented by Philippa's determination to marry Drogo. Had he been paying attention to the task assigned him by King Edward, he would have known when Drogo left the castle. He should have followed the baron and Killian when they left Oldwall; instead, he'd remained at the castle where he'd lured Philippa into a steamy tub of water, pleasured her with his hands, and in the process, nearly driven himself to madness.

Even now, Adrian should be exploring the castle grounds under the cover of darkness. But Philippa drew him to her like a siren who lured lost mariners to jagged shoals. Even if he wanted to, he couldn't stray far from her.

The damnable pity of it was, he didn't want to. Adrian's selfish need to possess Philippa warred with his desire to see her happy, to assist her in convincing Drogo she was a virgin, if that was truly what she wanted to do.

Worse, his urge to make love to her clashed with his fear of impregnating her. Conflicting emotions tormented Adrian each time he remembered Jeanne's fatal attempt at giving birth. He cared for Philippa too much to inflict such unfathomable pain and horror on her; indeed, had he anticipated the fatal consequences of loving Jeanne, he would never have touched her. It was his love that killed Jeanne!

But Adrian knew that if he couldn't have Philippa, he would go mad. *My God*, he cried silently, *tell me what to do!*

A breeze sighed in the corridor, and the narrow passage Adrian stood in pulsed rhythmically with each beat of his heart. His fingers curled into a fist, and his cheek pressed to the door. With one hand, he clung to the door for support, listening for the sound of Philippa's gentle snores. He was a shameless beggar, beseeching a queen to toss him a crumb. He was a hungry urchin, desperate for the tiniest signal of Philippa's existence. And he was awash in guilt for haunting her.

Unable to stop himself, he rapped on Philippa's door.

When, after a few moments, there was no response to his knock, he shoved the door open. Stepping inside, Adrian paused and allowed his eyes to adjust to the shadowy room. Then, he closed the door with a backward kick.

His candle threw a skirt of light around his feet, and scant starlight filtered through the thick window panes, but Philippa's bed was shrouded in darkness. Adrian moved to the end of her four-poster, extended his arm, and bathed the bed in candlelight.

Beneath a fur coverlet, her curvy form stirred.

"Philippa, are you awake?" The faint scents of lavender

and soap mingled with the smoky aroma of a dying fire. Glancing at the black tub-shaped shadow in the corner, Adrian recalled the look of horror on Philippa's face when Drogo's blood had splattered her tunic. He hardly faulted her for demanding a late-night bath; he just wished he'd arrived in time to join her.

"Go away." Philippa's wispy voice was full of mistrust.

As Adrian moved around the edge of the bed, his taper illuminated a chiseled profile at rest on a single, slender bent arm. Lying on her side, Philippa studiously avoided looking at him.

He sat on the edge of the mattress and placed the candle on a table. Then, he pressed the back of his fingertips to Philippa's cheek. Her shudder snuffed his ardor like a wet blanket.

"Does my touch repulse you so?" he asked, drawing back his hand. "Or do you fear me?" he asked more tenderly.

Burrowed deeper into the soft mattress, Philippa pulled the blanket up to her chin. Her bottom lip swelled, and her gaze fixed on some invisible spot on the opposite wall. "Why did you have to come here?" she asked, in so soft a voice Adrian barely made out her words. "I wish you never had come."

"I wish I had never come here, either," Adrian replied, hating the bitter sound of his words. Were he of a mind to be truthful, he might have added, *Because then I would never have fallen in love with you. I would never be forced to make the terrible decision whether to allow you to marry Drogo or to love you myself.*

At the fringe of Philippa's tightly shut eyes glistened a row of fat tears.

Adrian shook his head and sighed, frustrated by his inability to express what he felt. He wanted to tell Philippa about Jeanne. He wanted to unburden himself, and drink up some of her strength, to melt into her for comfort and succor.

But what good would that do? It would only expose to her his weakness, convincing her that he was less of a man than she'd previously thought. Pride was the stopper that kept his silent fears bottled up.

He would like to tell her why King Edward sent him to Sussex, and why he'd agreed to examine her maidenhead. But the questions such a confession would arouse were simply too painful to answer. Too much about his past would be revealed. Too many of his emotions would be exposed. Far better to conceal the truth, Adrian thought. He would rather have Philippa think him a cad than believe he was weak, tender-hearted, and unable to protect a woman he loved.

As he watched Philippa brush away her tears, distress pounded in his chest. He knew he had to say something, or else he had no reason to be in her room.

"I had no choice but to come here," he finally allowed. On the premise that good liars always stick as close to the truth as possible, he continued, "Like all men, I require food, clothing and shelter. In order to furnish myself the basic amenities of life, I must earn money. To do that, I must practice my trade. Given that it is generally illegal for men to practice midwifery, you could hardly expect me to refuse a legitimate offer of steady employment from an influential baron like Oldcastle."

"But you are specially licensed by the king to be a midwife. You could have remained in London and delivered babies there."

" 'Tis true," lied Adrian. "But a special license does not erase the stigma attached to a man who delivers babes for a living. Lords do not ordinarily seek out my services, and as I told you, I must have patients and fees in order to survive."

"What about the ladies? Do they shun you also?"

"Um, well, the ladies at court know of my expertise. I was never shunned in the boudoir of a woman writhing in the pain of childbirth."

Adrian refrained from adding that, among the wealthiest of London women, he was the most sought after midwife in England. Even when he practiced his trade in defiance of King Edward's law, quality women wanted him at their bedsides when their time drew nigh.

It was even fashionable to say one's child had been delivered by the handsome Sir Adrian. And, for the women involved, it was a reasonably innocuous infraction, since if the authorities discovered Adrian's presence, it was he who risked imprisonment, not the women whose babes he'd delivered.

Clearly, Adrian's evasive answers had heightened Philippa's suspicion. With a sniffle, she flashed him an accusing stare. "So, you thought to leave London because you tired of the prejudice you faced. But you weren't brought here as a prisoner, sir. You willingly accepted Drogo's offer of employment, even after you understood the terms of the bargain. You *agreed* to violate me!"

"Have we not resolved that issue, my lady?"

"Do you think I have forgotten that sordid episode?"

"I thought we were friends. I thought you had forgiven me." He extended his hand, palm up, but she refused to place her hand in his.

"What happened between us in the bathtub does not make us friends," she retorted. "I was tired and weak from the strain of helping Hilda birth her baby. I wasn't exercising proper judgment, and you took advantage of me, sir. You trifled with my emotions at a time when I hadn't the mental or physical strength to protest."

Philippa's damning words were like stones launched from a catapult. If she'd been a man, Adrian would have challenged her to a sword fight in exchange for her indictment. He prided himself on never having taken advantage of a woman. He'd devoted his life to taking care of them. But, in his heart, he knew that what he'd done was unforgivable.

Furious at himself and her, he resisted the urge to grab her shoulders and shake some understanding into her. He knew she was not a woman receptive to such violent persuasion, however. Lies and half-truths were the only weapons Adrian could use to combat her condemnation.

"Philippa, you know I didn't force you. Yet you refuse to admit that you took pleasure from my holding you, and touching you. What guilt scars your soul, woman? What past injury has so deeply wounded you that you must accuse me of molesting you, rather than accept the fact that you enjoyed being intimate with me?"

A quick intake of breath prefaced her rebuttal. " 'Tis shocking your lack of nobility. How dare you suggest that I enjoyed your touch."

"You didn't just enjoy it, Philippa. You loved it." He leaned closer to her, his arms bracketing her slender body. "You craved the release I gave you, and you will crave it again."

"No! You humiliated me in front of Drogo!"

"It was that oaf you intend to marry who took satisfaction from your humiliation," growled Adrian. "I only made love to you. I would never harm you."

"You violated me as surely as if you had robbed me of my maidenhead." Philippa's voice was strained now, high-pitched and taut with panic. "Indeed, how am I to know you did not tear my maidenhead yourself, destroying the evidence of my virginity so that I would not be fit to marry Drogo! You might well have sabotaged my marriage to satisfy your own perverted desire."

"Don't be ridiculous!"

"I was a virgin before you violated me. Now, you say that I am not!"

Heaving a sigh of frustration, Adrian beat back the impulse to bolt from the room. This wasn't the sort of conversation he, or any man, was comfortable with. Defending himself against Philippa's emotionally charged arrows was simply impossible.

He spoke only when his anger was in check. "Did you not hear me argue with Drogo against the wisdom of subjecting you to an examination? Did you not hear me attempt to forestall the man?"

When Philippa didn't answer, Adrian turned and leaned over her, his arms braced on either side of her head, his nose mere inches from her face. "Do you not know that I tried to protect you? Talk to me, woman!"

Wriggling deeper beneath the covers, she responded with stony silence.

In the distance, a wolf howled, its high-pitched wail a grim reminder of Adrian's animal need for Philippa, and the loneliness clawing at his heart. On the bedside table, the candle guttered in the chill that seemed to pervade the castle even on sunny days. Adrian was so near to Philippa that he could smell her, but he was miles away from convincing her that he meant her no harm!

"My lady," he managed through parched lips, "I fear that the effect you have on the four humours of my body might very well drive me insane."

"Perhaps you need a good leeching," she replied caustically.

Adrian reared back, stung by her persistent vitriol. "You asked me why I came to Oldwall Castle, and I will attempt to tell you once more. I was retained by your future husband as a midwife and physic. 'Tis an honorable position, and the monetary reward is handsome. I see no reason to apologize for coming to Sussex, my lady. As for my actions toward *you* . . . well, perhaps you regret the few pleasurable hours we have shared together. But, I do not regret them, so I will not apologize for what my heart has led me to do, either."

"Your heart? Were you following the commands of your heart when you violated my body on the fraudulent excuse of verifying whether I was a virgin?"

"That horrid examination was the price of my employment at Oldwall," said Adrian. "Had I refused—"

"Aye, you would have been sent back to London. Is that so terrible? Did you value your precious retainer at Oldwall over my honor and esteem?"

"Nay, my lady." Adrian's stubborn sense of pride made him unwilling to tell Philippa that if Drogo discharged him, he would be dead within a sennight. After a moment, he added, "Examinations of such a nature are not uncommon among quality folk wishing to ensure a pure bloodline."

"Drogo is hardly *quality*."

"Still, 'tis not unusual that he would require proof of your virginity. Had I refused to perform the service, someone else would have. You know that, and yet you wish to crucify me for carrying out my orders."

"You are surprised that I hate you?"

"What baffles me is that you wish so badly to marry Drogo, you are willing to lie about your virginity."

"I *am* a virgin!"

"Your body bears the scars of some fairly rigorous sex, lady."

"Liar!" Philippa cried, blinking rapidly.

Adrian propped his forearms on his thighs. A moment of tense silence passed while he laced his fingers and studied them as if they were the most fascinating things he'd ever seen. At last, he turned and stared at Philippa, catching her sea-green gaze for an instant before she looked away.

"My lady, you have no idea how deeply I regret that horrible examination. I understand how painfully humiliating it must have been for you. Especially since you are not the innocent maiden you are masquerading as."

"You understand nothing! You cannot possibly know how degrading it was to be *inspected* by a man as if I were some sort of livestock."

"Would it help you to know that I have examined numerous ladies under similar conditions?"

Philippa turned her scorching gaze on him, prompting Adrian to wonder which was worse, her accusing stare, or her annoying refusal to make eye contact with him when he spoke from his heart.

"What I should like to know is," she said, "how many such examinations have been performed on *you*, sir? By a member of the opposite sex? While a gawking spectator stood at the foot of the bed and yanked his willicock?"

"None, of course."

She rolled onto her back then, teeth clenched and eyes snapping. "Do you not understand why men are prohibited by law from practicing midwifery? You say that you comprehend my humiliation, but you know nothing because you are not a woman! You have never known the embarrassment of being handled like a piece of meat!"

Adrian started to take issue with that remark, but chose instead to remain quiet.

"You have never experienced the pain of squeezing an eight-pound babe from your body," she continued. "You are a man! Like every other man! And I hate—"

"Enough!" Adrian's patience snapped like a twig. Leaning down, he covered Philippa's mouth with his. He felt the softness of her lips, the clash of her teeth as she struggled to turn her head to the side. Her fists flew to his shoulders, but she was powerless to repel him. She gasped and cursed, but her words were muffled by the pressure of Adrian's kiss.

Sliding his hands beneath her, he gathered her in his arms, refuting her accusations with kisses, drinking in her anger as if it were a fortifying wine. Beneath the covers, she kicked her feet, but the harder she fought him, the tighter Adrian held her.

"No, I do not want to feel this way!" Philippa cried, writhing in his arms. Her head reared back, and she gulped in a huge breath of air. "Leave me be, sir. Do not trifle with me—I cannot stand it!"

Adrian lifted his head to look at her. Passion tightened Philippa's expression, but fear raged in her eyes. He ached to know what had happened to cause her to mistrust men so profoundly.

Holding her gaze, he lowered his head and gently pressed his lips to hers once more. Philippa whispered, "No," but her lips yielded. Kissing her, Adrian tasted the sweet posset she'd drunk before bedtime, the minty flavor of her breath, and the saltiness of the tears that had trickled down her face.

He cradled her head, supporting her weight as her back arched off the bed. When he slid his tongue into her mouth, he felt her tremble in his embrace. Then her fingers tightened on his shoulders and she clung to him like a frightened child.

Hungrily, Adrian explored Philippa's mouth. And as he held her and she clung to him, her responses quickened and intensified. Her fingers tangled in the hair on his nape. Her breasts crushed against his chest. A sort of physical greed overwhelmed him; Adrian ached to devour her. But when his urge to carry the embrace to more erotic heights seemed irresistible, he slowly lowered her shoulders to the mattress.

Blond hair, loosed from her braids, spilled across the pillow. Philippa stared up through glazed eyes, her lips parted. Then she closed her lids, swallowing hard as if to choke back a sob, and turned her head. Her pain was palpable, her sigh full of anguish. Adrian's heart twisted with pity while his body thrummed with desire.

He touched the back of his hand to her cheek, surprised at the warmth of her skin. When she flinched, he drew back, leery even of touching her. "Dear God," he whispered. "What has happened to you?"

The torment in Philippa's expression was visible despite the shadows. Pressing her lips together, she shook her head.

"Can you not tell me, Philippa? Can you not confide in me?"

"Nay, you are a man," she whispered.

"A man who loves you," he said, shocked to hear himself say those words.

He was even more shocked when Philippa's eyes flung open, and her fist shot out to strike him square on the jaw.

In the chill silence of the infirmary, Adrian gingerly touched the bruise on his jaw. He worked his jaw from side to side, still stunned that Philippa had thrown such a powerful punch. Not for the first time, he stood in awe of the physical strength a woman's body so often possessed.

Shaking his head, trying in vain to dispel visions of Philippa from his mind, he focused his gaze on the lifeless body before him. Belinda's pale flesh was as cold as the stone slab on which it reposed. Recalling her gratitude when he'd pleasured her, Adrian's sadness deepened. He'd have liked nothing better than to cover her body, prepare her for a decent, Christian burial, and retreat to his pallet for a night's worth of mind-numbing sleep.

But rest wasn't possible. Adrian had to finish his examination this night, despite his exhaustion. He was running out of time.

Starting at the top of her head, he meticulously inspected every inch of her. Belinda had obviously died of her throat wound. Unfortunately, the lacerations on Belinda's arms and hands indicated she'd not died quickly or easily.

With some effort, Adrian managed to lift and rotate Belinda's arms, now stiff and unyielding. On her palms were a series of deep slashes, evidently sustained when she raised her hands to fend off her attacker. Picturing her last few, terror-filled moments, a surge of disgust rose in Adrian's throat.

Continuing his examination, his disgust turned to pity, then to relief that he hadn't given in to his desire to bed her. It was clear that she was sick. She suffered from an infection rather common to whores, a virulent infectious disease that would spread to whomever she had sex with. Whoever had rutted with Belinda before she died was living with the incubus of a potentially deadly disease, himself.

As he wrapped the woman's body in a coarse winding sheet, something inside Adrian hardened like amber around the skeletal remains of an ancient beetle. Belinda's death would not go unavenged. Adrian would apprehend the villain and find justice for a woman whose life was spent servicing the needs of men.

Chapter Twelve

Propped against a bank of pillows and bolsters, Hilda cradled her infant to her swollen breasts. Her wan smile never quite reached her eyes, and her skin was as pale as a fish's belly, but a sense of serenity had finally descended in the temporary nursery on the upper floor of the keep. As her child suckled noisily, Hilda turned an inquisitive gaze on Philippa.

"So, what are ye goin' to do, then, my lady?"

Perched on the side of the bed, Philippa had spent the last quarter-hour staring dreamily at the baby girl nestled on Hilda's tummy. Occasionally, she reached out and stroked the soot-colored fur that capped the baby's head. But her thoughts were as distantly scattered as a yard full of frightened mice. When Hilda posed a question, Philippa jerked back to reality.

"What am I going to do? About what, Hildee?"

"About that man, that *midwife*, that saint of a man who delivered me babe and saved me from dyin'. Hadn't been for 'im, I'd a met me maker in a birthin' chair while Gertrude and them other old wives tied knots in every rope in the castle."

Unable to resist a weary chuckle, Philippa thought of the silly superstitions women attached to childbirth. Some believed that a woman in labor could be helped by wrapping about her middle a birth girdle, a long strip of parchment on which a prayer was written out. Others put stock in chanting, 'Tarla, farla, arlaus, tarlaus,' while a woman struggled to give birth.

"Hildee, I'm glad that Sir Adrian was present in the castle when you needed him. Knowing that he saved your life makes it easier for me to be civil to him."

For a long time, Hilda simply stared at Philippa. At length, she said, "So, you're just behavin' civil to 'im, is that what you'd have me believe?"

Heat suffused Philippa's cheeks. Was she so transparent that this woman could read her mind? They'd been friends for years, since Philippa had come to live in Drogo's castle at age ten. Frequently, they knew each other's minds and moods as well as their own. But secrets still remained between them. One of those secrets concerned Philippa's reasons for willingly accepting Drogo's offer of marriage. Another was the inexplicable attraction she felt for Sir Adrian Vale, a man she should, by all rights, despise.

A third secret was that he'd professed his love for her.

For which she had struck him with all her might. He *loved* her? Silently, Philippa scoffed at the notion. What sort of fustian was that? In no way did that man love her. He *could not*. He didn't even know her. He couldn't possibly guess her secret shame, even if he suspected from his physical examination that she wasn't a virgin. If he knew her—really knew her—he wouldn't even spit on her.

"I am indeed civil to Sir Adrian, but that is all," Philippa said, as off-handedly as she could. "He shows signs of being a skilled midwife and a compassionate physician. For those traits, I admire him. The fact remains, however, that Sir Adrian gladly participated in Drogo's shameful abuse of me.

Dear God, I believe he enjoyed it! How can I ever nurture even the tiniest speck of affection for a man who would do such a thing?"

Hilda clucked her tongue. "Lor, girl, I'm gettin' tired. And me mind's as cloudy as an old man's piss. But I know a good, strong buck when I see one."

"I suppose that's why you married Denys," Philippa riposted.

"Huh! Full of clever words, are ye? Well, ye may wear me down yet. But think on this 'ere ye make up yer mind, love. Sir Adrian had no choice but to carry out Drogo's instructions. And if he'd refused, you'd like to have been examined by some warty midwife with goat dung beneath her fingernails."

The thought sent a shudder through Philippa's body. But the thought of Sir Adrian's hands—clean, strong and gentle—elicited a different response, a heightening of awareness that moved over her like a heated vapor.

"Aye, Hildee, Sir Adrian was clean, at least. For that, I can be grateful."

"I've heard of midwives who treated their patients with less tenderness than a farmer treats a cow birthin' a calf," Hilda said. "Was Sir Adrian rough in the way he handled ye?"

"No." *On the contrary,* thought Philippa. His touch was disturbing because it *was* so soothing. Never before had she experienced the sort of sensations Adrian's touch roused in her. Though those feelings brought her pleasure, it was a pleasure wrapped in guilt. And the strength of her confused emotions frightened her.

"Did he say nice words while he touched ye?"

"Aye, and in the softest of tones, too. 'Twas belike he truly regretted what he had to do."

Recalling Adrian's husky assurances, Philippa's pulse began to race. He'd spoken so kindly that she'd even been able to block the grotesque sounds of Drogo pleasuring himself at the foot of the bed. God, but the notion of sleeping with that hideous little man, with his burnt hair and beetled eyebrows, repelled her. Now that she knew what it was to want a man, to truly desire a man's body and long for him to possess hers as well, how would she ever submit to Drogo?

"Then, how can ye say Sir Adrian enjoyed what he did to ye, child?" Hilda's voice, as cracked as a scullery wench's knuckles, betrayed her fatigue. " 'Pears to me the man was as gentle as he coulda been. Is it yer own feelin's that have turned ye agin him? Are ye angry at 'im on account of the fire he created in yer belly?"

Philippa met her friend's gaze and held it. "You don't think I liked it, do you? God's blood, Hilda! A decent woman doesn't talk about such feelings, much less desire them!"

"Seein' as I ain't a decent woman, I wouldn't know," replied Hilda, stroking the soft spot on the top of her child's head. "But I can tell you this, and ye'd best believe me! There ain't a nun in England who doesn't feel a hunger in her belly every once in a while, a hunger that only a man can satisfy. 'Tis a normal thing, Philippa. You oughtn't to feel you've sinned agin the Good Lord just because ye suddenly felt a certain need."

"Only men have those sorts of needs."

Hilda snorted, but her laughter was short-lived. Pain streaked her face, silencing her and filling her eyes with unshed tears. After a moment, when she'd caught her breath, she said weakly, "I think you've been more than civil to him, Philippa. The servants talk, you know. Gertrude couldn't keep a secret in a burlap bag."

Leaning closer, Philippa touched her friend's arm. "Are you all right, Hildee? Shall I fetch Sir Adrian? Would you like a bowl of mush, or a drink of wine?"

The nursing mother shook her head. "Listen to me, girl. Ain't nothin' worse than bein' tethered to a man ye don't love. 'Ceptin if it's being wed to a man who don't love *you*."

"I don't know what you're talking about, Hildee. Methinks

this fever has overset your mind. You're not thinking clearly. Don't you know that I'm bound to marry Drogo and become the lady of this castle?"

In a voice so faint, it was barely audible above the gurgles of her baby, Hilda said, "Has Sir Adrian sworn to Drogo you are a virgin?"

Unease roiled in Philippa's stomach. As much as she trusted Hilda, and as much as she *needed* someone to talk to, she couldn't bring herself to confess her shame. Besides, the older woman wouldn't understand. Philippa had never told anyone what Sir Faustus had done to her. And the stain of her mother's indiscretion had been swept under the carpet many years ago. Only Sir Casper Gilchrist's shame remained extant, as viable as any living, breathing creature that walked the earth. And Philippa wasn't about to reveal how her father had mortgaged his honor, or how she intended to buy it back.

"As it turned out, Hilda, I was having my menses when Sir Adrian examined me. He told Drogo he couldn't swear that I was a virgin."

"But he can't swear you *ain't*," said Hilda.

"No."

"Somethin' you want to tell me?" Hilda managed through bloodless lips. "Don't worry about me tellin' anyone else, love, fer I'll take yer secrets to the grave with me. I swear it!"

Choking back a sob, Philippa leaned over Hilda and her babe, wrapping them both in a silent, teary embrace. She wished so ardently that she could spill out her troubles to her best friend. Yet, she couldn't. The new mother's weak constitution couldn't withstand such a shock, Philippa thought. The disappointment Hilda would experience in learning of her friend's defilement would no doubt precipitate a depression that could seriously affect her and her babe's health.

But even if Hilda were strong as an ox, Philippa wouldn't easily reveal to her the awful secret of Sir Casper's disgrace.

Her father's shame was, after all, her own. And it was her life's ambition to erase that shame, not to perpetuate it.

"Have you decided on a name for your daughter, Hilda?"

The new mother shook her head. "I don't know her well enough to name her yet, now, do I?"

"Rest now, Hildee," Philippa whispered, laying her palm to the woman's burning cheek.

The fever that still raged in Hilda's body frightened Philippa even more than the prospect of mating with Drogo. As Hilda's eyes flickered shut, Philippa gently lifted the baby. Cradling the little girl in her arms, she paced the room. When a healthy little belch was achieved, she laid the child in her bassinet and called for Gertrude to keep a vigil in the nursery.

Suddenly, it seemed that Philippa had more worries than a dog had ticks. And, strangely, she could think of only one man, Sir Adrian Vale, who was man enough to help her solve them.

Drogo's solar, where the man had been confined these last twenty-four hours, smelled strongly of its occupant. That was why Sir Adrian repeatedly pinched the tip of his nose as he stood beside the baron's bed.

"I ought to have your ballocks on a platter for what you done to me," muttered the half-coherent baron before lapsing into a fitful sleep punctuated by violent snorts and snores.

On the other side of the bed, Sir Killian gave a harsh bark of laughter. "The king's physic, indeed! You damn near killed the baron. 'Tis only your good fortune that my liege-lord is strong enough to have survived your malfeasance. Nought but a quack would have hammered that arrow straight through his knee."

Exhaling, Adrian kept a tight rein on his emotions. Given the events of the last few days, he had no desire to be dispatched to London in disgrace. Not as yet, anyway. Before he left Oldwall Castle, Adrian was determined to avenge

Belinda's murder and discover whether Drogo was conducting raids into France.

More importantly, he intended to ensure that Lady Philippa Gilchrist's future was secure. He wasn't quite certain at what point he had begun to consider her his responsibility. Perhaps it was when he deceived Drogo by saying the virgin examination was inconclusive because Philippa had been having her menses. Or perhaps it was when he'd pulled her into the bathtub with him and realized that though she was evidently no virgin, her response to being pleasured was anything but experienced.

No, he wasn't certain when he'd assumed the role of Philippa's protector, but now that he had, there was no way Adrian could walk away from her without knowing she would be safe and happy.

Of his three objectives, securing Philippa's future would surely prove the most challenging. And puzzling. For, despite his admitted love for Philippa, Adrian remained steadfast in his determination never to marry, and never to impregnate another woman. Having dedicated his life to saving women from the dangerous perils of childbirth, he couldn't live with himself if he placed the woman he loved in harm's way.

So how was he to help her?

A disturbing thought suddenly materialized. If Adrian refused to certify Philippa a virgin, Drogo wouldn't marry her, of course. For a time, she would be safe from the consequences of pregnancy. But if Drogo didn't wed her, then Philippa would be forced to seek out another arrangement. Eventually, a decent man would ask for her hand. Of that, Adrian was certain, because Philippa was, after all, beautiful and sweet.

And, eventually, Philippa would become pregnant by another man.

The possibility of Philippa undergoing the rigors of childbirth filled Adrian with dread.

It occurred to him that he was powerless to protect Philippa from the trials and tribulations of womanhood. Pregnancy and child-bearing were the natural results of marriage and sex. He could no more prevent Philippa's having children than he could stop the rain from falling from the sky. Yet, the very idea she might experience the pain Jeanne had felt, the thought that she might succumb to an untimely death in the same manner Jeanne had, caused him to break out in a cold sweat.

Staring at Drogo's ugly face, ashen beneath the ruddy pallor of his infirmity, a terrifying insight seized hold of Sir Adrian. He had to help her! He had to rescue her from the specter of unhappiness that haunted her! If he did nothing else good in his life, then he had to know that he had given Lady Philippa Gilchrist the chance to know joy.

In that instant, when Adrian's course altered, and his emotions toward Philippa grew more richly textured, he experienced a sort of epiphany. He knew that he loved Philippa, yes, loved her with all his heart, but *not* with the consuming selfishness with which he'd loved Jeanne.

Rather, Adrian realized, with a conviction that bordered on religious fanaticism, he loved Philippa with a purity and selflessness that he'd never experienced before.

And, in his willingness to put aside his selfish desires, to focus purely on what was best for her, Adrian realized he loved Philippa more than he'd ever loved any woman. Any woman.

Was it possible? God, but he'd loved his sweet wife! But, Adrian's love for Jeanne, and his arrogant desire to create a child with her, had resulted in tragedy. It was he who had wanted children, not Jeanne. Two babes were delivered stillborn before the third was conceived. That should have been enough warning that Jeanne's body was not strong enough to bear children.

But when Adrian had insisted they try again, Jeanne had

willingly agreed. After all, she knew how badly he wanted a son. Her fulfillment came in loving *him*. Ultimately, her life had been sacrificed to his masculine urges.

He was older and wiser now. Perhaps for the first time, he knew what love really was. Never would he allow his own selfish needs to imperil Philippa's life. Instead, he would do what was right for *her*.

"Are you listening, man?" Sir Killian's voice cut through Adrian's jumbled thoughts.

"I don't wish to take issue with you, Killian," Adrian replied, forcing his attention to the situation at hand, "but had that arrow been cut from your leige-lord's leg in the manner he requested, he might very well have been crippled for life. Worse, he might have bled to death."

"So you say," retorted Killian. "But any fool can see the baron is suffering greatly. How do I know you didn't try to kill Drogo yourself? Good God, you nailed his leg to a wooden plank! The shock alone would have been enough to finish off a lesser man."

"He's a tough old bugger, that one," said Adrian, sitting on the baron's bedside.

His weight on the mattress caused Drogo to stir and open his eyes. "Damn, man, me leg feels like it's on fire!"

Adrian picked up his patient's wrist and measured his pulse. Then, he gauged Drogo's fever with a palm laid on his forehead. "Your injury was a serious one, my lord. Frankly, you are lucky to be alive."

A fetid grunt escaped the baron's lips. "I'm lucky I survived your malpractice, that's what I am!"

"If you think I am a quack, my lord, then mayhap you would like me to depart Oldwall Castle on the morn. I understand that Lady Philippa is quite knowledgeable about herbs and medicines. From what I have observed, the infirmary is quite well-stocked with powders and potions. And the local nuns are well-qualified to invoke the healing power of the saints. Would you prefer that the women be in charge of your recuperation?"

Drogo's face darkened. "Aargh! Are ye outta yer mind, sir? I wouldn't let no woman tamper with me body, not if I was lying on my death bed! Besides, you ain't told me yet whether Lady Philippa is a virgin."

Sir Killian, hands clasped behind his back, interrupted. "And that is what you came here for, isn't it, Sir Adrian? My friends at court assured me of your credentials. I wouldn't have retained you to conduct such a delicate examination had you not the king's endorsement. Tell me again, Adrian, what exactly is your title?"

The sparkle in Killian's gaze, as well as the mockery in his voice, grated on Adrian's nerves. He wasn't yet prepared to provoke Killian, however, so he spoke with as much restraint and civility as he could muster. "King's Physic, sir. I am specially licensed to attend to the ladies of the realm."

Killian's expression was smug. "Ah, yes. Indeed, you were highly recommended by the Marcher Lord Raeburn, that foppish frog de Champignac and Bishop Gramonti."

Drogo chuckled. "But Sir Adrian has yet to complete the task for which I retained him, namely to tell me whether Philippa's maidenhead is intact."

"How much longer before her menses are over and you can examine her again?" asked Killian.

"I am growing impatient," added Drogo. "As soon as you are certain that there is no infection in my leg, I want you gone from here!"

Adrian looked from Killian to Drogo, sensing a strong undercurrent of animosity. Could it be that they suspected he was King Edward's spy? Had Raeburn, de Champignac or Gramonti betrayed the king by revealing to Killian that Adrian was recommended as a midwife so that he could spy on Drogo?

"I thought you wished me to stay on, my lord," replied Adrian, "until Lady Philippa bore you a child."

"I have changed my mind, sir," replied the baron. "One of the village midwives will do for Philippa. The more I think on it, the less I like the idea of a man like you touching my bride."

"She isn't your bride yet," Adrian said, revealing too much of his feelings toward Philippa. He wished he could capture his words and swallow them, but it was too late.

Drogo's eyes narrowed to slits. "She will be, mark my words."

"What if my examination reveals she isn't a virgin?"

"That, sir, is a matter to be settled between Sir Casper Gilchrist and me. Her father promised me a virgin. . . . " Drogo's voice trailed off.

"And if Philippa isn't a virgin? How would that circumstance alter your contractual arrangement with Sir Casper?"

Drogo opened his mouth, but Killian spoke first. " 'Twould negate the baron's obligation to marry the chit, for one. But my liege-lord is a generous man, Sir Adrian. If it is found that Philippa's maidenhead is not intact, then some other arrangements for her will be made."

Drogo's crude laughter filled the gap created by Killian's stunning remark. "I might marry her anyway! Or, mayhap I would simply take her as a lover, without the benefit of marriage! Why buy the cow when you can get the milk for free, isn't that right, Killian?"

Adrian's exasperation surfaced. "What sort of nonsensical chicanery is this? What the hell difference does it make whether your bride is a virgin or not? Isn't it enough that she is willing to marry you, and that you love her? You do have some feelings of affection for Lady Philippa, do you not?"

An incredulous look smeared Drogo's features. "Are you such a knotty-pated simpkin that you believe a man must love a woman 'ere he takes her for his wife?"

Joining in the baron's laughter, Killian clapped his hands and stomped his booted foot. "Perhaps, Adrian, if you lose your license to practice midwifery, you can get on as the king's jester!"

Losing his temper would be counterproductive, Adrian knew. So despite the angry heat flooding his face, he smiled gamely. "Well, then, if you are intent on bedding the chit, within or without the boundaries of matrimony, perhaps I should be examining you, my lord, as well as the lady."

Drogo sobered. "What the devil are ye talkin' about?"

"I don't mean to step beyond my place, my lord. And if you have never touched the prostitutes who populate the castle grounds, then you are entirely without cause for alarm."

"Go on."

"But as a trained physician, I understand something of a man's urges. Good God, don't forget I was once a soldier myself! Men like us . . . *like you, that is* . . . well, we a need bawdy wench's body beneath us every now and then, don't we? Especially a randy fellow like you! It has been my observation that powerful men like you, my lord, often have the sex drive of a war horse in heat!"

"Yes, yes, I have sheathed me sword in many a wench's scabbard, sir. Don't be coy! What the hell are ye talkin' about?"

Swearing softly, Adrian rubbed his chin and looked away. "Just as I thought. A virile man like you has no doubted bedded many a leman."

"What of it?" snapped Killian.

"Well, in my capacity as physic here at Oldwall Castle, I have had the opportunity to examine several of the local prostitutes." Adrian hesitated, and pulled a long face. "And, zounds, but they do carry disease! Many diseases, some of the most virulent afflictions known to modern science!"

Killian leaned forward, clearly concerned, most likely for his own health more than for Drogo's.

The baron's face, if it were possible, faded to an even paler shade of gray. "Disease, man? What sort of disease?"

Adrian sighed. "The kinds that produce boils on your arse, incite fevers in your brain, and generally leave you with a feeling of malaise and lethargy. One of the diseases that is particularly rampant among the local whores will cause a man's bowels to move with an urgency that is most embarrassing and inconvenient!"

Killian's hand moved to his stomach. "I had the flux last week," he noted quietly.

Drogo swallowed hard. "I've got a boil on me arse that causes me great pain when I'm in the saddle. Do ye think I got it from havin' sex with some diseased wench?"

"Most likely," replied Adrian. "But that is not the worst disease I have encountered among the local prostitutes. There is another . . . but, of course, if you were suffering from the ill effects of that particular malady, you would already know it."

"What ill effects?" Killian and Drogo said in unison.

At length, Adrian said, "Understand that I don't mean to cause undue alarm, or frighten you away from the castle lemans. They need their coin, after all. They'd starve were it not for the patronage and generosity of the baron and his men."

"What ill effects?" demanded Drogo.

"Well, it seems that one of the women I examined . . . I can't remember her name . . . carried a certain disease that caused her flesh to shrivel and retract, to shrink as it were, until the most intimate parts of her body actually began to fall off!"

Killian gulped loudly. "A flesh-eating disease?"

Drogo's hands flew to his groin. "Parts of her body fell off?"

"You can imagine the ill effects this disease would have on a man," said Adrian. "In an advanced stage, absent any treatment at all, a man's parts would simply . . . fall off!"

In the moments following Adrian's pronouncement, while Drogo and Killian attempted to absorb the information the physic had provided, a long and crackly silence ensued.

Then, without ceremony, Drogo threw off his counterpane, and pulled up his coarse tunic to expose his genitals. "Go ahead, then, man, examine me! I don't want me willicock fallin' off!"

" 'Twould be a fate worse than death," agreed Adrian, suppressing a smile.

As Adrian leaned over Drogo's body, Philippa's words rang in his ears: *You have never known the embarrassment of being handled like a piece of meat*. Frowning, Adrian thought how painfully humiliated Philippa must have been during that dreadful examination. The guilt that assailed him was only slightly relieved by Drogo's present state of utter fear. That he might be in danger of losing his manhood horrified the baron. And because it did, Adrian couldn't help but be amused.

Of course, he didn't expect to find anything amiss with Drogo. He only wanted to find out whether Drogo showed symptoms of the disease he'd discovered on Belinda's body when he'd examined her. And, if in so doing, he managed to scare Killian and Drogo from the castle lemans for a few days, then that was all right, too.

What Adrian found instead was a rare abnormality that he knew from his tenure at Montpelier existed in a very small fraction of the adult male population.

Drogo's testicles were as tiny as grapes left in the sun to dry. One of them was drawn up so far into Drogo's body as to barely be visible. Gently palpating, Adrian satisfied himself that the man had not contracted syphilis. At least, no signs of the disease were evident. But, something very troublesome—something far more significant than Drogo's lack of venereal contagion—manifested itself.

"My lord," he asked, dread rising in his throat like bile, "Have you ever sired a child?"

Drogo's expression said it all. "Not that I know of. 'Course there's bound to be some little throw-off runnin' around the village with red hair and black brows. I've nailed quite a few wenches in me day, that's for certain."

"But none has ever reported to you that she was with child?"

Drogo frowned. It wasn't manly to admit that his seed, which by his own admission had been spilled rather injudiciously all over the castle grounds, had never produced a child.

But the truth of it was, that for all his whoring, Drogo had never impregnated a woman. That, and the condition of his shrunken balls, meant he probably never would.

Which in turn meant that if he married Lady Philippa Gilchrist, she would never get with child, never be subjected to the risks associated with childbearing, and never experience the pain and horrors of birthing a child without qualified medical assistance.

Adrian's heart squeezed. The last thing in the world he wanted was to inflict pain or hardship on Philippa. The last thing in the world he wanted was to hurt another woman the way he hurt Jeanne.

He loved Philippa. He would do anything to ensure her safety. Even if it meant certifying her as a virgin so that she could marry a man who would never get her pregnant.

Chapter Thirteen

In the vestibule just outside Drogo's solar, Philippa waited impatiently, tapping the toes of her buskins and toying with the jeweled cross that hung from her neck. She didn't dare knock at the door; indeed, her long-time practice was to stay out of Killian and Drogo's respective paths, drawing as little attention to herself as possible. But Sir Adrian she *did* want to see—desperately. Hilda's fever had worsened, and Philippa feared her best friend was weakening in the aftermath of her childbirth.

The door swung open and Adrian crossed the threshold with Sir Killian at his heel. Clearly failing to see Lady Philippa, the two men stood with their backs to her, conversing in hushed tones.

"I prithee, when can you take a look at my johnny, too?" asked Killian.

Philippa's ears burned, and she dipped her head in embarrassment, but she couldn't help smiling when she heard Sir Adrian's response.

"Good God, Killian, I'm truly quite busy just now! Drogo is a demanding patient, you know, and with all the extra duties piled upon me because of the epidemic among the whores—not to mention the monitoring of Lady Philippa's menses—well, I really can't say when I'll have a chance."

"Forget the whores!"

"Forget them? I thought it rather crucial to the health of your men that I document which girls are healthy and which ones carry the dread disease that I described to Drogo."

"Yes, yes," said Killian, "do that! But you must examine me first!"

"And there's Lady Philippa to think of. We mustn't forget that my primary obligation as Drogo's retainer is to determine whether his intended bride is a virgin."

"A turd in your teeth, man! Forget about Philippa for a moment! This is my johnny we're talking about. And I've bedded a few of the castle wenches myself. More than that braggart, Drogo, I can assure you!"

"Is that so?" Adrian lifted his dark brows and shot Killian an appraising look. "Did you by chance have sex with a whore named Belinda?"

Killian hesitated a split second. "Which one is she? The fat, dumpy one with the space between her front teeth?"

"That would be Cecily," replied Adrian.

"Why would a man in my position care to know the castle lemans by name?" Sighing, Killian looked at his boots. " 'Struth, I can't say whether I slept with Belinda or Cecily or the vicar's daughter. I only know that I've rutted with more than my share, and if there's some dread disease being passed from woman to man, then you'd best go about preparing me a remedy."

Adrian took a step toward the stairwell. "Remind me day after tomorrow, Killian, and I'll try to have a peek at your talleywacker."

Killian grabbed his arm. "I will be at the infirmary an hour before noon *tomorrow!* And you'd best be there, Adrian. *With a cure for this foul disease.* For, if anything does fall off, I'll have your head!"

With that, Killian shoved past Adrian and rushed headlong down the stairs where he could be heard shouting at a passing serving wench to bring him a tankard of strong ale.

Adrian remained at the landing, standing in semidarkness, with his broad muscular back to Philippa.

Moving out of the shadows, she said, softly, "Whatever in the world was that about?"

To her surprise, he wasn't the least startled by her presence. Turning, a slow smile spread across his face and he took in her full figure, from head to toe, with a frankly admiring gaze. "Killian is worried that his penis might fall off."

"I gathered as much." Unable to keep her distance, she walked toward him. She couldn't seem to pull away, or even to forget about him when they weren't together. Whatever invisible force it was that pinned the stars in the sky and held the water in the oceans kept Philippa coming back to Adrian, as well.

Arms crossed over her chest, she stood an arm's length from him, close enough to note that the dark stubble on his jaw line was turning to down, close enough to detect the aroma of clean sweat and soap on his woolen tunic. "But why does Killian fear losing his, er . . . manhood?" she asked, trying not to stare too ostentatiously at Adrian's handsome face.

"Can you keep a secret?" he asked, closing the small gap between them. Toe to toe with her, he brushed a wisp of hair from her cheek.

"Better than most," she replied. Better than you'll ever know, she thought.

"When I examined Belinda, I discovered that she had a disease. A nasty disease, to be sure, though I've never seen it make anything fall off a man."

Philippa shrugged in confusion.

"Listen well, and tell no one." Adrian made a dramatic show of looking around the tiny vestibule. No one was present, and no one could hear them, but he whispered nonetheless, perhaps to create a sense of intimacy, thought Philippa, or more likely to arouse her passions with his hot breath upon her neck.

"I have it on good authority that some of the castle prostitutes have become ill of late, and I am attempting to locate the source of the infection. Therefore, it was imperative that I examine Killian's genitals. Forgive me for being indelicate, but I examined Drogo's, too."

"Sir, you do not offend me," replied Philippa. "As I told you, I know the baron takes his pleasure with whores. I couldn't care less!"

"But like most men, Drogo and Killian were loath to submit to a physical examination—"

"Yet Drogo would have me probed like an animal," murmured Philippa.

"So, I devised a ruse," Adrian continued. "I gave them both a reason to want medical attention. I told them if they also came down with the dreaded disease, their bits might fall off! Of course, I wasn't entirely certain they would concern themselves with my warning. If they hadn't bedded any whores, I told them, they had nothing to worry about."

"But the fools incriminated themselves by unlacing their braies as quickly as they could, is that it?"

Adrian's chuckle kindled a tiny flame in Philippa's belly. But it was his velvety soft voice that sent shivers up her spine.

"Philippa, your quick wit is a worthy rival of your graceful beauty. My lady, you are the most compellingly alluring woman I have ever beheld." After a pause, during which he stared longingly into Philippa's eyes, Adrian added, "Why have you sought me out? Have you come to apologize for slapping my face?"

Reminded of her reaction to his avowal of love, Philippa's

face grew hot. She'd hit him because he'd threatened to destroy the tightly woven web of lies and denials that protected her heart. She'd lashed out at him because he was getting close to seeing straight into her soul and discovering her true identity. And she'd repelled him because if he ever really knew her, he would not love her.

She would rather reject him now, then be rejected by him later.

Chin to chest, she spoke in such a tiny voice that it sounded foreign to her ears. "I am sorry, Adrian. I never meant to hurt you."

"Nor did I ever intend to injure you, Philippa. Though I know I have."

"I spoke to Hilda," she began haltingly. "She is my best friend, and often when I converse with her, I gain insight into my own motivations and emotions. Hilda's lot in life has not been smooth. But she is a good judge of character, though she persists in defending that rapscallion husband of hers. And she listens well."

"That is truly the mark of a good friend."

"Hildee likes you."

"A huzzah for dear old Hildee." Adrian touched Philippa's chin, tipping her face upward, forcing her to meet his gaze.

Her breath caught in her throat, but somehow she managed to communicate her regret, even if her words did not flow easily. "Perhaps I judged you too hastily, sir, when I accused you of acting in concert with Drogo. I don't believe you wanted to participate in that tawdry scene. In truth, I believe you tried to save me from it, and when you couldn't, you tried to lessen the humiliation that I felt."

"You must believe that, Philippa."

"I . . . I am trying, Adrian. Sweet Mary, how I am trying!"

Grasping her upper arms, he pulled her to him. When he spoke, his eyes burned with a mesmerizing ferocity. "Would that I could keep you out of harm's way for eternity!"

"You can't, Adrian! No one can!"

"I would do anything to erase from your past whatever tragedies have scarred your heart!"

She shook her head, struggling against his tight embrace. "Why do you insist on looking so deeply inside me? Isn't it enough that you have explored every nook and cranny of my body? Must you peer inside my heart, as well?"

"How else can I know what will make you happy?"

"Why must you? Oh, Adrian, do not question me any further regarding my motives in wishing to marry Drogo! If you care for me at all, you must leave my past be! The iron bars that guard my heart are there to protect me."

"Are they protecting you, Philippa, or are they keeping you prisoner? Good God, girl, you've locked yourself behind a wall of pain and thrown away the key! Don't you see? I want to help you, not hurt you! I want to love you, not possess you!"

Pressing her palms on his tunic front, she pushed against his chest, an unyielding slab of muscle and flesh. Eyes tightly shut, she turned her head and willed him away from her. But instead of releasing her, Adrian easily enveloped her in the security of his embrace.

She wanted to hate him, wanted to banish him from sight and mind. Yet, as his arms surrounded her, and his lips found hers, Philippa's resistance was vanquished by a much more powerful need. Yes, Adrian's incessant interrogations jangled her nerves. Yes, his powers of perception threatened to blow apart her cozy little world. And, yes, his sexuality jeopardized her sanity.

But there was something strangely comforting about the way he rocked her equanimity. Sir Adrian Vale was strong and wise and good. He was gentle and kind, witty and intelligent. He was the only man, other than her father, who'd ever touched her in a way that didn't frighten her. He was a rock-solid man, and Philippa clung to him like a drowning woman.

He kissed her roughly, passionately, as if his hunger could not be satisfied. And the sound of his breathing, harsh and labored, filled the tiny vestibule, weighting the air with tension and erotic heat.

Her body, wracked by desire, melted in his embrace.

She felt his hand supporting her neck, his fingers clutching her nape. She gasped as he caressed the curves of her hips, cupped her derriere and pressed her body against his. Her body quaked when he massaged her breasts. His gentle pinching of her nipples drove her to a nearly frenzied state of excitement.

Adrian's excitement soared, too. Even through Philippa's tunic and surcoat, and the layer of coarse woolen clothes that he wore, his arousal was evident. In fact, to Philippa's mind, his arousal was formidable, intimidating and wildly intriguing.

And, perhaps the most remarkable of all her reactions, given that she had spent more than half her life in abject fear of the male body, was that Adrian's muscled body and throbbing manhood suddenly represented to her the promise of untold joy and unparalleled heights of happiness.

A thousand points of heat ignited beneath her skin, warming her body in places that only Adrian seemed able to reach. It occurred to her that before he touched her, she had never known anything about her own body. Now, it seemed she knew the secrets of the universe, or at least some of them. And she couldn't wait to learn more of what Adrian had to teach.

Philippa's heart pounded so fiercely she feared it would burst, and the accompanying sense of panic stole her breath away.

Adrian tore his mouth from hers, and whispered against her neck, "Come, Philippa, let us adjourn to your solar."

She wanted nothing more than to be alone with him, cling to him, explore with him this new world of eroticism they'd discovered. Weak from desire, she nodded. And a moment later, she was flat on her back in her bedroom, with the door safely latched and the rest of humanity exiled from her thoughts.

Naked, she lay beneath him, her breasts crushed against his chest. Supporting himself on his elbows, Adrian moved over her and lowered his hips between her thighs.

He'd already pleasured her with his fingers, bringing her to an exquisite release—twice—then holding her in his arms while she shuddered with emotion.

Now, his own body ached for release, and, with his manhood nudging Philippa's moist heat, and her knees squeezing his waist, his heart urged him to do what his brain knew was wrong.

"Make love to me," she whispered, clinging to his shoulders like a hungry waif.

Hesitating, he peered into her sparkling green eyes, awash with the tears that had accompanied her release. When her pent-up emotion spilled forth, she had sobbed, clutching at Adrian with the inner muscles of her body, bucking against his hand, burying her face against his chest, and crying out in torturous ecstasy. Never before had he shared such an intense physical experience with a woman.

Now, he ached to be inside her. Spilling his seed inside Philippa would be a profound experience, not merely because she was the most erotic creature he'd ever been with, but because he loved her so dearly.

All the more reason to stop himself from breaching her trust.

Abruptly, he rolled off her, lying on his side with his head propped on his hand. She turned to look at him, silently questioning his retreat.

"I can't," he whispered huskily.

"Is there something . . . *wrong* with me?"

Wrapping one arm around her waist, Adrian drew her closer to him, tucked her tightly to his chest. "Of course not. Dear God, you're as near to perfection as any woman I've ever seen. And I have seen many of them."

"Then, why?"

"I have no right to take you, Philippa." How could he explain his deepest fears to her? How could he tell her that in hurting another woman years ago, he'd lost his right to love anew? Philippa was so young, so innocent, so full of promise. And she had so much to offer a man. Some other man. A man who he now knew wouldn't get her pregnant and imperil her life.

"You belong to Drogo," he said at length.

"Not yet." Her chin jutted defiantly.

"Soon, you will be his wife," Adrian countered. "And if you are not a virgin, the baron will know."

"Not necessarily. You said yourself Drogo could be tricked into believing he'd ruptured my maidenhead."

Except that Adrian knew Philippa didn't have a maidenhead. Though now wasn't the time to remind her of that. Instead, he gently stroked her cheek, memorizing every detail of her features in preparation for the time when he couldn't hold her, couldn't smell her, couldn't feast his eyes on her.

" 'Tis not in your nature to be deceitful, Philippa, yet you harbor so many secrets in that heart of yours."

"I've given you everything that I have to give, sir. Why won't you give me what I want?"

"Aren't *you* afraid that I will get you pregnant?" he asked her.

For a long moment, she stared at him, then a slight smile curved her lips. At length, Philippa clasped Adrian's hand and studied his fingers. When he followed her gaze, he saw that his fingertips were stained russet, and beneath his nails were rims of dried blood.

"When did your menses begin?" he asked, surprised at the hoarseness in his voice. As a physic specializing in woman's medicine, he knew it wasn't *entirely* impossible for a woman to get pregnant during her period, but if her cycle was regular, it certainly wasn't likely.

"Just now," she replied. "Tomorrow the flow will be heavy. But, for today, 'tis very light."

"Are your menses very predictable?" he asked, shifting his weight.

Reaching down, she wrapped her fingers around his lengthening shaft. "Aye, every twenty-eight days, with nary a deviation."

Which meant, Adrian knew, that she was in the safest part of her menstrual cycle, and if she had sex now, it would be a minor miracle if she conceived a child.

His self-control quickly gave way to an urgent, primal need. Suddenly, his breathing deepened, and a sensation of heavy, throbbing urgency awakened in his groin. He wanted Philippa like he'd never wanted another woman, and after years of pleasuring himself, or paying whores to pleasure him with their lips, he craved the hot wetness of a woman.

Hovering over Philippa, he asked her, "Are you certain that you want this? Are you certain that you want me to make love to you?"

Wordlessly, she answered, stroking his flesh, cupping the most sensitive parts of his body. Then, when Adrian thought he couldn't stand it any more, she lifted her hips to meet his, and opened her legs to embrace him.

Slowly, Adrian moved into her, shocked by the pleasure her tight body yielded. Waves of pleasure washed over him as he pushed further into her hot, lush wetness. And when he felt her inner muscles respond and contract, he nearly lost control.

Between ragged breaths, while he tried desperately to slow his movements, he whispered, "I want it to last."

Philippa's spine arched, her mouth forming a little "o" of surprise. Locking gazes, she moved with Adrian in a rhythm as basic as fire, and as amazing to her as the first flickers of flame must have been to prehistoric men. 'Twas as if they were alone in the world, discovering by some divine revelation a magic that had previously been concealed.

Suspended in this brave new world, they gave themselves to one another. Rocking his body steadily within Philippa's, Adrian graduated from one plateau of arousal to the next. And with each thrust of his hips, she gasped, at last laughing with unabashed pleasure as he plunged his manhood as deeply inside her as her body would allow.

Any semblance of control that Adrian had attempted to maintain shattered. Moving faster, he laid his head in the crook of Philippa's neck and allowed his own pent-up emotions to explode without restraint.

Hugging his waist with her legs, Philippa cried out in startled delight. Her ragged breaths excited Adrian even more, and when he was certain she had reached the pinnacle of her excitement, he allowed himself the release for which he'd been starving.

Sweeping over him, his release was like a powerful storm, unleashed and uncontrollable. Adrian moaned with satisfaction as his seed escaped him, releasing with it years of physical repression. Shivering, he nestled against Philippa's neck, wishing more than anything else that he could melt into her.

With a sigh, she murmured something that sounded like, "I love you," but Adrian was already falling asleep and his mind was muddled.

Her arms wrapped tightly around him, blanketing him in a fuzzy security that seemed like . . . home.

Home.

Tenterden.

Jeanne.

The night she died in childbirth.

From somewhere deep in Adrian's subconscious those images of his wife toiling in childbirth, reaching for him, her eyes filled with stark terror, bubbled to the surface.

He awoke with a start, his body half-covering Philippa's,

his head resting on her breast. What the hell had he done? What the hell had he been thinking when he forgot his promise of celibacy and made love with this woman?

The fact she was unlikely to conceive made no difference. He shouldn't have done it; he shouldn't have put her at risk of getting pregnant even if the chances were infinitesimal.

His stirring awakened her, too. Lifting her head, she gazed dreamily at him. "Are you cold, Adrian?"

"Go back to sleep, my babe."

"Babe?" Her voice was groggy with sleep. "That reminds me. Hilda's fever has not abated."

He kissed her cheek, then crawled out of bed. "I will look in on her before I retire. But I must quit this room before Gertrude knocks on the door, or God forbid, Drogo sends Killian to fetch you."

But Adrian knew there wasn't much likelihood of Drogo summoning Philippa. The baron had yet to rouse completely from his own drug-induced sleep. And as for Killian, he was probably holed up somewhere all alone, bent in half and watching himself carefully lest anything fall off.

Bending, he planted another kiss atop Philippa's head. "Sleep well. I shall see you in the morn."

"Umm." Her gentle snores resumed before he'd even covered her naked body with the marten coverlet.

Before he left, he stoked the fire, concerned that she would awaken in the night and find her room too cold for comfort. At the door, Adrian turned and looked at Philippa, sleeping as peacefully as a child, her features cast in placid contentment. Knowing that he would ultimately entrust her to the likes of Drogo, in order that she might grow to be an old woman, gnawed at his gut. But the possibility that Philippa wouldn't survive her childbearing years was simply too horrid an alternative to face.

Hilda's body was bathed in sweat, her pillows drenched. Purple bruises shadowed her eyes, and deep creases furrowed her forehead. Beneath her counterpane, the woman's night rail was sopping wet and stained with the blood that continued to spill from between her legs.

Standing on the opposite side of Hilda's bed, rocking the newborn in her arms, Gertrude voiced the unanswerable question, "Is she gonna be awright?"

God only knows, Adrian would have said, but he wasn't certain how much Hilda could hear or understand. The new mother's body shuddered with fever, and her pallor was frighteningly gray. Her eyes fluttered open at random and she muttered barely comprehensible inquiries concerning her daughter, but otherwise she seemed to have lost much of her faculties, along with her ability to nurse her child.

Gertrude placed the baby in her bassinet, then stood beside Adrian. "Can you do anything for her, sir?"

He thought it odd that this woman, who had considered his presence in the birthing room shameful, now expected him to miraculously save Hilda's life. But he intended to try to do just that, despite the fact he felt Gertrude's newfound trust in him was a mite misplaced. She'd have done Hilda more good by getting to a chapel and bending her knee in prayer.

"Go and wake the other serving women. Tell them to prepare a posset with fortified wine for Hilda to drink. Then help with the buckets—Hilda needs to soak in a tub filled with hot water if her fever is to break."

When Gertrude left the room, Adrian looked among the phials and flasks he'd left on Hilda's bedside table. He'd often observed that when a patient was treated for her primary affliction, be it a wound or dread disease, then her fever abated naturally. Unable to point to any source or documentation that proved his theory, Adrian suspected that a fever was the body's way of fighting off illness. He therefore directed his attention to stanching Hilda's hemorrhaging.

By the time Gertrude returned with a ewer of spiced wine, he'd mixed a concoction of dried mustard, willow root and lettuce. Though Hilda was half-senseless, Adrian managed to lift her head while Gertrude poured the wine and medicine down her throat. Afterwards, the sick woman was put in a hot bath until so much sweat rolled off her she looked like she'd stood outside in a rain storm. When Hilda was bathed and freshly dressed, she was tucked in among fresh bed linens and covered with fur blankets.

Gertrude sat on a small stool beside the baby's bassinet, while Adrian dozed in a chair beside Hilda's bed. The night passed quietly, the sound of Hilda's shallow breathing underscored by her babe's occasional gurgles and mewls.

As his mind drifted toward sleep, Adrian thought of sweet Philippa and how much she loved her best friend, Hilda. Saving women's lives was what he'd dedicated himself to, and pulling Hilda through her arduous ordeal suddenly seemed the most important task he'd ever undertaken. He wouldn't leave the woman's side till her fever had broken, he vowed. He would not let Hilda, or Philippa, down.

His head had fallen to his chest, and his arms were crossed comfortably over his chest, when the door to Hilda's solar flung open.

The crash startled the babe, and awoke Gertrude, as well. Instantly alert, Adrian leapt to his feet just as a burly man wearing one of the most hateful expressions he'd ever seen crossed the floor.

"Hush, hush," cooed Gertrude, holding the babe against her shoulder. "Denys Terrebonne, you oughta be ashamed of yerself, barging in Hildee's sick room like a charging bull!"

Hilda's husband froze at the foot of the bed, his gaze swinging from Gertrude to Hilda to Adrian. When he looked at the physic who'd delivered his infant daughter, his lips pulled back in an ugly snarl. "I heard what you done to me wife."

"I didn't do anything to your wife," Adrian said.

"If I had known you defiled Hilda, I woulda' killed ye

below stairs, when I had the chance. The men been talkin' about what ye did. They're callin' me a jackass for allowin' it! And I can't ignore it no longer!"

"Your wife and daughter are alive, Terrebonne. You should be grateful for that."

"Thanks for nothing! Where is the little rat? Give her to me, and I'll drown her meself in the River Rother."

"You'll do no such thing. Gertrude, take the child below stairs, will you?"

"Ain't got no use for a split-tail," Denys said. But his gaze was full of hunger as he watched Gertrude gather up the child and leave.

"And I have no use for a man as ignorant as you," Adrian replied, his nerves taut.

From the leather belt that cinched his ragged tunic, Denys yanked a gleaming dagger. "You're an odd sort of fellow, sir. I'll take pleasure in cuttin' out yer tongue!"

Awaiting Terrebonne's advance, Adrian wondered whether the man had gained his experience in cutting out tongues in the prison tower of Oldwall Castle.

Chapter Fourteen

Glancing at Hilda, Adrian saw that her fever had rendered her oblivious to her husband's rantings. For that, at least, he was grateful. After what she'd been through, Denys Terrebonne's determination to murder their helpless child might just be enough to finish poor Hilda off.

As Gertrude scurried out the door with the baby in her arms, Adrian moved deeper into the center of the room, away from Hilda's bedside. Denys followed, and the two men slowly circled one another, their arms held warily at their sides.

Behind Adrian, a fire crackled, while outside the thick stone walls of the castle, a rooster loudly greeted dawn. Through the thick grease paper covering the windows in Hilda's small temporary nursery, a blurry wash of morning light softened the room's shadows. Adrian's muscles tensed and his senses sharpened. Fixing his gaze on Denys Terrebonne's bulging, slightly maddened eyes, the man who'd once been King Edward's favored knight calmly appraised his opponent and the dangerous situation he faced.

Denys broke the silence. "I oughtta kill ye for what ye done to me poor Hilda."

"For what? Saving her life and that of her child?"

"You know what I'm talkin' about! Mayhap she weren't no virgin when I married her, but she's been a good and faithful wife. She wouldna' let a strange man touch her if she'd been strong enough to fight."

"Your wife underwent a very difficult childbirth." Ever watchful for a signal that Denys was preparing to attack, Adrian nevertheless spoke to him in patient tones. "Your daughter came into this world feet-first, instead of head-first. That presents a very dangerous situation, both for mother and child."

"I heard you were a midwife, commissioned by the king, himself," said Denys. "The men at Oldwall 'ave been talkin.' They say yer a good fighter, too, or at least a crafty one. But I won't fall fer any of yer tricks. I'll beat you fair and square, I will, and we'll settle our score the way men should."

"With our fists?"

"With swords," said Denys.

A chord of irritation sounded in Adrian's voice. "Look, man, I'm a trained warrior. Do you really want to challenge me to a sword fight? Sweet heaven, don't you understand that I only touched your wife in order to help her?"

"Ain't no excuse fer touchin' another man's woman," argued Denys. " 'Tis shameful, and me honor demands that I fight you to the death."

"And what of Hilda and your child? What if you don't succeed in killing me? You'll leave behind a widow and an orphan. What good would you have done them then?"

"Hilda can hold up her head and be proud of her man."

"And your daughter?"

Denys blinked, his expression full of confusion and anger. Adrian almost felt sorry for the man, but any sympathy he might have had vanished when Denys finally put into words his jumbled up thoughts. "I tole you, I was gonna drown the little runt!"

"No, you will not," Adrian said through gritted teeth.

"She's my young'un, just like Hilda is my woman." Denys drew himself up, threw back his shoulders and planted his fists on his hips. "And I don't take lightly yer comin' into this castle and thinkin' ye can lord it over me, you with yer handsome face and silver tongue. A man's got a right to rule his own family, just like an overlord's got the right to rule his vassals."

"So, Hilda and the girl are chattel, is that it? You own them just like you own your pigs and chickens?"

Denys nodded. "It's up to me to decide whether I can afford to raise that little female whelp. I wanted a son, not a daughter. Hilda knew that, and she should have smothered the brat before it ever sucked at her breast. Instead, she's been piled up here in the baron's bed, livin' like a lady, neglectin' her wifely duties, and gettin' attached to that split-tail babe! All because of yer interference! And I won't stand for it! Do you hear me? You've all but cuckolded me, touchin' me wife's private parts, then turnin' her agin me!"

Sensing Denys's growing anger, Adrian patted the air. "Calm down, man. No one has cuckolded you. And Hilda will be happy to come home when she's well, provided you treat her as a husband should."

"I've been made the laughingstock of the castle grounds!"

Suddenly, Adrian's anger erupted. "Damn! Have you not a care for your wife's condition? The truth of it is, she might never regain her strength. When she leaves this room, it may very well be to go to her grave, man! If her body doesn't cease bleeding and her fever fails to abate, you'll find yourself a widower."

Anguish marred Denys's features. "Are ye tellin' me now that Hilda's gonna die?"

"Keep your voice down!"

In the split second that followed, Denys lunged, the tip of his dagger slicing through Adrian's tunic. A loud ripping sound and the coolness of air on his belly told Adrian he'd been cut. Acting on his warrior's instincts, he swung his leg up and out, kicking quickly but violently at the knife in Denys's hand. When Hilda groaned, Denys turned to look at his wife. Adrian snatched the dagger from among the rushes, and tucked it beneath his own leather belt.

Denys crossed the room, and bent over his ailing wife. "Can you hear me, Hilda?"

Standing near the hearth, Adrian said softly, "She's in a coma, Denys. I don't know whether she can hear you, but in the hopes she can, I strongly suggest you tell her whatever you want her to know."

Collapsing to the side of the bed, Denys clasped his wife's hand and bowed his head. Adrian, turning his back, afforded the couple a bit of privacy. He was painfully embarrassed by Denys's show of emotion, but he was wary of the man, too. Adrian didn't dare leave Denys alone with Hilda.

After a few minutes, Adrian turned, and said, " 'Tis time for you to leave, Denys. Hilda will be well cared for here."

Denys stood and stared at Adrian though red-rimmed eyes. "I challenge you to a sword fight, Sir Adrian. Day after tomorrow in the eastern field outside the castle walls. Be there with your second, or I will hunt you down and cut out your tongue."

"That is twice you have threatened to cut out my tongue," Adrian noted. "Is that commonly the method of punishment in Oldwall Castle's prison?"

"I wouldn't know," replied Denys. "I'm just a simple armorer. What goes on in the prison tower is none of my concern. Just meet me at Squire's Field at noon on the day after tomorrow."

"Are you certain, Denys? I'm giving you an opportunity to

change your mind. I won't tell a soul, I swear it. And your honor will not be tarnished."

Pausing at the door, Denys seemed to consider Adrian's offer. Then, he lifted his chin and shook his head. "No, I owe it to every man in this castle."

"Why? Am I so despised by the inhabitants of Oldwall Castle that killing me will make you a hero?"

Strangely, Denys's shoulders sagged, and Adrian had a glimpse of one of the most confused men he'd ever seen. Puffed up with his own sense of importance, yet terrified by the pressures of constantly having to prove his manhood, Denys was as dangerous as a loaded crossbow in the hands of a lunatic. A twinge of sympathy in Adrian's gut lessened his anger, but not his resolve: Denys Terrebonne would not be allowed to kill his babe, or take Hilda away from the protection of the castle keep before she'd regained her strength.

"You are well hated, aye," said Denys. "The whores of Oldwall are all in a twitter over ye, see. 'Tis as if they're under some sorta spell. Seems Belinda told them you took the time to pleasure 'er without ever stickin' yerself inside 'er. And they're demandin' that the rest of us do the same."

"Ah, that is sore punishment, indeed. No wonder I am the object of so much hatred."

Denys gave a derisive snort. "Yer an odd sorta feller, sir. 'Twill be my pleasure to dispatch ye to hell."

Smiling, Adrian mocked the man with a low bow. When he straightened, Denys was gone. The sounds of Hilda's breathing, shallow and labored, filled the room. As the din of knights breaking fast in the great hall filtered up the stairs, Adrian leaned against the mantel and breathed a heavy sigh.

He didn't want to kill Denys Terrebonne, but he would if he had to.

He didn't want to see Lady Philippa married off to Drogo, but he would endure that agony, too, if he had to.

A man of honor and duty, Sir Adrian Vale had never shied away from unpleasant confrontations. Offering up a silent prayer, he questioned a God who would put his character to so rigorous a test. All he wanted was to live out his days with the woman he loved.

All he wanted was precisely everything he could not have.

Philippa awoke slowly, stretching like a cat, yawning open-mouthed while she mentally catalogued the muscles in which soreness had settled.

Muscles that she never knew she had . . . sore in a manner that she'd never experienced.

Pulling the counterpane to her chin, she lay on her side, nose buried in a soft bolster still redolent with the scent of Adrian's hair. The smell of sex hung in the air, thick as treacle and just as sweet. Eyes closed, Philippa imagined Adrian's body moving over hers, his muscled arms surrounding her, his slender hips wedged between her thighs.

A faint sigh escaped her lips. Last night, Philippa had cast aside her distrust and succumbed to the powerful force that drew her to Sir Adrian. She wasn't certain what had inspired her to so brazenly ask the man to make love to her, but she had no regrets, no second thoughts, concerning last night's encounter. Indeed, if he were still in her bed, she would ask him to pleasure her yet again.

Breathing in his scent, she felt the stirrings of desire deep within her belly. Adrian had been so gentle, so tender . . . then he'd taken her with animal ferocity, rousing her excitement to fever pitch and holding her protectively while she'd shuddered her release. Philippa hadn't known sex could be like that.

Of course, she knew it was Adrian who made the sex so incredible. Rutting, simply for the sake of it, to satisfy an itch, as it were, wasn't an earthshaking event. Philippa felt sorry for women like Hilda, women who were married to men totally unconcerned about their wives' sexual happiness. The Denys's of the world were in far too great abundance; the Sir Adrian Vales of the world were in alarmingly short supply.

Morning deepened, burning the misty haze of sleep from Philippa's mind. She gazed at the opposite wall of her solar, seeing nothing but a stone scroll on which her future was depicted. Images of herself, helping servants bake bread in the kitchen, dispensing herbs and potions in the infirmary, assisting Sir Adrian as he attended births, flashed on the wall in colors so vivid, Philippa blinked with astonishment.

What sort of tricks did her mind play on her? Realizing the strength of her fantasies, apprehension clutched Philippa's heart. For those pictures on the wall, those imaginary scenes conjured by Philippa's deepest desires, were just that . . . *fantasies*.

She was engaged to be married to Drogo, Lord Oldcastle, and there was no going back on her word, or her father's word. She'd made a solemn vow to redeem her family's honor and it was that vow, that promise, that had sustained her faith these many years. To turn her back on that promise would be to lose her very identity. To renege on her obligation and duties would be to admit defeat. To take the easy way out of her predicament—to marry Sir Adrian—would be to confirm what Killian and his father Faustus had always said about her and her mother, that they were worthless women of low character and loose morals.

Marry Sir Adrian? Was that what her fantasizing brain had silently said? Philippa chuckled sadly as she threw off her counterpane and felt the cold floor with her toes. Why, the man hadn't even suggested such a thing! Just because he said he loved her, didn't mean he wanted to marry her.

Just because he had taken his pleasure with her didn't mean he loved her, either.

Yet, somehow, Philippa sensed that this man was different from other men. Years ago, she'd learned that sex was a

221

shameful, nasty affair, a frightening experience rife with pain and degradation. The man who'd taught her that was Faustus, Killian's father and Drogo's brother. She'd been but a child, and he'd cruelly abused her trust—and her mother's, she suspected.

But Sir Adrian had done something that Faustus never could; he'd won her trust and shown her that sex could be a magical, beautiful thing. He'd taken pains to give her pleasure, and rather than make her feel shame, he'd made her feel womanly and vibrant.

She wondered . . . was it pure fantasy to hope that Sir Adrian would somehow rescue her from the devilish deal her father had concocted with Drogo? Was it even remotely possible that Adrian would somehow save her from her hellish predicament?

He hadn't asked her to marry him. On the contrary, he'd said she belonged to Drogo.

And she did belong to Drogo. If she refused to marry him, she would set in motion a disastrous series of events. Bending over her basin, she splashed ice cold water on her face. Sobering, she realized it was dangerous to even dream of extricating herself from Drogo's snare.

A ray of sun penetrated her precious glass window, a symbol of the wealth she would enjoy as chatelaine of Oldwall Castle. A life of ease and leisure would be hers as Drogo's wife, to be sure. And, along with it, the knowledge that her father's honor had been redeemed.

But what of the price? Seated at a dressing table, staring at her foggy reflection in a piece of glass, Philippa slowly unwound her plaited hair. What was the price she would pay for this respectability, the erasure of this debt her father owed to Drogo and Sir Killian?

In the mirror, she saw herself married to the lord of Oldcastle. Sir Adrian was nowhere in this picture, nowhere in her future.

Yet, she knew in her heart that she loved him, and that she would never love another.

Life with Drogo would be miserable, but it would buy her mother's dignity, and her father's honor. On those intangibles, she could not place a higher value. If sacrificing her happiness was the price she owed to secure her family's good name, then she would pay it.

Besides, if Adrian ever knew the truth about her, he wouldn't want her anyway.

Oldcastle's infirmary, located in the bowels of the keep, was damp and cheerless. Enclosed by low ceilings and hard-packed earthen floors, the small compartment reeked of herbs and spices. The underground chill that permeated the stone walls served to preserve the bottled syrups lining the shelves, potions and electuaries and tonics, all carefully labeled in a small, flowing, feminine script that Adrian suspected was Philippa's handwriting.

Having witnessed her tirelessness in tending to Hilda, Adrian was hardly surprised that Philippa had been equally conscientious in obtaining a wide array of remedies for the castle's occupants. A generous store of medicinal provisions, including sugar, oils and even the expensive drug known as theriac, were at Adrian's fingertips. Scanning the shelves, he reached for several jars and bottles, setting them aside in the event he should find it necessary to mix a remedy for Sir Killian.

He felt Killian's presence before he heard him. Without turning around, Adrian said, "Good day, sir."

"You've got eyes in the back of your head, have you?" Killian's leather boots crossed the threshold and moved quietly through the rush strewn floor.

The atmosphere of the tiny infirmary acquired the crackling intensity of one man's hatred for another. Turning slowly, Adrian confronted the unalloyed hatred gleaming in Killian's narrowed gaze.

But Killian spoke with a civil tongue. "I own, you are a clever man, Adrian. Your mission here, however, will soon be complete."

"Less than a fortnight ago, you were eager to have me in Oldwall Castle. Now you are itching to see me go."

"Conduct the examination that Drogo has ordered." Killian's smile was as greasy as unwashed fleece. "Then, leave Oldwall as quickly as your horse will carry you. If you want to save your neck, that is."

"There is much for a physic to do within these castle walls. I had thought to remain here, tending to the sick, caring for the lord and lady . . . and for the children they might yet produce."

Killian jerked his chin at the well-stocked shelves. "Lady Philippa has tended the infirmary these last few years. She can continue to do so, and when matters outside her realm of knowledge present themselves, there is a respectable physic in the neighboring village."

"Then why wasn't he called upon to conduct the examination?"

"You are the only man in all of England who has the king's permission to touch the intimate parts of a female patient. Methinketh King Edward licensed you in this practice merely to amuse himself and his court, but that is none of my concern."

"Surely there is a midwife in the village who could have carried out Drogo's instructions." Adrian watched Killian's reactions, searching for a sign that the man was dissembling.

But if he was lying, he was doing so with skill. "No midwife in Sussex would dare conduct an examination on Lady Philippa. The very fact Drogo demands one suggests he has reason to believe she was violated. How many little old hags do you think queued up to take on the responsibility of examining Philippa, when they knew they might have the job of telling Drogo his bride was damaged goods?"

"Are you telling me that Drogo suspects Philippa is not a virgin?"

Killian's eyes were like slits in a basinet helmet. Peering at Adrian from beneath the visor of his low forehead and thick brows, he allowed himself a little smile. "Her mother was a whore."

"Watch your tongue, Killian." Adrian's fists coiled at his sides.

"I speak to you in confidence, sir, not with the intent to malign a dead woman. You see, Drogo and my father, Faustus, did what they could to protect the harlot's reputation. Her sin was not publicized, but was treated as a private matter between gentlemen. And Sir Casper Gilchrist, Philippa's father, tried—but failed—to remove the stain from his family's name."

"I don't want to hear any more of this drivel," Adrian growled.

"As a physic, you must know that daughters often bear the traits of their mother's personality, as well as her physical features. As for Philippa, it remains to be seen whether she is a Jezebel like her mother, Alison."

"That is enough!" Adrian's voice boomed through the tiny infirmary.

In the stillness that followed, Killian nodded contritely and stared at the floor.

At length, Adrian said, "You didn't come here to discuss Lady Philippa's mother."

"No, 'tis a far more pressing matter that brings me here."

Adrian nodded gravely. "Ah, yes, the matter of your willicock. Tell me, Killian, have you have had sexual intercourse with very many different women?"

"Of course I have!" Killian puffed out his chest, and crooked his thumbs in the leather belt that cinched his waist and held his dagger and purse.

Drawing up a low stool, Adrian sat at eye-level with Killian's middle. "Well, then, drop your braies, and let me have a look."

Killian tossed his belt on the marble slab where Belinda's lifeless body had lain just hours earlier. Then, he fumbled with his hose, untying them from his gypon, and sliding them down his bare, white legs. When he unlaced his loose-fitting woolen braies, they fell in untidy pools around his booted ankles. In the frigid air of the infirmary, he stood with his fists propped on his naked hips, ballocks shriveled, penis shrinking into the warmth of his body.

Adrian performed a thorough examination, including a urine analysis, widely considered the most useful diagnostic tool available to a physic. When Killian handed him the flask, Adrian stood and stoppered it with cork. Turning his back to his patient, he considered his findings. Clearly, Killian had the same venereal disease Belinda suffered from at the time of her murder. While this was not direct evidence that the man ever had sexual relations with the prostitute, it might be a small piece of the puzzle.

"Well, what about it, man? Do I have the flesh-eating disease you spoke of, or don't I?"

Facing Killian, Adrian shrugged. "I'm not certain. Are you quite positive you didn't have sex with the dead girl, Belinda?"

Killian's eyes narrowed. "I told you, I don't know one whore from the other!"

"In that case, you'd better consult with me in four or five days. Perhaps I can give you an answer then."

Yanking up his braies, tying his hose and grabbing for his leather belt, Killian was the picture of agitation. "What the hell do you mean, you might be able to give me an answer in four of five days? God's teeth, man, me bits could fall off before then!"

Smirking, Adrian replied, "Your body does show evidence

of a certain contagion, Killian, and for that I can provide a remedy. However, I will not know whether you have been infected with the flesh-eating disease until I have analyzed your urine specimen. That will take four or five days."

Killian spit on the floor, and folded his arms across his chest.

Witnessing the man's petulant childishness, a thin disguise for the fear showing in his eyes, Adrian felt a twinge of guilt. "Nothing will fall off in the next five days, Killian. However, if you refuse to take the cure and do what I proscribe, your brain will slowly rot. Lesions will form on your body, and, eventually, you'll even lose control of your muscles."

"Sweet Mary, mother of God." Killian crossed himself, and gulped. "Tell me what I must do."

Adrian reached for a flask of mercury, and poured some into a small brown bottle that he corked and passed to Killian. "Pour a gill of this into your ale each night, and drink it down. Continue that course for two weeks, and you should be cured."

Nodding curtly, Killian tucked the bottle into his leather purse. "I will come back in four days," he said, turning on his heel.

"Until then," Adrian warned, "You must stay away from the castle lemans. Until I have cured those women, they are not safe for you or your men."

"I shall pass the word along," Killian answered, pausing at the threshold of the tiny infirmary.

"Aye, and tell your men that I should like to examine anyone who slept with the woman Belinda. 'Twould be in the best interest of anyone who coupled with her to come to the castle infirmary."

Killian grunted, but was halfway down the dark corridor leading to the stairwell beneath the kitchens before Adrian resealed the mercury bottle. Replacing it on the shelf, he thought to tell the next purveyor who journeyed to London that a fresh supply of it should be purchased for Oldwall Castle. Given the propensity of Drogo's men to spill their seed indiscriminately among the castle prostitutes, he expected Belinda's disease to spread as quickly as the Plague.

At Hilda's bedside, Adrian bent over her, gently pulling her night rail down as he completed his examination.

"The bleeding has ceased," he said, tucking the counterpane around his patient's shoulders. "But she remains weak, and her fever has yet to abate."

"Can she hear us?" Philippa stood beside Adrian, so close he could feel her body tremble.

"Only God knows. But I have heard of patients emerging from deep sleeps of this sort, only to report they heard every word that was uttered around them. Therefore, I would suggest talking to Hilda."

Adrian paused, fearful of the impact his next words would have on Philippa, but mindful of his responsibility to prepare her for what he considered the very likely prospect of Hilda's death. "My love, if there is anything you should like to tell your best friend, you should do so now."

Blanching, Philippa grabbed Adrian's arm. A faint exhalation, as if she'd been punched in the stomach, escaped her rounded lips.

Gertrude, standing on the opposite side of the bed, Hilda's babe in her arms, whispered the Lord's Prayer. When she was finished, she asked whether she could take the child to the kitchen. "A wet nurse is needed, sir, and I must tell the women of the castle. Surely, there is some woman with enough milk in her breasts for two sucklings."

"You're a good woman, Gertrude." Adrian was somewhat relieved to see her go. Alone with Philippa, he could dare to touch her, to cover her hand with his, and support her as her legs wobbled beneath her tunic.

"Are you all right, my love?" he asked softly.

Was she all right? Closing her eyes, Philippa fought back the violent emotions churning inside her. No, she wasn't all right! Her best friend struggled to survive and Philippa was powerless to help her. The man she loved would hate her if he knew what she was about. A loathsome secret burned in her heart. And, the man she detested more than anyone else in the world was by all rights her future husband.

What more could be wrong with her life?

Chapter Fifteen

She clasped her hand over her mouth, choking on a silent sob.
On the chance Hilda could hear her voice, on the small chance
Hilda was aware of what was going on around her, Philippa
did not want to vent her anger and frustration here.

But when Adrian clasped her elbow and drew her body
toward his, her composure snapped.

As if the tears gushed from her very soul, Philippa pressed
her forehead to Adrian's chest and cried inconsolably. His
arms, strong and capable, surrounded her. His deep throaty
voice lulled and lured her, drawing Philippa into the open of
her own emotions.

Caressing her with sweet, tenderly spoken words, Adrian
found and touched a hidden patch of her heart, heavily protected territory that Philippa had assiduously hidden from the
world. Allowing her tears to flow, she fled gratefully to the
sanctuary he offered her. Like a criminal taking refuge in a
monastery, she thought not of her sins, but of her needs. And,

for once in her life, she thought she'd found a man willing to hide her from her pursuers.

Truly scared, Philippa cried. She clung to Adrian like a kitten clinging to the lofty branch of a tree. Afraid to look down, afraid to go higher, she simply hung on with her fingertips while all the emotion she possessed poured out of her.

" 'Tis all right, Philippa. I've got you now." Patting her back, he held her tightly.

Between sobs, she managed to say his name. "*Adrian*."

He held her while she cried, and when her tears had all been shed, he held her a while longer. At length, he tipped up her chin, forcing her to meet his gaze. "No matter what else happens," he whispered, "you must always remember, Philippa, that I love you dearly. Upon my word, I love you more than I've ever loved anyone."

She'd never told a man, other than her father, that she loved him. But the words came frighteningly easy. "I love you, too, Adrian. Oh, dear God, I love you! Promise me you'll never leave me! Promise me! I need you, can't you see? I need you!"

Gripping her hands, Adrian pulled back and stared hard at her. As his expression darkened, and his eyes grew cold, a chill rushed through Philippa's body. She didn't understand what was happening, but she sensed Adrian's retreat from her, his sudden withdrawal. It terrified her to feel his body go rigid beneath her touch.

When he spoke, his voice was as rough as the stone walls surrounding Oldwall Castle. "I love you, but—"

"But, what?" Philippa stood at arm's length, desperate to understand the drastic change in Adrian's expression. "You said you loved me!"

"I do." Releasing her, he half-turned. He ran his hand through his hair then gripped the back of his neck, massaging his muscles. Tension roiled from his body like vapor from a cauldron. Abruptly, he whirled to face her. "Philippa, I do love you! But, you're Drogo's woman, you told me that yourself."

She didn't want to be reminded. "I am not yet wed to the man."

"But you will be his wife soon enough. And then what will become of us? Can we forget that we loved one another? Forget we made love to one another?"

She shook her head, painfully confused. "Why must we forget, Adrian? You said you loved me—"

"Quit saying that!"

His angry voice was like a slap in the face. Brought up short, Philippa stood clutching the jeweled cross that hung around her neck. Everything Adrian said was true. She was obligated to marry Drogo, and, for her father's sake and her mother's honor, she would honor her debt.

Still, Adrian had said he loved her. And though he didn't really know her, couldn't possibly guess the terrible secret she kept hidden from him, he had at last convinced her that his feelings for her were genuine. She'd let down her guard, and she'd loved him in return. For one brief, fleeting moment, she'd even fantasized she was worthy of his love.

But, of course, she wasn't. She'd been wrong. Adrian's swift reaction to her avowal of love was overwhelming proof of how very wrong she'd been.

Her tears had long since dried up. A complete and utter feeling of worthlessness replaced them. Bowing her head, Philippa said, "I have been a fool. You're right, I am to marry Drogo, and there is no getting around that."

"There is no place for me in your life, Philippa. An honorable man should not make love to another man's intended bride."

"It did not feel wrong, Adrian. It felt . . . it felt very right."

"A vassal should not sleep with his lord's woman."

"You wanted me, and I wanted you. How could that have been wrong?"

"A knight of the realm should not violate a lady's sacred trust, Philippa. In taking my pleasure with you, I fell far below the standard of conduct I once swore to uphold."

"If you love me, how can you be so cold? Mayhap I will be the baroness of this castle, but why must you turn your back on our love?"

"I will not cuckold the man."

No, Philippa hadn't thought he would. And, once married, she didn't think she could bring herself to commit adultery, either. Perhaps, she hadn't thought it all out very clearly. But the fact remained, she loved Adrian. And, deep inside her, some instinctive need compelled her to risk, swear, promise or threaten anything to keep him at her side.

On a sigh, she whispered yet again, "You said you loved me."

He closed his eyes for a moment, and a cord of muscles along his jaw rippled. Then he looked at her, but it seemed to Philippa that it pained him to do so. "Aye, so I did. But I cannot take care of you the way Drogo can. And even if I could, you have professed to me your unshakeable determination to wed the man."

"But Adrian, I am no longer a virgin," she whispered. "What if he will not marry me now?"

"Drogo will never know you're not a virgin."

"You will lie for me?"

His nod was barely perceptible. "I want nothing more than for you to be safe and secure for the rest of your life, Philippa."

She thought to say she would never be happy without him, but that wasn't true, of course. Philippa's heart was broken and the pain knotting in her belly was, she speculated, far worse than the toils of childbirth. But she'd survived the first twenty years of her life without Sir Adrian Vale, and she knew she would survive the next forty without him.

Marriage to Drogo would be joyless, tedious and hard, but her life promised other rewards. So what if she never again experienced the exquisite physical joy of making love with Adrian? At least she'd had it once; that was more than most women had. Philippa knew she could find fulfillment elsewhere. She had her work in the infirmary, and she found pleasure in helping the sick and aged. She had friends. . . .

She had Hilda.

Turning to look at her dearest friend, Philippa felt a crushing sense of sadness. Suddenly, her own pain was insignificant.

Then, with a skillful ferocity born of experience, she tamped down her own desires and focused on the world beyond herself. Drawing herself up, she squared her shoulders and dried her eyes with the back of her hand.

"Can you save Hildee?" she asked.

"She is in God's hands now," Adrian replied quietly. "But, I will do everything I can for her, I promise you that. And if death does come for her, then I will see to it that she slips into her final sleep as peacefully and comfortably as possible."

Without looking at him, Philippa lowered herself to edge of Hilda's mattress. Gently, she caressed her friend's clammy cheek, unthinkingly repeating the very words Adrian had whispered to her. "I am here, Hildee. Don't worry, my friend, I am here."

"Her husband has challenged me to a duel of honor," said Adrian.

Philippa had already heard this news from the women below stairs. Though she'd never before felt pity for Denys Terrebonne, this time she feared for his immortal soul. There was no doubt in her mind who would win that contest. "Will you kill him?" she asked quietly.

Adrian stood beside her, so near she felt the warmth of his body, so close she felt the hardness of his leather booted leg against her skirts. "Have you forgotten, my sweetling, that Hilda might very well be able to hear every word we say?"

Perhaps it was the endearment Adrian used, *sweetling*, that reminded her of how gently he'd once loved her and how abruptly he'd thrust her away. Or perhaps it was the reminder of Denys Terrebonne's cruelty that stoked Philippa's anger. Whatever it was, something turned to ice inside Philippa's chest. Holding Hilda's hand, she nurtured a bitter hatred—hatred not for Adrian, but for the men whose actions conspired to deprive him of her.

When she spoke, her voice was cold and terse. "No, I did not forgot that Hilda might hear everything we say. On the contrary, I thought to relieve the poor woman of her burdens. No doubt she heard her husband threaten to drown their daughter when he was in this room last night. Gertrude heard it, and Denys Terrebonne has told everyone within the castle walls who will listen that is what he intends to do."

"Philippa, hush." Adrian squeezed her shoulder, but Philippa shrugged, shaking him off.

She looked at him. "I hope you kill him," she hissed. "I hope you slice off his head—"

"Philippa—"

"I hope you teach Denys Terrebonne and all the other men who live within these castle walls that they cannot treat their women like cattle, that they cannot abuse their wives and murder their children just because they are born girls!"

"Ah, sweetling," he murmured. But he took a step backward, his expression closed, his gaze hooded.

"Go away, Adrian. Just go away." Philippa lowered her head to Hilda's chest and held on to her friend as tightly as she dared. Hilda needed her, and she would stay there until the woman was recovered . . . or dead. "I don't ever want to see your face again."

Night descended uneasily. Outside the castle keep, rain and sleet buffeted the crenelated walls, furiously whipping the banner that waved from atop the highest tower. An occasional torch was lit, but quickly extinguished by blasts of arctic air. The lower bailey was empty, and the upper bailey deserted except for a skeletal crew of guards manning the portcullis that separated the two yards.

A strange silence, punctuated by the keening of the wind, settled over Oldwall Castle as Sir Adrian Vale stood beside Drogo's bedside.

The man's leg was healing, but slowly. A mild infection had set in, but Adrian had carried out a rigorous regimen of douching the baron's wound with wine, then dressing it in freshly boiled and dried linens. Though the man's injury would heal completely, he would suffer some stiffness in his knee for a long time to come, perhaps for the rest of his life. Presently, though, Drogo's chief complaint was headache and grogginess, the after-effects of the sedative Adrian administered to keep him calm and still.

Inside the great hall, the baron's soldiers moved and talked as if their limbs were tree-trunks and their tongues pudding. With their master lying in his sick-bed, and Sir Killian sequestered in his own chambers, their mood was gloomy and subdued. A rumor passed among them that a terrible infection had threatened to eat the flesh of Drogo's leg.

Killian was ill, too. Some suggested that he had contracted the pox, or perhaps the Plague, a notion that struck the soldiers dumb with fear. What sort of ill wind had blown into Oldwall Castle? they asked themselves. What sort of evil moved within their midst?

Some of the men blamed their lord's infection and Killian's illness on Sir Adrian's presence in Hilda's birthing room. Everyone knew it was a sin against God for a man to touch the private parts of a woman not his wife. For a practicing physic to attend the birth of a child—worse, to assist in the birthing of that child—was sacrilege.

Sir Adrian Vale's brazen act of defiance had provoked God to mete out the severest of punishments. It was no matter that the king had licensed Adrian to practice midwifery. It was heresy, and Killian and Drogo were paying the price for allowing and condoning the evil acts. As for the rest of the castle occupants, whatever fate befell their lords and masters would act to their detriment, as well.

Feelings of fear, hostility and resentment fermented like grapes in a cask. The soldiers in the hall looked for someone to blame for the oppressive atmosphere pervading the castle. And, aside from Adrian, the obvious scapegoat, they were beginning to say that Killian had committed mortal sin in bringing the male midwife to Oldwall, and that Drogo had made a grave mistake by not sending the man back to London forthwith.

Whispers that Adrian had put his hands inside Hilda's body slithered through the ranks like the asp in Eve's garden. It was an unspeakable offense, not only against God, but against the woman's husband. No wonder Denys Terrebonne was out for blood. The male midwife would be lucky if he left the dueling field with his head and shoulders still connected.

At last, the baron's trusted soldiers fell fitfully asleep in the great hall, their snores and grunts wafting up the steps like steam from a simmering pot.

Closing the door to Drogo's bedroom chamber, Adrian stood for a moment in the dark vestibule. Sensing the unease in the castle, his ears pricked and his senses heightened.

Instinct told him that his time was running out: Drogo, even in his drugged state of mind, had asked again when Adrian would examine Philippa. Killian would soon overcome his fear that a dread disease was going to rob him of his manhood, and then his dislike for Adrian would be full-blown.

With Killian dogging his every step, looking to condemn him for committing the most minor infraction of the castle rules, it would be nearly impossible for Adrian to complete his spy mission. And, with Philippa married to Drogo, he wouldn't be able to remain with the walls of Oldwall a second longer. To see the woman he loved wed to that brutish tyrant would be more than he could bear.

Adrian held his candle aloft, searching the shadows in vain. Though it had only been two nights previous when he'd found Philippa waiting for him there in that dimly lit passageway, it seemed an eternity had passed since then. So much had happened, his thoughts had undergone a revolution, and his heart had made a startling discovery.

And Philippa hated him.

Little wonder. He loved her, yet couldn't, or wouldn't, share his life with her. He'd made love to her against his better judgment, and in doing so, had made her as much a part of his body and soul as if she were his twin. But their love was impossible. When Philippa sought comfort from him again, he'd rebuffed her, reminding her cruelly that she was Drogo's woman.

Holding a single taper, Adrian climbed the stairs to Hilda's sickroom. Pushing open the door, he stood for a moment, his eyes adjusting to the even fainter light that spilled across the floor. The small compartment no longer had the ambience of a nursery, if it ever had. The suckling infant had been taken from the castle keep and entrusted to the custody of a village wet nurse. Infantile gurgles and wails had been replaced by Hilda's moans and fevered, incoherent ranting. Her illness weighted the air like greasy smoke.

The smell of dried blood and sickness was cloying.

At the foot of Hilda's bed, Philippa slept on a makeshift pallet. On her side, her hands folded beneath her head, she appeared as peaceful as a cherub.

Adrian crossed the floor and kneeled beside her. Her eyes fluttered open, widened for an instant, then narrowed. In her gaze, he saw nought but distrust.

Unable to resist touching her, Adrian stroked her cheek.

"You should go to bed, sweetling. *Your own bed.* Before you yourself fall prey to some illness or other."

Behind him, a fire crackled, throwing its amber light on Philippa's face. Still, the room was cold and the plank floor even colder. The shiver that ran through Philippa's body when Adrian touched her was testament to the pervasive winter chill that crept through Oldwall Castle.

Or was his touch repulsive to her?

Perched on his haunches, he drew back his hand. Philippa's silence pained him, but he could hardly blame her if she hated him. How could she be expected to understand his unwillingness to go to her bed again? How could she be expected to interpret his lack of interest in her as anything but cruel detachment? Or cowardice?

That Philippa might think him cowardly angered Adrian. He'd been as brave a soldier on the battlefield as any man had ever been. And, he'd risked life and limb to practice midwifery in defiance of King Edward's laws. Yet to the woman he loved, he was nothing short of a traitor, a man whose word could not be trusted. A liar. A dishonorable ruffian who would bed a woman he said he loved, then relinquish her to a man who didn't know the meaning of the word.

There was no use trying to explain. Adrian wasn't certain he understood his feelings well enough to put them into words. Rising, he said, "Has there been any change in Hilda's condition?"

"The fever has broken. Now she has chills that rattle her teeth."

Inwardly, Adrian felt his hopes for Hilda sink. Current medical science regarded fever as the disproportion of one of the body's four humors to another, an excessive amount of fire over water. But Adrian's observations had led him to doubt that theory.

Adrian had noticed that when the body ceased producing

fever, the patient often succumbed even more quickly to the illness attacking her. 'Twas as if the fever represented the body's attempt to fight off illness. Hilda's lack of fever might very well mean that she was getting well. On the other hand, it could mean her body no longer had the strength to fight for life.

He moved to the bedside and laid his hand on Hilda's forehead. Then he picked up her wrist and measured her pulse. At last, he pulled down the covers and inspected her body. Breathing noisily through her open mouth, Hilda never once opened her eyes or stirred. Even in the dim firelight, Adrian could see the pallid cast to her skin, and the hollows beneath her eyes. Tucking the covers around her shoulders, he bent low and whispered in her ear, "God bless you, Hilda. You are in His hands now."

There was nothing to do but wait.

He paused at the foot of the bed, looking down at Philippa. "The floor is not comfortable, my lady. You should get into bed."

She pushed off from the floor and stood toe-to-toe with him. "Very well. If you insist." Then, she got into bed next to Hilda, and curled up facing the woman.

She was silent as Adrian left the room.

Minutes later, he descended the stairs and moved stealthily through the great hall, stepping carefully around the soldiers who lay sleeping on the floor. Though he'd donned a hooded cape, freezing rain chilled him to the bone as he raced through the upper courtyard. At the portcullis, a soldier clad in a quilted gambeson and chain mail hauberk blocked Adrian's path with a lowered poleax.

"Who goes there?" barked the sentinel, his back to the grated archway.

" 'Tis Sir Adrian, my lord's physic. Let me pass, man."

"My orders are to let no one pass through this gate after the midnight hour."

Glancing up, Adrian noted that the guard stations on either side of the portcullis appeared unmanned. No doubt Killian's distracted state of mind and Drogo's illness were to account for this reduced state of security. If Adrian was ever going to make another bid at getting into the prison tower, tonight was the night.

"On whose orders do you forbid me entry into the lower bailey?" Adrian demanded.

"Sir Killian's," the man replied. "He'd 'ave me 'ead if I was to let you go through!"

"Haven't you heard there's a dread disease plaguing the harlot population? And there is evidence that the disease is passed from woman to man through sexual intercourse. As the castle physician, I am doing everything I can to prevent this contagion from spreading. Surely you understand."

With a nervous shuffle of his feet, the guard spat on the ground. "That don't change me orders. I cannot let you pass."

"But the whores are only in the lower bailey during the night hours! I must be permitted to speak with them!"

For a moment, it seemed as if the guard was going to relent. In the dim light of a torch, protected from the wind and rain by the overhanging eave of the guard tower, the guard's expression bore signs of confusion and weakness. A deafening crack of thunder seemed to galvanize his will, however, and at length, he said, "I'm sorry, sir. Sir Killian doesn't fancy having his orders disobeyed. And I've got a wife and children to think about. I can't afford to lose me wages."

Sighing, Killian nodded. He pivoted slowly, his hand slipping quietly inside his cape. But instead of retreating toward the castle, he whirled completely around, surprising the guard with a violent kick that sent the poleax clattering to the ground.

"Merde!" In his cumbersome chain mail, the guard bent over to retrieve his weapon.

In the next split second, Adrian snatched his dagger from beneath his cape. Grabbing a handful of greasy hair, he jerked the guard to full height. Then he pressed his blade to the sentinel's throat and pushed him toward the guard tower. As the two men ascended the steps, the guard cursed and swore, but inside the tiny parapet, he quickly cranked the lever that raised the portcullis.

When the gate was lifted, and his passage clear, Adrian shoved the man against the rough log walls of the guard tower, where he slid to the floor in a clumsy clash of chain mail. "Keep a keen watch, for I shall return before the sun rises and you must raise the gate for me then."

"What kind of fool do ye take me for? Why, as soon as Killian finds out you've defied his orders, you'll be a dead man!"

"And as soon as he learns you took coin in exchange for raising the portcullis, you'll be equally dead!" The gold coins that Adrian tossed at the guard clinked dully on his steel riveted hauberk. "You don't think I'll admit to having overpowered you, do you? God's teeth, man, I have more imagination than that! As King Edward's trusted knight, I shall swear you accepted my bribe willingly, that you even bartered for a higher price—"

"I have heard enough!" The man struggled to his feet. "My shift is over in two hours. If you're not back by then, you lousy bastard—"

"Don't worry. I'll be back before you go off duty." Adrian hurried down the stairs and through the open portal to the lower courtyard. Making his way to the prison gate, he squinted against the arrows of sleet that pummeled him. The starless night shielded him from the guards standing watch on the crenelated outer walls. But, the darkness obscured his vision, too. Only when lightning flashed across the sky did the deserted grounds light up.

Adrian couldn't resist a private chuckle. Clearly, the guard at the portcullis hadn't the sense God gave a billy goat. Even the least intelligent of men would have known that on a night such as this, the prostitutes were staying indoors.

He crept around the side of the stable where he'd earlier fashioned a crude wig from horse hair. Clever tricks would never budge those soldiers from their post again, Adrian knew. Clutching his dagger, he crouched low to the ground, waiting for the next burst of lightning. When it came, he saw that one of the guards held a short broadsword, while the other carried a dagger still sheathed in his leather belt. Their torch lights having been snuffed by the rain, they huddled in darkness outside the high wooden fence that surrounded the prison tower.

Two hours was all the time he had to get past the guards and into the tower. Adrian tossed a stone over the guards' heads, and when they turned toward the direction of the noise they heard, he approached from the rear.

"Who goes there?" one of the guards demanded, his back to Adrian.

"Go and see," suggested his companion. "I'll wait here."

Had the first guard been willing to investigate, Adrian most likely could have disabled his cowardly companion without injuring him, then entered the prison tower. But the men set about arguing over who would leave the relative protection of the prison perimeter. When Adrian stepped on a twig, they turned abruptly, weapons drawn.

"You're a dead man," muttered the first guard. He rushed Adrian with his dagger drawn.

It was two against one, but Adrian was the better fighter. In one quick movement, he leapt forward and cut his attacker's throat. As the scene was illuminated by a flash of lightning, the second guard brought up his sword and lunged. But,

Adrian easily deflected the intended blow with his own weapon, then dispatched his opponent with a well-placed thrust.

Through the gate he crashed, running through the tiny courtyard toward the prison tower. Pulling his hood low over his face, he banged his fist on the steel-studded oaken door.

The peep-hole slid open and another guard, not Wat, demanded, "Who the hell are you and what do you want at this ungodly hour of the night?"

Thunder rumbled and sleet fell in a slushy hammering on the stone path behind Adrian. " 'Tis cold as a pig's arse out here! Let me in, you foul-smelling pervert. I've a prisoner to question."

"Who goes there?"

Adrian hunched his shoulders and banged on the door again. In as gravelly a voice as he could muster, he replied, " 'Tis Killian, you idiot. Haven't you heard I've been confined to my quarters since that fool physic said my willicock might be wearing to a nub? I'm in no mood for your tomfoolery, now! Open this damn door before I have your empty head on a trencher!"

The peep-hold slammed shut, the latch was thrown, and the heavy door creaked open. Adrian lurched over the threshold, his dagger drawn. Making quick work of the dim-witted guard, he left him for dead slumped against the stone wall, his blood forming a dark puddle beneath the rushes.

He raced along the circular corridor, halting at the spot where he'd found the trap door embedded in the stone floor. He shuffled his feet in the straw until he felt his toe nudge the leather hide that covered the grate. Leaning down, he grabbed the iron ring and pulled the barred door ajar. The dank, fetid air that escaped the hole nearly knocked Adrian off his feet. He released the iron grate; it slammed to the floor with a terrifying clatter. Then, he grabbed a lit torch from a sconce on the wall and bent low over the smelly pit.

Rats, fleeing the splash of light, squeaked their indignation.

Cindy Harris

The sound of flapping wings overlapped the click-click-clicking of tiny talons seeking purchase on the stone walls. A premonitory shudder ran though Adrian's body, but still he leaned further into the sunken recess, throwing his torch light into the farthest corner, straining his eyes to discern the murky outline hunched there.

A rustle, then a faint moan, reached his ears. Quickly, Adrian descended the earthen steps. As torchlight illuminated the cell, a ghoulish array of chains, maces and other instruments of torture strewn came into focus. The smell of human excrement, blood and suffering accentuated the bitter cold. And, in the corner, sitting on the floor with his arms outstretched and his hands shackled to the walls, was the closest thing to a skeleton that Adrian had ever seen this side of the grave.

The man, emaciated and filthy, was naked except for a soiled loin cloth. His head, a skull, rather, on which it appeared a swath of onion skin had been tightly stretched, lolled to the side. Sunken cheeks and a neck as thin as cat-gut made his teeth look horsey and his eyes grotesquely large.

After thrusting his torch into a sconce, Adrian went to the man and kneeled beside him. Gently, he picked up the man's boney wrist and felt for a pulse. It was weak, but it was there. "How long have you been here, man?"

The man's jaw worked soundlessly. Nothing but grunts emerged from his thin, parched lips. Without looking into his mouth, Adrian knew that he had no tongue.

But, who was he? And what could he have done to have deserved such punishment?

Adrian didn't know, and didn't care. No human being, no matter how heinous his crime, deserved this sort of cruel torture. If the man had taken the life of another man, raped or maimed a woman or child, then English law demanded his life be forfeit. But, in Adrian's opinion, even that, the most severest of punishments, should have been meted out fairly and humanely. The man whose gnarled fingers Adrian held was clearly the victim of a perverted mind.

"Can you tell me your name? Can you write it in the earth?"

The man hardly had the strength to breathe. But somewhere, from deep within the recesses of his soul, he summoned the will to move his arms. A mirthless smile twisted the old man's lips as his thin wrists slipped easily from the cuffs attached to the wall. With listless agony, he touched his index finger to the filthy dirt beneath him.

Adrian scooted backward, watching the man's finger as it traced the letters that spelled his name. When the captive man was finished, even the chill in the room couldn't prevent the sweat that popped out all over Adrian's body.

In the damp, smelly earth of the hellish prison cell, the man had scratched out G-I-L. His shoulders slumped and his hand stilled. Moving his limbs just that much had drained him of the scant energy he possessed.

"Casper?" Adrian whispered.

The man's gaze flickered up. His glassy gaze focused on Adrian's and his head bobbed pitifully on his reedy neck.

The man in the prison hole, more dead than alive, was Lady Philippa's father, Sir Casper Gilchrist of Rye.

Chapter Sixteen

Adrian wrapped the old man in his cape, then carried him out of the prison in his arms. Sneaking across the lower bailey, he made it to the middle gate just as a shout went up near the prison. The guards had been found with their throats slashed, and a noisy ruckus commenced. From the watch tower, a herald trumpeted the warning signal, and beneath the thundering sky, a horde of soldiers trampled toward the grisly scene. Someone shouted, "Close the gates!" just as Adrian passed beneath the portcullis.

With groaning ropes and creaking pulleys, the grilled gate fell shut behind him. Inside the upper courtyard, Adrian glanced over his shoulder at the guard station, but the soldier who'd earlier taken his coin was shrouded in darkness, pretending not to see. The tumult in the lower bailey faded as Adrian hurried toward the castle keep.

Aware that the trumpet would have awakened Drogo's soldiers by now, Adrian avoided the great hall. Instead, he chose a back passageway that led to the steps descending to the underground infirmary. There, he laid Sir Casper Gilchrist on the same examining table where Belinda's body had laid. Then, he covered him with blankets and poured a drop of wine down his throat.

Sir Casper, his breathing shallow and bubbly, clung to life by the most tenuous of threads.

Above stairs, boots thudded and armor clashed as the soldiers in the great hall, informed of the murder in the lower bailey, donned their gear. Adrian guessed that Killian, closeted in his private chamber, was hearing now of this latest calumny. Reinforcements would be sent to the prison tower and security around the castle perimeter heightened. Given the recent strange goings-on in Oldwall Castle, a murderer would be rounded up and punished without delay. If Killian couldn't furnish his men with a scapegoat, he'd have a dangerously restless group of men on his hands.

And if Sir Casper were found in the infirmary, Adrian would be served up to Drogo like a roasted pig on a silver platter.

Resting fitfully beside Hilda, Philippa heard the door open and shut softly. No doubt it was Gertrude, come to inquire about Hilda's condition. Or, perhaps the servant intended to try again to persuade Philippa to return to her own bed chamber.

"Don't waste your breath," said Philippa, rising on her elbow. "Wild horses can't drag me from Hilda's side, so you might as well not try."

Turning her head, she gasped. Her body tensed instantly and her heart began to thud. For, at the foot of Hilda's bed, his gaze as black and penetrating as Philippa had ever seen it, stood Sir Adrian, a pile of blankets draped loosely over his arms.

His expression, both sad and menacing, inspired a dreadful wariness. Slowly, Philippa threw off her coverlet and stood. Her eyes lit on the bundle of tattered blankets Adrian held so gingerly. There was something strange about the way he held that armful of woolen throws and quilts, as if he held a baby swaddled in a winding cloth. Was it a rug he held, or were those bedclothes, especially prepared for Hilda's sick bed, rolled up for some odd reason in the shape of a pipe?

She thought he would never speak, and as for herself, she couldn't seem to find her voice.

"Philippa . . . " His roughened voice trailed. At length, he moved toward her, but she backed away, not wanting to be near him, not wanting to brush against his body.

Carefully, almost lovingly, he laid the bundle down on the bed. Then, he rearranged the blankets, exposing a face. The face of a man. A gaunt, terrifying face. As Adrian retreated a step, Philippa neared the bed, staring in horror. Her breath caught in her throat. The face, with its haunted gaze and sunken sockets was her father's. The pitiful bundle of rags was in reality a bundle of spindly limbs and brittle bones.

Falling to her knees, she laid her hands on her father's seemingly hollow chest. Sobs wracked her body. One strong hand clasped her shoulder. Another hand—weaker, palsied, but every bit as gentle and comforting—stroked her hair.

Sweet mother of God, her prayers had been answered. Philippa's father had returned for her at last.

She stood beside the bed, a tear-stained linen square knotted in her hands. Just before her father's eyes had fallen shut, he mouthed the words, "I love you, daughter." Though no sound had emerged from his lips, Philippa had understood.

When Adrian explained the cause for Casper's speechlessness, and the conditions in which he was discovered, she was shocked and sickened. "Oh, Papa, I love you, too," she assured him, holding his hand, careful not to squeeze his chalky bones too hard.

She was grateful when he slipped into unconsciousness; at least, he wasn't suffering.

Now, keenly aware of Adrian's presence, she looked down at her father and a deep, inconsolable despair settled on her shoulders.

Her father was supposed to save her when he returned. He was supposed to pay Drogo and Killian the heriot money he owed them for killing Faustus. That would have released her from her obligation to marry Drogo.

Necessity and honor had compelled Sir Casper to sell her into bondage; only he could buy back his daughter and restore the honor of his family name. Then, Killian and Drogo would release the mortgage they held on her father's share of the trading company, and her father would be rich again. Not only had Philippa dreamed this, she'd believed it.

Countless times she had pictured herself and her father as a family once more. She'd fantasized of marrying a man of her own choosing, a man she loved . . . a man like Sir Adrian.

But, if her father died, all hopes of escaping Drogo would vanish.

It seemed to Adrian that the humoral balance of the entire castle's population was off. Frozen rain besieged the stone walls like sharp arrows, or quarrels, fired from enemy crossbows. Wind rattled the wooden shutters and sliced through the rough stone walls. Peals of thunder shook the very foundations of the sturdy keep.

Morning came, and with it the vulgar laughter of scullery wenches serving breakfast in the great hall, soldiers laughing and stomping around the fire in the middle of the huge gallery, mongrels barking and growling as they fought for scraps among the littered rushes.

But the tiny infirmary was gloomy and cold, chillingly reminiscent of the pit in which Sir Casper Gilchrist had been imprisoned. Deep in the bowels of the rambling castle, it gave sanctuary to a man whose heart was as heavy as a ship's anchor. Sitting on a low stool, elbows propped on his knees,

Adrian cradled his head in his hands. Even in the thick of battle, he'd never experienced a blacker moment. Only the pain he'd felt at the death of his wife and child compared to the anguish he felt now.

He was tired. With a heavy sigh, he stood and stretched his aching limbs. Rubbing his hand down his thigh, massaging his stiff muscles, his mind flashed back to the horrors of the rack, grimacing at the memory. His body still bore the imprint of that torturous device. But his body would heal.

Adrian was quite certain his heart never would.

Hilda, whose eyes had miraculously fluttered open just before daybreak, burned with fever one minute, then shivered with cold the next. From the herbs and spices in the crockery lining the shelves, Adrian mixed a packet of violets, mallow and cloves. A hot, fragrant bath, and plenty of rest was all he could recommend for her.

Killian was suffering acute headaches and digestive difficulties as a result of his mercury treatment. After careful consideration, Adrian had prepared him a tonic that contained dried ginger, chamomile and mint.

His mind turned to Sir Casper, and for that unfortunate man, Adrian could offer little in the way of recuperative agents. Reaching for the opium bottle, Adrian smirked. Casper's body had been so emaciated that he'd easily passed for a bundle of bed clothes when Adrian had carried him through the great hall. Not a solitary soldier had looked twice at the roll of sheets and blankets in Adrian's arms. It would only be when Killian discovered Casper in Hilda's sickroom that hell would break out.

Pouring a goodly measure of opium into a small brown vial, Adrian hoped he could at least relieve some of Casper's suffering. Too weak to take food or drink, too frail to be cupped or bled, the man's fate rested in God's hands. Adrian tucked the vial into his brown leather pouch.

Last on his patient roster was Drogo. The baron's wound

was putrid. Infection had ravaged the flesh surrounding the entrance point of the arrow. Shoving aside the earthen leech vessel, Adrian found a glass jar filled with living maggots covered with a layer of coarse cheesecloth.

The baron wouldn't relish having a poultice of living insects on his knee, but Adrian knew it was the most effective method of excising the rotten flesh, while leaving the healthy tissue behind. With a sigh, he set the jar on the examining table beside his other remedies.

Footsteps padded down the dark corridor.

Looking up, Adrian saw the lumpy figure of Cecily the whore filling the doorway.

Relieved to see it wasn't Killian come to interrogate him, he smiled. "Good day, woman."

"You said I could pay you a visit if I ever needed your services." Cecily's affect was considerably more subdued than the last time Adrian had encountered her.

Gesturing for her to enter, he said, "What troubles you, Cecily?"

Her face was mottled with scarlet as she described her symptoms. Adrian, by now all too familiar with her complaint, poured a judicious amount of mercury into a bottle and explained the proper dosage. As an added precaution, he gave her a bit of the ginger and mint mixture he'd prepared for stomach ailments, too.

As she prepared to leave, Adrian said, "Cecily, you must tell the other prostitutes to pay me a visit."

"All of them, sir?"

"All of them." After a space, he asked her, "Have you heard any talk concerning Belinda's death?"

Her chin jutted proudly. "Cecily hears everythin', sir!"

Adrian fished in his purse, extracted a coin and flipped it to the woman.

Catching it expertly, she turned it over it in her chubby fingers. Then, she flipped it back. "Don't want your money, Sir Adrian."

"You would do all the women in this castle a true kindness if you told me what you knew."

"A kiss might nudge me memory."

Holding his breath, Adrian met the woman's squinty gaze. "I will not kiss you, Cecily. The truth is, I love another."

Her expression hardened. "Well, then. I can't help you, can I? Just as well." She turned and started for the door. At the threshold, she froze, slowly rounding on her heel. "Oh, to hell with it! If you want to know who killed Belinda the whore, ask Denys Terrebonne!"

Lurching forward, Adrian's hand shot out to stop the woman. But she was gone, lumbering down the passageway like a pickle barrel rolling downhill.

In Hilda's sickroom he emptied the contents of his leather medicine pouch, arranging the phials and packets atop the table beside the bed. Glancing at Philippa, slump-shouldered on a three-legged stool beside her father, he said, "You must get some rest."

"How can I rest?" she replied listlessly. Her hair was mussed and her tunic was crumpled. "How can I rest when my father and my best friend are very nearly dead?"

"You do them a disservice by refusing to sleep or take nourishment. Gertrude says you have eaten nothing in two days."

"I am not hungry." With her arms wrapped around her middle, and her cheeks sunken and shadowed, she looked like a starving waif. But her mouth set stubbornly and her green eyes flashed.

"Then eat to stay alive. If Hilda revives and finds you a skeleton, you will have done her more harm than good."

Adrian sat on the side of the bed opposite from Philippa

and her father. Picking up Hilda's wrist, he found her pulse was stronger than the day before, and more regular. "She is improving. But she is by no means assured of recovery."

Philippa's voice was scratchy and small. "I note you did not say, 'If your father revives. . . . ' You don't think he will, do you?"

Standing, Adrian looked into Philippa's beseeching gaze. "I cannot lie to you," he began, then thought how ridiculous a statement that was when in fact he was nought but a liar. He'd lied to Drogo when he said he couldn't conduct Philippa's examination.

Worse, he'd lied to Philippa when he told her it was honor and duty that kept him from making love to her. Damn, what a bald-faced lie that was! 'Twas cowardice that prevented him from taking Philippa as his woman! Nothing but sheer cowardice!

Coiling his fists, Adrian silently scoffed at his own perverted code of chivalry, his own false nobility. It was fine for him to tell himself that in rebuffing Philippa, he was behaving altruistically and selflessly. The truth was, he couldn't bear to risk losing another woman he loved. Losing Jeanne had nearly killed him, physically and mentally. Losing Philippa would rob him of his soul.

Killian's bellowing voice sounded from below stairs. The baron's liegeman banged on Drogo's door, entered, then slammed the door shut behind him. Staring at one another, Adrian and Philippa listened and held their breath. It was only a matter of time before Killian got curious and poked his head in this room. Or before Gertrude got careless and mentioned to one of the scullery wenches that there was a fragile little man sharing Hilda's bed and most likely dying right alongside her.

Duty and desire warred in Adrian's mind. Instinct goaded him; he hadn't much time remaining. Drogo and Killian were hiding something, something King Edward would surely want to know about. Prisoners with their tongues cut out languished in an abominable prison, guaranteeing silence in the face of Drogo's crimes. A murderer dwelled within the castle of Oldwall. And Philippa, daughter of Casper Gilchrist, was bound and determined to marry a man she loathed.

The mysteries seemed only to deepen.

"Stand." He stood beside her, his hand outstretched.

Slipping her hand in his, she rose on wobbly knees. God, but she hadn't realized how tired she was! When her legs buckled, Adrian caught her, drawing her into his embrace, supporting her weight as easily as if she were a feather.

Her heart skitteréd. She clung to him, fingers grasping his tunic, arms inexplicably winding around his neck. Before she realized what was happening, she felt his breath on her neck, his lips on her mouth, his teeth clashing with hers.

She hadn't the physical stamina to resist him. At least that's what she told herself. But, in reality, it was more that she needed him so badly, she couldn't deny herself the warmth that flowed through her body as he held her. Deep within her, an aching desire awakened, a matchless need so strong that Philippa felt powerless to repress it.

Pressing her palm to his face, she felt the texture of his skin, the coarse stubble of his beard, the liquid heat of his lips. She gasped and held on faster. While her body instinctively responded to the sensations enfolding her, her willpower slipped away.

He kissed her neck, her ears, ran his tongue along the sensitive skin of her shoulder. A wave of pleasure, accompanied by a ferocious desire, swept over her. Luckily, Adrian swept her into his arms at the same time, for Philippa's legs, as trembling as two mounds of pudding, refused to sustain her a moment longer.

He carried her out the room and down the steps, treading carefully past Drogo's solar. It was a miracle no one passed them in the corridor. But in her recklessness, Philippa wondered what would happen if Drogo discovered her with Adrian. At least he wouldn't want to marry her.

On the other hand, he would probably kill her.

Tossing her onto her bed, he gasped, "Philippa." Then, he quickly retraced his steps, closed and latched the door and returned to Philippa's bed.

They tore their clothes off, throwing tunics, stockings and boots to the floor. Then, in a tangle of limbs, they came together, their bodies hungry to join. Harsh breaths, murmured entreaties, and frantic pleas to God mingled in the dense, tension-laded air. Kisses, rough and urgent, rained down Philippa's neck, drawing shivers that rippled up and down her spine.

She pulled him onto her, wrapped her legs around his muscular thighs. Adrian's weight strained the bed-ropes and pressed her into the mattress, but she couldn't get enough of him, couldn't get close enough to him. Arching her back, she ground her body into his, crushing her breasts to his chest, molding her belly to his.

Suddenly, he drew back, rose on his knees. Philippa's heart squeezed, thudding to a halt. Shock and excitement poured through her—why was he staring at her like that, his eyes burning, his expression dark and fierce?

With one movement, he flipped her over. Cheek against the mattress, bottom popped up in the cool air, she was totally exposed. Fear, anticipation, and always, always, that hot, hot need gushing through her loins, overwhelmed Philippa. Adrian's hands caressed her buttocks, moving over them lovingly, slowly, *knowingly.*

She drew in a deep, ragged breath. A boiling, molten-hot well of desire swelled within her, but she didn't dare move, *didn't dare*, because nothing in her entire life had ever felt so good as the sensation she was experiencing now. Nothing had ever been more pleasurable, or more right.

And, though not an experienced lover, Philippa sensed that Adrian's desire was on the brink of completion. His breathing was quick and shallow, his language increasingly descriptive and intimate. Running his hand between her legs, widening the space between her thighs, he told her in graphic, exquisitely wicked detail, precisely what he was going to do to her.

Stroking her soft, moist flesh, he promised her she would like it. Expertly, he toyed with the most sensitive part of her anatomy. Philippa believed every word he said, believed it heart and soul. She wanted this man, every inch of him. Wanted him fiercely and desperately and wholly. Unable to restrain herself, she allowed her hips to sway, lifting her body just a bit, silently urging Adrian to take her.

From the corner of her eyes, she saw him reach for his leather pouch, tossed negligently on the bedside table. He rolled a skin-thin membrane of some sort down the length of his shaft. Then, grasping the soft, fleshy lobes of her buttocks, he drove into her. Deep and hard.

The swift, shocking pleasure that bolted through her was stunning. She cried out, tears stung her eyes, and something inside her came loose. . . .

With a firm hold on her hips, he drew her to him. She snuggled against his rigid muscles, ground herself into him. Reaching between them, she cupped his body, felt his fingers grapple with hers, felt his touch on her slick, hot skin, groaned with delightful pleasure-pain.

He moved in and out, his body slapping her backside, his fingers digging into her flesh. Philippa moved with him, her inner muscles squeezing, her pleasure cresting. When release overtook her, she buried her face in the mattress, having salvaged just enough of her senses to be able to stifle her screams.

Adrian's movements quickened, then he reached his climax, too, plunging deeper inside her than Philippa would have thought possible. He whispered her name, held her body tight against his for a moment, then sighed heavily. When they lay beside each other, he studied her through glazed, half-lidded eyes. She knew men favored slumber after swiving; that's what Hilda had told her. But Adrian didn't appear nearly as weary as Philippa felt. In fact, he appeared as alert as a cat, fascinated by what he saw.

"You have defied your lord, again, Sir Adrian," she murmured drowsily. She couldn't muster up the energy to be angry with him, even if she should have been. Tired, physically content and sexually sated, Philippa had gotten what she wanted from Adrian. If he left her bed this time, and never returned, she had only herself to blame.

"Aye." He brushed a wisp of hair from her forehead. "But, you need not fear pregnancy. I took precautions, and besides, you are still having your menses."

"You are an unusual man, Adrian."

His brows lifted. "I am? I prithee, what makes me so unique?"

Luxuriating in the warmth that lingered after their coupling, Philippa laughed easily. Turning on her side, she traced Adrian's jaw line, ran her finger over his lips, brushed her palm along his cheek. "You are a handsome man. As stunning as any woman I have ever seen. Yet you are as strong as an ox, and more fearless than a sensible man should be."

He chuckled. "Are you telling me I have no sense?"

"Do you still say you love me?"

"I do."

"Then, I say, you have no sense." They both laughed, though Philippa thought she saw a glimmer of sadness in his Adrian's gaze. "You are a knight of the realm, trained in the art of fighting, and yet you would rather deliver women's babes than seek glory on the battlefield."

"Ah, the ultimate contradiction."

"Have you killed many men, Adrian?"

A moment ticked by. Adrian's gaze blackened, then he answered softly, "Countless numbers, I fear."

A coldness penetrated Philippa's bones. Who was this man? A blackguard, or a healer? A killer, or a life-giver?

Drawing his hand, still fragrant with her sex, to her lips, she kissed his fingertips. Confusion embattled her weary mind. Adrian stroked her face, brushed her hair from it.

His hands, warm and strong, comforted her. But the hands that stroked and held her had once plunged swords and daggers into other men's hearts. Was the depth of Adrian's tenderness equal to the sorrow weighting his heart? Had she seen, hidden somewhere behind Adrian's cool mask of bravado, a glimmer of fear? Had she glimpsed a flash of fear when he replied, *Countless numbers,* or were her own eyes playing tricks on her?

"And have you delivered many babes into the world?" she asked him.

"Aye."

"Then, perhaps you have evened the score, Adrian. Do not punish yourself too severely. For, you are a good man—I know it. Even if you do not honor your allegiance to Drogo. And as for your unfortunate enemies, the men whose lives were forfeit to your greater fighting skills, consider this: For each life you were forced to take on the field of battle, you have delivered a new one into the world."

He shut his eyes tightly, growing very quiet.

When he finally looked at her, she was asleep.

But before Philippa's lids had fallen shut, she had seen the single tear that slid down his cheek.

And, in her heart, she ached for him.

Killian, standing beside Drogo's bed, stopped speaking mid-sentence when Adrian entered.

"How fares the baron?" Adrian asked, forcing a joviality that he didn't feel.

"As miserable as a pig on its way to the charnel house,"

replied Drogo. "My leg burns and my head hurts, too. I'm beginning to think you're trying to kill me."

"Were I attempting to murder you, my lord, you'd be dead by now." Adrian made quick work of removing Drogo's bandages. Then, he removed the jar of maggots from his leather pouch, and held them close to the candle that guttered on the bedside table. Inside the thick topaz-colored bottle, a small swarm of fat insects crawled all over each other.

"God's teeth! What in the hell is that?" Drogo recoiled, while Killian skirted the end of the bed and stood on the opposite side of the room.

"Your knee is badly infected, I'm afraid. The maggots will destroy the diseased flesh and leave the healthy tissue behind."

"You'll not put any putrid horse flies on me—"

"They are not horse flies, and I suggest you allow them to do their work, or else you risk the painful inconvenience of having your leg amputated when the infection has destroyed it completely."

"Flesh-eaters, are they?" Killian, having gone a bit green around the gills, swallowed hard. "What sort of gammon is this, Sir Adrian? First, you warn me that a flesh-eating contagion has loosed itself on the female population of Oldwall Castle, then you threaten to apply a poultice of flesh-eating flies to the baron's wound! You are a foolish mountebank if you expect Drogo to submit to this outrageous course of treatment."

"Would you rather your leg fall off?" Adrian asked the baron.

From the other side of the bed, Killian roared. "My lord, don't listen to him! He predicted my johnny would fall off. Well, I can assure you it has not!"

"The castle wenches will be happy to hear that, I am sure," said Adrian. "The sad fact remains that Drogo's wound is not healing properly. The maggots will consume the infection and he will not lose his leg."

In a pitiful voice, Drogo said, "I don't want to lose my leg, Killian. How'd I ever mount a horse without both me legs, much less mount a woman?"

"Good point," drawled Adrian, removing the bladder cover of the jar and unceremoniously dumping a load of maggots onto the baron's knee. "Try to keep still, now, that's it! Doesn't hurt much, does it?"

"Stings a bit," said Drogo, grimacing. " 'Tis the sight of it, and the sound, that is sickening."

With that, Killian lunged for the chamber pot tucked beneath Drogo's bed. Hunkered over it, he rid himself of his last meal, then slowly stood, his face now a paler shade of green. "You'll get what's coming to you, Sir Adrian. All your fancy tricks, smooth words and medical chicanery won't save you in the end, you know. I'll roast your ballocks on a spit before you leave here—"

Drogo, writhing in discomfort, cut off his liegeman's threat with a thundering admonition. "Shut up, Killian!"

Killian wiped his lips with the back of his hand. "He's been here long enough, my lord. Too long, in fact."

"On the contrary, there remains much for me to do here," answered Adrian. "Hilda is not yet recovered from her childbirth. There is some sort of scourge plaguing the prostitutes, and a murderer is loose within the castle walls. And, there is the matter of Lady Philippa. I have not yet been able to certify her as a virgin. I understand your hesitation to marry a woman who may have had relations with another man, my lord."

"The life of a serving wench means nothing to me," growled Drogo. "The lives of prostitutes means even less. However, the deaths of two of my most trusted guards mean something to me. I am not inclined to be lenient toward a retainer who refuses to obey castle curfews. You defied Killian's order last night, didn't you, Adrian? You killed two of my guards and Wat, the prison warden. Didn't you, Sir Adrian?"

"What precisely were you looking for, Adrian?" Killian's voice was rapier sharp. "As if I didn't know."

"I was looking for someone who could tell me who Belinda's last customer was."

In a mocking tone, Killian said, "Oh? Am I to believe, sir, that your investigation is confined to Belinda's murder? Or are you looking for something else?"

"Stolen French loot, perhaps?" suggested Drogo, winking at Killian.

"A stash of gold and jewels, maybe?" Killian laughed malevolently.

With sudden good nature, Drogo held out his hands palm up. "If you are looking for buried treasure, Sir Adrian, I am afraid you are wasting your time. Because there is none, you see. Drogo is an honest man. Drogo honors the Treaty of Brétigni and the fine French people across the channel. Drogo has no secrets from King Edward."

"It never occurred to me that you *did* have secrets from the king," riposted Adrian. But it did. Watching the quick exchange of glances between Drogo and Killian, he thought he detected a flash of nervousness. Drogo, in his taunting banter, had revealed more than he'd intended.

Killian cleared his throat. "I want you gone from Oldwall before tomorrow morn, sir. You are grating on my nerves and you are disrupting castle morale."

"Might I mention that, I have a duel to fight tomorrow afternoon." Adrian slanted Killian a rakish smile. "Fellow by the name of Denys Terrebonne. Thinks I have dishonored his wife by assisting her during childbirth."

"Umph." Pondering that, Drogo gave a bark of laughter.

Killian also appeared to give the matter of Adrian's duel

some thought. "Well then, you shall be gone the morning after the duel. One way or the other."

"That means you must examine Philippa this afternoon," said Drogo. "And I don't want to hear any nonsense about her monthlies. Examine her! Or don't, makes no difference to me. But if you don't inspect her maidenhead and certify her a virgin, then I shall consider the contract I entered into with her father null and void."

"In which case you will not marry Lady Philippa?" A picture, most unpleasant, was coming into focus in Adrian's mind.

"In which case she will be deemed unsuitable for the marriage bed!" Drogo pounded his fist on the mattress. "And all her father's stock that is presently held in escrow will be forfeit to me! Immediately!"

By way of clearing his throat again, Killian interrupted Drogo. In a voice as thick and sweet as treacle, he said, "I don't think the terms of your marriage contract are any of Sir Adrian's concern, my lord. Suffice it to say, Adrian, that your report will determine the course of Philippa's life. If she is not sworn to be a virgin, she will not marry Drogo."

Pausing for effect, Killian allowed the import of his words to sink into Adrian's head.

But Adrian, his mind spinning, easily predicted the words that next rolled from Killian's tongue.

"And she will be free to marry another man."

So, that's what they want, Adrian thought. They want me to say Philippa is not a virgin so that Sir Casper's shares of stock will be forfeit to Drogo.

Sighing, Drogo leaned back against his bolster and crossed his pudgy arms behind his head. "Ah, what a pretty little piece she is, too. 'Twould be a shame to lose her to another man."

"She will make some man a fine wife," Killian added.

Cold, hard hatred sliced through Adrian. Yet he steeled his expression and forcibly repressed his anger. He had much to sort out. If Killian and Drogo knew he'd been in the prison tower and killed the guards, why did they suffer his presence a moment longer? Why didn't they toss him in the dungeon, or cut off his tongue, or dispatch him to London forthwith?

Answers, slow and grudging, trickled through his brain. They needed Adrian. They needed him to prove Philippa wasn't a virgin so that Casper Gilchrist's shares in the shipping company would be transferred in sole, naked ownership to Drogo.

But what made them think that Lady Philippa wasn't pure?

Chapter Seventeen

Gertrude's excited voice jolted Philippa awake. "Hilda's roused from her sleep, my lady! Wake up, dearie, she's asking for ye!"

Instantly alert, Philippa threw herself out of bed and, with Gertrude's help, donned a straw-colored tunic and dark blue surcoat. Conducting her toilette in record time, she washed her face and ran a horse-hair brush through her tresses. Her fingers nimbly wound her pale yellow locks into plaits that she coiled and pinned above her ears. Then, she flew out the room and up the stairs to Hilda's converted chambers.

Her friend managed a weak smile when Philippa entered the room. "Lady, how is my babe?"

"Her lungs are strong, Hilda." Philippa kissed her father's sunken cheek before rounding the end of the bed. "Your daughter keeps half the village awake with her crying. Gertrude has gone to fetch her now so that you can hear her bawl with your own ears."

"And who, pray tell, is my current bed partner?" Hilda's voice was still hoarse, and her face as white as a birch tree.

Perched on the edge of the mattress, Philippa replied, " 'Tis my father, Hilda. I'm sorry if you were frightened to find a man in your bed when you awakened."

"In his condition, he isn't very frightening."

"No." Philippa held her friend's hand tightly. "No, he is very weak, Hilda. Adrian rescued him from the prison dungeon. We don't know how long he was there, or what tortures he suffered, or even why he was imprisoned."

"Has he not regained his senses, then? Can he not tell you what befell him?"

Beating back her emotion, Philippa replied tightly, "His captors cut out his tongue. He could not speak when Adrian found him. Then, he lapsed into a deep sleep and has not roused since he was brought here. Oh, Hilda, I fear he will never recover!"

With what little strength she had, Hilda squeezed Philippa's hand. "You must be strong, little chick. Your father has endured much hardship and he needs you now more than ever."

"I am helpless to do anything for him." Ducking her head, Philippa surrendered to her tears. "My life is ruined, Hilda! Always, I had hoped and prayed that Father would return from France." Between hiccoughs and gulping sobs, she poured out her troubles. "But now that he is back, nothing is changed! I am still bound to marry Drogo, if he will have me."

"What do you mean, if he will have you? The man would be a blasted fool not to want to marry you. You're young and beautiful! I don't care how rich that scoundrel is, where else will he find a woman as sweet and virtuous as you who is willing to share his bed?"

"But, Hilda, Drogo is dead-set on marrying a virgin!"

"You said you were. . . . " Hilda's voice trailed as her eyes rounded. "My God, child! Have you taken a lover behind my back? Well, good for you, if you have! You'll not hear a peep of disapproval from this old roundheels. Just be careful you don't conceive a child with your lover before you get pregnant with Drogo's spawn. I warrant the baron will be suspicious if his first born son don't have flamin' red hair and big bushy black brows."

Brushing away tears, Philippa whispered, "You don't understand, Hilda! Adrian knows I am not a virgin!"

"So it was he who broke you in, then! Well, just see if I go to sleep for a week again! Seems I missed all the fun!"

"No," Philippa groaned. "Listen! Adrian must swear to Drogo that I am a virgin, else Drogo won't marry me."

"Lucky you."

"But, I must marry Drogo!"

"Why, in heaven's name?"

Releasing a deep breath, Philippa regained her composure. It helped to talk to Hilda; she'd missed hashing over her life's complexities with her best friend. When she had someone to talk to, the world seemed so much less scary. "A very long time ago, when I was just a little girl, my father entered into a joint shipping venture with Drogo and Killian. And Killian's father, Faustus."

Hilda made a moué of distaste. "Aye, I seem to recall meeting the man. 'Twas many years ago. I was a young thing meself, servin' at the banquet table. Handsome man, as I recall. Like Killian. When I placed his trencher in front of him, he pinched me arse."

"Be glad that's all he did to you." Philippa pulled her hand from Hilda's clasp, and hugged her shoulders. Her chest ached with the weight of her confession, but as she forced the words, it became easier to accept the awful truth. And, perhaps, to forgive herself. "There was a terrible row between the men. Well, between Faustus and my father, that is. My father accused Faustus of raping my mother."

"Child," Hilda whispered, "you don't 'ave to tell me."

"Faustus claimed my mother made overtures toward him. That it was she who seduced him. He called her a she-devil."

"Your father's honor was at stake."

"Just so. But, I don't think my father would have killed Faustus if it were only his wife's virtue that was impugned. You see, my father was a peaceful man. He didn't want to fight. He knew my mother was innocent, and he didn't care what his peers thought of him."

"Your father had another grievance against Faustus."

"Yes." Closing her eyes, Philippa saw a young girl cowering in the corner of her bedchamber. A man's shadow loomed over her. The child whimpered, but when the big hands lifted her to her feet, the child somehow separated from her body and floated to another place, a happy sun-drenched place where no one could hurt her.

"And you, just a child," Hilda said, understanding all.

For a long while, Philippa sat quietly, remembering the awful pain and humiliation she'd suffered at Faustus's hands. Sitting with Hilda, she reminded herself she was safe now, the odious monster was long dead.

She glanced at her father, jaw slack, scrawny chest rising and falling at far too infrequent intervals. Casper Gilchrist's anger when he'd learned Faustus had attacked his wife was formidable, even frightening. But when he'd discovered that his daughter had been defiled, he'd gone crazy. Truly crazy.

"He killed him." Philippa recalled the horror of knowing that her father had plunged a sword into Faustus's neck. *Because of what she'd told, because she'd divulged the secret that Faustus had warned her against telling.*

Guilt, remorse, and utter shame had swallowed the young girl. And when Faustus's relatives appeared at Casper's doorstep to collect their kinsman's death money, she saw herself as having been responsible, not only for Faustus's death, but Casper's financial ruination as well.

Staring at a hole in the floor boards, she continued.

"Faustus was dead and his son wanted retribution. Killian demanded his heriot, swearing that his father had been murdered without just cause. Drogo, championing Killian's cause, agreed."

"Did your father pay the heriot?"

"He hadn't the money, he'd sunk all his capital in the shipping venture, you see. And my mother, gone mad from learning that her child had been . . . well . . . "

"Go on," said Hilda, gently.

"My mother died soon after Faustus was killed. Father said she couldn't bear the shame, that she'd lost her mind. And I think she had."

"You must have been sorely confused. Taking the blame on yourself, feeling that you'd ruined your parents' lives."

"Killian and Drogo devised a scheme meant to enable Father to repay them." A bitter smile tugged at Philippa's lips. It all seemed so cruel now, so calculated. Any scrivener's apprentice would have recognized the contract drafted by Drogo and Killian as unconscionable, even ruinous to Casper. But at the time, Philippa had thought her father very noble and wise when he sat at the big trestle table in Oldwall Castle's great hall, head down, brow furrowed, as he scratched his quill across the foolscap.

And that was all it took. Drogo owned her then.

"What were the terms of the agreement?" Hilda asked. "Where is the contract now? Perhaps there is another way out of it."

Philippa shook her head. "Father couldn't raise the necessary sum for the heriot, so Drogo advanced him a portion of the amount that was owed to Killian."

"Which made your father indebted to Drogo."

"Yes, but a balance was still owed to Killian. So, Father was forced to put his shares of the shipping company into escrow. Killian and Drogo held a mortgage on Father's interest in the joint venture."

"But, that wasn't enough for Drogo," suggested Hilda.

"That's right. He demanded further collateral."

"You." The older woman, sucking air through her teeth, shuddered.

With a sigh, Philippa nodded. "Me. I was to be raised in Oldwall, beneath the scrutiny of Drogo. I was to be trained to be the chatelaine of the castle, groomed to be Drogo's wife, as it were. Fatted like a calf prepared for the slaughter. The only stipulation is that I am to be relieved of my obligation to marry Drogo if Father repays his debt to Drogo, compensates Killian for Faustus's death, and redeems his interest in the trading company."

"Which isn't very likely to happen now," Hilda said wryly, frowning. "Wait a minute, you said Drogo wants to marry a virgin."

"Aye."

"But he must know you are not a virgin, if what Faustus did to you was made known. And it must have been if Casper Gilchrist killed him for it."

"Father never publicly accused Faustus. You see, it shamed us all. 'Twas bad enough the crime had been committed. It would have been far worse if my shame became common knowledge. Father never could have married me off, not to a respectable man, anyway. Indeed, had Drogo known of my . . . condition . . . he would not have offered to marry me."

With a catch in her voice, Philippa slanted a half-sympathetic, half-bewildered gaze at her father. "No one, aside from Mother and Father, knew what Faustus had done to me. That is why Father mounted such a feeble defense when Killian demanded the death tax be paid."

Hilda shook her head. "Pride goeth before a fall, the good Lord says. Sir Casper Gilchrist of Rye had too much pride, dear. For which you have paid a terrible price."

"But, now, Hilda, I must marry Drogo!"

"Why, child? For God's sake, run away from here! Run

away with that handsome knight, Sir Adrian. From what you've said, he's taken a liking to ye. Ye could do a far piece worse than he, my dear."

Hearing the sounds of an infant wailing in the great hall, Philippa patted Hilda's hands. "No, my friend. I have spent my life plotting to redeem my family's honor. And if I must marry Drogo to do so, then that is my lot in life."

"Foolish girl!" But Hilda's voice gentled as her daughter's crying voice neared. "Have you forgotten that you must convince Drogo of your virginity before there is to be a wedding?"

"I have not forgotten," Philippa replied. "I have already taken care of that little problem."

Adrian will lie for me, she thought. *He wouldn't dare not!*

That he hadn't suggested fleeing from Drogo and from this awful marriage caused her heart to ache, but she found some relief in the fact that he was willing to fraudulently document her purity. She'd come to terms with her fate. If Adrian couldn't—or wouldn't—rescue her from Drogo, the least he could do was help her buy back her father's good name and swear she was a virgin.

Gertrude, trudging up the steps, invoked the name of God, shushed the baby as she passed the door of Drogo's solar, then chuckled when she made the upper landing. The instant servant and child crossed the threshold, a keening cry split the air.

Hilda's face glowed from within as her child was placed in her arms. Cradling her daughter against her chest, she exuded maternal contentment.

Sharing her friend's happiness, Philippa smiled through her tears. Bolstered by the knowledge that Hilda would survive, she stood, her strength renewed. Pausing, she thought to discuss Denys Terrebonne's challenge to Adrian, then decided the woman had heard enough unpleasantness for the time being. What Hilda needed was rest, peace, and quiet time with her child.

Philippa went to her father and kissed him. If the baby's cries couldn't wake him, she feared nothing would. But a strange sort of peace had settled over her. Hilda was right; her father had laid a tremendous burden of guilt on her. Departing the sickroom, she wondered what it would feel like to cast off her yoke of guilt, to live without the stain of dishonor on her soul and the sword of retribution hanging over her head.

Her mother's dying words to her had been, "It wasn't your fault, Philippa."

But Philippa had never believed it.

She thought of Adrian's kindnesses, his whispered urgings breathed against her neck. A fire ignited her blood each time she imagined his naked body, his strong sex plunging into her. Hadn't his loving felt good . . . and right? Hadn't he made her feel loved? Hadn't he proven that there were good men in the world? And that she was worthy of being loved by one of them?

Could it be that she was, in fact, worth more than the number of pounds owed to Drogo and Killian by her father?

She'd never thought of it before, but Philippa suddenly wondered if there was another way out of her contractual and moral obligation to wed the lord of Oldcastle, that abominable man, the greedy villain who had conspired in stealing her childhood.

With his bandaged leg propped on a stool, Drogo presided over the long, elevated table at the far end of the great hall. He'd been too restless to remain in bed an hour longer, and, against Adrian's advice, had ordered a banquet and descended from his solar. A snoutful of good French wine not only improved his spirits, but helped numb the pain in his leg. Scratching his crotch, he scanned the room for wenches and thought he might even be up for a little bed-play later on.

Two more tables ran the length of the room, and while servants scurried about with trenchers of food and ewers of ale, the baron's knights ate, arm-wrestled, told jokes and celebrated the return to table of their liege-lord.

On Drogo's right sat Killian, morose and pensive. Turning to him, Drogo said, "What the hell's the matter with you? You've hardly uttered a word all night."

Stroking his chin, Killian said, "I don't like it, I just don't like it. We've got to get rid of Vale. At once!"

Adrian entered the hall, and approached the baron's table. Killian and Drogo, their heads together, were engaged in earnest conversation. Meeting Killian's gaze, Adrian nodded, then, made an abbreviated, begrudging bow in deference to Drogo.

Killian and Drogo's whispered conference abruptly ended. Leaning to his left, Drogo spoke to Denys Terrebonne—who inexplicably had been promoted to a place of honor at the baron's table. "Well, man, here's your competitor come straight from the birthing room. Or was it the nursery you was overseein' tonight, Sir Adrian? Have you taken to wet nursin' your little charges?"

Rewarded for his wit with a ripple of laughter muffled by mouths full of tripe, pheasant and nightingale, Drogo happily slapped his meaty palm on the table. "Are you prepared for tomorrow's combat, Sir Adrian? I know that Denys Terrebonne is, and if you haven't heard it before now, he's a worthy opponent, this one."

Denys, basking in such rare praise, quaffed another tankard of ale and laughed heartily. "You won't best me this time, sir. One of us will die tomorrow. Best say yer prayers tonight, that's my advice."

Biting his tongue, for he would have liked to box this simpleton's ears and tell him what a fool he was, Adrian stepped nearer the table. "I shouldn't relish the thought of rendering your babe fatherless, Terrebonne. But I intend to defend myself and my honor, if I must. And if I have to kill you to preserve my own life, I will."

"Haven't you killed enough of Drogo's men?" Killian asked menacingly.

Drogo's black bushy brows shot up. "What sort of trouble have ye got yerself into now, sir?" he asked puckishly.

Adrian remained silent. This was clearly a dialogue between Killian and Drogo, a shared joke at his expense.

"He's like a rooster in the hen house, that one," purred Killian.

Drogo played along. "You don't mean to say the pretty midwife has been partaking of the castle wenches, do you?"

"Why, Belinda, the whore who died, couldn't quit talking about him. Said he knew more about a woman's body than a man had a right to."

"Oh, when did you converse with Belinda?" Adrian inserted smoothly.

Killian's expression hardened instantly. "You're not so clever as you think, sir! Enjoy your last evening in this castle, because tomorrow we'll be measuring your body for a casket. You'll rue the day you defied Drogo's orders and stuck your nose in business that didn't concern you."

"You haven't been sneaking around the prison tower again, have you?" Drogo slanted Adrian a falsely indulgent smile. "Because if I hear you are responsible for killing three of my manservants, Drogo will be very, very unhappy."

So they knew. Which meant they also knew Adrian had rescued Sir Casper Gilchrist. Then, why hadn't Killian already ordered Adrian's arrest? Why hadn't Drogo sent his knight to Hilda's sickroom to search for the missing prisoner?

The atmosphere in the great hall shifted from one of frivolity to tense wariness as Drogo's knights detected their lord's hostility. Denys Terrebonne, so pleased to be seated at his master's table, studied Adrian with murderous disdain. Killian leaned back and enjoyed the gamesmanship.

"Perhaps it was a mistake to bring you to Oldwall Castle," Killian remarked at length. "But you will soon enough be returned to London, where, with the king's indulgence, you may catch as many noble ladies' babes as you like."

" 'Tis what you want, isn't it?" Drogo asked. "To return to London?"

"I came here to practice medicine," Adrian replied. "My work is yet incomplete."

"You came here to spy on me!" the baron roared. "And you think I'm fool enough not to know it. Well, I'll not ignore your little midnight sorties to my prison tower any longer. Drogo knows what you're about, sir! You're a damn spy and bloody well I know it!"

Killian cleared his throat and laid a restraining hand on Drogo's meaty arm. "Enough," he said quietly. "Tomorrow will determine Sir Adrian's fate. If he lives, he can return to London and report to his superiors, whoever they might be, that he has found not a single ingot of French gold in Oldwall Castle. That's what you're looking for, isn't it, Adrian? Evidence that Drogo has conducted illegal raids into France?"

Caught off guard, Adrian held his tongue. If Drogo and Killian knew he was a spy, knew he'd killed three prison guards and rescued Casper Gilchrist, why wasn't his corpse hanging in chains from a gibbet?

A deep undercurrent of secrecy and evil ran beneath the surface of their hostility. Drogo and Killian clearly intended to use the situation at hand for their own nefarious purposes. Feeling like a mouse perched on the edge of a spring trap, Adrian glared at them.

"And if he doesn't survive his battle with Denys?" Drogo mused.

"Then Sir Adrian will trouble us no more with his snooping," Killian replied.

Having vented his anger, Drogo had grown tired of toying with Adrian. Signaling his boredom, he reached for a joint of mutton. "Tell me something, Adrian," he said around a mouthful of food, "Have you examined Lady Philippa yet? Or have you been too busy mucking out me dungeons?"

Denys's snicker was quickly cut off by a sharp look from Killian.

"I am prepared to deliver my report concerning the lady's virginity," Adrian said, indicating his respect, not for Drogo's authority but for Philippa's good character, by a dip of his head.

"Not a bloody moment too soon." Drogo's sharp teeth ripped at the greasy drumstick he held in his fist. "So what do you say, Sir Adrian? Is Lady Philippa a virgin or no?"

The feast in the great hall was in full swing. Drogo's confinement had been a period of agitated depression for the castle retainers. But the baron's return to apparent health had jolted the men from the doldrums and into a mood of lusty joyousness.

The clang of pewter tankards and the boisterous laughter of knights drifted up the stairs to where Philippa stood outside the door to Drogo's solar. Inhaling the dense, smoky aroma of spit-roasted fowl, she closed her eyes. Her mouth watered at the thought of the sugary confections sure to grace the banquet tables. Despite her hunger, however, Philippa had sent word to Drogo that she did not feel well and would not be attending the banquet.

She had other matters to attend to.

Heart thumping wildly, she pushed open the door to Drogo's bedchamber. Starlight poured in through the arched window cut high in the rough stone walls. Allowing her eyes to adjust to the dim light, Philippa scanned the room. Her gaze lit on the jewel-encrusted casket that graced the mantelpiece.

She crossed the room and reached for it, held the box in trembling hands. Inside was the contract that her father had signed, mortgaging his young daughter to a ruthless opportunist, encumbering his family's fortune as well as its honor.

Running her fingertips along the intricately carved panels, she turned. Almost reverently, as if it held some great treasure instead of the papers that formalized her servitude, Philippa placed the box on Drogo's four-poster bed. Holding her breath, she raised the thick oaken lid.

A thick sheaf of foolscap rustled beneath her fingertips. Squinting, Philippa swore softly. She needed more light. Tucking the papers beneath her arm, she quickly lit the candle beside Drogo's bed. Then she held the papers close to the flame, and read.

"The terms of the contract are clear, are they not?" The voice slid through the room like a snake.

Gasping, Philippa whirled to face Sir Killian, nonchalantly leaning against the doorway, arms folded across his chest. The picture of male cockiness, he emerged from the shadows like an unfolding nightmare. His smirk, the twinkle in his eyes, the very ease with which he approached her sparked a panic in Philippa's chest.

"Aye, the contract appears iron-clad, sir."

"As the document's author, I accept your compliment." He stood so near to her that she could see his white teeth gleaming, could smell the mint on his breath.

" 'Twas no compliment." Despite her fear, Philippa fought to meet Killian's stare. "This is the most unconscionable, unfair and one-sided agreement I have ever heard tell of. This . . . this . . . this *contract* as you call it is in effect nothing more than a sales receipt! My life exchanged for your silence!"

"Well, now, I believe the arrangement was a little more complicated than that." Killian snatched the papers from Philippa's hand and tossed them onto the bed. Then, he brushed the back of his hand along her cheek. "But, I wouldn't expect a woman to understand such legalities. Don't trouble yourself as to matters outside your purview, my lady. That agreement is perfectly legal. And it is binding on your father as well as you."

Philippa turned her head, recoiling beneath Killian's touch. For a moment, he froze, his hand hovering in the air. She slanted her gaze at him, anticipating a blow or a slap. Instead, he lowered his arm. A slow, oily smile full of evil promises spread across his face.

With a sigh, as if he regretted the unpleasantness of their conversation, he scooped up the papers and tucked them beneath his leather belt. "There is no room for argument on this matter, Philippa. Your father killed mine."

"Faustus raped my mother, and. . . . " Philippa clamped her lips shut. How could she accuse Faustus of molesting her and at the same time assert her fraudulent virginity?

"And what?" Tilting his head, Killian studied her from top to bottom. "Speak now, wench, or forever hold your peace."

"Nothing."

"Your mother, dear, was the village whore. 'Twas not my father who sinned against her. Rather it was she who snared and seduced him." Shrugging, he added, "It pains me to speak so bluntly to you, but you have forced the issue by challenging the contract. That is what you intended to do, isn't it? Why else would you sneak into Drogo's solar and purloin the contract?"

"I have as much right to read it as anyone else. More so, since I am the object of these contractual arrangements."

"Perhaps. Or perhaps you meant to burn the documents and disavow your obligation to marry Drogo."

"I have never attempted to shirk my duties." Philippa's cheeks burned with indignation. "For whatever reason, whether from some perverted sense of loyalty, discretion or honor, my father chose to negotiate with you and Drogo after he killed Faustus—when, according to law and custom, he had every right to kill the man."

"I do not concede that issue," Killian replied.

"Be that as it may, you demanded a death tax from my

father. And he was willing to pay rather than continue a notorious and potentially scandalous feud with your family."

"I suppose he knew it was impossible to successfully defend the rather tattered virtue of his women."

His women. Philippa's mind reeled. How much did Killian know of what transpired between Faustus and Casper?

Anger and humiliation emboldened her. Her voice caught on a sob, but she refused to retreat in the face of Killian's cruel charges. "My father loved us! Mother was a kind and virtuous woman! She would never have willingly slept with your filthy father! Never!"

"Then why did Casper Gilchrist agree to the death tax?" Killian countered smoothly. "If your mother was such an innocent matron, why would Casper Gilchrist have mortgaged his shares in the shipping company to me, and his daughter to Drogo?"

"Because you and Drogo tricked him!" The words, ripped from her soul, were laden with hurt and venom. "You tricked him into believing that he could save me from the stain of Mother's dishonor, a stain that spilled solely from your father's evil deed. You took everything my father owned in exchange for silence. Silence about a crime that *your* father committed."

Touching his heart, Killian spoke with unreal sincerity. "Philippa, dear, this was an arm's length deal if there ever was one. Your mother should have ridden backwards on a donkey's back through the village. 'Tis the accepted punishment for adultery."

"She never committed adultery."

"My father was like any other man, defenseless against the wiles of a she-devil. Your father killed an innocent man. As his son, I was entitled to recompense."

"I hate you!"

Killian pushed on in a harsh staccato. "Casper couldn't afford to pay, so Drogo loaned him the money."

"And I wound up engaged to Drogo!"

"Whilst I agreed never to publicly accuse your mother of her wanton misconduct."

Burying her face in her hands, Philippa cried, "You impudent bastard, you act as if you did my parents a favor! But Mother died of a broken heart! She died a miserable woman! Your cruelty drove her mad!"

"Guilt drove her mad, Philippa. Face the facts."

Uncovering her tear-streaked cheeks, Philippa glared at Killian. "My mother was guilty of nothing!"

Lightning-quick, Killian grabbed her arm, pulled her to him, and pressed a kiss on her lips.

Rearing back, Philippa slapped his face. "Don't you touch me, you filthy animal! I hate you!"

But her vitriol fueled Killian's lust. Grinning, he reached for her again, and when she batted his hand away, he lunged for her, surrounding her in a bear-hug and forcing another kiss on her mouth.

Fighting his embrace, Philippa turned her head. Killian's touch was vile, the very thought of his mouth on hers made her stomach turn. But the harder she fought, the tighter he held her. At last, she was pinned against his body, her feet kicking desperately at his booted ankles, her arms crushed helplessly against his chest. She twisted and writhed, but his rough kisses scraped her neck even as his fingers grappled her bottom.

"You are your mother's daughter, aren't you, little one? A whore's daughter is nought but a whore herself, isn't that right, Philippa?" Grinding his hips, he prodded her belly with his arousal. "You want it, don't you? And you've been wantin' me to give it to ye ever since you came of age!"

In the vestibule outside Drogo's solar, a floorboard creaked. In the next instant, Killian's eyes widened and his expression froze in a rictus of surprise. Then, he seemed to float backwards, his arms releasing Philippa, his fingers grasping air.

His body fell in a heap to the floor.

Adrian stepped over him and swept Philippa up in his arms. "Are you all right? Say the word, and I will kill the bastard. If he has laid one finger on you—"

"No, no, I am all right." Shamed, Philippa closed her eyes and clung to Adrian.

Planting a kiss on her head, he whispered, "Everything will be all right, sweetling. I would die before I would let that man harm one hair on your head."

Behind them, a dazed Killian struggled to his feet. Shaking his head, he stumbled a bit. Then, he rubbed his neck as if to determine the extent of the damage done to him. Mottled imprints in the shape of Adrian's hands ringed his throat.

"I did not do her any damage." Killian's sarcasm was evident even through his hoarseness. "So you needn't run a sword through my gullet."

"Perhaps I will have another opportunity." Turning, Adrian held Philippa snugly in his embrace, as if to shield her from danger.

Killian chafed his hands and dusted off his knees. "She had no business here in Drogo's solar, snooping through his papers."

Adrian's gaze shot to Killian's. "She's going to be his wife, isn't she?"

Chuckling, Killian nodded. "Then you'd better release the lady, hadn't you, sir? Before her future husband catches you fondling his bride, eh?"

Slowly, Adrian's arms slid from Philippa's waist. As he stepped away, her heart emptied and grew heavy. A great distance opened up between them, a chasm she couldn't breech with her entreating glances. Why did Adrian retreat from her? Why wouldn't he look at her?

Answering her silent question, Killian said, " 'Twas quite a festive moment in the hall, my lady, when Sir Adrian announced you were indeed a virgin, fit to marry the baron. Perhaps you heard the huzzah that went up among the knights."

But Philippa could hardly breathe, much less respond to Killian's jibe. So, Adrian had lied and told the baron that she was a virgin. How very helpful of him, how very chivalrous!

Marriage to Drogo had always loomed in her future as an unpleasant threat, a punishment removable by her father's return. Adrian's actions, however, had made her marriage a present reality. And, with her father near death and unable to repay his debts, the wedding was sure to go forward. As soon as Drogo decided upon a date, Philippa would be joined in holy matrimony to a man she despised.

A sense of betrayal settled on her shoulders like a leaden mantle. Keenly aware of Killian's presence, she held her anger in check. But her stomach was a knot and her face burned with emotion.

Still, what had she expected Sir Adrian to do—tell the truth and condemn her to a life of ignominy and impoverishment? Had she really expected him to swear to Drogo that she was not a virgin?

Hadn't he done precisely what she'd begged him to do?

A coldness, like some wintry frost, swept through her soul, burying the tiny buds of happiness and desire that she'd so recently—and so lovingly—sown with Adrian.

Brushing past him, she met his gaze and hesitated. Some dark emotion she couldn't identify burned behind his eyes, but his jaw was solid stone.

"Sir, I wish to thank you for your honest testimony regarding my chastity."

"I did what I thought was right, my lady."

She lifted her chin a notch, determined to maintain her dignity even if her soul had been ripped apart. "I pray that you return from tomorrow's duel without injury."

"Then you pray for Terrebonne's death," said Killian.

"I pray for no man's death." *Except Drogo's,* Philippa thought, unable to deny her murderous hatred for the man.

With one last accusatory glance in Adrian's direction, Philippa walked proudly from the room. But in her own chamber, where Hilda and her babe lay sleeping in her bed, she collapsed beside them, exhausted, too sad even to cry another tear.

Half-asleep, Hilda murmured, " 'Twas kind of you to allow me the luxury of sleeping here, my lady."

"That little girl cries too much to have her share a bed with a sick old man. Besides, I thought you might be unsettled by the notion of sleeping beside a dying man."

"Thank you, Philippa." A few seconds later, Hilda's gentle snores resumed.

Philippa touched the baby's hand, smiling when the tiny fingers instinctively wrapped themselves around hers. Something about the child's sweet smell, her gurgles, her total dependence, eased the pain in Philippa's heart. Closing her eyes, she prayed for strength and wisdom and guidance.

She'd spent too many years waiting for her father to show up and rescue her. Now, she realized, she'd have to figure out a way to rescue herself.

Chapter Eighteen

Daylight washed the sky in shades of gray. Outside the castle walls, a barren scrap of hard-packed dirt had been converted overnight into a tournament field. Cold winter wind whipped the blue and gold banners flying above the hastily constructed wooden lists. Servants, knights and village people packed the viewing stands while vendors hawked roasted chestnuts, sugared plums and strips of meat impaled on wooden sticks.

Wedged between Sir Killian and Drogo, Philippa shivered beneath a fur-lined cloak. Each time Drogo nudged his elbow in her side, she hugged herself tighter. Killian's rude leers served to deepen her quest for independence. The sure smugness with which they discussed Sir Adrian's impending defeat galvanized her determination to escape their tyranny.

For too long, Philippa had allowed her fate to be controlled by others. Now her heart was in full rebellion. She didn't know how or when she would escape Oldcastle—and she wasn't counting on Adrian to save her—but she knew she wouldn't acquiesce to marrying Drogo. She'd die before she crawled into the marriage bed with him.

Trumpeters heralded the combatants' arrival. Cheers and huzzahs erupted among the spectators as first, Denys Terrebonne, and then, Sir Adrian Vale, rode onto the field.

Dressed in full tilting armor, minus only their helmets, they stood straight in their saddles. Pausing before the baron, they pledged to fight fairly, honorably and to the death. Drogo gave them his blessing and declared that the victor would be rewarded the sword and all possessions of the slain man. Another cheer rumbled through the crowd as Denys and Adrian faced one another, extended their arms and briefly joined the knuckles of their gauntlets.

Denys yanked his elaborately armored destrier away from the viewing stands and cantered toward the northern edge of the field. Even in armor he'd fashioned himself, he seemed ill at ease on a horse he could never afford. Clearly, his part in this tournament had been underwritten by someone else. Adrian hesitated, his gaze fastened on Philippa. A titillated murmur rippled through the viewers in response to this brazen display of affection and respect.

Now or never, thought Philippa. Standing, she unwound a scarf of dark bark blue silk from around her neck. She tossed it to Adrian. It fluttered through the air, and he caught it in his iron mitten. For a moment, while his war horse whuffled and pawed the ground impatiently, he stared at her, defiantly, possessively . . . yearningly. Her heart ached and fear tunneled its way through her bones, but never in her life had she been so proud or so at peace.

Still unable to stand easily, Drogo grumbled with displeasure.

Killian sprang to his feet and pressed his lips to Philippa's neck. "Sit down, my lady, or else I will give orders to have the impudent scoundrel disemboweled on the spot."

"Upon what charge?" she whispered, never tearing her gaze from Adrian's.

"Rape. Fornicating with the baron's woman. Trespassing and abducting Drogo's prisoners. Murdering his soldiers. You name it, Philippa. Adrian has committed more than one crime for which I could order him drawn and quartered. Now sit down!"

Slowly, she sank to the hard bench. Adrian galloped to the opposite end of the field where his page awaited. The young boy assisted him in strapping on his helmet and tying Philippa's colors onto the tip end of his lance.

It was then that Philippa realized what deviltry had been committed. Glancing at both combatants' lances, she shivered in horror. Leaping out of her seat, she threw up her arms, signaling to Adrian. His helmet turned in her direction, but before she could open her mouth, Killian clamped a hand over her lips and pushed her back to her seat.

"One word out of you, my lady, and you'll share your lover's fate."

"You've tricked him!" But her words were cut off by the point of a dagger pricking at her ribs. Gasping, Philippa stared into Killian's cold, demonic eyes. "My Lord," she whispered, yanking her arm from his grip.

"Even God can't help him now." Killian chuckled, his body flush against Philippa's, so close that he could control her easily with the threat of his dagger.

Suddenly, the viewing gallery sucked in a collective breath of surprise. Philippa gaped at the sight of Adrian sliding off his horse. A clearly confused page fumbled with helmet straps, gauntlets, and greaves. A puddle of armor fell to the ground.

When the only protective clothing he wore was a cuirass and mail skirt, Adrian remounted. Outbursts of astonishment, along with shouts that the man was insane, spread like wildfire through the crowd. Angry knights who had wagered their money on Adrian spat on the ground and wished him a quick trip to hell.

The trumpeters blasted the signal to begin the joust.

Denys Terrebonne goaded his borrowed beast with pricket spurs. Adrian, leaning forward in his saddle, squeezed his horse's sides with strong, unprotected legs.

The horses' hooves thundered down the narrow jousting lane. Philippa, forgetting the dagger pressed against her ribs, half stood. Excitement brought Killian, and indeed all the spectators save Drogo, to their feet. As the combatants picked up speed, drawing nearer to the center of the field, some of the onlookers saw what Philippa had seen.

"Look! Sir Adrian's lance has a coronel on the tip!"

An old woman cried, "But Denys's lance has a sharp one."

"Foolish oaf," said Killian, under his breath. "Without his armor, he's a dead pigeon. Denys has only to plunge his lance into the man's bare flesh and the tournament is over!"

"How dare you outfit Denys Terrebonne for a joust of war!" Philippa's voice, as well as her legs, trembled. "You knew that Adrian carried a blunt-tipped lance, yet you armed Denys with a deadly, sharp-tipped one."

Killian's hand tightened around her upper arm. "All is fair in love and war, my lady."

On opposite sides of the wooden tilt, the horses bore down on each other. As the men moved toward the moment of impact, time slowed to a torturous drip. Philippa's senses, heightened by suspense, drank in the sight of Adrian's dark hair, his fine shapely head and intensely brooding gaze. Even from a distance, even in the midst of crisis, she was moved by his power, his overwhelming aura of masculinity. Desire quickened inside her. Her love for him swelled to near bursting in her heart. Her breasts burned for his lips; her body pined for his touch.

Denys, his lance firmly anchored to his armored breast-plate, took dead aim at Adrian's head.

The ground shook beneath the pummeling of hooves. Philippa's ears rang with the roar of the crowd. Thirty yards separated the horses, then twenty, then ten, until, at last, the horses were practically upon one another. Adrian threw down his lance, drew his short sword from his belt and hunkered low behind his horse's head. As the combatants passed on either side of the wooden tilt rail, Denys's lance, long and unwieldy, slid clean over Adrian's head.

A quick shift in his saddle brought Adrian level with his opponent. His sword clashed loudly against Denys's breast-plate, knocking him from his mount.

The crowd went wild.

Adrian drew his horse up short. Nostrils flaring, the beast turned, chomping at the bit, eager to charge again. But Adrian held the reins tautly, riding slowly back to the center of the field.

Trapped in his bulky armor, Denys writhed helplessly, the whites of his terrified eyes gleaming through the slit of his helmet visor.

Shouts of "Kill him!" and "Finish 'im off!" rose from the bloodthirsty spectators.

Dismounting, Adrian slapped his horse's flank and sent it pounding off to the edge of the field where Denys's mount was held by a page. He kneeled down and, with his knee on Denys's breastplate, unstrapped his opponent's helmet and cast it aside. "Have you had enough of this foolish combat, Terrebonne?"

Denys's jaw worked and he spat in Adrian's face.

Lightning quick, Adrian pressed the tip of his sword to Denys's bobbing Adam's apple. Instantly, the man stilled.

"Go ahead, then, kill me. I wouldn't show an ounce of charity to you if we was in opposite positions. We're sworn to be bitter enemies, we are, and there's no place on the battlefield for softness. Besides, you've already disgraced me woman. You might as well 'ave made me a cuckold, too, for all the shame I've suffered. If I can't hold me head up, I'd just as soon you chop it off!"

"You prefer being beheaded to suffering a bruise to your inflated pride, is that it?" Adrian nearly felt sorry for the man. Leaning closer, he said, "There is another way, you know, Denys."

"Ain't no other way." With a deep breath, the man closed his eyes. "Go ahead, kill me."

Glancing up, Adrian took note of Killian's absence in the stands. His gaze swung to Drogo who looked slightly piqued, but not unduly concerned that Denys Terrebonne might be about to lose his head. Which perplexed Adrian because he thought he had figured out the source of Killian's and Drogo's resentment toward him.

Then, he met Philippa's stare and a fresh wave of pain shot through his body. Seated beside the baron, she stared back at him, tears streaming down her cheeks, hands clasped to her heart. She didn't know yet that her father had died quietly, just minutes before Adrian took to the field. And she didn't know what Casper Gilchrist had revealed in the moments before his death. Unable to speak, the old man had opened his eyes and with his last drop of strength, clutched a quill and scratched out three words on a sheet of foolscap.

Loot.

Cheated.

King.

It had taken Adrian a moment, but before Casper Gilchrist breathed his final breath, he'd pieced together the puzzle.

There was just one more detail he needed to know, for Belinda's sake as well as his own.

With the crowd screaming and begging for blood to be spilled, he spoke quickly. "Denys Terrebonne, we can help each other. You have something I want, and I have something you need."

Denys opened his eyes. "If it's me wife you want, take her. She ain't let me touch her for nigh on nine months, anyhow!"

"Well, thank God for that!" At least poor Hilda wouldn't have contracted Belinda's disease through Denys.

"You have nothing I need." Even pinned to the ground, Denys refused to beg for his life.

"You need the cure for your disease, man."

"What disease? Ain't got no disease!"

With poorly concealed impatience, Adrian explained that if Denys had slept with Belinda, he had contracted a very serious contagion. "The disease won't kill you . . . anytime soon, that is. But, if you don't take the cure, you'll one day die a very painful death. And you'll inflict this agony on every woman you sleep with until you've rid your body of the contagion."

"And you're willing to give me the cure?" Denys asked skeptically.

"Aye, as soon as you've done my bidding. Now listen carefully, because we haven't much time. What I need from you is twofold. The first is a question. It has to do with Belinda—"

"I didna' kill that whore, I swear it!"

"I didn't say you did! But Cecily says you were with her when her last customer engaged her. I'm certain that the last man who swived her also murdered her. I want you to tell me who that man is, Denys!"

"Damn that Cecily! Her's mouth as wide as her—"

"Forget Cecily, Terrebonne! Do you want to live, or do you want me to slice your head off right now! You hear that crowd, don't you? They're bleating like sheep for me to finish you off. I was the odds-on favorite, after all!"

"And if I tell, what good will it do me? You might let me live this day, but the man who killed Belinda would just as easily kill me. And he will if he finds out I told!"

"But, he'll never know, and if he does, it won't matter by then. Because as soon as you get off this field, I'm sending you to London with a missive for the king. It's part of our bargain. Your life and the remedy you need in exchange for your naming Belinda's killer. Then, you must ride to London as fast as your horse will take you. When you return, it will be in the company of the king's men, for I assure you when he reads the letter I am sending with you, he will dispatch a small army to Oldcastle. And then, I will give you the curative that will make your willicock healthy again."

Gulping, Denys agreed to the terms of the bargain. "Sir Killian Murdoch killed Belinda," he said as Adrian's sword lifted from his throat and a folded letter slid between a gap in his armor.

Catcalls and derisive boos filled the air when Denys, aided by his page and Adrian, scrambled upright. The combatants approached the gallery and stood beneath the stand where Drogo and Lady Philippa sat.

"My lord, Denys Terrebonne and I have reached an amicable conclusion to our dispute." Turning to Terrebonne, Adrian fell on one knee and bowed his head. "Having committed a grievous injury to Denys Terrebonne's person, I hereby submit my most humble apology."

"Er, which I readily accept," stammered Terrebonne.

Drogo bellowed his disapproval. "God's blood, this ain't no way to fight a duel! 'Twas meant to be fought to the death, you knaves!"

Adrian rose to his full height and faced the baron. "If you will permit me, my lord, I must, as a licensed physic of the realm, decline to take the life of another man. 'Twould be an affront to my oath as a practitioner of the healing arts."

"Poppycock!" With a huff, Drogo crossed his arms over his chest. "I won't have it, I say. I simply will not have it!"

A raucous cheer from the onlookers enforced Drogo's

appraisal of the situation. Someone yelled, "What kind of sissy arse are ye, Terrebonne?"

To which, Denys responded under his breath, "Must I let ye slit me throat to prove I'm a man?"

Adrian would have chuckled, but for the sudden restless murmur that rippled through the crowd. Killian waded through the throng of people, then bent to Drogo's ear. When he'd finished whispering, he stood beside the baron and swept the spectators with a quelling gaze. A hush swept through the stands.

Philippa's strong, reassuring gaze warmed Adrian's heart.

But the words that rolled from Killian's tongue chilled his bones. "Sir Adrian Vale, it is my grave duty to inform you that you are under arrest and are hereby condemned to death by torture."

"What is the charge, sir?"

In the stands, simple village people, knights, servants, wenches and vendors froze. Scanning their slack-jawed faces, Adrian saw them as the landscape of a dream, an unreal tableau painted on his mind. Time stood still, muting every voice, every gasp, every exclamation of surprise.

He met Philippa's shocked gaze, saw her mouth form a tiny oval and her skin bleach white. The urge to rush to her, to scramble through the wooden stands and hold her in his arms was nearly irresistible. But he didn't dare put her life in danger. Instead, he threw back his shoulders and faced his accuser. Without fear, without regret. For, he knew in that instant, down deep in his heart, that Philippa's love for him was real and sacred.

No matter what happened now, he would go to his grave, secure in the knowledge that he had loved her, too.

And wasn't loving a woman the most noble act of chivalry a man could perform?

Intoning the words, Killian puffed out his chest and stared

at Adrian with barely concealed malice. "I hereby charge you with the murder of Sir Casper Gilchrist of Rye."

Only Denys Terrebonne heard Adrian's response. "Go now, ride fast and hard. Take the fastest, strongest horse you can find in the stable, don't worry about the consequences. And don't stop before you make London, Denys. My very life, perhaps the lives of everyone in this castle including your wife and child, depend upon you."

Denys ducked his head. "Mother of God, I don't want them to die!" he whispered, then turned and ran.

"A right fine coward he turned out to be," muttered Drogo.

Killian threw out his arm, indicting Adrian with an accusing finger. "Seize him!"

Guards and knights, Drogo's trusted retainers, swarmed from the stands and over the wooden barrier. In seconds, Adrian was surrounded by soldiers, bereft of his sword, restrained on either side by Killian's minions.

Philippa's voice rang out, clear and confident. "No! I forbid you to arrest Sir Adrian!"

Drogo's astonishment lifted his bushy brows and raised his voice. "What the hell are you babbling about woman? If you don't sit down right now and shut that hole in yer head ye call a mouth, I'll slap the devil outta ye!"

"I won't let you hurt Adrian . . . and I won't marry you!"

"Oh, you won't will you?" A beat passed while Drogo pulled at his chin, considering Philippa's act of defiance. At length, he said, "Well, if that's the way you feel, my lady, it's off to the dungeon with you, too. Casper Gilchrist is dead now, and there's nothing he can do or say to help you. By virtue of my contract with him, I now own everything he once possessed, including you, you little minx. But that don't mean I have to tolerate your backtalk! Guards! Take the lady to the prison tower and throw her in the cell with her precious baby doctor."

At once, Philippa felt strong hands close around her upper

arms. Minutes later, she was hustled through the doors of the prison tower and shoved down a short flight of steps into a small, foul-smelling cell. Adrian landed on the hard earth beside her. Before the iron grate clanged shut and the light extinguished, she met his black, anguished gaze.

For all her bravery, she'd earned nothing but a terrifying death sentence. For all her independence, she'd won nothing but imprisonment. For all her love, she'd found nothing but darkness.

Cold earth enclosed them. Above their heads, heavy footsteps and shouting faded to silence. Smothered in blackness, huddled against the stone walls, the sound of their breathing filled the tiny chamber.

In the depth of his voice, she heard raw emotion. "Dear God, I'm sorry Philippa. Please believe me: *I did not kill your father.*"

"I know. 'Twas only a matter of time before Killian found him and finished what he'd started."

"He's known for days where Casper Gilchrist was. I should have moved the man, but there was nowhere else to hide him. I didn't mean to draw you into this. I didn't mean to put you in harm's way."

She found his hand, closed her fingers around his. "I made my decision freely." After a space, she added, " 'Tis odd, but I am wondering what sort of torture Drogo has in store for us. Perhaps he will press us beneath a pile of stones, slowly crushing the life from our bodies."

Adrian released a ragged sigh. "Please, don't. . . . "

"But, don't you see? It doesn't matter, because I feel as if a wall of stones were just removed from my chest. I feel liberated, Adrian! Free! Free from the tyranny of my father's dishonor, free from the oppression of my self-imposed shame."

"You have no cause to feel shame, Philippa."

"No, and I never did." She laid her head on his shoulder. "If only I had realized it before. If only I hadn't spent years trying to redeem my honor. You see, I thought it was my fault that Mother lost her mind and Father lost his money. And I thought it was my responsibility to make it all right."

She told him the story, then, of how Faustus had ruined her mother, then robbed her of her innocence. Her mother had gone mad, and perhaps her father had, too, in his own way, for instead of publicly charging Faustus with a crime, he'd simply killed the man.

"I might have killed him, too," muttered Adrian.

"But when Father refused to voice why he'd taken Faustus's life, I got it in my head that part of the blame was mine. There was something so shameful about what had happened, Father couldn't even name the crime. So, it had to be my fault."

"No, sweetling, it wasn't."

"If Father was willing to give everything he owned in order to pay the death tax, and to buy Killian's silence, then my only chance at redemption was to perform under the terms of that odious contract. It never occurred to me, until you came along, Adrian, that I could escape my prearranged fate, that I possessed a free will of my own, that I was . . . " Her voice trailed. In the darkness, she was free to cry, but she didn't want Adrian to hear.

"It's all right, now," he whispered, drawing her into his arms.

"You changed everything, Adrian."

"No, Philippa, I changed nothing. You merely recognized your value as a woman. You were always good, always worthy. You just didn't know it."

"And might never have if it hadn't been for you. You're a good man, Sir Adrian. Strong and brave . . . and very desirable. I never thought a man like you could love me. I thought that if you knew what had happened to me—"

"Shhh. Don't you know, my lady, that it only makes me love you more?"

Snuggling closer to him, she pressed her face in the crook of his neck. The nearness of his body infused her with warmth. She adored this man, wanted him, loved him with a fierceness that frightened her.

And the wonder of it was that she could love at all.

"Ah, Philippa. 'Tis I who am unworthy of you. I am just a man, after all, a man who was arrogant enough to think he could control his lustful desires by taking a vow of celibacy."

"You? A vow of celibacy?" Philippa couldn't suppress the tiny giggle that bubbled to her lips. "Don't you know that waste is sinful, Adrian?"

His fingers stroked her hair, and his voice was pensive and faraway as he told her about Jeanne. "I thought it was my fault, I hated myself for getting her pregnant."

"Didn't she want to have children?"

"Not particularly."

"But, I do, Adrian! I love babies, and if we ever get out of here, I want to have *your* baby."

She heard him swallow, heard the pain in his rasping voice. "Don't you understand, Philippa, I couldn't bear it if anything happened to you. If something happened during childbirth—"

"You are not God, Adrian." Her voice had taken on a firmness that surprised even her. "And you are not responsible for the decisions that God makes."

"Aye," he whispered.

"Moreover," she said in a lighter tone, "having just discovered that I am capable of choosing my own fate, I truly resent your presuming to make that decision for me. My urge to have children is a strong one, Adrian. 'Twould be wrong for me to repress it. Just as it is wrong for you to attempt to repress your sexual desire."

When he whispered her name, his voice was laden with

such fondness and gratitude that she melted closer to him. "Dear Philippa. God knows I love you. More than anything else in the world."

"And I love you, Adrian." Reaching up, she felt the moisture on his cheeks. She wet her fingertips and tasted the salt of his tears. "So much so that I'd rather die with you in this dark, dank cellar than marry Drogo."

He kissed her lips, gently at first. "Don't worry, sweetling, you won't die. Not if Denys Terrebonne keeps his promise."

"What promise is that?" she asked, her pulse skittering.

"He's gone to fetch the king's men, my dear. Drogo and Killian will cease to be a threat to us, once the king learns of their treachery."

She could hardly breathe as Adrian ran his beard along her sensitive neck. Between gasps, she said, "What treachery?"

"I'll try to explain." Unable to see, she thought he leaned his head against the rough stones. "King Edward and a small contingent of his courtiers sent me to Oldwall Castle as a spy."

"You mean you're not a licensed midwife?"

"Oh, I am! But I was hanging on the rack when Edward pardoned me in exchange for my agreement to spy on Drogo. The ruse was perfect, you see, and Killian, who was in London at the time seeking a midwife to perform your examination, was quick to take me into the fold."

"Yes, I can see where he would be. Drogo was having a difficult time persuading the village midwife to perform the examination. She feared her head would be cut off if she said the wrong thing, or even if Drogo was dissatisfied on his wedding night . . . for any reason."

"I should have seen it then. Killian was a little too quick to retain me on Drogo's behalf."

"What do you mean?"

"It was a conspiracy." Adrian tightened his grip on Philippa's hand, as if in need of an anchor, a rope to cling to while he told of his own betrayal. "The king knew that Killian and Drogo were stealing from the French. He knew because he was participating in the profits. He'd given them private sanction to violate the Treaty of Brétigni, but he couldn't very well tell his courtiers that, could he?"

"So, he sent you to spy on Killian as a means of appeasing his advisors?"

"Exactly. I was meant to declare you unfit to marry into the bargain."

"They knew—"

"Of course, they knew. Faustus, no doubt, bragged to his son about his evil misdeeds. Which is why, when I swore you were a virgin, it irritated the hell out of Drogo. You see, he wanted me to swear you weren't a virgin, so that he and Killian could declare your father's fortunes as their own. *According to the contract.*"

"He must have been shocked when you lied."

"Aye." Adrian chuckled bleakly. "Killian suspected I was in love with you. He was sure I would swear you weren't a virgin, if for no other reason than to have you myself. As soon as I had done so, he intended to dispatch me to London at once."

"Where you would tell the king, more importantly his courtiers, that you'd found no evidence of smuggling."

"Exactly. For even if I had stumbled across the truth, Killian knew I wouldn't dare accuse Drogo, not after I'd run off with his woman. That is why, after I forced my way into the prison tower and rescued your father, Killian turned a blind eye. He was merely biding his time."

"But you did find evidence of smuggling, didn't you?"

"Worse, I found a prison full of men whose tongues had been cut out to prevent them from speaking of Drogo's crimes. Killian has taken great pains to silence his enemies. So he thought he was quite safe in bringing me to Oldwall. In addition, the French loot is very well hidden."

"Do you know where it's hidden?"

"I do now. Your father told me. Or rather, I guessed it and he nodded. We're sitting atop of it, sweetling."

The thought of sitting atop a horde of gold and treasures brought a slight smile to Philippa's lips.

"What the king doesn't know," Adrian continued, "is that Drogo and Killian have been cheating him out of his rightful percentage. Just like they cheated your father."

"Dear God, imagine how angry Edward would be!"

"Yes." With a sigh, Adrian drew her back into his arms. "We might as well get as comfortable as we can, Philippa. We are going to be here at least four days, perhaps longer, depending on how fast Denys can ride."

Curling up beside him, her legs thrown over his, she thought how strange it was that she'd found peace and safety in a dungeon prison. "How can you be certain Denys will even go to London?"

"Oh, he will go to London, and he will return. I have promised him a dose of mercury when he gets back. I'm afraid he has contracted a rather serious contagion, you see. From one of the prostitutes."

Philippa laughed. "I think I understand. Yes, I am sure he will return." But, after a pause, she added, "What if he does not return in time? What if Drogo decides he is weary of our living, and kills us before Denys returns with the king's men?"

"Drogo will not kill me before his leg is completely healed. And Killian will not kill me before he has finished the regimen of mercury I ordered for him."

"Men are such vain creatures." Philippa rested her head on Adrian's hard chest and wrapped her arm around his waist. The next four days would be difficult ones, she knew. But, with Adrian beside her, she could survive anything. With Adrian loving her, she knew she would be all right.

* * *

Adrian marked the time by the change of guards outside the prison cell door. After four nights, he forced himself to stand, stretching his muscles as best he could. Though his stomach ached with hunger and his mind was cloudy with fatigue, anger burned in his veins, awakening his senses, sharpening his fighting instinct.

The thunder of hooves entering the outer bailey reverberated through the tiny cell. Denys Terrebonne and the king's men had at last arrived.

"Philippa, wake up! The time has come!"

He pulled her to her feet just as a great crash sounded above them. The prison tower had been breached by the king's men. Drogo's men shouted obscenities, but their retreat was clearly audible. The clash of swords and the pounding of footsteps grew closer. Adrian pulled Philippa close, then pushed her behind him, determined to shield her from harm no matter what fate befell him.

Her arms wrapped around his middle; her soft breasts were crushed to his back. He felt her flinch as the cell door crashed inward. Torchlight lit the room, burning on Adrian's unaccustomed eyes the image of a man filling the door frame.

Killian's voice echoed through the chamber. "Drogo told me to kill you days ago, and for once I should have listened to the old devil!"

Slowly, Adrian's eyes adjusted to the light. Shoving Philippa further behind him, he stood tall. "Why didn't you kill us then, Killian? What in God's name were you waiting for?"

Killian's grin was strangely drunken looking. "For the same reason I didn't kill Sir Casper, I suppose. I liked the idea of having a man's life in my hands, knowing that I could kill him at any moment, knowing that every breath he drew was at my whim."

"I pity you, Killian. No soul is as cruel and twisted as you

303

are without having been victimized by someone even more perverted. You drew strength from Casper's suffering. You sucked the life from him, growing fat from his pain, like a leech. But you were stupid! Too stupid to kill your enemies when you should have. And now you have waited too long to kill us!"

"It is not too late!"

The man's face was tinged with gray and deeply lined. Perhaps he'd consumed too much mercury in an effort to expedite his recovery. And his eyes, red-rimmed and glazed, seemed to dance with demonic glee. When Killian laughed, it was a high-pitched convulsion that made Adrian chudder.

"How much of mercury have you drunk?" Adrian asked.

But Killian ignored the question. He shoved his torch in a crude wall sconce, then yanked a dagger from his belt.

Adrian's skin prickled with tension. Behind Killian, and outside the prison tower, a battle for control of Oldwall Castle raged. If Drogo's men prevailed, Philippa and Adrian were as good as dead. If the king's men won the day, Killian would be hung from a gibbet before nightfall. But, whichever side took the castle was at the moment immaterial. Killian or Adrian would die inside this prison cell before the fight outside finished.

Despite the dullness that four days of captivity had brought to his senses, Adrian felt Philippa slip from his fingertips. In his peripheral vision, he saw her shadow move along the dank prison wall. She skirted the room as Killian lurched toward Adrian.

A quick sidestep took Adrian out of range, but the dagger's tip still gleamed in the flickering light. Moments ticked by as the men cagily circled one another. Then, Killian, arm outstretched, leapt toward Adrian once more.

This time, the knife slashed Adrian's tunic, burning a trail across his flesh. Adrian touched his belly and felt blood oozing from his wound. In his diminished condition, tired and hungry, a cloud of confusion enveloped him. Killian's weapon jabbed at him again, and Adrian threw up his arm, deflecting the blow. The dagger fell to the earthen floor with a heavy thud. Throwing himself at Killian, Adrian slammed into the villain and against the wall. His head hit the stones, and a blinding pain shot through his temples. The hard dank earth beneath his feet seemed to sway. The walls surrounding him spun like an eddy in a rain-swollen creek. Shaking his head, Adrian turned and pressed his back to the cold rough stones and drew in a deep breath.

Eager to press his advantage, Killian scrambled forward, pulling from the leather lace tied around his leg a short knife, one more suitable for gutting fish, Adrian thought vaguely, than a man. Barely shoving off the wall in time to avoid being pricked in the heart, Adrian stumbled across the room. But, his feet were as unsteady as his attacker's. Backing away from Killian's little knife, Adrian tripped and fell.

On his back, he stared up into Killian's leering smile. The man seemed to hover above him, suspended, fading into double images, then sliding back into one body. Adrian's head ached and his eyes refused to focus. Instinctively, he scuttled backward, but Killian was astride him in a flash.

The knife was small, but sharp enough to slit a man's throat. Killian arched his back and raised his arm, knife clutched in his fingers, blade-point aimed at Adrian's throat. But, Adrian, still half-dazed, possessed enough of his warrior's instinct to catch Killian's wrist in mid-air. The two were suddenly frozen in a silent struggle, Killian's weight shifting forward in an effort to bring his knife down into Adrian's body, Adrian's arm muscles straining to hold Killian's wrist.

Then, a rustle sounded from behind Adrian's head. He felt the cold metal of Killian's dagger slide beneath his free hand. Philippa had kicked the fallen dagger toward Adrian.

"Kill him, Adrian!" she whispered.

Her voice, raw with pain and fatigue, imbued Adrian with

newfound strength. His gaze focused and his muscles came alive. Wrapping his fingers around the hilt of the dagger, he swept his arm up and plunged the blade into Killian's chest.

Shock and bewilderment registered on the knight's face. He gasped as his fingers released the small knife, allowing it to fall to the floor. Like wine leaking from a broken cask, the man's life force slowly faded from him, until he slumped sideways. Sliding off Adrian's body, he collapsed.

Propped on his elbows, Adrian listened as the battle raged above him. Somewhere in the eastern corner of the castle yard, a battering ram hammered away. Horses' hooves thundered across the ground and swords clanged harshly as the fray continued. Women screamed and men hurled oaths at one another, but inside the prison tower, no voices cried out. With a shudder, Adrian thought of the tongueless wretches shivering in their cells, awaiting their fate. He had to see about them. He had to get up, move, help Denys Terrebonne and the king's men as best he could.

His body ached as he scrambled to his feet. But, when he stood, Philippa gently pressed herself to him, her cheek against his chest, her arms around his waist. Wordlessly, he held her, clung to her, drew her willowy body as close to him as he could.

After a moment, he said, "You must stay here, Philippa, until the fighting is over."

"No!" She clung more fiercely to him. "Do not leave me!"

"But I must free the prisoners," he said softly. "And, then, I must find Drogo. I have a bit of business with the baron that cannot wait any longer. There is something I want to get from him. Something you should have."

"No! No, Adrian! Wherever you go, I must go, too!"

Clasping her shoulders, Adrian peered into her face. He must explain to her that her safety meant more to him than anything, and that until the battle above ground was finished, she was safer in the prison cell, behind a locked door, where none of Drogo's men would bother to look for her.

But, Denys Terrebonne's voice cut him off. "Sent Killian to the devil, did ye? Sorry he got 'ere before I found him. Woulda' liked to do the bastard in meself to tell the truth!"

"Are your men in danger of being bested?" Adrian asked.

A wide smile spread across Denys's grimy face. "They've just now taken the castle. Stormed the great hall and captured Drogo. Got him tied up like a pig on a spit! Damn, but that man can swear a bloody—"

"There's a lady present," Adrian reminded him, hugging Philippa tighter to his body.

Without turning her head, Philippa whispered against Adrian's chest, "Is Hildee all right?"

"Aye, and I want to thank ye both for tendin' to her." The catch in Denys's voice surprised everyone in the room. "And fer lookin' after me little girl. Hildee tells me we've named her Adriana, after the man what helped bring her into the world. Seems a mouthful of a name to me, but if the wife likes it . . . well, I guess she's deservin' of a little happiness."

Stepping into the tiny prison cell, Denys pulled a leather pouch from his belt and extracted a crumpled paper. "Here's somethin' you might be interested in. Drogo was tryin' to burn it when the king's men rushed into his room. Don't know what it is, bein' as how I can't read, but I snatched it from the flames anyhow. Though it might have somethin' to do with your business with the king."

Adrian took the proffered paper, charred around the edges and badly damaged from the effects of being crushed into Denys's pouch. Despite the paper's condition, however, it remained the embodiment of the dreadful negotiations that had imprisoned Philippa in a private cell of shame and fear. His heart pounded as he passed the contract to her. Their fingers touched as she received it. Then, as a huzzah went up in the courtyard, signaling the end of the battle, Drogo's defeat, and the king's capture of Oldwall Castle, she stepped out of Adrian's embrace. Without looking at him, she turned, crossed the room and held the paper to the torch flame.

As it burned, Adrian studied her proud, straight spine, her tangled flaxen hair and her squared, defiant shoulders. No longer a victim, Philippa Gilchrist was truly the bravest woman he'd ever known.

Epilogue

Nine Months Later

Philippa gave one last final push. "Damn you, Adrian! I have changed my mind! This hurts like hell! I . . . don't . . . want . . . to . . . have . . . a . . . baby!"

But by the time her head had fallen to the pillow, and the pain of the contraction had subsided, Adrian's gentle laughter reminded her how deeply she loved him. And how badly she did want his child.

Looking down, she saw the writhing, wriggling little pink body in Adrian's hands. A lusty cry split the air.

" 'Tis a girl, Philippa, a beautiful perfect, baby girl!" Tears streamed down his cheeks as he cleaned the baby, swaddled her, then laid her on Philippa's breast.

Hilda, who had been at her side throughout her pregnancy and during every excruciating moment of labor, wiped her face with a cool, wet cloth. "A little friend for my tiny

Adriana. She's lovely, my lady. Just lovely! I'm going to run tell Denys, if you don't mind. He'll want to know."

As the baby suckled, Adrian sat on the edge of the bed, one hand cupping the top of his daughter's head, the other caressing Philippa's cheek. " 'Tis a miracle," he whispered.

"I suppose so." He'd been attentive and fretful throughout her pregnancy, but even so, she'd never expected this degree of emotion from him. "One of many miracles this past year. Who'd have thought the king would reward you by granting you Oldwall Castle?"

"Who'd have thought that I could have such a beautiful, warm, loving wife. . . . " He kissed her lips, her bare breast, the baby's soft, downy crown. "And such a fine, healthy babe."

"Denys Terrebonne will be happy to hear you've produced a daughter. He will see it as vindication of his own masculinity. After all, he's spent this last year refashioning himself into a coarser version of you."

"Should I be flattered?" Unable to take his eyes off his daughter, Adrian chuckled.

"I think so. Denys's change of heart certainly has made Hilda a happier woman, and for that alone, I am grateful."

"As I am." Looking at his wife, his incredible wonderful wife, who had just done this amazing, miraculous thing, Adrian shook his head. "As I am grateful for so many things. You, most of all. And our daughter. I never thought I could love this much, Philippa, or this deeply. It frightens me."

She understood. "Me too."

"What shall we name her, sweetling?"

Philippa smiled. "Would you like to name her Jeanne?"

His eyes flooded. Finding no words to express his emotion, Adrian bent over his wife and child, enveloping them, protecting them . . . needing them.

And Gold Was Ours
Rebecca Brandewyne

In Spain the young Aurora's future is foretold—a long arduous journey, a dark, wild jungle, and a fierce, protective man. Now in the New World, on a plantation haunted by a tale of lost love and hidden gold, the dark-haired beauty wonders if the swordsman and warrior who haunts her dreams truly lived and if he can rescue her from the enemies who seek to destroy her. Together, will they be able to overcome the past and conquer the present to find the greatest treasure on this earth, a treasure that is even more precious than gold. . . .

____52314-0 $5.99 US/$6.99 CAN

Dorchester Publishing Co., Inc.
P.O. Box 6640
Wayne, PA 19087-8640

Please add $1.75 for shipping and handling for the first book and $.50 for each book thereafter. NY, NYC, and PA residents, please add appropriate sales tax. No cash, stamps, or C.O.D.s. All orders shipped within 6 weeks via postal service book rate. Canadian orders require $2.00 extra postage and must be paid in U.S. dollars through a U.S. banking facility.

Name_____
Address_____
City_____ State_____ Zip_____
I have enclosed $_____ in payment for the checked book(s).
Payment <u>must</u> accompany all orders. ❑ Please send a free catalog.
         CHECK OUT OUR WEBSITE! www.dorchesterpub.com

Fairest of Them All

Josette Browning

A true stoic and a gentleman, Daniel Canty has worked furiously to achieve the high esteem of the English nobility. Therefore, it is more his reputation than the promise of wealth that compels him to accept the ninth earl of Hawkenge's challenge to turn an orphan wild child into a lady. But the girl who's been raised by animals in the African interior is hardly an orphan—and his wildly beautiful charge is hardly a child. Truly, Talitha is a woman—and the most compelling Daniel has ever seen. But the mute firebrand also poses the greatest threat he has ever faced. In the girl's soft kiss is the jeopardy which Daniel has fought all his life to avoid: the danger of losing his heart.

___4513-3 $5.50 US/$6.50 CAN

Lady of the Night

Cordia Byers

Manacled to a stone wall is not the way Katharina Fergersen planned to spend her vacation. But a wrong turn in the right place and the haunted English castle she is touring is suddenly full of life—and so is the man who is bathing before her. As the frosty winter days melt into hot passionate nights, she realizes that there is more to Kane than just a well-filled pair of breeches. Katharina is determined not to let this man who has touched her soul escape her, even if it means giving up all to remain Sedgewick's lady of the night.

___4404-8 $5.99 US/$6.99 CAN

Dorchester Publishing Co., Inc.
P.O. Box 6640
Wayne, PA 19087-8640

The CHANGELING BRIDE

LISA CACH

In order to procure the cash necessary to rebuild his estate, the Earl of Allsbrook decides to barter his title and his future: He will marry the willful daughter of a wealthy merchant. True, she is pleasing in form and face, and she has an eye for fashion. Still, deep in his heart, Henry wishes for a happy marriage. Wilhelmina March is leery of the importance her brother puts upon marriage, and she certainly never dreams of being wed to an earl in Georgian England—or of the fairy debt that gives her just such an opportunity. But suddenly, with one sweet kiss in a long-ago time and a faraway place, Elle wonders if the much ado is about something after all.

___52342-6 $4.99 US/$5.99 CAN

SAINT'S Temptation

DEBRA DIER

Seven years after breaking off her engagement to Clayton Trevelyan, Marisa Grantham overhears two men plotting to murder her still-beloved Earl of Huntingdon. No longer the naive young woman who had allowed her one and only love to walk away, Marisa will do anything to keep from losing him a second time.

___4459-5 $5.99 US/$6.99 CAN

Dorchester Publishing Co., Inc.
P.O. Box 6640
Wayne, PA 19087-8640

Please add $1.75 for shipping and handling for the first book and $.50 for each book thereafter. NY, NYC, and PA residents, please add appropriate sales tax. No cash, stamps, or C.O.D.s. All orders shipped within 6 weeks via postal service book rate. Canadian orders require $2.00 extra postage and must be paid in U.S. dollars through a U.S. banking facility.

Name_____
Address_____
City_____ State_____ Zip_____
I have enclosed $_____ in payment for the checked book(s).
Payment <u>must</u> accompany all orders. ❑ Please send a free catalog.

Exquisitely beautiful, fiery Katherine McGregor has no qualms about posing as a doxy, if the charade will strike a blow against the hated English, until she is captured by the infuriating Major James Burke. Now her very life depends on her ability to convince the arrogant English officer that she is a common strumpet, not a Scottish spy. Skillfully, Burke uncovers her secrets, even as he arouses her senses, claiming there is just one way she can prove herself a tart . . . But how can she give him her yearning body, when she fears he will take her tender heart as well?

___4419-6 $5.99 US/$6.99 CAN

Dorchester Publishing Co., Inc.
P.O. Box 6640
Wayne, PA 19087-8640

Please add $1.75 for shipping and handling for the first book and $.50 for each book thereafter. NY, NYC, and PA residents, please add appropriate sales tax. No cash, stamps, or C.O.D.s. All orders shipped within 6 weeks via postal service book rate. Canadian orders require $2.00 extra postage and must be paid in U.S. dollars through a U.S. banking facility.

Name_____
Address_____
City_____State_____Zip_____
I have enclosed $_____ in payment for the checked book(s).
Payment <u>must</u> accompany all orders. ❏ Please send a free catalog.
        CHECK OUT OUR WEBSITE! www.dorchesterpub.com

VELVET & STEEL
Sylvie Sommerfield

Commanded to marry a Saxon heiress in order to secure her lands for his king, Norman knight Royce, Sword of William, does not expect to find the lovely creature who stands before him. Her defiant eyes the color of cornflowers on a summer day reveal intelligence and gentleness. For once, Royce is struck speechless—and he knows that he will be the one to spark the fire that will set this maid aflame with desire. He is the largest, most intense man she has ever encountered. But it is his gaze that both unnerves her and touches her soul: His golden eyes glance over her body and heat her to the very core of her being. For though he is the Sword of William—a knight so passionate and powerful on the battlefield, legends tell his tale—Lynette sees the pain behind his handsome visage, and knows that she will be the one to heal the wounds of his tormented past.

___4576-1 $5.99 US/$6.99 CAN

IONA

MELANIE JACKSON

Isolated by the icy storms of the North Atlantic, the isle of Iona is only a temporary haven for its mistress. Lona MacLean, daughter of a rebel and traitor to the crown, knows that it is only a matter of time before the bloody Sasannachs come for her. But she has a stout Scottish heart, and the fiery beauty gave up dreams of happiness years before. One task remains—to protect her people. But the man who lands upon Iona's rain-swept shores is not an Englishman. The handsome intruder is a Scot, and a crafty one at that. His clever words leave her tossing and turning in her bed long into the night. His kiss promises an end to the ghosts that plague both her people and her heart. And in his powerful embrace, Lona finds an ecstasy she'd long ago forsworn.

___4614-8 $4.99 US/$5.99 CAN

Rejar

DARA JOY

Lord Byron thinks he's a scream, the fashionable matrons titter behind their fans at a glimpse of his hard form, and nobody knows where he came from. His startling eyes—one gold, one blue—promise a wicked passion, and his voice almost seems to purr. There is only one thing a woman thinks of when looking at a man like that. *Sex.* And there is only one woman he seems to want. *Lilac.* In her wildest dreams she never guesses that bringing a stray cat into her home will soon have her stroking the most wanted man in 1811 London....

__52178-4 $5.99 US/$6.99 CAN